A Long

The Secon

This first edition is published in Great Britain
2019 by Friston Books.

This book is a work of fiction and the characters and events in it
exist only in its pages and in the author's imagination.

A catalogue record for this book is available at the British Library.

ISBN 978-1-78926-198-1

Printed and bound in the UK by BookPrintingUK.

The Ruslan Shanidza Novels

The Price of Dreams
A Long Night of Chaos

To the memory of Josip Reihl-Kir.

Ksordia-Akhtaria

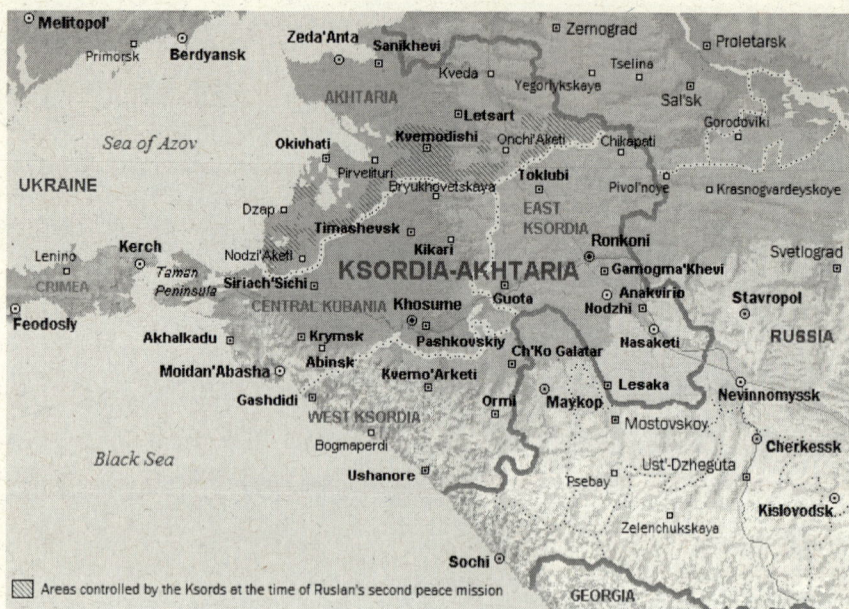

Areas controlled by the Ksords at the time of Ruslan's second peace mission

May 1992
Southern Akhtaria

Chapter One

THE FOUR men lay on the road, not daring to move. The rain pounded down upon them, but they stayed where they were, face down on the tarmac. Only after several minutes did one of them have the nerve to raise his head to see if the gunmen were still there.

'Sergo,' he said, 'they've gone.'

Sergo Lionidza looked up.

Mikhel Inalipa cautiously raised himself to his hands and knees. He looked at the car, which sizzled and bubbled. He could smell petrol and was surprised it hadn't exploded when Mingrelsky shot it up.

He got to his feet, crouching down low.

'Be careful,' hissed Lionidza.

'They've gone, I'm sure of it.'

Lionidza raised his considerable weight to his hands and knees. 'Where's Ruslan?'

Mikhel looked all round. 'I don't know. I can't see him.'

'Maybe he's down there,' said the Ksordian village leader.

'I'll have a look.'

Mikhel tried to stand, but he still didn't dare to straighten up. It wasn't quite dark, and he was scared Mingrelsky and his men might see him. He shuffled his way to the edge of the road and looked down into the gloom.

He couldn't see Ruslan anywhere.

Perhaps he had managed to escape.

A fork of lightning flashed across the sky and Ruslan flickered into view. He was down the embankment, where the impact of the bullets had thrown him, lying upside-down on his back, his head right near the bottom.

The sight of him came as a crushing blow to Mikhel.

It was true.

They had really shot him.

The thunder growled and rumbled, and Mikhel started to climb down and then slipped and skidded to the bottom.

He crawled over to where Ruslan lay. The rain had washed away most of the blood, but Mikhel could just make out the dark marks on his chest and his flank where the bullets had hit him.

Another thunderbolt lit up Ruslan's face. It had the pallor of death. His eyes were half open, and his mouth and nose were full of blood.

Mikhel crossed himself and put his hands on Ruslan's eyes to close them. As he did so, Ruslan seemed to blink, ever so fleetingly.

He couldn't believe it. He put his fingers to Ruslan's throat and felt for a pulse. Yes, there it was.

'You're alive! Jesus Christ, you're alive!'

He wanted to shout up to Lionidza and the others, but he thought of the gunmen. They couldn't be far away.

He looked at Ruslan again. He would have to put him in the recovery position quickly before he drowned in the blood that was collecting in his mouth and nose. He put Ruslan's left hand by his face and then scrambled up to reach his legs. He leant over and took his right knee and raised it. Then, with one hand under his knee and one on his shoulder, he pulled Ruslan onto his side and tipped his head back.

Blood poured from Ruslan's mouth and nose. And then it stopped, with no coughing or any sign of breathing.

Mikhel put his ear down by Ruslan's mouth.

Nothing.

He felt for a pulse again.

Yes, it was still there.

A pulse but no breathing, Mikhel was sure of it.

He would have to do the kiss of life. He rolled Ruslan onto his back again, pinched his nose, put his mouth down onto Ruslan's bloody lips and blew.

The air wouldn't go in.

Puzzled, Mikhel took another breath and tried again.

He blew as hard as he could, but hardly any air went in.

He tried one more time. He pinched Ruslan's nose, put his mouth to his lips and blew. Still the air wouldn't go in properly. He felt Ruslan's pulse again. Yes, it was there, but there was no sign of breathing, and he couldn't even give him the kiss of life.

Why? What was wrong?

Then he realised: it had to be the drowning reflex. The blood from Ruslan's chest wounds had trickled down his windpipe and sent his throat muscles into spasm. Air couldn't get in or out. Any air Mikhel had managed to blow into him had probably gone the wrong way.

'Hell and damnation.'

There was only one thing for it, and he would have to be very quick.

He rushed up the slippery embankment.

By now, Lionidza and the village leaders had come over to look. They were crouching in the puddles at the top.

'Is he dead?'

Mikhel ignored the question. 'Have any of you got a knife?'

'What?'

'Have you got a sharp knife?'

'No.'

'There must be one somewhere.'

'Well, there's the vegetable knife in the lunch box,' said Lionidza.

'Thank God for that. Have you got a ball-point pen?'

'What the hell do you want a pen for?'

'Have you got one?'

'Yes,' said Lionidza, taking one out of his jacket. 'Here.'

'Right. Keep it and go down to Ruslan. I'll get the knife.'

Still bending low, Mikhel ran to the car.

The boot was locked.

Where were the keys?

He rushed round to the front. The door was open and they were in the ignition. He grabbed them and opened the boot.

The vegetable knife was in the lunch box, just as Lionidza had said.

Mikhel grabbed it and splashed his way across the road and down the slippery embankment. Lionidza and the Akhtarian village leader were by now kneeling next to Ruslan.

'Oh God,' Lionidza said. 'What are we going to say to Tamara? Her plane's landing in an hour.'

Mikhel was too busy feeling for Ruslan's pulse to listen. It was still there. He tried the kiss of life again, but the air still wouldn't go in and Ruslan's lips were turning blue.

Lionidza was still speaking: 'I really thought we could do it. I thought we could stop another war. Honest to God, I didn't think they'd kill him.'

'He's not dead. He's still got a pulse.'

'He has?'

'Yes, but he can't breathe. He's suffocating.'

Mikhel's fingers felt their way up and down Ruslan's throat from his Adam's apple to his collar. When he was sure he had his windpipe, he held onto it with his left hand and raised the knife in his right.

'Have you got that pen?'

'What are you doing?'

'A tracheotomy. Get the pen.'

'It's here.'

'Right, take the top off and take the middle out. You have to turn it into a tube.'

Lionidza did as he was told.

Mikhel closed his eyes. 'Please, God,' he said, 'give me this one thing and I'll never ask you for anything again. I swear it. Absolutely never.'

Then, holding the blade between thumb and fingers, he pushed the knife into Ruslan's throat just below the Adam's apple. The blood that had collected in his windpipe gushed out over Mikhel's fingers and the rain washed it away.

'Give me the pen.'

Lionidza handed it to him, and Mikhel thrust it into Ruslan's throat.

Ruslan coughed several times through the pen, and his lips began to lose their deathly blue.

Mikhel looked up at his horror-struck companions and down at the pen. It had worked. Jesus Christ, it had worked. He had never done a tracheotomy before, except on plastic dummies in training. Thank God it had worked.

Then he noticed that Ruslan's breathing had stopped. The pen was filling with blood.

'Sergo, get his knee and bend it up. Not that one, the other one.'

Lionidza took the other knee and pulled it up.

'Okay.' Mikhel addressed the Akhtarian village leader. 'Now you take hold of his far shoulder. That's good. Now the two of you have to pull him onto his side. Are you ready? Okay. Slowly.'

Lionidza and the Akhtarian pulled Ruslan over while Mikhel kept hold of the pen in his throat.

Ruslan coughed and blood spurted through the pen.

Lightning flashed again.

'God's nails,' said Lionidza. 'Look at his back.'

There was an enormous exit wound where the bullets had smashed their way through. The bleeding didn't seem as bad as Mikhel would have expected, though, and the uninjured side of Ruslan's chest was on top, so he guessed that he should be able to breathe as long as he didn't move.

'Put your jacket over the wound to keep the rain off it,' Mikhel said.

Lionidza took off his jacket and did so.

The three men looked at each other as the thunder rolled again.

'Now what the fuck do we do?'

'One of us has to get help,' said Mikhel. 'The others have to stay here and keep this pen in Ruslan's throat.'

'I'll see if our radio's working.'

'It's fucked. Mingrelsky shot it to pieces. One of us has to run for help.'

'You'd be much faster than either of us,' said Lionidza.

'Okay, you take the pen. Pinch his throat. That's it. Keep it still. Now hold it right there. Make sure it doesn't move. If it falls out, you have to shove it back in, but not too far.'

'Okay.'

'If you get tired, ask him for help,' said Mikhel, indicating the Akhtarian leader.

'I will.'

'And if Ruslan can't breathe, you've got to suck the blood out, but without moving the pen.'

'Yes okay, I've got it.'

'Right.'

'Be quick.'

'Shall I go to the Akhtarians?'

'No. Too far. Go to the Ksords.'

'But what if Mingrelsky's there?'

'You just have to hope he isn't. Hurry up.'

'Okay.'

Mikhel climbed up to the top.

'What's happening?' asked the Ksordian village leader.

'You go down and help them.'

Mikhel set off through the pouring rain. After a while, his old knee injury started to nag at him, but he pushed himself on. He had to get help quickly while Ruslan was still alive.

Lightning flashed and lit up the straight road ahead of him. It couldn't be far now. Then the thunder came with a bang and Mikhel flung himself to the ground. For an instant he thought the Ksords up ahead were shooting at him.

He picked himself up and started to run again, a little more slowly now. What if the Ksords had heard the gunfire when Mingrelsky and his men shot Ruslan? They would be very jumpy right now, and when they saw him coming, they might easily take him for an Akhtarian.

He had better start shouting.

'Don't shoot...I'm a Ksord...Don't shoot.'

This slowed him down even more, but he had to do it. He wouldn't be able to save Ruslan if he were dead.

Lightning streaked across the sky once more, and three Ksordian militiamen flashed into view, maybe 200 metres up the road, pointing their rifles in his direction.

Mikhel raised his hands and stopped running.

'Don't shoot...I'm a Ksord...Don't shoot.'

He walked towards them, shouting out his mantra at the top of his voice. The thunder rolled, and then Mikhel could make out their voices above the din of the rain.

'Who are you?'

'What are you doing here?'

'Don't shoot...I'm a Ksord...I'm with Ruslan Shanidza.'

They were closer now. He could make them out clearly. They still had their guns pointing at him.

'I'm a Ksord...Don't shoot.'

He stood still and waited for them to come up to him.

'I'm with Ruslan Shanidza.'

'What's going on?'

'Ruslan's been shot,' he panted. 'About eight hundred metres down that way.'

'Is he dead?'

'I don't think so...Sergo Lionidza and both village leaders are with him...You have to get help...Please.'

Seven Weeks Earlier

Chapter Two

RUSLAN LOOKED out of his window as the plane flew over Taganogsky Bay towards the northern mouth of Russia's quiet river, the Don. He was heading for Rostov, now Russia's only major port on the Black Sea since the demise of the Soviet Union. For in the three and a half years since he and Tamara had gone to live in England, the world had turned upside-down. Gorbachev's reforms had snowballed out of control, Communism had collapsed and the Soviet Union had been dissolved.

So it was that Ruslan entered Russia as a foreigner rather than a citizen of a fraternal Soviet republic, though he had to use his old Soviet passport in order to do so.

'What's the purpose of your visit to Russia?' The immigration officer leafed through his passport as she spoke. She had not yet so much as glanced at him.

'I'm on my way to Ksordia-Akhtaria.'

'So why didn't you fly direct?'

'It's much cheaper to fly here and then take the train.'

'But you can't take the train to Ksordia-Akhtaria. There's fighting on the border.'

'I know. There isn't any fighting near Stavropol. I'll go that way.' Ruslan was in fact heading to where the fighting was heaviest, but the immigration officer wasn't to know that.

'You do a lot of travelling.'

'Yes, I'm an athlete. I used to represent the Soviet Union.'

The immigration officer looked at him for the first time. Ruslan took it for granted that she would like what she saw: the tanned face of a fit and healthy man in his early-thirties with deep brown eyes that were beautiful, as Tamara would occasionally remind him in their more intimate moments.

'What kind of athlete?'

'A marathon runner.'

'Are you famous?'

'I'm world champion.'

'Seriously?'

'Yes, and Olympic champion. Unfortunately, I only got silver in the European Championships, so I keep quiet about that one.'

The immigration officer looked impressed. She stamped his passport and handed it back to him. 'You can always save yourself the price of a bus fare and run to Stavropol.'

As he entered the dimly-lit baggage hall, Ruslan was none too pleased to spot his suitcase already on the carousel. He decided to ignore it and wait at the wrong carousel for ten minutes. He was early for his cloak-and-dagger rendezvous with Sergo Lionidza, and it was important not to go through customs too soon.

Ruslan was very aware of just how much he owed Lionidza, who had protected him during the Soviet era and had made it possible for him to compete abroad. Without Lionidza's help, he and Tamara would never have obtained the exit visas that allowed them to go and live in the West.

And now Ruslan was here to pay him back, though he wasn't entirely sure how.

He glanced at his watch. It was almost four o'clock, time to play the part of a confused traveller who suddenly realises that he is at the wrong carousel. He pushed his trolley to the notice board, scratched his head, swore in Russian, picked up his suitcase and headed for customs.

Once out into the arrivals hall, he shook his head at the unofficial taxi drivers who swarmed around him. He spotted Lionidza standing at the coffee bar, still dressed like an *apparatchik* from the Soviet era.

For an instant, they made eye contact, but Ruslan quickly looked away and walked on.

A moment later, he heard Lionidza's voice: 'Ruslan...Ruslan!'

He turned round.

'Oh hello, Comrade Lionidza, sir.'

'Call me Sergo. Nobody says, "Comrade" these days.'

Sergo? That was an unexpected honour.

The two men exchanged four kisses.

'What are you doing here?' Lionidza said it in Russian, which Ruslan considered a bit over the top.

'I'm trying to get home,' he said, obediently speaking Russian. 'What about you?'

They switched to Ksord-Akhtarian and discussed the supposed purpose of their journeys. As if by coincidence, it turned out that they would both be staying the night in Rostov, so Lionidza suggested that they share a taxi.

That single word that is the same in every language animated all the taxi drivers around them, but Ruslan and Lionidza shook their heads. They made their way to the official taxi rank, where they would be sure of a random driver who just happened to be next in' the queue, a driver who would neither understand Ksord-Akhtarian nor be employed by any of the two or three secret services who might be interested in their conversation, which could begin in earnest as soon as they had given the driver his instructions.

'Thank you for coming, Ruslan. I'm very grateful.'

'I just hope I can help.'

'How long are you here for?'

'I asked my university for unpaid leave until Easter. They haven't actually had time to consider it yet, but I think it'll be okay.'

'Well, if we can't sort this mess out in four weeks, you might as well give up and go back to England. Now tell me, did you phone that Russian reporter like I said?'

'Yes.'

'And?'

'He's coming with a camera crew.'

'Excellent. Sergei Ivanov's a very good friend to have. He's had *blat* up to his eyeballs since he covered Boris Yeltsin during the coup.' (Lionidza used the Russian word *blat* to talk about Sergei's recently acquired influence in high places.) 'Now this evening you're going to have to make a lot of phone calls.' He took a small notebook out of his pocket and opened it. 'You'll need Ksords and Akhtarians and Tatars too. TV's most important, but you also need some press. These are the people to call. I've put their work numbers on the left and their home numbers on the right. And call this guy: he's a photographer and he's good.'

'Okay.'

'You need some pro-democrat press. Have you got Nina Begishveli's number?'

'No, and in any case, I'd rather not call her. It'd be a bit awkward.' (Democrat leader Nina Begishveli had been Ruslan's lover some ten years earlier.)

'Aren't you in touch with her?'

'No.'

'So do you have any contacts among the democrats?'

'Not really. I'll phone that singer, Leila Meipariani. She'll know who to call.'

'You've got her number?'

'No, but I can call Fatima Dzemileva. She'll have it.'

'Okay. Now when you make your calls, whatever you do, don't mention my name.'

'Why not?'

'Well, I'm not exactly the most popular person in Ksordia-Akhtaria right now. Even Comrade Zikladza's seriously annoyed with me since I resigned from the government.'

'So you're not going to be at the press conference?'

'No.'

'And you won't be coming to the border with me?'

'No.'

'What are you going to do?'

'I'm going to Zeda'Anta. The Akhtarians may not like me very much, but they might be willing to talk to me.'

'Okay.'

'Do you know what to say to the press when you call them?'

'More or less, but can you remind me what I'm supposed to do when I get to the border?'

Chapter Three

FIVE DAYS Before Ruslan's arrival, Comrade Besiki Zikladza, Ksordia-Akhtaria's fallen Communist ruler, had scowled at the reports on his desk. So the Akhtarians had finally done it, had they? They had declared independence. The bloody morons. Did they seriously think the Ksords would let them get away with it? Not with nearly half a million Ksords living in the south of the country, they wouldn't.

The Ksords would send in the army and drive the Akhtarians out of the south, and then they would let them have their independent state, a shattered rump filled with destitute refugees.

After that, thanks to those Akhtarian morons, that treacherous cretin Shakman Korgay would be able to present himself as the hero of the hour, the saviour of the Ksords, the man who had seen off the 'Rebel' threat.

Fucking Korgay.

Zikladza's blood still boiled every time he thought of him.

God's nails, he hated that man.

Korgay owed Zikladza everything. He was a nothing until he had taken him under his wing. Nothing. A nobody. Just a has-been of a wrestler, and he hadn't even been any good at that. He never won a single tournament outside Ksordia-Akhtaria, and he didn't make the Soviet team, not even once.

That man owed him everything.

Everything.

And how did he repay him?

By stabbing him in the back first chance he got.

Son of a slut.

Zikladza wished he could think of a way to stop him.

There had to be something he could do.

A way to piss on Korgay's plans.

But how?

How could he do it?

How could he stop him exploiting the situation in Akhtaria?

He could get in there first.

Yes, that was it. Get in there first.

Now how was he going to do that?

Maybe he could persuade the Federal President to send the army into Akhtaria straight away, before Korgay had time to react. Not to start a war but just to force the Akhtarians to the negotiating table.

Yes, that would do it.

Not an invasion. No, just seize some strategic points. Maybe the border posts on Akhtaria's frontier with Russia. Yes, that would be good.

Then the Akhtarians would have to negotiate. And if he could dominate the negotiations and reach a deal with them, he could knobble Korgay and finally begin the long road back to power.

Comrade Zikladza sat back in his leather chair.

Yes, he had found a way forward, a way to fight back. It would be good to be in control again for the first time in more than two years, ever since Korgay had shafted him.

Remembering how that cockroach had betrayed him filled Zikladza with rage once more. Korgay's anti-bureaucratic revolution? What a joke. Totally opportunistic revolution more like. Korgay didn't have a principled bone in his body.

But even then Zikladza might have found a way to outmanoeuvre him if that imbecile Gorbachev hadn't come up with his stupid multi-party elections. How was the Party supposed to win when every demagogue in the country was at liberty to stir people up and promise them the earth?

The elections were a catastrophe. The Party lost more than two thirds of its seats at both federal and regional level.

He had expected this defeat to be the end of him, but it wasn't.

All those bloody democrats and nationalists, they hadn't dared to kick him out of the government, let alone arrest him. They were so scared of Korgay that they gave Zikladza three seats in the cabinet just to make sure Korgay didn't dominate.

They thought they didn't need to worry about Zikladza.

He was no threat.

Just a toothless old dinosaur.

Well he would show them he wasn't finished yet. He would force the Akhtarians to negotiate and frustrate that traitor Korgay. And then he would find a way to shit in the democrats' and nationalists' shoes too.

He smiled and sat back.

But then he had a thought.

What if the Akhtarians misinterpreted his actions? What if they thought he was sending the army in to crush them, not to stymie Korgay? They might attack the troops at the Russian border. That would be a disaster.

Maybe he could send the Akhtarian leadership a secret message.

But no, he had no reason to trust them. And they had no reason to trust him for that matter. After all, he had had most of them locked up during the Soviet era.

No, if the Akhtarians attacked the army, he would need something else, a way to extricate his troops without mounting a full-scale invasion. He would need someone he could use but who wasn't associated with him. A useful idiot who would do what he wanted but who wouldn't know that he was calling the shots.

Who?

It had to be someone the Akhtarians would trust and someone the Ksords trusted too.

For several minutes, Comrade Zikladza racked his brains.

Who could it be?

Who?

Then he smiled. He had the perfect candidate, or rather Sergo Lionidza did.

He buzzed his receptionist-cum-mistress: 'Can you give Sergo a call? Tell him I'd like a word.'

Chapter Four

AS HE lay in his hotel bed unable to sleep, Ruslan reflected on other times he had made a big splash when he arrived in Ksordia-Akhtaria. The first had been his triumphant return after he won Olympic gold in 1988. He had been staggered by his reception. The streets of Khosume had been lined with cheering crowds all the way to Victory Square, where 40,000 or more had turned up to welcome him home as a national hero.

He and Tamara had posed for photographs with all the Communist big fish, including Ksord-Akhtarian Party boss Comrade Zikladza and his two closest advisors, Korgay and Lionidza. Korgay had quite obviously been bowled over by Tamara, who was a striking young woman with jet black hair and a pale complexion, high cheekbones and a strong Anatolian nose. Korgay couldn't keep his eyes off her and cornered her for some considerable time during the reception that followed. Ruslan and Tamara laughed uproariously about it afterwards.

The authorities sent them on a victory tour of the other three regional capitals in East Ksordia, West Ksordia and Akhtaria. They were keen to use their Ksordian Olympic champion and his photogenic Akhtarian wife to send out a message of Ksord-Akhtarian unity in an effort to cool the nationalist passions that were beginning to bubble under the surface.

Neither of them had any great love for the Communists, but they shared their fear of a resurgent nationalism and the havoc it could wreak in a multi-ethnic republic. It was, after all, just seven months since they had witnessed the rape and murder of Armenians at the hands of a nationalist mob in Azerbaijan.

Ruslan's second great homecoming took place two years later with his silver medal from the European Championships. Ruslan had experienced the race as a traumatic defeat, made all the worse by the fact that it wasn't the first time Giovanni Bardolini had outfoxed him in a major tournament.

Bardolini had ignored all the other runners and treated the race as a contest between just the two of them. He stayed three paces behind Ruslan throughout, stalking him, unnerving him and infuriating him. It was the most frustrating race Ruslan had ever run because he knew after ten kilometres what would happen: Bardolini would overtake him near the end and beat him, and there would be nothing he could do to stop him.

Ruslan half expected his countrymen to jeer him when he took his medal home, but his reception was every bit as rapturous as after his Olympic victory. Perhaps this was because a love of heroic failure was burned deep into the Ksordian psyche, hardly surprising in a country that had been ruled by a succession of foreign overlords for the last 600 years and where every attempt to regain independence had ended in disaster.

The Ksords' archetypal hero was their last king, Wirustam II, who was remembered not for any victories but for his desperate last stand against overwhelming odds during the Tatar invasion. The Ksords' great national epic, *The Downfall of the Kuban Kingdoms*, told how, the night before battle, the prophet Elijah appeared to Wirustam as a white eagle and offered him the choice between craven surrender and a heroic death that would inspire his people forever.

'Wirustam, great King of Ksordia
Tomorrow two destinies are yours to choose.
If it's a white beard and grandchildren you hope for,
Then stable your horses, stand down your men
And walk into the enemy camp at daybreak.
Surrender your standards, hand over your sword
And ask the heathen invaders for mercy.
They will be mild in their dispensation
And will set you to rule your ravaged kingdom
As a vassal, a knave and a collector of taxes.

'But if you desire eternal glory,

Then draw your army around you
In the field of red-breasted geese,
And set your standards in the ground
With the noble diamonds of your brother.
There you shall die with sword in hand
And your crown will be lost amid the slaughter.
But remember that even a long life is fleeting
And a martyr's glory will last forever.'

Wirustam chose to fight, and the next day he and his army stood their ground and were cut down to a man.

But, however much the myth of King Wirustam permeated his thinking, Ruslan felt like a failure rather than a hero when he returned from the European Championships with only a silver medal. And he couldn't understand why he should be welcomed home by tens of thousands of adoring fans when Nina Begishveli and other dissidents had been greeted by at best a hundred or so supporters when they returned from their prisons and labour camps. In his eyes, these people were genuine heroes who had gone to prison rather than surrender their principles, while he had abandoned his in order to further his running career.

By now, the Ksordia-Akhtaria that welcomed him was a very different place. The Communists' monopoly of power had collapsed and, in a development Ruslan viewed with some alarm, a new strongman had emerged to lead the Ksords.

That man was Shakman Korgay, the senior Communist who had been so taken by Tamara in the aftermath of his Olympic triumph. For almost 20 years, Korgay had been one of Comrade Zikladza's closest collaborators. But then, in the spring of 1989, he had turned against him in the most dramatic fashion.

It all started innocuously enough: textile workers in East Ksordia had gone on strike over unpaid wages. The police weighed in, and some of the strikers were given a thrashing. Comrade Zikladza sent Korgay to deal with the situation. He told him to take a conciliatory approach and bring the strike to a speedy end.

Instead, much to everyone's astonishment, Korgay denounced the police and denounced Zikladza and put himself at the head of the strike.

The effect was electrifying. With a heady brew of *perestroika* and Ksordian nationalism, Korgay set off a massive wave of strikes and demonstrations that rapidly brought him control of both Party and state in East Ksordia. Then he bussed tens of thousands of supporters down to West Ksordia and took control there too.

When he prepared to send his hordes to Akhtaria, an ugly confrontation loomed. Akhtarian nationalists vowed to throw back this 'Ksordian invasion', and it was only at the last minute that Comrade Zikladza's police intervened to halt Korgay's convoys.

For the next nine months, Ksordia-Akhtaria was ruled by two opposing Communist governments: Comrade Zikladza's old-style Communists controlled Central Kubania and Akhtaria, while Korgay's 'reformists' ran East and West Ksordia. Were it not for the restraining hand of Moscow, their rivalry might easily have led to civil war.

In March 1990, Moscow ordered multi-party elections throughout the Soviet Union. Comrade Zikladza was unable to fix the results and lost his remaining strongholds. Nationalists swept to power in Akhtaria, and an unlikely coalition of Ksordian, Akhtarian and Tatar nationalists took over in Central Kubania. Meanwhile Korgay consolidated his hold on the rest of the country.

It took more than a month of negotiations to form a government for Ksordia-Akhtaria as a whole. With a professor of economics at its head, the new cabinet was little more than a collection of enemies. It included nationalists of every hue, plus radical democrats (led by Nina Begishveli) and both Comrade Zikladza's and Korgay's Communist factions. In any case, it had very little power. The regional governments undermined it at every opportunity.

Just like after his Olympic victory, Ruslan's post-European Championship procession made its way through the cheering streets of Khosume to a massive reception where he and Tamara

24

would stand and smile for the cameras beside almost every senior politician in the republic.

Only three big players failed to turn up. To Ruslan's relief, Korgay chose not to be enticed out of his East Ksordian lair. Ruslan guessed that he had no desire to be seen with an athlete associated with Lionidza, by now the sole remaining confidant of his enemy Comrade Zikladza. Akhtarian leader Baykan Eristov, who famously disapproved of mixed marriages between Akhtarians and Ksords, saw no reason to greet a returning Ksord. And Nina Begishveli preferred not to meet her former lover and his now pregnant wife.

When Ruslan got a moment alone with his old friend the Tatar leader Yakub Bovin, he gave him a message for Nina: 'Tell her I'm cross with her. She should have come.'

Ruslan's third great triumphal homecoming came in the summer of 1991, when he and Tamara brought their six month-old baby son home to present him to their families. For such a proud father, this felt like his greatest triumph of all.

But this time, they made sure that details of their visit were kept quiet. Tamara had no desire to appear in public or to have any press or TV cameras at their baby's baptism. In the event, it was a good job the media weren't there because the whole thing turned out to be a disaster.

It all started well, with the two extended families together for the first time since their wedding. Ruslan's relatives were delighted that the ceremony would take place in their home village and that the baby would be chrismated into the Ksordian church, thereby bestowing a Ksordian identity upon him.

In return for this concession, Tamara had insisted that he be named Shota and that everyone should know that this was in honour of the Akhtarian Partizan of that name that had helped defend the village against Akhtarian Rebel raiding parties during the Great Patriotic War.

After the service, they held an enormous party to celebrate. That was when things started to go wrong. One of Tamara's cousins got into an argument with some local youths. He told them the wartime Akhtarian Rebels weren't anything like as bad as Ksords liked to pretend, not a sensible thing to say in a village where they had massacred 127 civilians, most of them women and children.

Within minutes a fight had broken out, with seven or eight young men on either side having a real go at one another. Ruslan and others intervened to pull them apart, but that wasn't the end of it. Some of the locals decided to vandalise all the Akhtarian guests' cars. They tore their wing mirrors off and kicked in their lights.

Ruslan and Tamara were mortified, as were the older generation on both sides. Those who could remember the war exchanged kisses and best wishes at the end, but their sons and grandsons continued to exchange insults.

That night, Tamara told Ruslan that she was too frightened to remain in Ksordian territory, so next day they drove to her parents' flat in Zeda'Anta, where she and Shota would spend the summer while he went off for altitude training in Georgia.

In the second week of August, Ruslan and the Soviet team headed for the World Athletics Championships in Tokyo. But before the competition could begin, their preparations were interrupted by news of a coup d'état by Communist hardliners in Moscow.

The athletes and their coaches crowded around TV screens desperate for news. To his surprise, Ruslan recognised one Russian reporter whose footage made it onto CNN. This was Sergei Ivanov, who had helped rescue him and Tamara when they had been arrested for fighting with Vakhtan Mingrelsky almost 14 years earlier.

The coup divided Soviet team between those Russians and Ukrainians who supported it and the rest, including everyone from other ethnic groups, who regarded it as a catastrophe. Ruslan heard rumours of fights breaking out between supporters and opponents of the coup, though he never witnessed anything of the kind himself.

His main concern was Tamara and his family's safety, and he spent half the day frantically trying to phone them. It wasn't until the next day that he was able to get through to Tamara. She told him that Ksordia-Akhtaria was calm and he should get back to his training.

She said that Comrade Zikladza had publicly backed the coup. She had seen him on TV with Lionidza by his side as he read out a statement of support. All this was predictable enough, though it saddened Ruslan to be reminded that his mentor Lionidza was one of *them*.

More remarkable was what Tamara told him about Shakman Korgay, who was supposed to be Ksordia's leading Communist reformer. It was several hours before he said anything – he was obviously waiting to see which way the wind was blowing – and he then made a broadcast on East Ksordian TV in which he proclaimed his support for the coup.

Ruslan was flabbergasted. This was opportunism of such astonishing crassness that he almost admired Korgay's nerve.

When the coup disintegrated on the third day, Ruslan was relieved and overjoyed. Not only had the hard-line Communists failed, but Korgay had made the most spectacular miscalculation. His reformist and nationalist allies would now desert him, and his destabilising influence on Ksord-Akhtarian politics would surely come to an end.

Ruslan had worried that the coup would distract him from his preparations for the marathon, but in the event he experienced its failure as a massive boost to his morale.

He had devised a bold, almost reckless plan for the World Championship marathon that involved three separate surges in a single race. In the first, which started at around 20 kilometres, he caught up with the leading pack. Five kilometres later, he surged again until he had built up a commanding lead.

He knew that the best runners would catch up with him, which Suleyman Ahmadi of Djibouti and Hiroyuki Tomizawa of Japan did just before the 38-kilometre mark. He let them overtake him but made sure he stayed within striking distance until, half a kilometre later, he surprised them with his third and final surge. They were unable to keep up, and Ruslan knew that gold would be his provided he could maintain a good pace for the rest of the race.

What he didn't realise was just how difficult this would prove to be. Those last three kilometres would prove to be the most excruciating of his running career. He had never known such pain. Even his beatings at the hands of Vakhtan Mingrelsky couldn't match the torture he inflicted upon himself that day.

Whenever he thought about it afterwards, it astonished Ruslan that he had managed to keep going. The only thing that got him through it was the memory of his humiliation by Bardolini the previous year and his determination never to be beaten in the final stages of a race again.

Long before he reached the stadium, his face had set in an agonised grimace, but somehow he kept up his pace until right near the end, when he very nearly collapsed. He used his last milligrams of strength to heave himself across the winning line. Then he staggered a few more paces and fell to the ground. The track officials summoned paramedics, who were so concerned that they placed an oxygen mask over his face and stretchered him out of sight of the cameras.

Tamara, like almost the entire population of Ksordia-Akhtaria, watched in horror as Ruslan was carried away. It was fully twenty minutes before he emerged, pallid and unsteady, supported by the arm of his coach Mikhel Inalipa. The whole stadium gave him a standing ovation, as did Tamara in her parents' flat 8,000 kilometres away, tears streaming down her cheeks.

Ruslan regarded this World Championship gold as his supreme achievement. He knew he would never be able to do anything like that again and wondered whether the time had come for him to quit.

Back in Ksordia-Akhtaria, he received his most triumphal welcome yet, and this time he felt he deserved it. The crowds lining the streets were thicker and more ecstatic than he had ever seen them, and his convoy's halting progress through the surging crowds in Victory Square was genuinely scary.

The Akhtarian leader still saw no reason to greet a returning Ksord, but the other political big fish that had missed his last triumph turned up. Korgay was there, smiling, slapping backs and laughing at everyone's jokes. He was as obsequious as ever towards Tamara when he greeted her, but this time he had politicians he needed to fawn on, so she would be spared his attentions for the rest of the evening.

Far more important to Ruslan was the presence of Nina near the end of the long line of dignitaries who waited to have their photograph taken with him. It would be the first time he had seen her since the last day of their trial more than nine years earlier.

She looked older than her 39 years, but she had kept her slender figure and still showed the poise that Ruslan had always appreciated. In fact, he thought she looked fabulous, though he also took pleasure in the fact that she was nowhere near as good looking as Tamara.

Nina had brought along her latest lover, a distinguished sociologist with whom, scandalously, she cohabited quite openly.

'Hello Nina, long time no see.' Ruslan was very aware that Tamara was watching, as was half of Ksordia-Akhtaria on TV.

'Hello Ruslan.'

Flashlights flashed as they exchanged four kisses.

'It's good to see you again.'

'You too.'

'This is my wife Tamara.'

'Hello. Nice to meet you.'

'Nice to meet you too.'

The two women shook hands.

Nina introduced her 'partner' and then it was time for Ruslan and Tamara to move down the line. He didn't have another opportunity to speak to Nina that evening, but he was delighted to have seen her at last and hoped it wouldn't be another nine years before they met again.

Back in England, it was difficult for Ruslan to follow events in Ksordia-Akhtaria. His only sources were friends and family and the occasional newspaper article they posted to him. But one thing was clear: he had grossly underestimated Shakman Korgay and his ability to bounce back from his failure to back the winning side in the Moscow coup.

Korgay reinvented himself as an out-and-out Ksordian nationalist and started to push for full independence, which came at the end of the year when Boris Yeltsin dissolved the Soviet Union.

As a youth, Ruslan had longed for the day when Ksordia-Akhtaria would become independent, but now he looked on in trepidation, aware of Aleksander Herzen's warning from the previous century that the collapse of empire and dictatorship could easily lead to 'a long night of chaos and desolation' rather than the spontaneous flowering of liberty.

It was certainly an astonishing situation. Ksordia and Akhtaria hadn't been independent since the Tatar invasion of 1238, apart from the short-lived Pan-Kuban republic of 1918-19 and the Rebel Akhtarian state set up by the Nazis.

Now Ksordia-Akhtaria was an independent Federal Republic, but Ruslan doubted that even half its inhabitants identified with it. Many Ksords dreamed of 'Ksordia United With Korgay', while most Akhtarians longed for a state of their own without him. The only community who were wholehearted in their desire to keep Ksordia-Akhtaria together were the Tatars, just 12% of the population, who felt safer in a multi-ethnic state and who feared the consequences of conflict between the Ksords and the Akhtarians.

The Tatars, together with the democrats and some moderate Ksordian and Akhtarian nationalists, hoped to turn Ksordia-Akhtaria into a loose confederation. But more militant nationalists would have no truck with that idea. They wanted separation. Unfortunately, however, Central Kubania and southern Akhtaria were such an ethnic mishmash that Ksords and Akhtarians inevitably had very different ideas about where the border between them should lie.

Korgay now made an audacious move. He surprised everyone by arranging a meeting between his militant Ksords and the Akhtarian leadership. He proposed that they should bypass the Tatars and the Federal Ksord-Akhtarian government and carve the country up between them.

Unfortunately, the meeting was a disaster. The Ksords' territorial demands were so extreme that the Akhtarians took fright. They decided to declare independence at once and try to secure international recognition before Korgay could consolidate his grip on Ksordia.

But a unilateral Akhtarian declaration of independence was not something that the large Ksordian communities in southern Akhtaria were in any way inclined to accept. This was hardly surprising, since the last time they had been subjected to Akhtarian rule was under the Rebel state set up by the Nazis in 1942.

The Rebels had persuaded Himmler that they were descendants of the Black Sea Goths and therefore an offshoot of the Master Race. They proceeded to purge their state of the Ksords who made up a quarter of its population, unleashing a genocidal campaign that slaughtered 100,000 Ksords in the space of less than four months.

And now, 50 years later, the Ksord-Akhtarian Federal Republic stood on the brink of civil war.

It was on Friday 13th March that the British media became aware of the existence of Ksordia-Akhtaria. That night's TV news carried a 30-second report that covered Akhtaria's unilateral declaration of independence and showed footage of Federal troops driving north through hostile crowds to seize the border posts on Akhtaria's northern frontier with Russia.

Ruslan and Tamara tried to phone home, but they couldn't get through until the next afternoon when Tamara finally managed to speak to her sister. She reported that so far fighting was confined to the Russo-Akhtarian border posts, where Akhtarian police and nationalist militias were attacking the Federal troops (she referred to them as 'Ksords'). The whole of Akhtaria was seething with rage, and everyone was expecting a full-scale Ksordian invasion at any minute.

Ruslan spent half the evening on the phone but was unable to speak to his family. By ten he gave up. It would by now be one in the morning in Ksordia-Akhtaria and it was time to let his relatives sleep. He and Tamara turned on the TV to see if there was any more news.

Five minutes later, the telephone rang. To Ruslan's astonishment, it was Lionidza. He sounded somewhat the worse for drink and spoke of his despair at the turn of events. Sending troops into Akhtaria was an act of madness that could spark all-out war between the Ksords and the Akhtarians. He had resigned from the government in protest.

Lionidza explained what had happened. The Federal President had sent the troops in as a way to force the Akhtarians back to the negotiating table, but the whole thing had backfired and now the Akhtarians were attacking the Federal troops.

'The terrible thing is that everybody wants the fighting to stop, but nobody dares to call it off. Everyone on the Federal side can see that their army's fallen into a trap. The troops on the border can't fight their way back to Ksordian territory and there's no way the Federal army can march across the whole of Akhtaria to rescue them.

'But the Akhtarians are desperate for the fighting to end too. They haven't got a proper army and they're just not ready for a full-scale war. Both sides want a ceasefire, but neither of them has the balls to be the first to call a halt.'

This was where Lionidza thought Ruslan could help. 'You're a hero to everyone in the country. You're the only person who every community admires: Ksords, Akhtarians, Tatars, the lot.'

He begged Ruslan to return home and go to where the fighting was fiercest and say, 'This is insanity. It has to stop.' The politicians and soldiers could then use his presence as an excuse to call a ceasefire and start talking. He was sure it would work.

Tamara refused to express an opinion about how Ruslan should respond to Lionidza's request. 'It's your decision,' she said.

'But it will affect you.'

'I know, but it's your decision.'

But Ruslan would never forget her face as he said goodbye to her at Heathrow Airport. He felt that nothing he had ever done had hurt her so deeply. 'Remember that I need my husband and Shota needs his father,' she told him. 'Make sure you come back to us in one piece.'

Chapter Five

THAT EVENING, Russian reporter Sergei Ivanov checked into the same hotel as Ruslan, and the two bumped into each other at the breakfast buffet next morning, the first time they had met for almost 14 years. They embraced like old friends, and Ruslan invited Sergei to sit with him.

'I never got a chance to thank you for helping me and my friends after our little spat with Vakhtan Mingrelsky.'

'Glad we were able to help. In a funny kind of way, I owe you too.'

'You do?'

'Yes, you helped me get my first big byline. It was your little escapade that got me suspicious when Aleksander Mingrelsky resigned. Everyone said it was because of his womanising but I just knew it had to be something to do with his son, and so I kept digging and digging until I found the story.'

'I didn't know he was a womaniser.'

'God yes. He had a terrible reputation for chasing after Party members' wives.'

Ruslan laughed. 'Was it easy to get your story printed?'

'My editor loved it. Apparently the censors were none too happy, but they didn't actually have a good reason to stop us.'

'It made my day when I read it. I bought copies for all my friends.'

Sergei laughed. 'And I hear you and Mingrelsky junior's paths have crossed twice since.'

'Bloody hell. You're well informed.'

'I interviewed Nina Begishveli last year. When I said how I'd met you, she went off the record and told me.'

'I didn't know she knew, about the second time, I mean.'

'Well, she does. Did you know Mingrelsky junior beat her up too?'

'No? When?'

'About three months after she got out of prison.'

'Ah yes, I heard she was beaten up. She was quite badly hurt, wasn't she?'

'Two broken ribs.'

'I never realised it was Mingrelsky. Presumably the KGB were behind it.'

'Probably, but she said she felt there was a kind of personal element to it, almost like he was giving you a thrashing by proxy.'

'Really?'

'You want to be careful of him. You know he's got his own private army now?'

'So I hear. Look, can you keep this about Mingrelsky off the record?'

'Sure, but when you go public, you do it through an exclusive interview with me, okay?'

'It's a deal.' Ruslan changed the subject: 'What about Natasha? Are you still in touch with her?'

'I see her every other weekend, when I pick my daughter up.'

'Oh, right. Is she still working as a journalist?'

'Yes, she edits the women's page in *Nezavisimaya Gazeta*.'

'That's good. So how old's your daughter?'

'Eleven, and then I've got another little girl with my new wife. You're still with Tamara, right?'

'Yes, we've got a little boy now.'

'How old is he?'

'Fifteen months.'

'That's a nice age.'

'He's so cute.'

'Is Tamara still in England?'

'Yes. I'm hoping I won't be here for long.'

'Do you like it over there?'

'It's great. Life's so easy: you never have to queue, everything works, the summer's not hot, the winter's not cold. Have you been there?'

'No, only to West Germany.'

'England's a funny country, though. They should wrap it up and put it in a museum. They've still got their Queen and all their Lords, and they don't use metres or litres. It's like the last two hundred years never happened.'

'What about the English? What are they like?'

'They keep themselves to themselves a bit, but they're okay.'

'Is it true that they're a nation of hypocrites?'

'Oh God, yes. They're the biggest liars on the planet. Tamara worked as a doctor before she had her baby. She always said her patients would come in, and she'd say, "How are you?" and they'd always say, "Fine thanks."'

Sergei laughed.

'I mean, what's the point of going to see the doctor if you're fine? So she'd have to say, "How can I help you?" and then they'd say, "It's my sinuses doctor, they're killing me."'

'Yes, that's what I've heard. Aren't they funny?'

'They even train their kids to lie. I've seen it. They've got this sort of tradition, if a child crosses his fingers like this,' Ruslan crossed his fingers and held them up, 'they can tell any lie they like. We used to babysit for our neighbours sometimes, and their kids were always doing it to us.'

Sergei's camera crew had just come down for breakfast, so Sergei introduced them. They joined Ruslan and Sergei round the table, and their conversation quickly moved on to their finest hour, when they filmed Boris Yeltsin standing on a tank outside the White House parliament during the Moscow coup. Ruslan felt flattered to be covered by such an illustrious crew.

He held his press conference that evening. Russian TV news covered it, but Ruslan was unable to pick up any Ksordian or Akhtarian channels, so he had no idea what impact if any he had had back home. He thought of phoning his half-brother Giorgi to ask but decided he would rather not explain himself to his nationalistic relatives quite yet.

Early next morning, he set off for the Russo-Akhtarian border in a hired Zhiguli Fiat. The drive should have taken little more than two hours, but the camera crews who accompanied him lengthened the journey by demanding that he stop so they could film him driving past all the big landmarks on the way. But they showed their value when he encountered the massive Russian military presence near the frontier. Without Sergei's *blat*, the Russian army would never have allowed Ruslan to proceed beyond Zernograd.

By now, he was feeling more and more nervous. He thought that if it weren't for his press companions, he would have been very tempted to turn his car round and head back to England. However, his fear of public humiliation was proving stronger than his fear of the war zone he was nearing.

Two kilometres from the border, the convoy reached a Russian command post. By now, the noise of the fighting was very audible indeed. A Russian sergeant told Ruslan the Akhtarians we attacking the Ksord-led Federal troops with small arms fire, and the Federals were replying with small arms, RPGs and the occasional mortar round.

The sergeant took Ruslan and Sergei to meet his captain, who already knew why they had come. 'I'll call up the Federals,' he said. 'We get on well with them, unlike those Akhtarian bastards.'

Ruslan found this confusing: both Lionidza and Sergei had told him that the Russians and Akhtarians were allies.

The Captain led them into a tent, where he began to speak into a field radio. 'This is Russian Bear. This is Russian Bear calling the Federal forces. Do you read me? Over.'

After a few minutes of this, a Ksord-Akhtarian accent crackled over the airwaves. 'Federals here. What's happening, Russian Bear? Got those whores for my men yet? Over.'

The Captain grinned. 'Ever heard of Ruslan Shanidza? Over.'

'Of course I have. Over.'

'Well, he's here with me and he wants to speak to you. Hold on a second.'

He handed the microphone to Ruslan.

'What rank is he?'

'Senior Lieutenant.'

'Hello,' said Ruslan, speaking Ksord-Akhtarian. 'Senior Lieutenant?'

The Russian captain gestured to Ruslan, who said, 'Over' and clicked the switch on the microphone.

'Hello?' replied the Senior Lieutenant in a strong West Ksordian accent. 'Is that really Ruslan Shanidza? Over.'

'Yes. Over.'

'What the fuck are you doing here? Over.'

Ruslan had rehearsed this conversation many times: 'I've come to see if I can negotiate a ceasefire between you and the Akhtarians. Over.'

'You're joking. Over.'

'No, I'm not. Over.'

'Why? Over.'

Ruslan had his answer ready: 'Because I don't think it's right that young conscripts should get killed just because the politicians have cocked things up. Over.'

'My orders are to hold onto this border crossing. Over.'

'I'm not saying you should surrender. I'm just saying we should see if we can arrange a ceasefire. Over.'

'Yes, but how the fuck are you going to do that if I refuse to surrender? Over.'

'I've got some ideas, but I don't think we should talk about them over the radio. Can I come and join you? Over.'

'Are you serious? Over.'

'Very. Over.'

'You're fucking mad, do you know that? Over.'

'But you'll let me come, right? Over.'

The Federal Senior Lieutenant agreed and said Ruslan could bring the press and TV with him, as long as there were no Akhtarians among them.

The Russian Captain then called up the major commanding the Akhtarians, whose brusque manner showed that he disliked the Russian intensely. Ruslan wondered what was behind this.

'What the fuck are you up to, Shanidza?' the Major asked. He was obviously going to be difficult, but he agreed to let Ruslan come over, but not by car: 'I don't want you delivering supplies to the Ksords (as he called the Federal forces).'

The TV camera crews wanted to bring Sergei's outside broadcast van over, but when Ruslan called the Akhtarian Major to get clearance, he refused to allow it.

After a quick lunch that everybody was too nervous to eat, Ruslan filmed short interviews in Ksord-Akhtarian, Tatar and Russian.

'Have you noticed?' Sergei said as they prepared to set off. 'Nobody's fired a shot since you got here.'

'Maybe I should quit while I'm ahead.'

He swung his borrowed Russian military rucksack onto his shoulder and took his first steps along the flat, straight road that led to the war.

Chapter Six

RUSLAN THOUGHT they must have looked an odd procession, with him in front, a white flag in his hand, and the TV cameramen and photographers scurrying around him, trying to get shots that made it look as if the rest of his media circus weren't there. He hoped he didn't look as frightened as he was feeling.

They encountered the last group of Russian troops 100 metres from the frontier, which was marked by a dull white, blue and green triband – the flag of both the Ksords and the Ksord-Akhtarian Federal Republic they dominated.

Soon they came across their first Federal troops, all East Ksords but for their Tatar sergeant, sheltering along the embankment by the road. They made Ruslan and his companions leave the road and clamber down the embankment, and then they led them to the village of Betkio. A number of Akhtarian civilians were still there, sitting outside their wooden houses. Ruslan guessed that the Federal forces kept them there to prevent the Akhtarians from shelling the village, though whether they had any shells was another question.

Ruslan's escorts separated him from the press and took him to one of the few brick houses in the village. There he encountered the Senior Lieutenant and two other officers, both of them West Ksords. They greeted Ruslan warmly and invited him inside.

'Do you want to correct your coffee?' asked one of the officers, holding a bottle of vodka over it.

'No thanks. Too much of a health freak.'

The Senior Lieutenant filled Ruslan in on what had been happening.

'We came here last Thursday. There were just two Rebel customs officers and we sent them to fuck donkeys. Then the next day the Rebels attacked, and we've been at it ever since.' (Like many Ksords, he called all Akhtarians 'Rebels', an appellation most

Akhtarians found deeply offensive but which a growing minority embraced enthusiastically.)

'Has anyone been killed?'

'Yes, we've lost two men and two more badly wounded. We got the Russians to take them. But we've killed at least half a dozen Rebels.'

'What about your supplies?'

The three officers looked at each other and laughed. 'By rights, we should only have five or six days' ammo left, but we did a deal with the Russians. They let us send forty men south through Russian territory. Then we nipped back into Ksordia-Akhtaria and raided a Rebel village. We commandeered fifteen cars and vans, loaded them up with TVs, videos, fridges and what have you, and then we sold the lot to the Russians in exchange for ammunition.'

'We sent nearly all our men on that raid,' another officer said. 'The Rebels could have just walked in here if they'd known.'

The three officers all smiled broadly, confident that Ruslan, as a Ksord, would approve of their exploits.

'What happened to the civilians there?'

'Nothing. We never laid a finger on them.'

'There was one guy who got thumped, but he asked for it.'

Ruslan was relieved. Any atrocities would have made his task much more difficult.

'So what are you planning to do?' the Senior Lieutenant asked.

Ruslan leaned forward. 'Can I be completely frank? I mean, we're all intelligent men, we're all Ksords, so there's no need to donkey shit, okay?'

The three officers nodded.

'Okay, let's start at the beginning. Who sent you here and why?'

'Korgay: we're here to stop the Russians supplying the Rebels.'

'Wrong. Korgay had nothing to do with it.'

'Who says?'

'Sergo Lionidza. He says the Federal President sent you here to prevent Akhtarian independence.'

'And Korgay?'

'He's quite happy for Akhtaria to be independent. He just wants to bite a few chunks out of it.'

'The Ksordian bits.'

'Yes, the Ksordian bits.'

The Senior Lieutenant looked sceptical. 'So how come Korgay's people didn't walk out of the Federal government, like Lionidza and the Tatars and your old girlfriend?'

'Korgay can't be seen to take a soft line with the Akhtarians, so he had to go along with it. But he doesn't give a damn about these border posts. What he cares about is southern Akhtaria.'

'You mean North Ksordia.'

Ruslan smiled. 'It doesn't matter what you call it. Korgay knows he needs his forces down there, and he won't let the Federal army come a hundred kilometres across Akhtarian territory to dig you guys out of the shit.'

The three officers frowned.

Ruslan continued: 'It's Korgay that matters now. Comrade Zikladza's had it. Korgay'll make sure Zikladza gets all the blame when you surrender and that'll be the end of him.'

'Who says we're going to surrender?'

'Boris Yeltsin. He wants to rub the Ksords' noses in it.'

The officers said nothing. Everybody knew that the Russian President hated both Zikladza and Korgay because of their support for the Moscow coup. The cosy relationship between the Federal troops and the Russian Captain was just a temporary business arrangement.

'So if we're in such deep shit, why should the Rebels want to come to a deal?'

'Everyone wants a deal. The Akhtarians are desperate to avoid all-out war. Comrade Zikladza will go for anything that saves him the humiliation of you surrendering, and Korgay has to make sure Zikladza can't pin any blame on him. Think about it. All these people knew I was coming here, but have any of them tried to stop me? They could have, but they didn't.'

'And what about you, Shanidza? What's your angle?'

'You know I'm married to an Akhtarian? Well I don't want a war. If it happens, it'll tear our families apart. It might even tear us apart and I don't want that.'

'And that's your angle?'

'That's my angle.'

'And what's this deal you want to arrange?'

'What are your orders?'

'To hold onto this border crossing.'

'And what are the Akhtarians' orders?'

'To take control of the border, I suppose.'

'And to open it up,' added Ruslan.

'Yes, maybe.'

'Well then, that's easy. Your orders and their orders aren't incompatible.'

The three officers burst out laughing. 'Of course they're fucking incompatible.'

'No they're not. All you need is joint control of the border crossing until the politicians come up with a proper deal.'

'What? You want us to share control of the border with the Rebels?'

'Yes.'

'You must be fucking joking. Two of our men have died to keep those cockroaches out.'

At that moment, Ruslan lost his cool.

'I'll tell you what's happened here: two of your lads have had their lives snuffed out because the Federal President's a stupid dinosaur who thinks Ksordia-Akhtaria can be held together by force. That's two Ksordian mothers who've lost their sons, and do you know what for? Well, I hope you do, because I don't.

'And just tell me this, those young lads of yours out there, how many more of them have to die? Because some of them will, won't they? If you don't make some kind of deal, more Ksordian lads are going to die, and maybe even that Tatar sergeant. And then in a week or ten days, you're going to surrender anyway. And when that happens, I hope you can look your dead soldiers' mothers in the eye and tell them why their sons' deaths weren't a complete waste, because I don't know what I'd say to them.'

Ruslan stopped, his whole body quivering. He felt a complete idiot. He'd been doing so well and then he had lost his temper.

He stared into space and hoped that he hadn't blown it.

The Senior Lieutenant got up from his chair and walked over to the window. He took out a cigarette and lit it. He spent some time smoking it, blowing the smoke forcefully onto the glass so that it made a circular pattern on the window before it dissipated.

He turned round and spoke to Ruslan. 'Look, we'll lend you a car, and why don't you go and talk to our Rebel friends and see what they might agree to? We haven't agreed to anything yet, and don't go giving them the impression that we have. But it might be worth seeing how amenable they are.'

Ruslan tried not to show his anxiety about what kind of reception the Akhtarians might give him. If Ksordian paranoia was a legacy of the Rebel genocide, the Akhtarians' folk memories gave them every reason to adopt a fearful and fearsome posture of aggressive defence.

When the Red Army 'liberated' Ksordia-Akhtaria from Nazi occupation, Stalin visited upon the Akhtarians the 'Great Repression', a devastating collective punishment for the depredations of the Rebels.

The first wave was the systematic massacre of anyone even remotely connected to the Rebels. Whole families were caught up in the ensuing bloodbath, with more than 20,000 Akhtarians slaughtered in a matter of weeks.

But it was not until the following year that the Akhtarians felt the full force of Stalin's terrible vengeance. Every single Akhtarian man, woman and child was rounded up and deported to Soviet Central Asia, leaving them utterly destitute thousands of kilometres from their homeland.

By the time Khrushchev rehabilitated the Akhtarians and allowed them to return home, hundreds of thousands had died. Almost every family had lost loved ones. And those who found Ksords occupying their homes when they returned were unable to dislodge them.

So Ruslan was not at all surprised to find the Akhtarians hostile. He suspected this was compounded by the fact that where the beleaguered Ksords in the Federal Army saw him as their salvation, the Akhtarian troops, most of whom were in fact policemen rather than soldiers, obviously feared he would deny them their hard-earned victory. They pointed their guns at him as he drove up to their checkpoint, and they gave him and his Russian and Tatar press companions a thorough search before they allowed them to proceed.

The major commanding them, who was a real soldier, shared their hostility. 'Those Ksords are just fucking bandits. They've killed three of my men, and you know what they did in Tsipnag'Maisi? They stole everything the people had, and anyone who protested got the shit kicked out of them.'

Ruslan suggested joint control of the border crossing, but the Major wasn't interested.

'No fucking way. My orders are to fuck them over, and that's exactly what I intend to do.'

Ruslan had an answer lined up for this eventuality: 'So is that it? Shall I tell the press that the Ksords wanted to make a deal, but the local Akhtarian commander was determined to keep fighting?'

'You can tell them whatever you want.'

'Are you sure your political masters want me to give that message to the Russians and the Tatars?'

'Shall I tell you what, Shanidza? Why don't you go and bugger a goat? Go back to the fucking Ksords before my men remember that you're a Ksord too and start taking pot shots at you.'

Ruslan was stunned. He hadn't expected his peace mission to end so abruptly. Within minutes he found himself frogmarched to his car and seen off by jeering Akhtarian policemen. Humiliated and utterly bewildered, he had no idea what to do next.

Chapter Seven

AS HE drove back to the Federal positions, Ruslan realised that his only hope was to contact Lionidza and ask for advice. But the Federals' telephone lines had been cut off, so he would have to go back into Russia. He would refuse to speak to the press. Retreating to Russia in front of their cameras would be such a humiliation that he couldn't bear the thought of explaining it to them.

'Our Akhtarian friend doesn't want to make a deal,' he told the Ksordian Senior Lieutenant. 'I need to call Zeda'Anta to see if I can get someone to twist his arm.'

The Senior Lieutenant gave Ruslan and the press three cars to drive back into Russia and then radioed the Russians and the Akhtarians to get clearance for them to make the journey.

'We start shooting in 30 minutes,' the Akhtarian Major said. 'So they'd better be quick. And make sure you don't sell the villagers' cars to the fucking Russians.'

The Senior Lieutenant's grin indicated that this was exactly what he had arranged to do.

Once back in Russia, Ruslan tried all the numbers Lionidza had given him, but he was unable to locate him. All he could do was leave messages and wait for him to call back. In the meantime, the fighting had started up again, and Ruslan busied himself with keeping as far away from the press as he could.

Lionidza didn't phone until nearly seven. 'I'm not surprised the Akhtarians don't want a ceasefire. After all, they're the ones defending their homeland, and sooner or later the Federal troops are going to have to surrender.'

'So what can I do?'

'Nothing. Just thank your lucky stars you've got me. I'm meeting one of the Akhtarian President's key advisers first thing tomorrow. Maybe he can help.'

'I certainly hope so.'

'Things are going better than you think. You're going to be on the nine o'clock news on just about every channel in the region.'

'Big deal.'

'It is a big deal, Ruslan. The press are the best weapon we've got. Give them a quick interview in time to get it on the news. Say exactly what you threatened to say: the Federal commander was willing to negotiate, and you understand there are people in Zeda'Anta who want to make a deal, but the local Akhtarian commander's opposed to any ceasefire.'

Ruslan did as he was told. His press and TV companions then edited and filed their reports.

Half an hour later, Sergei Ivanov came up to Ruslan. 'All is not lost.'

'You think so?'

'Listen...the Akhtarians have stopped shooting.'

Next morning, the Akhtarians radioed soon after eight. 'Can you come over? The Major would like a word.'

Ruslan drove across in his hire car, followed by all the press, including both Ksords and Akhtarians and Sergei's outside broadcast van. The Federal troops cheerfully waved them through but the Akhtarian police were still menacing.

Their Major was in a foul mood, but it was obvious that he had been ordered to come to a deal. 'Look, I might be prepared to discuss a ceasefire, but they'd have to pull back from the road first, and they have to pull out of the village too, without looting the bloody place.'

'Do you want to talk to the Federal commander directly, or do you want me to act as intermediary?'

'I'm not talking to that piece of shit.'

In his Rostov taxi, Lionidza had given Ruslan a crash course in negotiation techniques, and he now put what he had learnt into practice. He broke the negotiations up into different strands, with one about control of the village and others about the border, the road, the villagers, where the front line actually lay and compensation for those whose possessions had been 'commandeered'. Lionidza had told him to search out areas where he could get them to agree and then, having built up a degree of trust, to begin to deal with disputed areas.

The negotiations dragged on all day, and the two commanders tested Ruslan's patience to the limit by quibbling about almost every little thing. Even when the broad principles of the agreement had been settled, the details proved very difficult: who had how many unarmed observers where, which flag was to be flown where, who would be the first to inspect vehicles as they crossed the border.

It took eleven trips across the lines before the deal was finalised, and then Ruslan had to endure a long wait while the Federal Senior Lieutenant crossed into Russia to telephone his superiors. Finally, they gave their consent, and Ruslan escorted the Senior Lieutenant over to the Akhtarian side, where he and the Major saluted and shook hands.

To Ruslan's surprise, there turned out to be no animosity between them. Each commander congratulated his opposite number on various clever moves he had made during the fighting, like the managers of two football teams having a beer together after a match. The men who had been maimed and killed suddenly seemed very unimportant to them.

Then they all smiled for the cameras and signed their ceasefire agreement in good time for the nine o'clock news.

Afterwards, an elated Ruslan gave a press conference and then telephoned Tamara to tell her of his first success. He tried and failed to contact Lionidza and then returned to the village for the night. He felt safer surrounded by Ksords, despite the fact that the Akhtarians had stopped pointing their guns at him and started asking for his autograph instead.

The following morning, the Senior Lieutenant passed on three requests from Federal commanders to help negotiate ceasefires with the Akhtarian forces besieging them. Ruslan decided to go first to the village of Tavkhacha, 35 kilometres to the west.

The fighting there had been particularly severe, as this border post was on the Rostov to Ronkoni highway, a major artery of communication. A dozen men had been killed and many more injured.

The negotiations, however, went smoothly. In fact, there wasn't a great deal for Ruslan to do. Both sides were keen to make progress, and by three in the afternoon, they had produced a draft agreement.

While they were waiting for clearance from their superiors, Ruslan received a telephone call from Lionidza, who was delighted to hear that things were going so well.

'I'm not quite sure where to go next. The only place they're still fighting is Kuneti. Maybe I should go there.'

'No, don't touch it with a barge pole. The Federal troops raped several women there and the Akhtarians are after blood.'

'But surely that's the kind of place I need to go to most.'

'No. You can't afford to fail. You need to build up momentum.'

'So what do you suggest?'

'Go to Khosume. Our dear friend the Federal President wants to see you. Your work at the border posts is done. It's time to get the politicians talking.'

The drive down to Khosume, the Federal capital, came as a revelation to Ruslan. He had never seen so many flags in all his life. Northern Akhtaria was awash with the red and yellow diamonds so cherished by Akhtarians and so hated by Ksords. Further south, the tribal identity of every town, village, shop or farm was evident from a distance: red and yellow diamonds for Akhtarians and dull tribands for Ksords. As Ruslan crossed into Central Kubania, another flag began to compete: the bright green, white and red of the Tatars.

A naive visitor might imagine this festival of long suppressed nationalisms a thing of beauty, but Ruslan recognised it for what it was: the harbinger of civil war. The greater the variety of flags, the more devastating the conflict would be when it came.

It was the graffiti that did most to bring the danger home. The Ksordian slogans were bad enough, but militant Akhtarians had taken to scrawling a single letter guaranteed to drive any self-respecting Ksord berserk: Φ – the Cyrillic 'F' for Fyetnarebi, the pro-Nazi Akhtarian Rebels who had murdered more than 100,000 Ksords during the Great Patriotic War.

'God's nails,' Ruslan said to himself. 'This whole place has gone mad.'

Chapter Eight

RUSLAN ARRIVED in Khosume that evening, and the state of the city shocked him. Flags and graffiti were everywhere, while the shops looked emptier than ever and scarcely one streetlight in four was working. It seemed to him that the competing governments of Ksordia-Akhtaria had better things to spend their meagre finances on than guns and ammunition.

He stayed the night with his Tatar friends the singer Fatima Dzemileva, her husband Murad and their children. Murad persuaded him to watch Ksordian TV once the children were in bed. After the news, which was crude propaganda in its own right, there was a documentary about the Rebel genocide, in which film of the wartime Rebels and their atrocities was intermingled with modern-day film of Akhtaria's new President addressing a sea of red and yellow diamond flags, Akhtarian troops and paramilitaries in training and posters of Rebel leaders on sale in Akhtarian markets.

Ruslan said, 'This is brilliant propaganda. I can feel it getting to me, even me. God only knows what it does to people like my mother.'

'They have this kind of programme almost every night,' said Murad. 'Korgay's whipping the Ksords into a frenzy, and Akhtarian TV's a mirror image on the other side, with documentary after documentary about the Great Repression.'

'What about Tatar TV?'

'A paragon of truth and moderation.'

Ruslan looked unconvinced.

'It is compared to the other two.'

The next morning Ruslan got up early and went for an hour's run before his meeting at the Presidential Palace. He wondered if he was getting out of his depth. This time he wasn't meeting politicians as a triumphant athlete but as a peacemaker or diplomat or whatever he was now. He wasn't expected just to smile and shake hands for the cameras. He was expected to end a war.

To his astonishment, a crowd of several hundred supporters was waiting to greet him. The police escorted him through them before he had a chance to decide whether or not he should make a speech.

Soon he found himself following the frail looking Federal President up a long, circular flight of stairs to a large, ornate room, where the Federal war cabinet was waiting to receive him. They were sitting under a photograph of Lenin, the first Ruslan had seen since leaving Russia.

'Have you met my colleagues?' said the President. 'This is our Foreign Minister, Comrade Zikladza.'

'Yes, we've met. Hello sir.'

'Hello again, young man.'

Ruslan dutifully shook hands with Ksordia-Akhtaria's former Communist ruler.

The President introduced the other two ministers in his war cabinet: an elderly Tatar ally of Comrade Zikladza's, and a short, angry looking man from Korgay's Socialist Party.

With the exception of Korgay's man, who scowled throughout, they were all very friendly and polite to Ruslan. They thanked him for everything he had done at the border and nodded meekly as he spoke about the need to co-operate with moderate Akhtarians.

The Federal President cleared his throat and said, 'We in the war cabinet have discussed the situation, and the majority of us...' he paused and looked at Korgay's man, 'the majority of us feel that the time has come to withdraw the Federal Army from Akhtaria. We'd be grateful if you could go to Zeda'Anta for us and negotiate that withdrawal.'

Ruslan looked from the Federal President to Comrade Zikladza. Their eyes pleaded with him to say yes.

'Will you order an immediate ceasefire?'

'Yes.'

'In that case I'll do what I can.'

'There must be no humiliation,' said Comrade Zikladza. 'The Federal Army mustn't surrender, and they must be allowed to leave Akhtaria with all their weapons.'

Ruslan nodded. 'Will you send a spokesman to Zeda'Anta?'

'No need. Sergo Lionidza's already there.'

Next day, Ruslan drove up to Zeda'Anta, another bankrupt city of power cuts and shops with empty shelves, and now the beleaguered capital of newly-independent Akhtaria. He stayed with Tamara's parents, whose flat overlooked a cemetery. Ruslan wondered if there were any plots there that might lie empty as a result of his actions that spring. He hoped so. It was a terrible tragedy for young men to die just as their country was coming back to life after a long, harsh winter.

Lionidza came to pick him up next morning to take him to meet the Akhtarian president. As Lionidza's sleek Chaikas headed towards the city centre, Ruslan took a deep breath and said, 'I know.'

'Know what?'

'I know that you're working for Comrade Zikladza.'

Lionidza flinched. 'What do you mean?'

'Don't donkey shit me, okay? He gave it away. You've been working for him all along, haven't you?'

'What are you talking about?'

'So do you deny it?'

'Yes, I'm in touch with him. That doesn't mean I'm working for him.'

'So how long have you been in touch?'

'Since soon after I came here. The Akhtarians asked me to phone Comrade Zikladza and the Federal President. They needed to know if you and I could get official backing from the Federals. They would have looked pretty stupid if they'd ordered a ceasefire and the Federals hadn't reciprocated.'

Ruslan gave Lionidza a hard look. 'So who are you working for?'

'Well now I'm working for the Federal President. So are you. He's asked us to dig him out of the shit, remember? But that's only in the last few days. I had a bloody great row with the President

52

when I resigned from the government, and I quarrelled with Comrade Zikladza too, if you must know. He threatened to kick me out of the Party.'

'So if you and Comrade Zikladza fell out, how come you managed to kiss and make up so quickly?'

'I got my wife to phone his wife.'

Ruslan laughed contemptuously.

'What's so funny about that? They've been friends for nearly thirty years.'

'It's not the first time I've heard stories about Comrade Zikladza's wife, you know.'

'Sorry?'

'When I had that fight with Aleksander Mingrelsky's son and Sergei Ivanov was trying to get us released, well the KGB told me the Moscow press would never print anything because Comrade Zikladza's wife had powerful relatives there.'

Lionidza smiled. 'I know about that. It wasn't Sergei Ivanov that got you released, it was Comrade Zikladza.'

'Who says?'

'Comrade Zikladza told me himself, years ago.'

'Oh yes? How come?'

'Ivanov wasn't trying to free you. He was trying to make the front page.'

'That's not what the people in my sanatorium said.'

'Come on, don't be so naive. He's a journalist. What ambitious journalist ever gives up a big story out of the goodness of his heart? He wanted his byline, and his editor wanted to break a big scandal to show the world how daring he was, never mind that it might damage the best leader that Ksordia-Akhtaria had ever had. Well fortunately for us, Comrade Zikladza's wife had a brother there. Which paper was it?'

'Literaturnaya Gazeta.'

'That's right, *Literaturnaya Gazeta*. He was a sub-editor or something. He tipped Comrade Zikladza off, so Comrade Zikladza stepped in and told Aleksander Mingrelsky to drop all charges.'

'The staff in the sanatorium told us Mingrelsky made a deal with Ivanov.'

Lionidza shook his head. 'What do they know?'

Ruslan was bemused. He had been steeling himself for a big confrontation with Lionidza about who he was working for and whether he had lied to him and used him, and Lionidza hadn't just brushed it all off, he had managed to undermine one of Ruslan's most cherished memories in the process.

Ruslan decided to give him the benefit of the doubt. After all, whatever Lionidza's motives, there was no way he could negotiate an end to the war without him.

At the Presidential Palace, an official ushered them in. 'The President will be here in about five minutes. The plan is for you to meet him, the Foreign Minister and the Defence Minister in front of the press. Then perhaps you and the President can make a short statement before we go off for talks. Is that agreeable?'

Lionidza nodded. 'Yes, that's fine.'

The official left them to prepare their statement.

'I can't do it,' said Ruslan.

'Can't do what?'

'I can't shake hands with their Defence Minister in front of the cameras.'

'What are you talking about?'

'For Christ's sake, Sergo. He's a Rebel. I can't shake his hand in front of the cameras.'

Akhtarian Defence Minister Nartshu Sulkavidza was a hate figure among the Ksords. His father had been a senior Rebel commander during the Great Patriotic War and had been responsible for appalling massacres of Ksordian civilians. When the Germans retreated, he and his family had fled with them, eventually making their way to safety in Canada.

Lionidza had no sympathy for Ruslan's worries. 'I don't care if he's the devil incarnate. Rule number one of negotiation is that you smile and shake hands in public, and then you go for their throat in private. Now stop being stupid and let's agree on this statement.'

Ruslan allowed Lionidza's words to carry him along, though he found it very difficult to pay any attention to the statement Lionidza was suggesting.

Soon the official came back and ushered the two of them into a large room full of reporters and camera and sound crews, where he led them to a small podium at the front. Ruslan viewed the camera lights and the flashlights of the photographers with a mounting sense of panic. If he shook Sulkavidza's hand, his mother and Giorgi would see it on the TV news. How could he ever explain it to them?

'I can't do it,' he whispered to Lionidza.

'You have to,' he hissed back.

'I can't. I'll do it in private but not in front of these cameras.'

It was too late. A door opened at the other side of the room, and Baykan Eristov, the Akhtarian President, stepped in. Still tall and powerful, despite his 75 years, Eristov had risen to prominence during the early 1970s, when he led a campaign for Akhtaria to become a fully-fledged Soviet Republic in its own right. Eventually, he was expelled from the Party and spent the next 15 years in and out of prison, only to emerge as the leader of a wave of Akhtarian nationalism when *glasnost* finally reached Ksordia-Akhtaria.

Behind President Eristov came his urbane Foreign Minister, the acceptable face of the Zeda'Anta government.

Defence Minister Sulkavidza brought up the rear. A thickset man of 60, with wavy grey-black hair and bushy eyebrows, Sulkavidza had returned to his father's native land shortly before the 1990 elections, brandishing the financial clout of the militant Akhtarian diaspora. Unlike President Eristov, who would condemn Rebel atrocities even if he constantly cast doubt on their extent, Sulkavidza idolised the Rebels.

He also actively wanted war. He was fond of saying that a nation can only be forged with blood. Akhtarians had to kill and die for their independence or it would have no meaning.

And now there he stood, not far from Ruslan, who would soon be expected to shake his hand.

Eristov was first. He shook a dazed Ruslan's hand under a hail of flashlights. Next, Eristov shook Lionidza's hand, and only then did the Foreign Minister offer his hand to Ruslan (Ksords and Akhtarians shared a superstitious terror of more than two people shaking hands across each other's arms).

Finally, Ruslan was faced with the hateful figure of Sulkavidza, his hand outstretched.

'I'm sorry, Mr Sulkavidza. It's very difficult for me to shake the hand of a man who expresses admiration for the Rebels. They slaughtered eight members of my family, seven of them women and children.'

There was pandemonium. The camera lights flashed and the reporters blurted out a mass of questions. Sulkavidza's face betrayed shock and fury as he withdrew his hand.

President Eristov directed a black look at Ruslan, a look that would appear on many of the following day's front pages. 'We will begin our negotiations now. And we very much hope that our guests have come to talk seriously rather than to insult us.'

The reporters turned their attentions to Ruslan, who somehow managed to trot out Lionidza's statement, whose platitudes included a call for political leaders on both sides to behave cautiously and responsibly.

Once they were all out of sight of the cameras, Eristov rounded on Ruslan. 'Cautiously and responsibly? God's bollocks, Shanidza, you've got a lot to learn. You don't begin negotiations by publicly insulting the other side, you know.'

'Do you know what happened to my family in the war?'

'And do you know what happened to mine in the Great Repression?'

'I can guess. I've got an Akhtarian wife, remember, and I know what happened to hers.'

'You Ksords are all the fucking same. Rebels this, Rebels that. What the Rebels did was nothing compared to what happened to us.'

'So when they shot my mother's babies, that was nothing, was it? When they shot my father's wife and children, that was nothing? And you expect me to shake the hand of a man who goes round saying how great the Rebels were? No way. My mother would spit in my face if I did.'

'My government's a democratic government that reflects all shades of Akhtarian opinion, and Nartshu Sulkavidza is a senior minister in that government. Anyone who insults him insults the nation he represents.'

'And anyone who includes him in a government insults the Ksords his father murdered.'

'Take that back, son of slut,' Sulkavidza yelled in his odd Canadian accent.

'The composition of the government of Akhtaria is strictly a matter for the Akhtarians,' said Eristov.

'So the Ksords who make up a quarter of your population have no say? No wonder they're on the brink of insurrection.'

'Take back that you say about my father, son of slut.'

Ruslan thought Sulkavidza might hit him at any moment, until Lionidza stepped between them. 'Comrades, gentlemen. We're supposed to be here to end a war, not to start a new one.'

'He has to take back that he say.'

'Leave it, Nartshu,' said Eristov. 'He isn't worth it.'

'He's insult me and he's insult my father. I suppose to just take it?'

'No, you're supposed to leave it. Lionidza's right. I'm glad Zikladza's got the brains to send someone with a bit of sense. Perhaps we'll ignore our bungling amateur and address ourselves to the professional, shall we?'

The five men sat down on opposite sides of a desk, with the official to one side, ready to take notes. Ruslan felt humiliated once more. He felt used and useless and just wanted Lionidza and Eristov to complete the negotiations as soon as possible so that he could get out of that nightmare of a meeting and fly back to England on the first possible plane.

Chapter Nine

COMRADE ZIKLADZA actually came out of his office to greet Lionidza, a rare honour indeed. If Lionidza had merely been shown in without delay, or if Comrade Zikladza's receptionist-cum-mistress had chatted with him while he waited, he would have known that his boss was very pleased with him. But for him to come out to greet him, that was almost unknown.

Lionidza stood up and straightened his tie. Zikladza embraced him and kissed him, then led him into his office and closed the door.

'Sit down, dear friend, sit down. You've done a splendid job. Congratulations.'

'Thank you, comrade. I just hope you can get our little ceasefire deal through the Federal cabinet.'

Zikladza smiled and settled his hands on his stomach, his long fingers intertwined. 'We will and we won't, if you see what I mean.'

'How's that?'

'Korgay's got enough people in the cabinet to vote it down, but he doesn't want to. He's planning to get some of his nationalist friends to resign before we take a vote, then his people can vote against it safe in the knowledge that they won't stop it passing.'

'But of course you'll get blamed for betraying the motherland.'

'Exactly. And only then will he bring down the Federal government.'

'Is there nothing you can do to stop him?'

'No, not without sabotaging your ceasefire.'

'Pity. Do you think Korgay will be able to set up a new Federal government?'

'No. We'll vote against. The Tatars and Nina Begishveli will oppose him because he's too much of a nationalist, and then nationalists like Orbeliani and Kakhi will oppose him because they think he's still a Communist.'

Lionidza snorted his derision. 'So there'll be no Federal government?'

'No, but never underestimate how cynical Korgay is. My guess is that he'll start a war just to make the nationalists rally to the flag.'

'It wouldn't surprise me.'

'But there may be a way to shit in his shoes.'

'Yes?'

'Do you think your young athlete might be able to help us out again? Is he still in Ksordia-Akhtaria?'

'Yes, he's gone to spend a few days with his mother. But there's something you should know.'

'What's that?'

'He guessed that I was working for you.'

'Oh dear.'

'I think I managed to sow a few doubts in his mind.'

'You think so?'

'I think so. But he doesn't really trust me.'

'Not to worry, there may be a way round that little problem.'

'What's that?'

Comrade Zikladza tapped his nose. 'All will be revealed. Now I had a very interesting talk with some army officers the other day. Did you know that in the old Soviet Army, they said that West Ksords made the best officers and Tatars made the best NCOs?'

'Really? Ruslan said he came across a lot of West Ksords and Tatars.'

'Yes. You know that place where some Akhtarian women got raped? That was the only place where our troops weren't commanded by West Ksords. I now know all about West Ksordian blood feuds and how they view any attack on a woman as deeply shameful.'

Lionidza smiled. 'I hope you aren't going to tell me that we should reintroduce the blood feud as well as capitalist speculation.'

Zikladza laughed. 'No, but the interesting thing is that the Akhtarian army has no West Ksords and no Tatars, which means they've got a massive shortage of both officers and NCOs. So they aren't in any state to fight a war.'

'Really?'

'Yes. Remember, they didn't capture a single border post, despite the fact that their troops were motivated and outnumbered our boys. But Korgay has a problem too: if he uses the Federal army as a purely Ksordian army, then all the Tatars will desert. That'll leave the army without two thirds of its NCOs. Think about it, Sergo. An army can't fight without NCOs.'

Zikladza leaned forward: 'Let me tell you what's going to happen. Korgay needs a war to help him form a government, so he'll create a Ksordian insurrection in southern Akhtaria. But then all the Tatar NCOs will desert, and Korgay will find that the military need him to play for time so that they can get the army ready to fight. And the Akhtarians will need to play for time too, because their army's not ready to fight either.'

'And you think me and Ruslan might be able to get a peace process going in the meantime?'

'Yes. What you need is something fairly nebulous that everyone can sign up to.'

'A promise to be good if the other side are good too?'

'Exactly. Get your young athlete to make Korgay and the Akhtarians sign up to it. Meanwhile you go to Moscow and Kiev and meet a few of our old friends who still have *blat*. Get Russia and Ukraine to sign up too, and most importantly, get them to restrain their allies down here.'

'Do you think Moscow and Kiev will co-operate?'

'If you can show them it's in their interests.'

'Do you know?' said Lionidza. 'I think this could work. Both sides go along with us to play for time, and meanwhile we lock them into a peace process.'

'A lot would depend on your young friend being a bit more diplomatic than he was when he met Sulkavidza.'

'He's a quick learner.'

'I hope so. We have to frustrate Korgay. We'll never be able to restore Socialism if that cockroach is in power.'

Lionidza nodded.

'Now,' said Zikladza, 'there is one other problem.'

'What's that?'

'You, my dear friend.'

'Me?'

'Yes. People still associate you with me. The Akhtarians don't care, but your young athlete won't co-operate with you if he thinks you're working for me. Nor will Korgay, and nor will the Russians. Boris Yeltsin's a vindictive son of a slut, and he hates me almost as much as he hates Korgay.'

'What are you saying?'

'When Korgay's people table a vote of no confidence in the government, I'm going to say it's your fault that we had to agree to such terrible ceasefire terms. I'm going to say you cocked up the negotiations with Zeda'Anta.'

Lionidza stared at his boss in horror.

'Then,' said Zikladza, 'you're going to make a very angry speech. Call me a stupid old fool. Say I'm completely out of touch, that Akhtarian independence was inevitable and I was an idiot to support sending troops in, that sort of thing. You have to be very rude. The next day, I'll call a Politburo meeting. Probably the best thing would be if you don't turn up, because we're going to expel you from the Party.'

'Please Comrade Zikladza, don't do that.'

'It's the only way.'

'Oh no, please no.' There were tears in Lionidza's eyes. 'The Party's my life. All my friends are in the Party. I met my wife through the Party. Please, don't kick me out.'

'Sergo, don't you see how things have changed? In a few days, we won't be part of the government any more. We may even have to go underground, just like in Lenin's time. We're a revolutionary organisation again, and that means some of the most important comrades will have to operate on the outside. I'm sorry, dear friend, that's how it has to be.'

Events now moved very quickly. As Comrade Zikladza had predicted, the Federal government fell, but Korgay didn't have enough support to create a new one. Then, on the last day of March, the Ksord-dominated police in Kvemodishi mutinied against their new Akhtarian commanders. This triggered off the 'North Ksord

Insurrection', a bloodless uprising that quickly seized control of the Ksordian areas of southern Akhtaria.

Lionidza contacted Ruslan the day after his supposedly furious row with Comrade Zikladza. Quite how he got hold of the telephone number of Ruslan's mother's neighbour was something Ruslan never quite understood.

Ruslan had no desire to work with Lionidza again. He didn't know whether he could trust him, and he felt the last day of their peace mission had made a fool of him. But, as Lionidza pointed out, they had achieved something together. Amazingly enough, they had actually stopped a war.

And Lionidza was right: peace was very far from secure. Their success in the 'War of the Border Posts' would count for nothing if Ksords and Akhtarians went on to slaughter one another over 'North Ksordia'.

Lionidza was very good at stroking Ruslan's ego: 'People will listen to you,' he said. 'You had an amazing impact at the border…Everyone knows you're genuine…There's nobody else who can do it.'

So Ruslan agreed to drive his hire car down to Khosume and meet him without making any promises. And then, before he knew it, Lionidza had somehow persuaded him to join a second peace mission. Lionidza's daughter would run their office in Khosume, and Ruslan would ask Murad to help with fundraising (he desperately needed a salary if he and Tamara weren't to exhaust their savings).

Ruslan suggested 'Four Principles for Peace' as a framework for resolving the conflict:

1. Nobody is to be forced out of their home
2. Nobody is to be forced to live in a state that is not in some sense theirs
3. All military activity (including troop movements) is to be frozen
4. All disputes are to be settled by negotiation in a spirit of goodwill.

Three days later, he found himself addressing a large fundraising meeting. A good fifth of those present were Tatars from the arts and the entertainment industry, and a similar percentage were Armenians, a small but relatively wealthy minority that held Ruslan in high esteem. There were representatives of the new business class, independent trade unionists, student activists and members of various anti-Korgay political parties. The meeting was a great success and raised enough money to pay generous salaries to Ruslan, Lionidza and his daughter.

After the meeting, a young man came up to Ruslan with a message from his father, Ruslan's former coach Mikhel Inalipa, who offered to act as his driver.

'Wow, that's brilliant,' Ruslan said to him. 'I'd love to work with your father again.'

'He's in West Ksordia at the moment, and he says he'll need a couple of days before he can join you.'

Ruslan thought it would be good to have a companion who wasn't Lionidza: somebody he could trust.

Back at her house, Fatima had another message for him. 'Can you phone Nina?'

Ruslan's heart skipped a beat.

'Hello, Nina Begishveli.'

'Hello, Nina. It's me.'

'Hi, Ruslan.'

'So how are you?'

'Not bad, you know. Busy, stressed, tearing my hair out, but enjoying it in a masochistic kind of way.'

'That's good.'

'And how are you?'

'Not running as much as I should and sort of getting sucked into things over here.'

'So I hear. That's what I rang you to talk about.'

'Yes?'

'First of all, congratulations. You did a fantastic job at the border posts.'

'Thank you. A lot of that was Lionidza, behind the scenes.'

63

'Yes, so I hear. The other thing I wanted to say was to warn you.'

'About what?'

'I hardly know where to begin. Let's start with Lionidza. Don't trust him, Ruslan. Since when has he been such a pacifist?'

'People change, Nina.'

'He was always one of the worst Communists. His sort turn into hard-line nationalists, like Korgay, not pacifists. It doesn't add up.'

'Look, we all know about Lionidza's past, but right now he's working to try and prevent a war. That's a fact and I need him. I'd be lost without him.'

'Yes, well don't trust him. He's got his own agenda.'

It occurred to Ruslan that Nina's phone might be bugged, either by Comrade Zikladza's secret police (if he still had any) or by Korgay's. He decided to tailor his reply for Korgay's ears. 'He probably wants to get back into power, and maybe our peace plan is just a way of making himself useful to Korgay. I don't care about that, Nina. I'm just trying to stop a war.'

'But you won't get peace as long as Korgay's in power. He can't bear to share power with the leaders of other ethnic groups. That's why he has to stir up trouble.'

'We have to try, Nina. I don't see anyone replacing him, so I have to work with him. I'm not part of the opposition. I'm just trying to help the Ksordian and Akhtarian leaders communicate with each other.'

'Fair enough, but there's other things you need to be careful of. All the Ksords loved it when you refused to shake Sulkavidza's hand, but the Akhtarians didn't and Sulkavidza certainly didn't. That man's really dangerous, Ruslan. He's quite capable of ordering your murder.'

Ruslan said nothing.

'Be very very careful,' Nina continued, 'especially when you're crossing from Ksord-held territory to Akhtarian-held territory. It would be very easy for either side to shoot you and pin the blame on the other.'

'Yes, I've already thought about that. I'll be careful, don't worry.'

'The problem is, the more successful you become, the more dangerous it'll get. There are plenty of nutcases on both sides who'll be happy to kill you if you look like you're getting in the way of their little war.'

'So are you telling me to give up and go home?'

'No, I'm not. I think you're right to try, no matter how hopeless it is. In fact you're probably the best hope we've got right now. But you know what really scares me?'

'What?'

'You.'

'Me?'

'Yes, you. What if there comes a time when you have to choose between giving up and getting yourself killed in a blaze of glory? What will you choose?'

'Don't worry. I've become quite pragmatic in my old age.'

'I hope so, Ruslan. I really hope so. Just remember that you're not King bloody Wirustam. You're no good to anyone dead.'

Chapter Ten

THE NEXT morning, Ruslan received an invitation to meet Korgay himself. He dearly wished Lionidza would accompany him into the monster's lair, but he was already on his way to Moscow to meet senior Foreign Ministry officials.

Murad lent Ruslan a very flashy Mercedes Benz, and he drove it to Ronkoni, a city every bit as destitute as Khosume and Zeda'Anta. Political graffiti was everywhere, with more than 30 political parties competing for wall space, as if the Ksords were trying to make up for 70 years of being allowed only one.

Just as ubiquitous was the burly image of Korgay, his hair dyed black and swept back. And on every poster of him there were the same four Cyrillic letters: 'KTKT', *Ksordia Twaksa Korgaytan Tad* (Ksordia United With Korgay), the favourite slogan of the vast crowds that had swept him to power just three years earlier.

At the East Ksordian Presidential Palace, Korgay greeted Ruslan with four kisses, a tight embrace and enquiries after Tamara.

'Did she give you a son?'

'Yes.'

'That's good.'

Korgay and Ruslan made brief statements for the cameras, and then Korgay led him to a cabinet room dominated by portraits of Lenin and King Wirustam II, a curious juxtaposition if ever there was one.

Korgay introduced four of his senior colleagues, two of whom Ruslan had encountered previously: his man in the now defunct Federal war cabinet and his tall, skinny Minister of the Interior, the former KGB colonel Tengiz Alavidza.

'We've met, haven't we?' Ruslan said as he shook hands with Alavidza.

'Yes, I think we have, but I can't remember where.'

'A long time ago, in West Ksordia. There was that business with Alexander Mingrelsky's son.'

'Oh yes, that's right. You've got a very good memory, young man.'

Ruslan said nothing about the time Alavidza had come to gloat at him in KGB headquarters. As Lionidza would say, better to smile and be polite to the member of Korgay's inner circle who was undoubtedly an enemy.

After the greetings were all finished, Korgay said with a wink: 'I hear you and Sulkavidza nearly came to blows.'

'I would have had him.'

They all laughed.

Korgay invited everyone to sit down. He looked intently at Ruslan. 'So, tell me, what's your attitude to the North Ksord Insurrection?'

'I have a lot of sympathy. You can't expect Ksords to roll over and accept rule by a government that includes people like Sulkavidza.'

'And do you think North Ksordia should be part of Akhtaria?'

'The Four Principles for Peace are not an answer to that question. They're a framework for you and the Akhtarian leadership to try to negotiate the answer. If they want the North Ksords to stay in Akhtaria, they'll have to make a lot of concessions. First and foremost, they'd have to give them real autonomy.'

'And they'd have to get rid of their flag,' said Korgay. 'That's a Rebel emblem.'

Ruslan avoided committing himself on this point. 'They'd have to distance themselves from the Rebel tradition, like the West Germans did when they outlawed the swastika and made holocaust denial a crime. Eristov would have to crack down on the neo-Rebels and kick the likes of Sulkavidza out of his government.'

'I know Eristov. He'd never make that kind of concession.'

'In that case, he'd have to cede territory, but we would have to guarantee the rights of Akhtarian civilians in the areas we control.'

Korgay raised an eyebrow at this. Then he asked his companions if they had any questions for Ruslan.

Alavidza asked, 'What's Lionidza's role in all this?'

'Lionidza's an old contact from the Soviet era. He sponsored me then and he's working with me now. He's in Moscow today, trying to get the Russians to support the Four Principles and stop arming the Akhtarians.'

Raised eyebrows all round. This was obviously news.

'People always used to think of him as Comrade Zikladza's man.'

'Yes, but they seem to have fallen out quite spectacularly.'

'And what do you think Lionidza's real aims are?'

'I should think in the long term he wants to park his backside on the seat of a ministerial Chaikas once more.'

Everybody laughed at this.

'And what about you?' asked Alavidza. 'Where do you stand in terms of Ksordian politics?'

'I'll give you the same answer as I gave Nina Begishveli.' Ruslan thought he detected in Alavidza's eyes an indication that he knew all about his conversation with Nina. 'I'm trying to be neutral, and I'm trying to facilitate negotiation between those who are in power. In Ksordia, that means you, Mr Korgay. In Akhtaria, it means President Eristov.'

Alavidza hadn't finished. 'And what's your attitude to Nina Begishveli?'

'On a personal level, she's an ex-girlfriend, as you know, and I'm very fond of her. On a political level, she's not in power, so I'm not that interested in her. The same goes for the rest of the opposition.'

'You've been honest with us, Ruslan,' said Korgay, 'and I appreciate that. But you have to understand that responsibility for the destiny of the Ksordian nation has now fallen onto my shoulders. That's a heavy responsibility and I take it very seriously. The Ksords can't afford to enter this conflict with one hand tied behind their backs. We might be prepared to negotiate with Eristov on the basis of your Four Principles, but we won't be bound by them unless and until Eristov agrees to be bound by them too.'

Ruslan did his best to hide his elation. 'I think your position is entirely reasonable.'

However, the crisis continued to deepen. That night came reports of the first serious fighting of the North Ksord insurrection. Quite who fired first was unclear, but more than a dozen men died in a battle over a bridge.

Meanwhile, Korgay set about consolidating his power. An assembly of Ksordian leaders from the various regions met and elected him 'Executive President' of a new Ksordian Provisional Government, which would have its capital in his power base Ronkoni, rather than in Tatar-dominated Khosume.

This government had no basis in legality, and the Ksordian opposition refused to recognise it. The Tatar leadership, for their part, were reported to be apoplectic with rage.

Almost the first act of Korgay's Provisional Government was to send Federal Army 'peacekeepers' into all the Ksord-controlled areas of Akhtaria. Expecting fighting to break out at any minute, Ruslan telephoned Lionidza in Moscow.

Lionidza was very blasé about it. 'Korgay's only sending a token force north. The Akhtarians won't attack.'

'How can you be so sure? They did last time.'

'I've had a very productive meeting with the Russians. They say that as long as Korgay accepts our Four Principles, they won't give the Akhtarians enough ammunition to launch an offensive.'

'Christ, how on earth did you manage that?'

Lionidza laughed. 'First rule of negotiation, show your partner that what you want fits in with what he wants.'

'I thought the first rule was to shake them by the hand in public and go for their throat in private.'

'Well, that too. You have to remember, the Russians and the Ukrainians are just using the Ksords and the Akhtarians as bargaining chips in their wider negotiations with each other.'

'So the fate of Ksordia-Akhtaria depends on the state of Russian-Ukrainian relations?'

'To a certain extent, yes, and that's not necessarily a bad thing. They both want to manipulate the crisis, but neither of them wants it to get out of control. So if the Russians restrain the Akhtarians, there's every chance that the Ukrainians will restrain the Ksords.'

Meanwhile Ruslan and Nina's old friend Yakub Bovin, who by now was leader of the Tatars and President of the Central Kuban regional government, reacted angrily to the news that Federal Army 'peacekeepers' were to be sent into Akhtaria. 'Since the Ksords have hijacked the Federal Army,' he said, 'the Central Kuban police will no longer co-operate in the search for deserters and draft dodgers.'

This was an open invitation to desert, and some 5,000 Tatars took it up at once, along with the remaining Akhtarians and more than a few Ksords. Their commanders didn't dare to resist this mass defection, for fear of driving the Tatars into the arms of their Akhtarian enemies. But the loss of so many Tatar NCOs crippled the Ksords' army. Their supreme commander pleaded with Korgay to play for time, saying that it would be at least a month before his troops could be ready to fight again.

Sulkavidza, the Akhtarian Minister of Defence, desperately wanted to attack the Ksords. 'We need to hammer them now,' he told President Eristov. 'Smash them before they recover from loss of Tatars. There never better time.'

His military commanders were horrified at the thought: 'We'd have to annihilate the Ksordian army in the first five days,' they told Eristov. 'If we don't, we'll have shat in our own shoes because we'll have used up all our ammunition.'

Needing to play for time, the Akhtarians invited Ruslan up to Zeda'Anta for talks. His old coach Mikhel Inalipa had by now joined him. An athletic looking Ksord in his late forties, Mikhel had been a promising runner until injury forced him to retire. He had then trained as a paramedic, but he found the work too stressful and became a coach instead. Ruslan was delighted to see him again. The two men had always got on well, and Ruslan was sure he could trust him absolutely.

Ruslan remembered Nina's warning about crossing over the front line, so he asked Mikhel to drive the long way, going from East Ksordia to Russia and then from there into Akhtaria.

When President Eristov and his Foreign Minister greeted Ruslan in front of the cameras, Sulkavidza was nowhere to be seen.

He turned up soon enough, however, once Ruslan was ushered out of sight.

The two men shook hands stiffly.

When the others sat down, Eristov remained standing and launched into a lengthy rant about the perfidiousness of Ksords in general and Korgay in particular. 'How can I be expected to trust that lying scumbag?' he asked again and again. 'One minute he says he accepts your Four Principles, the next minute he goes and invades my country.

'I mean, look at your Principles. "Principle One: Nobody is to be driven from their home." Oh yes? Tell that to all the Akhtarians who've had to flee Kvemodishi for their lives. "Principal Two: Nobody is to be forced to live in a state which is not in some sense theirs." Bloody Korgay tried to snuff our state out right from the word go.

'And what about the others? "Principle Three: All military activity (including troop movements) is to be frozen." Well, that's a joke, isn't it? He accepts this Principle one day, and the next day he orders his whole fucking army into Akhtaria. And what's the fourth one? "All disputes are to be settled by negotiation in a spirit of goodwill." Negotiate? With that fucking cockroach? You must be joking.'

Eristov's rant seemed to last an eternity, but eventually he slowed down and began to speak at a more normal volume.

'I can understand your feelings Mr President,' Ruslan said when Eristov finally sat down. 'I'd be the first to agree that the situation is alarming. I'm not asking you to trust President Korgay now, today.'

'It's a good job you're not, because I wouldn't trust him a millimetre.'

'I can understand that, Mr President. What I'm asking you to do is to enter a peace process that allows you to test the sincerity of the other side.'

'Sincerity? Fucking sincerity? He doesn't know the meaning of the word.'

'Mr President, I'm not here to represent President Korgay. I'm just trying to open up a channel through which the two of you can communicate. I'm trying to find a way for you and the Ksords to rebuild trust through actions.'

Eristov scoffed.

'Mr President, President Korgay hasn't yet entered the peace process, but he has agreed to do so if you will too.'

'And you believe him?'

'It's not a question of whether anyone believes him. It's a question of whether you're prepared to enter into a peace process that'll give you the opportunity to put his words to the test.'

Eristov's eyes narrowed. He looked at his colleagues and then picked up a sheet of paper.

'We're going to make this statement: "The Akhtarian government believes that Ruslan Shanidza's Four Principles for Peace may be a good starting point for negotiations. However, we will not enter into any negotiations with the Ksords unless and until they begin to implement these Principles on the ground."'

Ruslan was astonished. What was the point of Eristov's rant if he had already decided to accept the Four Principles? But he managed to hide his feelings and say the right thing: 'I think what you say is eminently reasonable.'

That evening, however, Akhtarian TV announced that almost 15,000 troops were to move south to be nearer to the front lines. This came as a heavy blow to Ruslan. It seemed that every time anyone agreed to his Principles for Peace, they then turned round and stoked the fires of war.

Chapter Eleven

RUSLAN TELEPHONED Lionidza, who advised him to go to Dzap in the southwest, where the local Akhtarian police chief had invited him to help negotiate a series of local ceasefire accords between Ksordian and Akhtarian villages. 'You've done a brilliant job with the politicians,' Lionidza said. 'Now do some work from the grass roots. Get a few successes under your belt first, then go and meet the leadership of the North Ksord insurrection.'

Ruslan went back to the front line reluctantly. He didn't like the idea of trying to mediate between nervous soldiers and militiamen who were armed to the teeth.

Dawa Tetradza, the police chief in Dzap, was a tall man in his early forties with a handsome and gentle face. Ruslan took to him immediately.

'It's a great pleasure to meet you,' said Tetradza, in the lilting tones of the Coastal dialect. 'I'm a great admirer of everything you've done since this whole business started.'

'It seems to be one step forward two steps backward at the moment.'

'I wouldn't worry too much about the deployments. They know they may have to freeze troop movements before long, so they're trying to get a decent number of men up near the front first.'

'Has there been any fighting round here?'

'None, thank God. The Rebels hardly touched this area during the Great Patriotic War, and Akhtarians all got their property back after the Great Repression. People have always got on fine and everyone's anxious to avoid conflict.'

Ruslan explained his strategy to Tetradza: Lionidza would try to get the Russians and the Ukrainians to restrain both sides from above, while he attempted to create pressure for peace from below. 'I'm hoping to do the same here as I did on the Russian border and get some of the local commanders to make ceasefire agreements.'

'Well, you've come to the right place.'

Over the next few days, the two of them supervised the signing of several mini-peace treaties. Ruslan's role was fairly minimal. The villagers trusted each other, and Tetradza had already done much of the groundwork. Ruslan's presence spurred them to sort out tricky points such as the control of disputed road junctions, and everyone was keen to be photographed with him at their signing ceremonies.

To Ruslan's intense relief, nobody pointed their rifles at him when he crossed from one side to the other. The Akhtarians were just as well disposed to him as the Ksords. Here at least he felt safe.

Meanwhile Lionidza reported excellent results from Kiev, where the Ukrainians had agreed to support the Four Principles and refrain from arming the Ksords, provided the Russians stopped arming the Akhtarians.

Lionidza told Ruslan it was time for him to go to Kvemodishi to meet Mataa Bogiani, the leader of the North Ksord insurrection.

Bogiani, a quiet man in his late fifties, had been the Kvemodishi police chief until the Akhtarian government sacked him as part of its purge of Ksords. He got his revenge by organising the police mutiny that sparked the North Ksord insurrection. Bogiani had personal memories of the Rebel genocide. As a young boy he had narrowly escaped a Rebel raiding party. However, he was no anti-Akhtarian bigot. His first wife had been Akhtarian, and he frequently said that their desire for a state of their own was legitimate, but so was the desire of the North Ksords to stay outside it.

Bogiani greeted Ruslan cordially and invited him to address the North Ksord Assembly the next day. The Assembly was a collection of some 200 local big fish: party and militia leaders, representatives of villages and towns, senior policemen, top businessmen, trade unionists, students and intellectuals.

It convened in a theatre in the centre of Kvemodishi. Ruslan shared the stage with Bogiani and half a dozen others. Bogiani pointed out to him some of the major figures in the Assembly.

Several village leaders he had met during his negotiations near Dzap gave him a cheery wave. He was glad to see friendly faces.

Ruslan spotted a tall, athletic man in combat uniform who seemed to radiate confidence and charisma as he strode into the theatre. It was Vakhtan Mingrelsky, and this was the first time Ruslan had seen him since he broke his leg with a hammer almost nine years earlier.

He and Ruslan caught each other's eye. They looked at each other for a few seconds, but no greeting passed between them.

'Friend of yours?' Bogiani asked.

'I wouldn't say that, but I do know him.'

'He's bad bad man,' Bogiani whispered. 'One of the crazies. I've spent most of my working life putting people like him behind bars.'

There were three cameras from North Ksordian TV. The debate wouldn't go out live, but edited highlights would be broadcast on the evening news.

Bogiani tapped the microphone and called the Assembly to order. Proceedings began with two minutes' silence, followed by a rousing rendition of the Ksordian national anthem.

> *Men of Ksordia, our ancestors' word lives on,*
> *As long as their sons' hearts beat for the nation.*
> *The spirit of Ksordia lives, it will live for centuries.*
> *The fires of Hell threaten in vain,*
> *The crash of thunder is in vain.*
> *Now let the north wind cover all with ice,*
> *Let the rocks crack, the oaks break, let the earth shake.*
> *We will stand steadfast through all the ages,*
> *Like the burial mounds of our ancient kings.*
> *Let every traitor to his homeland be damned.*

Bogiani introduced Ruslan, who stood up to polite applause. All the notes for his speech were on a single sheet of paper. Next to it, he placed a newspaper and a borrowed copy of the Ksords' great epic poem, *The Downfall of the Kuban Kingdoms*.

'Do you know?' he began. 'In some ways, life was easier in the Soviet era. When you had to make a speech, you just started with the word "Comrades". These days it's all changed, and I've been out of the country for a long time, so I'm not sure whether to say "Ladies and Gentlemen" or "Friends" or "Assembly Members". Perhaps the best thing is just to say: "Fellow Ksords."'

This brought applause from half the audience.

'Because I want to start by reminding you that I'm a Ksord. I'm not neutral in the conflict between Ksords and Akhtarians: I'm a Ksord.'

Almost everybody applauded this.

Ruslan went on to talk about how the Rebels had slaughtered his parents' families, and how his father had defended his village.

'I was weaned on a hatred and a fear of the Rebels. Nothing that has ever happened has changed that. I stand here shoulder to shoulder with you in your struggle against the threat of a return of the Rebels.'

This brought Ruslan the biggest round of applause so far.

'But, and here there is a "but", I make a distinction between those Akhtarians who are Rebels and those who are not.' He talked about the Akhtarian Partizan who had fought alongside his father, and about Tamara, who had said on their first date that the Rebels were evil. 'So the distinction I make is this: ordinary Akhtarians are no better and no worse than people of any other nationality, and we can and should try to come to a deal with them. But those who identify with the Rebels are our enemies, and we have the right to defend ourselves against them.'

Almost everyone applauded this. Ruslan hoped they remembered the first sentence as they applauded the second.

'I'm not here as a pacifist. If you have to fight, then I'm with you. I'm not a very good shot, I'm afraid. Perhaps you can use me as a runner.'

Some people laughed.

'But I haven't come here to fight. I've come to try and make peace, because I believe that a just peace is possible. And if we can, then we have a duty to try and make that peace. If you'll bear with me, I'll give you some reasons why we should try and avoid war.

'First reason: it's quite simple, really. If there's a war, a lot of people will get killed. How many Ksords have died so far?' Ruslan looked at Bogiani.

'Twenty-nine.'

'Twenty-nine? That's a lot, mostly young lads who had their whole lives in front of them. That's the whole front row here, gone. That's twenty-nine mothers who've lost their sons. Can you imagine the pain of that? To bear a child, to devote your life to bringing him up, and then just as he's ready to make his way in the world, bang. He's gone.

'Now think what's going to happen if we have an all-out war. How many Ksords will die then? A thousand? Ten thousand? Twenty-nine thousand? How many mothers will lose their sons? And how many sons will lose their mothers? You can be sure the civilian population won't be safe, not by a long stretch.

'So if you want war, look at all your male relatives, especially the young ones. Which one are you prepared to sacrifice? Pick one, and tell his mother that you're prepared to sacrifice him.

'And remember that people don't just get killed in wars, they get injured too. Twenty-nine Ksords have died, but how many have been injured? Probably about fifty or so. Think about the human body and where people get hurt, you know, the nasty injuries that do happen in war. Brain damage that turns young men into drooling vegetables, spinal injuries that turn them into cripples, jaws blown off, faces burnt off. And let's call a spade a spade and name the injury that every man dreads: testicles shot off.

'Well then, if you're gung-ho about war, think again about all the young men you know and pick one. Not one that you hate, one that you get on with. Pick one, and go up to him and tell him that you're prepared for him to get his testicles shot off.'

Everyone in the theatre was silent. Ruslan knew that he had them.

'Second reason. Now before I speak, there are two things I need to say. Firstly, if this was being broadcast live, I wouldn't say this, because this is Ksord speaking to Ksord. This isn't for Akhtarian ears. So people from the TV station, don't broadcast this bit, okay?'

Some of the audience applauded.

'You're not going to like my second reason. I'm not going to tell you what you want to hear. I'm going to tell you what you need to know. My second reason's quite simple, really. War's a very risky business and the good guys might lose.'

There were shouts of protest from the audience.

'Now on paper, we should win easily. How many Ksords are there? About four and a half million. How many Akhtarians? Less than two million. So it should be easy, shouldn't it?

'But military victory isn't just a question of numbers, is it? It's a question of morale, quality of the troops, leadership, weapons, munitions and outside allies who'll stand by you when the going gets tough. So let's look at it, objectively. Let's weigh up us against the Akhtarians in terms of these things.

'Now I've spoken to a lot of people since I've been here: soldiers, army officers, militia leaders, village leaders. And one thing's pretty clear: the North Ksord troops are good.'

The audience applauded the North Ksord troops.

'Their morale is high, and in fact their commanders have told me some of them are a bit too eager to get at the Akhtarians. Now we've also got paramilitary groups like Vakhtan Mingrelsky's White Eagles.'

Applause for the White Eagles.

'Now I bet Mingrelsky's men are good fighters. They're all volunteers and they're motivated.'

Mingrelsky caught Ruslan's eye and raised an eyebrow.

'Okay, now what about the enemy? When I was at the border, I spoke to lots of Ksordian officers, and the bad news is that they all said the same thing. They said the Akhtarian troops were good. They were badly led, but they were motivated and they took risks.

'And do you know what they said about their own troops? They said the North Ksords were good...'

More applause for the North Ksords.

'...and the East Ksords, the West Ksords, the Central Kuban Ksords? Shall I tell you what they said? You're not going to like it, but this is what they said. They said they were useless. That's what they said. They were all useless. They didn't want to take risks. They were keeping their heads down because, and this is the crucial point, because they didn't want to get their heads blown off in somebody else's war.'

Again there were shouts of protest from the audience, but Ruslan used his microphone to drown them out.

'Let me prove it to you.'

He waved a three day-old edition of the pro-Korgay newspaper *Kerda Ksordia*.

'Maybe you've read this. If you've got it at home, have a look at page five. There's an interview with General Napashidza, and this is what he says. Apparently, we should be able to raise an army of a hundred and thirty thousand. Do you know how many men there are in the Ksordian army? Just seventy thousand. That's seventy thousand out of a hundred and thirty thousand. It's not me saying this, it's General Napashidza.

'Take Timashevsk as an example, only about seventy kilometres from here. Do you know what percentage of young Ksords are dodging the draft? According to General Napashidza: thirty-five percent. In Khosume it's forty percent, in Ushanore forty-eight percent, and in Ronkoni it's fifty-five percent. Shall I repeat that? In Ronkoni, the capital of a united Ksordia, fifty-five percent of young men would rather go into hiding than come here and fight.'

There were cries of 'Shame' from the audience.

'Remember, these are General Napashidza's figures, not mine. And those who don't dodge the draft, you can bet your bottom kopek a lot of them just want to keep their heads down and stay alive. And the reason is, and I find this just as disturbing as you do, the reason is that we Ksords are a very fractious bunch, aren't we? We want a united Ksordia, but when it comes to it, there are a lot of Ksords from outside North Ksordia who don't think this is their war. They think it's your war, and they aren't willing to risk their lives for you.'

There was pandemonium, with 20 or 30 Assembly Members shouting at Ruslan, gesturing angrily, calling him a traitor and a defeatist. Others called on them to hear Ruslan out.

'Like I said, comrades, I'm not here to tell you what you want to hear. I'm here to tell you what you need to know.'

It was more than a minute before Ruslan could continue.

'Right, let's compare our Army and the enemy's in other ways, shall we? Leadership? There we have a distinct advantage. The Soviets always said that West Ksords made the best officers.'

Applause for West Ksordian officers.

'Now with NCOs we have a problem. NCOs are the backbone of an army, because you sometimes need the men to be more scared of their NCOs than they are of the enemy. Now we have a problem because we've lost the Tatars and they were very scary NCOs.'

Laughter and a ripple of applause.

'But the Akhtarians haven't got enough officers or NCOs, so there we have an advantage. You know what Sulkavidza's doing to find new officers and NCOs? Recruiting Russian mercenaries, Afghan veterans who've developed a taste for fighting. He'll get them as well, so my guess is that our advantage in this department will only last a few months.'

'Equipment? We have the advantage. Munitions? We have a big advantage at the moment, a very big advantage. Particularly now, because the Russians have said that if we accept the Four Principles for Peace, they won't give the Akhtarians enough ammunition to launch a big offensive. That's very important, because it means you can negotiate from a position of security. As long as you're talking, the Akhtarians can't attack you, because they haven't got enough ammunition.'

'Now, talking about the Russians, that brings us to the question of external allies. The Akhtarians have got the Russians and we've got the Ukrainians and the Georgians. Now, let's be clear about this, the Russians couldn't care less about the Akhtarians, and I can say this because this won't be broadcast, okay please TV people? The Ukrainians and the Georgians couldn't care less about us.'

Ruslan half expected to be heckled at this point, but he wasn't.

'So why are the Russians helping the Akhtarians? It's pure politics. At first, they just wanted to use Akhtaria to bully us back into their orbit. But that backfired on them, because we moved closer to the Ukrainians. That's a nightmare scenario from the Russian point of view, because they don't want control of the Taman

Peninsula to go to an ally of Ukraine. They want to make sure their ships have free passage from Rostov to the Black Sea.

'So now the Russians have two options: either they promote peace and try to wean us away from the Ukraine that way, or else they arm the Akhtarians to the teeth, make the war spread into Central Kubania and get them to seize the Taman Peninsula.

'At the moment, they're backing the peaceful option because they think it's a more viable strategy. And it's cheaper. My guess is that they'll continue to do so for as long as they think it'll work.'

The audience was silent and attentive.

'And why are the Ukrainians and Georgians helping us? With the best will in the world, we can forget the Georgians. They just want us to take a bit of flack so the Russians won't give them such a hard time in Abkhazia.

'The ally that matters is Ukraine. So what do they want? Well, they want Crimea – all of it. And a good share of the old Soviet Black Sea Fleet, and they want the Russians to keep their hands off the Russian-speaking parts of Ukraine. And the Ukrainians are using us to give the Russians a hard time. We're just a bargaining chip, and when the Russians have given them the deal they want, the Ukrainians will discard us. Make no mistake about this: the Ukrainians couldn't care less about the Ksords.'

There was no heckling now. Everybody knew he was right, though perhaps they hadn't had the fickleness of Ukrainian support spelled out so openly before.

'So as I say, war's a risky business. Now this is Ksord speaking to Ksord, and it isn't for broadcast, but my guess is that we would have to win an absolute victory in the first few months while we still have an advantage in terms of officers, equipment and supplies. If we don't win then, and the Russians will do their best to make sure we don't, then we'll be in deep trouble.'

Ruslan paused to let his message sink in.

'If war's unavoidable, then we have to fight and we have to run the risk of losing. We have to hope the Ksords from outside North Ksordia turn out to be more willing to fight than they are now. We have to hope the Ukrainians don't ditch us too soon, and we have to hope the Russians don't help the Akhtarians. And hope not too many of our young men are maimed and killed. But I ask you this, as leaders of the North Ksords. What if war isn't unavoidable? What if you can get what you want through negotiation?'

Nobody heckled, much to Ruslan's surprise.

'So this is where the Four Principles for Peace are intended to act as a guideline. I'm sure you all know of them. Principles Three and Four are a mechanism, freezing military activity and talking rather than fighting. The important ones are Principles One and Two.

'"Principle One: Nobody is to be driven from their home." I wrote this with the interests of the North Ksords in mind. Not long ago, President Korgay met the Akhtarian leaders, and they tried to agree on a border between the two countries. I believe both sides were sincere in this effort, but they failed, because the distribution of Ksords and Akhtarians is such a hotchpotch. Any border has to put some Akhtarians in Ksordia or some Ksords in Akhtaria.'

There were rumbles of discontent from the audience.

'Now one solution is a so-called exchange of populations.'

Shouts of 'Kick all the Rebels out!'

'Now you can drive the Akhtarians out if you fight a war and win it. But what if the Russians make sure you don't? What if there's a stalemate? What then?'

The heckling started in earnest. Ruslan had to shout to make himself heard.

'Think about it. A year of war, stalemate, a bankrupt economy, supplies of munitions low, the Ukrainians have done a deal with the Russians, the Ksords outside North Ksordia getting war-weary. What exchange of populations will start to look very attractive to them?'

Suddenly the hecklers were silent. The kopek had dropped.

'If there's a stalemate, what exchange of populations will begin to look attractive outside North Ksordia? Think about it. I'm not saying President Korgay would ever betray you like this, but he could find himself replaced by someone who would. If that happens, the losers will be you. All the Akhtarians will be driven out of Central Kubania, and you'll find yourselves driven out of North Ksordia and into their old homes. Except they'll burn their houses and slaughter all their livestock rather than hand them over to you. So you have to be very clear about this, no exchange of populations. Nobody is to be driven from their home.'

Some people applauded. Only one person heckled. Ruslan pressed on.

'The other crucial Principle is Principle Two. "Nobody is to be forced to live in a state which is not in some sense theirs." Now people like Sulkavidza, he wants to violate Principle One, he wants to drive you out. He'd probably rather slit your throats, but he'd settle for driving you out. Eristov can probably just about tolerate the idea of you still living here, but he wants to violate Principle Two. He wants to make you prisoners of a state that isn't yours. Because Akhtaria isn't your state, is it? It's theirs, not yours, and that's why you've risen up against it. And frankly I don't blame you.'

About half the audience applauded.

'What's the first sentence in the new Akhtarian constitution? "The Republic of Akhtaria is the homeland of the Akhtarian people." In other words, it's not your state, so why should you agree to live in it?'

This was greeted with a wave of applause from everyone except the diehards.

'You had no say in drawing up the constitution, and it explicitly excludes you. Now if they'd involved you in drawing it up, if it said something like: "This is a democratic republic that belongs to Akhtarians and Ksords and so on," well, it might be a different story. But they didn't, did they?

'Number two: that flag, the red and yellow diamonds. Now I hate that bloody tea towel as much as anyone in this room.'

This brought applause and cheers.

'Every time I see it, I just think of the Rebels.'

More applause.

'As you know, my wife's Akhtarian. She's genuinely anti-Rebel, but one thing we've learnt not to discuss is that flag.'

Laughter.

'If we do, she goes on about how it's an ancient symbol of Akhtarian nationhood and so on and so forth. You know what they always say. Well, Mr Bogiani has been kind enough to lend me his copy of our national poem, *The Downfall of the Kuban Kingdoms*. I'm going to read you a bit. This is the bit where the Ksordian King is visited by the prophet Elijah in the shape of a white eagle.'

Ruslan stopped and looked at Mingrelsky.

'Mr Mingrelsky, perhaps you know it.'

Laughter and applause. Even Mingrelsky smiled.

Ruslan read the text out loud:

> 'But if you desire eternal glory,
> Then draw your army around you
> In the field of red-breasted geese,
> And set your standards in the ground
> With the noble diamonds of your brother.
> There you shall die with sword in hand
> And your crown will be lost amid the slaughter.
> But remember that even a long life is fleeting
> And a martyr's glory will last forever.'

'Did you catch that bit in the middle? I'll read it again:

> 'But if you desire eternal glory,
> Then draw your army around you
> In the field of red-breasted geese,
> And set your standards in the ground
> With the noble diamonds of your brother.'

The Assembly was silent. No Ksord would ever dare to interrupt a reading of their great epic poem.

'So who's the brother and what are the noble diamonds? The brother is King Murman of Akhtaria, who's already been killed. The poem always refers to him and Wirustam as brother kings. And the noble diamonds? That's the Akhtarian flag, because King Wirustam's army at the Field of Red-Breasted Geese contained the remnants of the Akhtarian army. Now, I've never told my wife, so I'd appreciate it if the TV people didn't broadcast it. But it's true. The diamonds really are an ancient Akhtarian symbol, not just a Rebel symbol, and the Downfall describes them as noble. I still can't stand that bloody flag and I think you should try to negotiate it away, but personally, I wouldn't be willing to get my testicles shot off over it.'

The audience was silent. Perhaps they couldn't believe that anyone would dare to enter the North Ksord Assembly and describe the Akhtarian diamonds as noble. Or else they were shocked to hear that their national poet had already done so.

'Third reason why Akhtaria's not your state, and this is much more serious than the flag: the Rebel tradition. You don't need me to tell you. You know what Sulkavidza's father did not far from here. He killed thousands: men, women and children. You don't need me to tell you that Sulkavidza's proud to be his father's son, and yet that's the man that Eristov's put in charge of his army.

'You don't need me to tell you that there's a militia called the New Rebel Brigade, or that you can buy 1940s Rebel posters at any market in Akhtaria. You don't need me to tell you that you can see the Rebel "F" painted on walls all over Akhtaria, or that Eristov can't bring himself to criticise the Rebels without saying "but" and quibbling over numbers. You don't need me to tell you that he's thinking of calling his new currency the Otter, just like the Rebels did in 1942. You don't need me to tell you this. You don't need me to tell you that Eristov's republic is not your state because it's suffused with the Rebel tradition. No wonder you rose up against it.'

Two thirds of the audience applauded. Ruslan assumed the others were waiting for him to say 'but'.

He didn't do so quite yet. Instead he contrasted Akhtaria with the way West Germany had purged itself of its Nazi past.

'Fourth reason why Akhtaria isn't your state? How many Ksords have been purged from their jobs? Hundreds, maybe thousands. Senior policemen? Sacked. Civil servants? Sacked. Judges? Sacked. Heads of state enterprises? Sacked. Eristov has made it very plain that there's no future for you in his republic. No wonder you rose up against him.'

Applause.

'So it's perfectly obvious what you should try and do. You should try and negotiate your way out of this republic and into a united Ksordia.'

Applause.

'Negotiate, if you can. Avoiding war, if you can. Local ceasefires, confidence-building measures, protecting Akhtarian civilians, freezing troop movements. Remember the Russian promise: if we negotiate in good faith, they won't give the Akhtarians enough ammunition to launch an offensive. You can negotiate from a position of security.

'But here's another dilemma for you. What if? What if the Akhtarians try to make their state your state too. What if they refuse to shift the border, but they agree to change the constitution and make it as anti-Rebel as West Germany is anti-Nazi? What if they get rid of the flag, if they send Sulkavidza back to Canada and ban the Rebel parties and militias? What if they make genocide denial a criminal offence? What if they reinstate all the Ksords who've been sacked? All of them, every last one. What if they give you real autonomy and the right to fly the Ksordian flag and carry Ksordian passports and give you cast-iron guarantees of your place in this country? If they do all that, will you still go to war?

'It would be a dilemma, wouldn't it? I think it would be really difficult. But what I'm saying is that you should talk. Talk yourself out of Akhtaria if you can, but with absolutely no exchange of populations. And if you can't do that, then brace yourselves and drive a bargain so hard that it'll make Eristov weep and it'll drive Sulkavidza out of politics and preferably out of the country forever.

'Negotiation isn't an easy option. It's a hard, hard option, and your leaders will need nerves of steel to see it through. But maybe, just maybe, it can leave you safe in your homes in a state which is in some sense yours, and best of all, with all your young men alive and well.'

Ruslan sat down, exhilarated.

Perhaps a third of the audience sat stony-faced or shouted abuse and another third applauded politely but without much enthusiasm. The rest cheered and gave him a standing ovation.

He felt confident the majority would be willing to give his peace process a chance. After all, Korgay would have told Bogiani that he needed to play for time. He also knew that there was no way he could go back to comfortable obscurity in an English university after this.

He had become a politician.

He was home to stay.

Chapter Twelve

THE KNOCK on the apartment door didn't come until nearly eleven. Lionidza's elderly friend Jeltkov scolded his excitable dog. Then he nodded to his wife, who got up from her armchair and walked slowly to the door. She opened it just a little and looked at the two men outside.

'Shush. Don't say anything.'

Mrs Jeltkov nodded and let them in. The older man took off his coat and hat, revealing the familiar face of Ksordia-Akhtaria's fallen Communist ruler.

'It's good to see you again, Comrade Zikladza.'

'Good evening, Sergo. I hope your exile from the Party hasn't been too hard on you.'

'I'm fine. It's difficult for my wife, though.'

'It won't be forever.'

The two men embraced and exchanged four kisses.

Lionidza introduced his hosts, and then they and Zikladza's bodyguard retreated to the kitchen, leaving the two old comrades alone in the living room.

'So how's your young protégé?'

'Doing surprisingly well. Everyone's agreed to his Four Principles.'

'You want to be careful. He isn't one of us.'

'I know.'

'We mustn't build him up too much. He might turn on us. Have you got anything on him?'

'Pardon?'

'You know: sex, speculation, bribery.'

Lionidza shook his head. 'He's pretty straight.'

'Keep your eyes open for anything we can use. You know he's in touch with Nina Begishveli?'

'You're joking.'

'No I'm not. She's approached Korgay. She says she'll help him form a legally constituted Federal government if he promises to stick by your Four Principles.'

'God's nails. Ruslan never told me anything about that. Still, it might not be a bad thing. It would lock Korgay into the peace process.'

'But would it help our long-term aim? Never lose sight of the fact that we're working for the restoration of Socialism.'

Lionidza nodded. 'Yes, of course.'

'So what happens now?'

Lionidza shrugged. 'I'm going to take a singer to work with us in Kvemodishi.'

'Who's that?'

'Leila Meipariani.'

'Never heard of her.'

'She translates Tatar songs into Ksord-Akhtarian. She's half Tatar, half Ksord.'

'So what's she going to do? Sing for peace?'

'She's going to open an office for us in Kvemodishi. It's a well-known fact that singers make first class bureaucrats.'

The two men laughed at the ridiculousness of it all.

Leila Meipariani was a beautiful young woman with long, permed hair, a voluptuous figure and a mischievous grin. As Lionidza drove her towards Kvemodishi, she was irrepressible, like a little girl on her way to the seaside, very excited at the prospect of meeting Ruslan Shanidza once more.

'I sang at his wedding, you know. You should have seen his wife, she was so gorgeous.'

Then, for Lionidza's benefit, she launched into the song she had sung there.

'Give me daffodils in the springtime
As a token of your love
Hold my hand in the gentle sunshine
While the birds sing their songs for us.
We'll walk together in the fairs and markets,

And let everyone see that we are one.'

Lionidza smiled. He had quite liked that song when it first came out, though he was less than thrilled by her friendship with Nina Begishveli and other leading democrats.

Previously, Ruslan and Mikhel had been sharing a room in a cheap guesthouse near the centre of Kvemodishi, but with the arrival of Lionidza, North Ksord leader Bogiani found them a large house on the outskirts of town, plus a housekeeper to shop, cook and clean for them. Lionidza warned the others that she would almost certainly be spying on them too. 'She may plant bugs in the house, so if we have a sensitive discussion, we should either go into the garden or maybe turn the TV up or something like that.'

Leila insisted on having three telephone lines installed: one that would only be used for incoming calls from Ruslan and the team, one for incoming calls from contacts and one which she would use for all outgoing calls. Her role was to act as their secretary, but Ruslan soon came to feel that she was in fact their manager. She arranged their diary and dealt with the many requests they received to help mediate local agreements. He would often ask her, 'How many gigs today?' and be astonished at how well she had arranged them to minimise travelling time.

He was happy to allow Lionidza to dictate their negotiating strategy. Sometimes Ruslan would act as front man, but often he would sit back and let Lionidza take over. He came to admire Lionidza's skills as a negotiator and his ability to cut through the nonsense that angry or disingenuous villagers and militiamen spouted.

However, he found living in the same house as his colleagues something of a strain. Lionidza and Leila filled the house with smoke, and Lionidza had clearly never done any housework in his life. He left every plate, cup or glass exactly where he had used it and no amount of nagging from Ruslan and Leila could persuade him even to dump them in the kitchen sink.

Ruslan was also surprised at how much he drank. He had beer with dinner every night and would hit the vodka not long afterwards. He never seemed to get particularly drunk, but Ruslan doubted that he ever went to bed sober. Lionidza's drinking didn't stop Ruslan admiring him, but he wasn't sure how much he liked living with him, and he certainly didn't know how much he could trust him.

Leila meanwhile, showed herself to be every bit as obsessive about her music as Ruslan was about his running. She would play her guitar whenever she wasn't working, eating or sleeping. If Ruslan and Mikhel wanted to watch sport on TV, which they did any chance they got, she would retreat to the dining room under protest and strum away there.

As well as the efficiency with which she managed their peacekeeping mission, Ruslan came to admire her ability to get to know all the big players in the region very quickly. He also found her very attractive and wasn't sure whether the feeling was mutual or whether she was just one of those outgoing women who make almost every man they meet think she fancies them. But whatever the case, self control was a strong point of any marathon runner and Ruslan was confident that his marriage vows weren't in any danger.

His fitness levels, however, were. Bogiani's police had warned him that it was too dangerous for him to go running every day. He had to confine himself to mobility exercises and hope that his peace mission wouldn't last too long.

Ten days after her arrival, Leila sent them to the town of Sagobeskila, where Colonel Bebur Chikradza, commander of the Ksordian Second Motor Rifle Regiment, had come to make contact with an old friend who led the Akhtarian forces in nearby Natsopeli.

Chikradza was a large, gruff West Ksord who knew Lionidza well and took Ruslan into his confidence at once. 'My troops are in no state to fight. Not that the other side are any better. If fighting starts, it'll just be a bloody mess: a lot of people killed but neither side strong enough to take advantage. But a few more weeks and Korgay might think we're ready to attack.'

He sent Ruslan over to the Akhtarian side with proposals for demarcation lines and joint patrols that would at least ensure that fighting didn't break out by accident.

When he had a spare moment, Ruslan telephoned Tamara in England.

'You've been on TV over here,' she told him.

'Really? I haven't seen any British reporters.'

'They showed an interview in Russian, and they said you were a beacon of sanity in a country gone mad.'

Ruslan laughed and told Tamara about the progress he was making and about his growing optimism that war could be avoided.

'You know it's Easter next weekend. It doesn't look much like you'll make it back to London for the start of next term.'

'No, I don't think it does.'

'You're not coming back, are you?'

'Not if you'll agree to come over here.'

'I told you. Whatever you decide, I'll agree to it.'

'Then will you come?'

'Of course.'

'Brilliant. I can't wait to get my hands on you again.'

Tamara laughed. 'You mean you can't wait to speak to me and to see your beautiful little boy again.'

'Yes, that too. But I really can't wait to get my hands on you.'

'I look forward to it. Where do you want me to come to? Khosume or Zeda'Anta?'

'It's up to you.'

'I'll go to Zeda'Anta and stay with my parents. It'll take me a week or two to arrange everything. I want to sell as much as I can over here. We're a bit short of money, you know.'

'Leave some money in the bank over there and just bring dollars. Roubles are useless.'

'Okay.'

The next day was spent shuttling between Natsopeli and Sagobeskila, and in the evening Ruslan escorted Chikradza over to meet his old comrade and sign a ceasefire accord in front of the cameras. Later that evening, after they had toasted their success perhaps a little too thoroughly, Mikhel drove them back to the Ksordian lines.

A young officer stopped them at a roadblock.

'Excuse me, Colonel Chikradza, sir. Have you heard the news from Dzap?'

'No? What's happened?'

'That police chief, sir, the one who's been negotiating the ceasefires. He's been shot dead.'

Mikhel drove Ruslan and Lionidza to Dzap the following morning. Dawa Tetradza had been murdered by one of his own policemen. When arrested, the assassin had confessed at once, saying that Tetradza was a traitor who deserved to die.

Ruslan and his comrades spent that afternoon and evening racing round the nearby villages, shoring up the ceasefire accords and urging everyone to stay calm. The next day, Leila joined them as they escorted six local Ksordian leaders to Dzap for Tetradza's funeral, taking with them a wreath from Bogiani.

Several thousand people lined the route of the funeral cortege as it made its way to a recently reopened church in the centre of the town. Hundreds of Akhtarian police were in attendance, along with the Akhtarian Minister of the Interior. Ruslan turned down an invitation to attend the wake. He was anxious to get his Ksordian companions back home safely before nightfall.

As he left the church, he kissed Tetradza's two sons and his teenage daughter. Then he found himself face to face with his widow. She took his hand and inclined her head towards him. They exchanged four kisses.

'I'm so sorry, Mrs Tetradza. Your husband was a fine man.'

'He said the same about you.'

'We won't give up. We'll carry on what he started.'

He began to move his hand away, but she gripped it firmly and looked him in the eye. 'Be very careful, Ruslan Shanidza. They'll kill you next.'

Tetradza's murder unnerved Ruslan, and he wondered whether his widow's words might turn out to be prophetic. That evening, he turned up the TV and asked the others whether they thought it was too dangerous to keep crossing from one side to the other.

'I don't know,' said Lionidza. 'I've been asking myself the same question.'

Leila asked if they had thought about getting an armed bodyguard.

Ruslan shook his head. 'It's not possible. Whenever I approach a roadblock, I always get out of the car with my hands up. Then I open my jacket and say, "Look, we're not armed."'

'God's teeth, that sounds pretty scary.'

'It is, but we need people to be able to trust us.'

'Then your best protection could to be the press. I could make sure there are plenty of press on both sides before you cross over, preferably TV.'

'You think that will be enough?'

'It's not for me to judge.'

Ruslan turned to Lionidza.

'I really don't know,' he said. 'To be honest, I'm getting more and more nervous. I fucking hate it when we approach roadblocks, if you'll pardon my language, Leila. You never really know how they're going to react.'

'So do you think we should to stop?'

'I suppose either we use the press to protect us or else we give up and go home.'

'So which option do you prefer?'

'What do you think? You're the one most likely to get shot.'

Ruslan thought for a moment. 'Well, we're getting somewhere, aren't we? It would be a shame to give up now.'

Lionidza nodded.

'What about you Mikhel? What do you think?'

'I think we should carry on.'

'Leila?'

'I'm not out there, so it's not my decision. But I'll stay here until you think it's time to stop.'

'Then we carry on.'

Later that evening, Leila went out into the garden. Ruslan joined her and spoke to her in Tatar. 'Can I ask you a question?'

'Yes?'

'Do you think we can trust Lionidza?'

Leila laughed. 'Before I came here, my friends told me to be very wary of him. One minute he's a real hard-line Communist and the next minute he's a pacifist. It seems a bit odd.'

'I know. There was one time just after I'd finished at the border posts when I was convinced he was working for Comrade Zikladza. I can't remember exactly what Zikladza said, but I was sure he gave it away. I challenged Lionidza about it but he had a really convincing answer to everything.'

'He's a politician. It's his job to have a convincing answer to everything.'

Ruslan smiled. 'So what do you think now, after seeing him in action?'

'I like him.'

'Do you trust him?'

She thought for a moment and then said, 'Yes. He seems pretty genuine to me.'

'That's good. I just wanted a bit of feminine intuition.'

'Can I ask you a question? How come you speak such good Tatar?'

'My home village is surrounded by Tatar villages and I had lots of Tatar friends when I was a boy. My first girlfriend was a Tatar.'

'Oh yes? I suppose it's a good way to learn a language, the horizontal approach.'

'I was only about thirteen, so I don't think we ever went horizontal.'

Leila laughed. 'Is that why you're such an internationalist? Because of all the girls you've had?'

'I haven't had that many.'

'No? Never had a Russian?'

Ruslan shook his head. 'Ukrainian yes, Russian no.'

'What about English? Had any English girls?'

'Certainly not. I'm a happily married man.'

'I'm pleased to hear it.'

On Good Friday, Ruslan and Lionidza, plus two cars full of press and TV, went to an isolated Akhtarian village near Sagobeskila, where they helped negotiate an accord with the surrounding Ksords. The next day, they crossed into Akhtarian-held territory and drove to Onchi'Aketi in the east, where tensions had been raised when somebody fired a rocket at a nearby Ksordian village. Rumour had it that Nartshu Sulkavidza, Akhtaria's neo-Rebel Defence Minister, had fired the missile himself.

The situation was too tense to resolve in a single day, so Mikhel arranged for them and their press companions to stay the night in the Ksordian village. Ruslan called Leila to give her their contact number.

'Guess what,' she said, 'there's a programme about you on Akhtarian TV tonight.'

'Something to look forward to. What time?'

'Eight.'

'Fame at last, eh?'

At the appointed time, Ruslan and his companions settled down in a nearby bar to watch the programme. They very quickly realised that it was going to be hostile: dark music accompanied images of Ruslan shaking hands with Korgay and North Ksord leader Bogiani but refusing to shake Sulkavidza's hand. The opening title was stark: 'Ruslan Shanidza Unmasked – a Special Investigation.'

The programme began with the 'standard' view of Ruslan: the great Ksordian athlete who had married an Akhtarian, the man who had gone to prison rather than testify against his dissident friends, the internationalist so horrified by the pogroms he had witnessed in Azerbaijan that he was risking everything to prevent war between Ksords and Akhtarians.

'This is a carefully cultivated myth,' said reporter Yemish Baratov, a senior newsreader on Akhtarian TV. 'We shall show you that Ruslan Shanidza is in fact a fanatical Ksordian nationalist and an enemy of the Akhtarian people. His only disagreement with Korgay and Bogiani is over tactics. He shares with them the aim of destroying the territorial integrity of the Akhtarian republic.'

Ruslan and Lionidza looked at each other.

The programme started with Ruslan's father, 'a Stalinist Partizan'. Then it swung into an attack on Tamara, saying how happy she was to have their son chrismated as a Ksord. It cut to her cousin who had started the trouble at Shota's baptism, resplendent in Akhtarian Army uniform, Kalashnikov on his knees: 'Tamara's forgotten her identity. She's more like a Ksord these days: always banging on about the Rebels.'

Next, they showed an old photograph of Ruslan, Nina and some of her co-conspirators in the Ronkoni Committee for Truth. Among them were two whom the reporter described as Ksordian nationalist extremists.

'That bit's true,' said Lionidza. 'Iya Cristavi's in the Radical Party, and that priest's in the Ksordian Renaissance.'

'Christ's nails. I used to really like them.'

The reporter now attempted to prove that Ruslan had been a KGB informer all along. 'How many dissidents were allowed to travel abroad freely during the Soviet era? How many unreliable people represented the Soviet Union in international competition? How many people were ever charged with anti-Soviet agitation and found not guilty? The answer to all these questions is only one: Ruslan Shanidza.'

He then read out some of the statements Ruslan had made to the KGB during interrogation.

'The only reason Ruslan Shanidza was so blessed was that he was a KGB informer, a far cry from the noble young man who was prepared to go to prison rather than testify against his friends.'

Next, the programme demonstrated that Ruslan was himself a militant Ksordian nationalist, using heavily edited extracts from his speech to the North Ksord Assembly.

'...I do want to start by reminding you that I'm here as a Ksord. I'm not neutral in the conflict between Ksords and Akhtarians: I'm a Ksord.

'...if this was being broadcast live, I wouldn't say this, because this is Ksord speaking to Ksord, this is not for Akhtarian ears.

'I was weaned on a hatred and a fear of the Rebels. Nothing that has ever happened has changed that. I stand here shoulder to shoulder with you in your struggle...

'...that flag, the red and yellow diamonds. Now I hate that bloody tea towel as much as anyone in this room.

'Because Akhtaria isn't your state, is it? It's theirs, not yours, and that's why you've risen up against it. And frankly I don't blame you.

'So it's perfectly obvious what you should try and do. You should try and negotiate your way out of this republic and into a united Ksordia.

'And if you can't do that, then you'll have to fight.

'...the Rebels are our enemies, and we have the right to defend ourselves against them.

'...we should win easily. How many Ksords are there? About four and a half million. How many Akhtarians? Less than two million.'

Lionidza signalled Ruslan to over to a corner where their press companions couldn't hear them. 'Did you really say all that? God's bollocks, Ruslan. What on earth were you playing at?'

'For Christ's sake, Sergo, they've edited it.'

'Yes, but you gave them the ammunition.'

Ruslan shook his head and said nothing.

'Anyway,' said Lionidza. 'there's no way we can ever show our faces in Akhtarian-held territory after this. They'd kill us. We might as well give up and go home, because you've shat in your own shoes, Ruslan. You've shat in your own shoes big time.'

Chapter Thirteen

NEITHER OF them spoke for an eternity. Some reporters asked for their reaction to the programme but were rebuffed. Lionidza ordered some vodka. He clearly intended to drink his way to oblivion. Ruslan sat staring into space, consumed with hopelessness and fury.

So much for his great career as a politician.

He got a message from the house where he was to stay the night. 'There was a phone call for you, someone called Leila.'

He called her back using the bar's payphone.

'Hi, Leila.'

'Hi, Ruslan. Did you see it?'

'Christ's nails, yes.'

'You have to come back to Kvemodishi at once. I've been in touch with Bogiani's secretary. He says he'll give us a complete video of your speech. You can use it to show how they quoted you out of context. I rang Murad. He's coming here tomorrow with a thing for editing videos.'

Ruslan said nothing.

'I phoned your mother's house. Your brother was there. He said he'll come up with your father's certificate of rehabilitation. That'll prove they lied about him being a Stalinist. He'll meet Murad in Timashevsk, and they'll come up together. Can you think of anything else?'

'I don't know.'

'Come on, Ruslan. What else can you use?'

Ruslan blinked and shook his head. Leila was right. He wasn't beaten yet. This was just a stumble in the middle of a long race, and he would show them that it would take more than a TV programme to beat him.

'I know,' he said, 'get Giorgi to bring a photo of me after the KGB broke my leg.'

'Okay. Anything else?'

'Yes, if someone I was on trial with could make a statement to say that I wasn't KGB. But not Nina Begishveli.'

'For God's sake, Ruslan. This is an emergency. Nobody cares about your bloody love life.'

'That's not why. Nina's too anti-Korgay. I can't afford to be associated with her. Why don't you get Yakub Bovin to make a statement? He was in prison with me.'

'Yes, good idea.'

'Do you have Nina's number? She'll have Yakub's home number.'

'I've already got Yakub's home number. Anything else?'

'Can't think of anything. Leila, thank you. You've saved us tonight. I thought we'd end up eating shit.'

'We're not out of it yet.'

'We soon will be. Can you organise a press conference? And get Bogiani to let Akhtarian TV and press come. I don't want them to have any excuse for not broadcasting my reply.'

The next morning, Lionidza still felt angry with Ruslan for throwing it all away with his nationalist rhetoric. But he was also angry with himself. He should never have let him go to the North Ksords alone. And now Ruslan and that flirtatious little airhead Leila Meipariani seemed to think that all they had to do was call a press conference and rebut the allegations and all would be well.

And who had they invited to help them? Two bloody Tatars!

As if that would cut any ice with the Akhtarians.

Ruslan and Leila were thrilled that Tatar leader Yakub Bovin was actually coming up to appear at their press conference in person, but Lionidza most certainly was not. How was he supposed to get himself readmitted to the Party if he had to appear next to such a fanatical anti-Communist?

Lionidza reluctantly agreed to sit through the whole of the Akhtarian broadcast again, while Ruslan and Leila made a list of all the lies. Then they played a video of Ruslan's speech to the North Ksord Assembly. Lionidza watched this with some interest. He had to admit that it had been an effective speech, though the nationalist rhetoric had provided easy ammunition for the Akhtarians, especially calling their flag a tea towel. Ruslan should have been more careful there, and he shouldn't have made such reckless attacks on Sulkavidza.

Reinforcements arrived at midday: Lionidza had never met Ruslan's friend Murad and his half brother Giorgi before, and he was surprised at how warmly they greeted him. Yakub Bovin, on the other hand, was no more than icily polite. When he showed the others photographs of his tiny baby daughter, he didn't even bother to let Lionidza see them.

As the afternoon progressed, however, Lionidza's mood gradually lifted and he started to contribute ideas and suggestions. He also remembered that far from being an airhead, Leila was a very shrewd operator indeed.

And Ruslan himself was turning out to be far more capable than expected. Lionidza couldn't help but admire the Machiavellian streak revealed by his secret contacts with Nina Begishveli.

By the time the press conference started, Lionidza knew that it would be a triumph. Giorgi, Yakub Bovin and Lionidza himself would prove that Ruslan had never worked for the KGB. Then Ruslan would use video clips very cleverly edited by Murad to demonstrate how completely Akhtarian TV had distorted his words.

The only question was whether the Akhtarians would broadcast it. And therein lay the gamble that worried them all, because Ruslan would finish the press conference with a very aggressive statement: 'It's clear that the Akhtarian TV programme was a tissue of lies made by people who want the peace process to fail. Tonight at nine o'clock, everyone in the region should tune in to Akhtarian TV news. If that broadcast doesn't show in minute detail how yesterday's programme slandered me, then everyone will know that the Akhtarian government has chosen to go to war.'

Yakub left soon after the press conference, but before going, he invited Ruslan outside.

'Don't tell Lionidza, but...'

'Why don't you trust him?'

Yakub looked at Ruslan as if he were an imbecile. 'Because he's one of *them*. He's still working for Comrade Zikladza, you know.'

'Oh, come on.'

'He is. Do you think I haven't got reliable sources of information?'

'Do you know what, Yakub? I couldn't care less. I just know that I wouldn't have achieved anything without him. Not a thing.'

'Maybe, but I've got some information for you, and I don't want Zikladza to know, so that means I don't want Lionidza to know.'

Ruslan nodded.

'We're in touch with Korgay, us Tatars, the democrats, moderate Ksordian nationalists like Orbeliani. We're offering to help him form a legally constituted Federal government. We've told him we'll support it as long as he supports your Four Principles.'

'Is Nina in on it?'

'It was her idea.'

'This is fantastic. Do you think it'll happen?'

'It's difficult to say. It's still very tentative at this stage. It depends how much Korgay wants a legally-constituted government.'

'It would be a big prize if he could woo you away from the Akhtarians.'

'It certainly would.'

'Let me know what happens.'

'Okay, but don't say anything to you-know-who.'

Despite what he said to Yakub, the thought that Lionidza might still be working for Comrade Zikladza came as a shock to Ruslan. What was he up to? Didn't he believe in the peace process? Was the whole thing just a way of undermining Korgay so that Comrade Zikladza could make a comeback?

But what about Lionidza's blistering attack on Zikladza in the Federal Assembly? And hadn't Zikladza expelled him from the Communist Party? Ruslan found the whole thing difficult to believe.

He decided to ask Leila what she thought. He motioned her into the kitchen, turned on the taps and, whispering in Tatar, told her what Yakub had said.

'Yakub has his ears to the ground. If he says Lionidza's working for Zikladza, then it means he is.'

'So what's he playing at?'

'Why don't you challenge him?'

Ruslan thought about it and shook his head. 'No, we need him, don't we? And in a sense it doesn't matter what his motives are, he's brilliant at what he does and there's no way we can prevent this war without him. Believe it or not, I don't actually do that much negotiating. I'm just his front man half the time. But if he's using us, well two can play at that game. We can use him until the threat of war has receded and then we dump him and join forces with the democrats.'

'Ooh you're such a turn-on when you get all conspiratorial.'

Ruslan smacked her on the bottom.

She looked at him, grinned and walked back to join the others.

He stood there for a moment, bemused. Where had that come from, the slap on her behind? It had certainly set his pulse racing, and he suspected it had done the same to her. He had better calm down and control himself. And he had better get the thought of her very shapely backside out of his head.

At nine o'clock, they all crowded round their television to see what the Akhtarian news would say.

'Tonight we are pleased to present a special Easter documentary on the history of Christianity in Akhtaria,' the disembodied voice of the announcer said. 'The news will be shown at ten o'clock.'

'What?'

'For fuck's sake!'

Lionidza laughed. 'Can you imagine what's going on in Zeda'Anta? They must be in a real panic.'

They turned over to watch the Ksordian TV news, which featured Ruslan's press conference prominently and accurately. They then turned back to watch the religious documentary, a programme so appalling that everyone was sure they would never have broadcast it if Ruslan's press conference hadn't landed them in it.

'It's a conspiracy,' said Leila. 'They've put this on to send everyone to sleep so we don't know what their bloody news says.'

'It's also complete fiction,' said Ruslan. 'I mean, all this crap about sixteenth century Akhtarian nationalists. There was no such thing.'

'Oh no,' said Murad. 'Don't let him start.'

By the time the news began at ten o'clock, Ruslan and his friends were feeling nervous again. They all cheered when they saw that the newsreader wasn't Yemish Baratov.

'That's a good sign,' said Lionidza.

And then, nothing.

The first ten minutes was an account of President Eristov's day: meeting dignitaries, inspecting troops, conferring medals and eating Easter lunch in his ancestors' graveyard. Then came a largely fictitious story about ceasefire violations by Ksordian troops near Onchi'Aketi, plus film of training manoeuvres and passing-out parades.

'They're not going to mention it,' said Leila.

'They will. They've got no choice.'

It didn't come until 20 minutes in.

'Evidence has emerged of a complex operation by the Ksordian Security Police to destabilise negotiations while shifting the blame onto the Akhtarian government. Our special correspondent Shad Ratiev takes up the story.'

Ratiev told how a mysterious Georgian had given Akhtarian TV a video with extracts from Ruslan's speech, together with what was alleged to be his KGB file. 'Any reporter will know how difficult it is to establish whether or not such items are genuine, and Akhtarian TV began an extensive investigation to check the truth of these potentially explosive revelations. Unfortunately, such an investigation takes a long time, and a small group of reporters and editors grew impatient, fearing that they would be scooped if they didn't broadcast the story quickly.'

'They're going to make Baratov carry the can.'

'Ah, don't you feel sorry for him?'

'Shush!'

'...contained a number of factual errors. There is in fact no evidence that Ruslan Shanidza was ever a KGB informant during the Soviet era. Indeed, Central Kuban President Yakub Bovin, who was his co-defendant at the 1982 trial of Ronkoni dissidents, categorically stated this afternoon that Shanidza behaved with integrity throughout that period. There is evidence that the KGB in fact attempted to stop Shanidza running competitively for the Soviet Union, but that they were foiled in this by Shanidza's friends in the Soviet military and the Ksord-Akhtarian Party leadership.'

'What about the photographs?' said Ruslan.

'Didn't mention my name, did they?' said Lionidza.

'Shush!'

'...now know that the extracts from Shanidza's speech distorted the tone and content of his remarks. Though he did use strong anti-Akhtarian rhetoric, Shanidza did in fact urge the Ksords to try to resolve the current crisis through peaceful negotiation. In a statement this afternoon, President Eristov said that he believed that Akhtarians can and should continue to work with Shanidza for peace.'

Cut to film of Eristov.

'Following the latest investigations, I would urge all Akhtarian forces to continue to co-operate with Ruslan Shanidza. In doing so, we have to remember that by his own admission, he is a Ksordian nationalist, but I believe his desire for a negotiated settlement is genuine.'

Cut back to Ratiev.

'The Managing Director of Akhtarian TV has issued a statement expressing regret that last night's programme failed to live up to the high standards of truth and honesty that Akhtarian TV has set since its inception last year. An internal inquiry will be held and those responsible for the programme will be suspended until the inquiry's findings are published.'

They turned the TV off and sat in silence for a moment.

'What do you think?' Ruslan asked. 'Is it enough?'

Lionidza nodded. 'Just about.'

Life now became much scarier for Ruslan and his companions, who started to receive death threats on a daily basis. Ruslan didn't mention them in the letters he sent to Tamara, but he wrote about them in the diary he was keeping. (It was addressed to her, so it avoided any mention of the smack on Leila's bottom.)

His peacemaking work in the front-line communities was now far more difficult. The Akhtarians were more wary of him, and many were angry that he had insulted their flag. Some Ksords were angry too, believing that he had blamed their intelligence service for the attack on his peace mission. Where Ruslan had once felt confident that ordinary people trusted him, he was no longer sure.

He and Lionidza were anxious to withdraw from the front line and begin negotiations at government level, largely for reasons of safety, but also to move the peace process forward. It couldn't remain at the grassroots forever.

Ruslan invested a lot of hope in the secret talks between Korgay, the Tatars and the moderate opposition. However, just five days after the broadcast, massive riots in the Ksordian capital wrecked any possibility of a deal.

The trouble had started a week earlier when Korgay closed down a radio station that supported Kakhi Djebuadza, the wild man of the Ksordian right. Kakhi (as Djebuadza was universally known) organised a protest demonstration for Saturday 25th April, and the moderate opposition leaders felt compelled to join in. The closure of the radio station was just the kind of heavy-handed authoritarianism that would make any deal with Korgay very difficult to sell to their supporters.

The demonstration was a remarkable event in that it brought all the factions of the Ksordian opposition together for the first time ever. The turnout was enormous, the largest crowd in Ronkoni since the huge rallies that had brought Korgay to power.

Quite how the violence started was unclear. Opposition spokesmen blamed police provocateurs, while the authorities (and, in private, many opposition leaders) blamed Kakhi, saying that he was using the demonstration to attempt a *putsch*.

Whatever the explanation, by mid-afternoon, the centre of Ronkoni was the scene of a massive pitched battle between the police and tens of thousands of demonstrators, many of them armed with clubs and iron bars. By five o'clock, the police had lost control. The rioters attacked businesses owned by government cronies and ransacked the headquarters of Korgay's Socialist Party, burning it to the ground.

The government sent in troops. The demonstrators marched towards them, calling on them to turn their guns on the 'Bolshevik' Korgay. The soldiers fired a volley over the heads of the crowd, who responded with a hail of stones. The troops then panicked (or moved on to the next stage of Korgay's dastardly plan, according to one's preferred version of events) and fired right into the crowd. As the demonstrators retreated in terror, tanks, troops and police surged forward in a fearsome display of violence.

Some 33 people died that day, 28 demonstrators, three policemen and two Socialist Party members whose charred remains were found in their headquarters. More than 500 were arrested. Most were released after a few days, many after a good thrashing, but more than 100 people, including most of Kakhi's senior colleagues, faced serious charges. Kakhi himself was repeatedly beaten over several days and then suddenly rushed to hospital. His wife wasn't allowed to see him, so severe were his injuries.

The events of 25th April reverberated around the whole of Ksordia-Akhtaria, polarising opinion and splintering the Ksordian opposition. Korgay's enemies believed that his government was now a dictatorship in all but name, while his supporters felt that he had only just avoided being overthrown by Kakhi's fascists. The Akhtarians braced themselves for trouble and the Tatars looked on apprehensively.

Ruslan and Lionidza knew that April 25th meant that any chance of talks between Korgay and the Akhtarians had gone. Korgay would have to adopt an ultra-nationalist tone until he felt safer at home.

By now, Ruslan was beginning to lose his nerve. After a hard-eyed Ksordian militiaman ran a finger across his throat as Ruslan's car drove past, he almost told Lionidza and Mikhel that it was time to give up. He wondered why he didn't. Perhaps because he felt obliged to stand by those who still supported his ceasefires. Perhaps because he didn't want to let his companions down. If he had asked them, however, he might have discovered Mikhel and Leila were both very frightened and only stayed on out of loyalty to him.

A few days later, some Akhtarian villagers called on Ruslan to remove a unit of extremist Ksordian paramilitaries who had taken control of a road junction in contravention of a local agreement. Ruslan and his companions were very wary of extremist paramilitaries, and they travelled first to the nearest Ksordian village, where they got the entire village council to accompany them to the junction. Even then, the paramilitaries refused to budge.

Ruslan raised Colonel Bebur Chikradza, the local Ksordian commander, on his field radio. 'Go and piss your pants away from the front line,' Chikradza told the paramilitaries. 'If you sons of sluts cause any more trouble, I'll have you all shot.'

As they boarded their cars to leave, they swore at Ruslan and called him a traitor. 'You're dead meat,' they shouted.

That evening, Nina telephoned: 'Ruslan, is your line safe?'

'I doubt it.'

'Okay. I'm going to give you a safe number here. Find a safe phone and call me as soon as you can.'

Ruslan took down the number and they went to a nearby bar. While Ruslan spoke with Nina, Leila made sure the jukebox kept playing, and she, Mikhel and Lionidza positioned themselves so that nobody else could get near him.

'So how are things, Nina?'

'Rapidly going pear-shaped. You can forget about our talks with Korgay. No chance.'

'Yes, I guessed.'

'I don't think it would have ever come to anything. Korgay would never place his government at the mercy of us and the Tatars.'

'Well, thanks for trying.'

'Ruslan, I haven't rung about this. Do you remember when you first started, I told you the time might come when you have to choose between giving up and getting killed?'

'Yes?'

'Well, that time's come.'

'What makes you say that?'

'Remember your old friend Vakhtan Mingrelsky?'

'How could I ever forget him?'

'He's planning to kill you.'

Ruslan was silent for a moment. Then he asked, 'Who says?'

'Yakub.'

'How does he know?'

'The Tatars have good sources and they say Mingrelsky's been given the green light.'

'By who?'

'Tengiz Alavidza, I should think.'

'Alavidza?'

'Probably. Rumour has it he's Mingrelsky's controller.'

Ruslan took a moment to digest this. 'You know Alavidza was the KGB officer I insulted in Bogmaperdi?'

'I know.'

'Do you think it's personal?'

'I don't think so. Yakub's sources say a faction within the Ksordian leadership thinks they're ready for war and they want you out of the way.'

'And how do you know these sources are telling the truth?'

'Yakub's desperate for you to succeed. Why would he say anything that might make you give up if he wasn't sure it was true? You've got to get out of there.'

Ruslan thought for a moment and then said, 'Nina, this is off the record, but I get death threats all the time. Today some paramilitaries gave us a real fright until we got a Ksordian colonel to scare them off.'

'Ruslan, get this into your head: this isn't some bunch of paramilitary half dicks. This is Korgay's Minister of the Interior. He's decided he wants you dead and he's sending his favourite psychopath to kill you.'

Ruslan was silent.

'You have to get out of there.' Nina sounded close to tears.

'I can't just cut and run.'

'I knew you'd say that.'

'I'll have a chat with Lionidza and the others. We are taking precautions you know.'

'Ruslan, don't listen to bloody Lionidza. Just get out of there.'

'He's got no more desire to get shot than I have.'

'Let's not argue about Lionidza. If you stay there, you'll get killed. It's that simple.'

'So what am I supposed to do? Give up?'

'Yes.'

'I can't do that. A lot of people in front-line communities are relying on me.'

'You're no good to them dead.'

'Yes, but I can't just abandon them.'

'Ruslan, stop trying to be King bloody Wirustam. You've got a wife. You've got a child. You haven't got the right to get yourself killed in a blaze of glory.'

'It's not a question of that. I have obligations. People are relying on me. I can't just give up and go home.'

'Well why don't you go and see Korgay?'

'God's teeth, I never expected you to suggest that.'

'Well why not? He might like to have a chance to play the statesman, you never know.'

'All your friends in the opposition will hate me if I see Korgay.'

'So what? You're not part of the opposition. You're just trying to stop a war, remember?'

'Yes, I do remember and maybe you're right. Thanks, Nina.'

'Promise me you'll stop crossing from one side to the other.'

'I'll do what I can.'

'That's not good enough, Ruslan. You have to promise me.'

'I'll do what I can.'

Chapter Fourteen

MUCH TO Ruslan's surprise, Lionidza liked the idea of going to see Korgay, and the two of them asked Bogiani to set the meeting up. The answer came two days later: 'President Korgay's too busy to see you. Maybe in a couple of weeks, when things have quietened down.'

'This is bad news,' said Ruslan. 'Now what do we do?'

'What can we do? We carry on here.'

'Shouldn't we go and see the Akhtarian government?'

'And what are we going to say to them?'

'So you think we should keep crossing the lines?'

Lionidza had no answer to that question.

'Can I make a suggestion?' said Mikhel.

'Yes?'

'When we cross the lines, we make them hand us over.'

'How do you mean?'

'Let's say we go from the Ksordian side to the Akhtarian side, the local Ksordian leader escorts us half-way and then hands us over to the Akhtarian leader.'

Ruslan looked at Lionidza.

'Would they agree to do that?'

Mikhel said, 'Well, if they don't, we don't cross.'

'You could insist on TV cameras,' said Leila. 'That would be another layer of protection.'

'So you think we should carry on?'

Leila raised her hands and shook her head. 'I don't have a vote. It' not my life on the line.'

Ruslan looked at the other two.

'Either we carry on or we give up,' said Lionidza. 'I don't see a third alternative.'

'And what do you think we should do?'

'It's not me that Mingrelsky and Alavidza want dead.'

'If they spray the car with machine gun fire, you could end up just as dead as me.'

Lionidza thought for a moment. 'If we do most of our travelling in Akhtarian territory, that would make it harder for Ksordian extremists to shoot us. And why don't we insist that the local leaders from both sides always escort us all the way across?'

'Not half way?'

'No. Both leaders, all the way.'

'Will they be willing to do that?'

'That's up to them. We just say we're getting more and more nervous about crossing because of all the threats we get. If they want us to help them out, that's what we insist on. My guess is that Mingrelsky won't be allowed to kill local Ksordian leaders.'

'Okay,' said Ruslan. 'I vote to carry on, at least for the time being. But anyone who wants to is at liberty to give up and go home.'

Ruslan was reluctant to be the first to abandon his mission, but truth be told, he was beginning to lose faith in the whole peace process. He couldn't see how their network of local ceasefires could last much longer without some movement at the top.

Even the weather seemed to be against them: it had been dry and sunny for weeks. Ruslan longed for some rain to dampen the spirits of those on the front line and drive them indoors.

And he still didn't know how far he could trust Lionidza. Was he really working for Comrade Zikladza? Or was he just in touch with him? Everything Lionidza said and did seemed to be so much in line with what Ruslan was trying to achieve. And it wasn't as if he wasn't risking his own life too.

Surely he wasn't faking it.

What worried Ruslan most was the fact that Tatar leader Yakub Bovin was convinced that Lionidza was working for Zikladza. If Yakub believed this, perhaps Korgay and the Akhtarian leadership thought so too, in which case they might think that the whole peace process was just a plot to undermine them and restore Zikladza.

But Ruslan didn't say anything to Lionidza. He wasn't sure why. Perhaps because he would just get a politician's answer if he did, or perhaps because he couldn't help but defer to the man who had been his mentor and protector for so long. There was also a sense in which he felt he was using Lionidza almost as much as Lionidza was using him. After all, when their peace mission ended, he would align himself with Nina and the democrats, not the Communists.

He decided not to discuss Lionidza with Leila any more. He was by now nervous of getting too close to her and doing something he would later regret.

Ruslan sometimes thought back to that evening almost 14 years earlier when Mingrelsky and his cronies had come looking for them on the beach. Tamara had wanted to run, but Ruslan had insisted that they stand their ground and fight.

He wondered if that had been a pivotal moment in his life. If they had listened to Tamara that night and run away, Mingrelsky's honour would have been satisfied and he would have had no need to attack them again.

And what about Tengiz Alavidza? He would never have tried to recruit Ruslan as a KGB informer and Ruslan wouldn't have heaped abuse on him. He had often wondered if Alavidza had anything to do with the trap the KGB set for Nina, Yakub and the others. Was it some kind of revenge on Ruslan? Could their arrest and imprisonment have been an indirect consequence of that fight on the beach?

And where would he be now if he had run away that night? He might even have become an historian rather than an athlete if his arrest hadn't cut short his academic career. He could be teaching in a Ksord-Akhtarian university and researching into something obscure, maybe land ownership patterns in the middle ages. The thought of that made him smile.

And would he now be married to Nina?

No, that wasn't a possibility. Their relationship wouldn't have survived. She was already involved in dissident activities back then and would have got herself arrested sooner or later. And in any case, they weren't right for each other. He understood that now.

Three years after his release from prison, Ruslan had a brief fling with a Ukrainian athlete. They had liked each other very much but had never quite fallen in love, and he remembered her words after their relationship fizzled out: 'It would never have worked. We're too similar. We're both obsessives with big egos. What we need is someone who's sane, someone who isn't desperate to be a superstar.'

How lucky he was to have found just such a woman. Tamara was a brilliant doctor and she worked hard, but she wasn't driven like he was, nor was she ruled by her ego. In her eyes, work was work and home was home, and family would always come first. She kept him grounded and tolerated his obsessions, but she would always be the one who held them together.

Nina could never do that. She was as obsessive as he was. It was her tragedy that she was drawn to charismatic men with egos as powerful as her own when what she needed was someone modest who would be content to stay in the background and let her hog the limelight.

Even now, with his life in danger, Ruslan had no regrets about the way things had turned out. Tamara was everything he could hope for in a wife, and he adored her and the son she had given him. He had his two gold medals, which he might never have won if things had been different. And he could never regret the fact that he now had the chance to help prevent a war that would be an absolute catastrophe, even if he owed that opportunity to Lionidza's machinations.

He most certainly had no wish to die. He had Tamara and Shota to live for, and he hoped that he was laying the foundations of a future career in politics. But he didn't see how he could simply drop everything and run. It wasn't a question of some King Wirustam-style martyrdom complex as Nina seemed to think. It was just that too many people had placed too much faith in him. He couldn't suddenly abandon them.

He decided that if the worst came to the worst and he had to die, he would do so with dignity. He knew Mingrelsky wouldn't be content with shooting him from afar. He would want to see the terror in Ruslan's eyes and gloat.

Well, he was determined not to give him that pleasure. He would make sure he didn't go to pieces or grovel or beg for his life. So in the small hours, he sometimes visualised the moment Mingrelsky came for him, trying to rehearse a noble death. This was hardly conducive to sleep, but it helped him to cope, and he could always catch up with sleep during the day as Mikhel drove him from one place to another.

North Ksord leader Mataa Bogiani gave them an armed policeman outside their house, and they continued to follow their new ultra-cautious policy when crossing to and from Akhtarian-held territory, but the strain of constant death threats was taking its toll on all of them. Mikhel and Leila became increasingly irascible, while Lionidza drank himself into a stupor every night. Ruslan too was irritable and found it impossible to sleep sober, though he was nowhere near as bad as Mikhel or Lionidza.

Ruslan and Lionidza took to arguing about politics almost every evening.

'Communism isn't dead,' Lionidza would say. 'It isn't a political party. It's the eternal longing for justice and equality. You'll never abolish that.'

'Dream on, Sergo,' Ruslan would reply. 'Communism's as dead as a dodo. There might be other challenges to capitalism, but they'll come from eco-warriors, nationalists and religious nutcases, not Communists.'

'You're wrong. Communism is the rational organisation of society. If that isn't possible, then what's left? Just muddling through, that's all we can ever hope for. Just muddling through.'

'Maybe that's all we ever could hope for.'

One evening in their Kvemodishi house, they all got even more drunk than usual. Lionidza staggered off to bed at midnight. Soon after, Mikhel made his excuses and left Ruslan and Leila sitting on the sofa together.

'Do you want another beer?' she asked.

'Shall we share one?'

'Okay.'

She put her hand on his knee to lift herself up and walked unsteadily towards the kitchen. Ruslan watched her as she went, and decided that he really did approve of her backside very much indeed. As she returned and took a swig from the bottle, he stared appreciatively at her ample breasts and her face, with its excellent mixture of Tatar and Ksord.

She handed the bottle to him and remained standing while he took a swig. As he did so, he enjoyed the thought that a little of her saliva might enter his mouth.

He felt the first stirrings of arousal.

He looked up at her and they both smiled. She knelt down in front of him and put her hands on his knees.

That was when he remembered that he was married.

Hell and damnation! What am I doing?

He took hold of her arms: 'Leila, I'm really drunk. I'd better call it a night. See you in the morning.'

The next day, after breakfast, Leila went out into the garden. Ruslan joined her there.

She spoke to him in Tatar. 'What are you going to say? That you're sorry about last night?'

'Yes.'

'Sorry what? Sorry that you led me on or sorry that you didn't have the balls to go through with it.'

'I'm sorry I gave you the wrong signals.'

'Bullshit. You wanted me and don't pretend that you didn't.'

'I'm married.'

She snorted her derision. 'I thought you were special, Ruslan Shanidza. Do you know that? I really thought you were special. Well you've gone down in my estimation, I can tell you.'

With that, she stormed back into the house, but then she turned round and came out again. 'You know what? I hope you'll always regret that you didn't have me, because you'll never get a second chance.'

Ruslan felt wretched, but he also felt relieved. He hoped he hadn't permanently ruined his friendship with a woman he liked and admired, but he counted himself lucky that he hadn't wrecked his marriage. Tamara could read him like a book, and if he had been unfaithful to her, he knew that she would realise it the instant she saw him.

In the event, having put him in his place, Leila soon reverted to her usual cheerful self. But three nights later, as he lay in bed, Ruslan heard the sounds of lovemaking coming from Mikhel's bedroom.

This came as quite a surprise. Mikhel had been married for more than 20 years and Ruslan regarded his wife as a friend, but he didn't feel he was in any position to judge. He wondered whether Leila had jumped into Mikhel's bed as a way of getting at him. If that was the case, so be it. He was sure Mikhel wasn't complaining, and at least his own wedding vows would be safe for the duration.

Ruslan wrote about Leila and Mikhel in the diary he was keeping for Tamara but, regarding the circumstances that led to their affair, he only said that he was surprised.

Desperate to find some way to advance the peace process, Ruslan and Lionidza arranged to meet Tatar leader Yakub Bovin in Khosume. They hoped he could act as an intermediary between the Ksords and the Akhtarians. They would then travel up to the Akhtarian capital on the Tuesday, arriving in time for Ruslan to meet Tamara when she and baby Shota came back from England. Perhaps President Eristov would meet them, and after that they might even have something to say to Korgay.

Ruslan wasn't optimistic, however. The only thing that gave him hope was the fact that the Russians and Ukrainians still seemed to want to restrain their allies.

Lionidza, Mikhel and Ruslan drove to Khosume on the Sunday. Ruslan stayed with Murad and Fatima and their young family, and for a few precious hours, he managed to leave politics behind and enjoy playing with the children.

He got up early next morning and went for a half-hour run. He was shocked at how out of condition he was and promised himself he would run more often.

When he got back, Fatima told him to call Leila.

'Ruslan, the Ksords have taken Khidmabani. Both sides want you to come and sort it out.'

'Where the hell's Khidmabani?'

'Near Pirvelituri.' (Pirvelituri was a key strategic town linking Akhtarian-held territories in the north and the southwest.)

'Do we have an agreement there?'

'No, but Khidmabani's ninety percent Akhtarian.'

This was a dangerous escalation: it was the first time either side had seized a town predominantly inhabited by the other.

Ruslan telephoned Lionidza, who was no more enthusiastic than he at the prospect of a return to the ethnic borderlands, but they both felt they had no choice but to cancel their meeting with Yakub Bovin and head north. They hurried to Kvemodishi in Lionidza's car. Mikhel would catch up with them later.

'I just hope Korgay hasn't decided to start a war,' said Lionidza. 'He might think he can blitz the Akhtarians and win it before the Russians have time to react.'

As they drove towards the frontier between Central Kubania and Akhtaria / North Ksordia, however, they saw no evidence of troop movements and no indication that the Ksords were preparing a major offensive.

They arrived at their Kvemodishi office shortly after one. Leila, as usual, had been busy. 'Mikhel should be here in an hour or so. Bogiani's given us a number for making international calls. I've spoken to Moscow and Kiev, and they're waiting to hear from you, Sergo. Yakub Bovin says he'll phone Korgay and Eristov and try and get them both to cool it.'

Lionidza called Moscow and Kiev, while Ruslan phoned the Akhtarian Foreign Minister, who agreed to try to calm things down from his end. 'You'd better be quick, though,' he warned Ruslan. 'The Ksords have only got a company of light infantry in Khidmabani, and we've got them surrounded. If they try to send reinforcements, it could all turn very bloody.'

Mikhel arrived soon after two and they set off. It was the hottest day of the year so far and surprisingly sticky for the first week in May.

'We could do with a thunderstorm,' said Lionidza.

They crossed over into Akhtarian territory near Natsopeli with the help of Colonel Bebur Chikradza and his friend in the Akhtarian military.

Once they reached Khidmabani, Ruslan and Lionidza got the local Akhtarian commander to brief them. He said 60 Ksords had arrived just before dawn, seizing the town centre and all the routes out of town before anyone knew what was happening. The Akhtarian police and some civilian militiamen attacked one of their roadblocks, and the Ksords promptly dropped their rifles and ran. They then abandoned all their other roadblocks at the edges of the town and retreated to the centre.

Meanwhile, the local Akhtarians had telephoned their army, who sent a 400-strong infantry combat battalion. Their commander had given his men strict instructions not to shoot and then contacted the Ksordian commander, who agreed to call in Ruslan.

The two commanders escorted Ruslan and his companions over to the Ksords, who took them to the police station where they had set up their headquarters.

'What do you want us to do?'

'Just get me and my men out of here, okay?'

Ruslan and Lionidza met the leader of the Ksords on the town council. He was distraught: 'We had no trouble with the Rebels till these idiots turned up. They've shat in our shoes big time.'

'We'll get the TV cameras in,' said Ruslan. 'Say that you've always got on well with the local Akhtarians. Don't use the word "Rebel" okay? Then say you want the Ksordian troops out, but it would be good if they could leave a couple of unarmed observers behind to make sure everything's okay.'

'Right.'

'And say you want the Akhtarians to promise no reprisals.'

'Yes.'

'And they have to keep their paramilitaries out of town.'

'Okay.'

The TV camera crews came in and duly recorded interviews with the Ksordian councillor and with Ruslan, who stressed the need to make sure that this 'misunderstanding' didn't lead to the outbreak of war.

Ruslan went back to the Akhtarian commander, who told him the government was sending the Foreign Minister to negotiate. He was relieved that it wasn't their Defence Minister and was hopeful that he might still be able to get to Zeda'Anta the next day in time to meet Tamara and little Shota.

When the Akhtarian Foreign Minister arrived, he agreed to allow two unarmed Ksordian police observers to stay in the town, provided the Ksordian Army got out by ten o'clock the following morning.

'You've done a good job, Ruslan,' he said.

'Not yet I haven't. I still have to persuade the Ksordian leadership to let them leave.'

'They haven't got much choice, have they?'

'Not really, no.'

If the North Ksord leadership reluctantly accepted Ruslan's *fait accompli*, more militant Ksords did not. On television that evening, Vakhtan Mingrelsky denounced the agreement and called Ruslan a traitor to his nation.

'I think our days at the front lines are coming to an end,' Lionidza said when he saw this. 'Even if Mingrelsky wasn't planning to kill you before, he's just announced open season on you now.'

Chapter Fifteen

Ruslan, Lionidza and Mikhel spent the night in Khidmabani and stayed to supervise the departure of the Ksords. After that, they joined the local Akhtarian leaders for breakfast.

'What are you going to do next?' asked the Mayor.

'I'm going to Zeda'Anta tonight. My wife's due to fly in from England this evening.'

'Look at that grin on his face,' said the Mayor. 'You can see exactly what he's got planned for tonight.'

Everybody laughed.

Just then, Ruslan caught the eye of an official who had walked into the room.

'Dr Shanidza,' he said. 'The Ksords want you to go to a place called Moreni.'

'Moreni? Didn't we negotiate an agreement there?'

'Yes,' said the official, 'but now the Ksords claim the local Akhtarians have occupied some farm buildings in contravention of your agreement.'

'What do you think, Sergo?'

'I don't know. Maybe one last one for the road?'

Ruslan looked at Mikhel, who nodded.

'Okay, in for a kopek, in for a rouble. Let's do it.'

Just outside Moreni, the Ksordian military had set up a field hospital. Ruslan and Lionidza viewed this with alarm. It meant somebody senior thought this dispute could lead to serious fighting, though fortunately there was no sign of troop reinforcements.

The local Ksords were furious with their Akhtarian neighbours. They showed Ruslan their copy of the local ceasefire accord, which clearly placed the disputed farm buildings under Ksordian control.

Ruslan raised the Akhtarians on the radio. 'What's going on? Over.'

'There used to be several Akhtarian workers on this farm, so we've come here to protect their interests. Over.'

'What the hell are you playing at? Over.'

'We're just standing up for our rights. Over.'

Ruslan looked at Lionidza. He made sure his radio wasn't broadcasting and then said: 'They're playing silly buggers, aren't they? Just copying what the Ksords did at Khidmabani.'

'We've got to stamp on this, Ruslan. Otherwise we'll have silly buggers all over the place trying to renegotiate their deals.'

'Are Akhtarian TV there? Over.'

'No, we told them to go and piss their pants somewhere else. Over.'

'Well we're not coming unless we can bring Ksordian TV with us. Over.'

'No fucking way. Over.'

'Then we're not coming over to you. We've got no guarantee of our safety. Over.'

'What are you talking about? We'll guarantee your safety. Over.'

Ruslan looked at Lionidza and Mikhel, who both shook their heads. 'Look, we get death threats all the time, and the press are the only protection we've got. If you want us to come over there, you've got to let a TV camera crew in. Otherwise we're not coming. Over.'

'Okay, but it has to be Akhtarian TV. No Ksords. Over.'

'Right. Get them to call me on the radio when they arrive. Over and out.'

The Akhtarian camera crew didn't return until four o'clock, by which time the weather had turned. The clouds were so heavy that it was almost dark. Lightning was flashing in the distance, and the first drops of rain were beginning to fall.

'This rain's good news,' said Ruslan. 'It'll keep everyone indoors for a day or two. But I tell you what: as soon as the rain stops, we stop crossing the lines like this. It's just too dangerous.'

Lionidza and Mikhel nodded their agreement. One of the local Akhtarian leaders drove across and he and a local Ksordian leader called Valentin joined them as they crossed in their car. By the time they reached the Akhtarian positions, it was raining heavily.

'I didn't like that bit in the middle,' said Mikhel.

'Where?'

'About half a kilometre back there. The road dipped, and for about a hundred metres we were invisible from both ends.'

Ruslan shrugged and looked at his watch. Tamara would be arriving in just over three hours. He hoped her plane wouldn't fly into a thunderstorm.

The local Ksordian leader Valentin waited with Mikhel in the car as Ruslan and Lionidza went to negotiate with the Akhtarians, who admitted that they had taken over the farm buildings in retaliation for the Ksordian incursion into Khidmabani. They said they were disgusted that Ruslan had rewarded them with two observers. 'If they can renegotiate their agreement, so can we.'

'God's teeth,' said Ruslan. 'I can't believe my ears. Number one: you and the local Ksords actually have a fucking agreement, negotiated clause by clause and signed by you. In Khidmabani there was no agreement for the Ksords to renegotiate. So the situation there was completely different.

'Number two: which fucking planet are you on? You think the deal in Khidmabani favoured the Ksords? Don't be fucking stupid. Your Foreign Minister's on cloud nine. He's rubbed the Ksords' noses in it. The two observers are just a face saver for the Ksords. They're the big losers in Khidmabani.'

The Akhtarians looked stunned. Ruslan had never spoken to them like this before. Lionidza was holding his right hand in front of him, the five fingers extended as far apart as they could go. (He and Ruslan used three basic hand signals during negotiations: a clenched fist meant 'be harder with them', extended fingers were an instruction to ease off, and the English children's crossed finger gesture meant 'they're lying'.)

The Akhtarians asked Ruslan to let them discuss the matter among themselves. They kept him waiting for almost two hours as the weather got progressively worse. Before long it was pouring with rain, and Ruslan and his companions listened as a fierce thunderstorm approached.

Just as the storm reached them, the Akhtarians emerged and agreed to back down. 'Let us keep our lads there overnight. That's our face saver. We'll pull them out first thing in the morning.'

'Okay,' said Ruslan. 'I'll put that to the Ksords.'

He, Lionidza and the Akhtarian village leader hurried out and ran through the driving rain to the car, where Mikhel and the Ksordian leader Valentin were waiting.

'I hope your lot agree to this straight away,' Ruslan said to Valentin. 'I'm so sick of crossing the lines. I just can't do it any more.'

'I know how you feel,' said Lionidza.

As they drove into the heart of the thunderstorm, Ruslan felt the road dip. This was the stretch of road Mikhel didn't like.

A fork of lightning shot down in front of them. The thunder boomed almost at once.

'Oh fuck,' said Lionidza. 'There's something on the road ahead.'

Ruslan looked up, suddenly afraid.

Someone had put what looked like farm machinery across the road. Behind it stood four men with masks and Kalashnikovs.

This was it. They had finally come for him.

Oh God no.

Not now.

Not when Tamara was just over an hour away.

Mikhel stopped the car.

'Get out,' shouted a masked voice. 'Keep your hands up.'

It was Mingrelsky, no doubt about it.

Oh God, thought Ruslan. I'm so sorry, Tamara.

I'm so sorry to do this to you.

'Move,' shouted Mingrelsky, pointing his gun at Ruslan.

Stay calm, Ruslan told himself. Stay calm.

Don't beg, don't grovel.

Keep your dignity.

He got out of the car and felt the cold rain penetrate his clothes almost at once.

'Which one of you is the Rebel?' Mingrelsky shouted.

Valentin pointed to the Akhtarian village leader: 'Him.'

One of Mingrelsky's men took hold of the Akhtarian and pulled him away from the others.

Were they going to shoot him?

'Stand over there the rest of you and turn round.'

Fuck, he's going to shoot the rest of us. He'll leave the Akhtarian alive so everyone will blame the other side.

'Mingrelsky, don't shoot the others,' Ruslan heard himself say. 'You don't need to. Just shoot me.'

Everyone stopped.

'It doesn't make any difference. It's just me you want. If they lie down in the road.'

Lightning blazed across the sky, and Ruslan saw the desperation etched on Lionidza's face.

'Lie down Sergo. Fucking lie down for God's sake. You too Mikhel, and you Valentin. Just fucking do it, will you? On your face.' He turned to the Akhtarian village leader. 'You too.'

They all lay down as the thunder roared.

Ruslan looked at Mingrelsky: 'See? You don't need to kill them. Shoot the car engine up. We've got a radio in the front. Shoot that up too. Then you don't need to kill them. It's just me you want.'

Mingrelsky turned and Ruslan watched in horror as he emptied a magazine into the car. He could almost see the bullets flying out of the gun and ripping through the car, knocking out its lights and causing the engine to hiss.

Any minute now and he would do the same to him.

Ruslan felt so afraid and so alone.

He wanted to run.

He wanted to beg for his life.

He wanted to ask Tamara and Shota for forgiveness.

But no, it was too late.

This was where it would end.

All that was left was to die with dignity.

Die with dignity.

Oh God, this is hard.

This is so hard.

The other three gunmen stepped forward. Mingrelsky hung his rifle on his shoulder and pulled out a Makarov pistol.

They all aimed their guns at Ruslan's chest.

He had rehearsed this so many times. Step a little to the side just before they shoot.

Now.

One shot rang out and almost instantly three more.

The impact of the first bullet threw Ruslan backward, causing two of the assassins to miss. Ruslan landed head down on his back on the embankment.

The gunmen all climbed down.

Lightning flashed again as Mingrelsky aimed his pistol at Ruslan's chest.

The thunder drowned out the sound of his shots.

Then he and his men ran off and disappeared into the dusk.

Chapter Sixteen

THE NEWS that Ruslan had been shot stunned everyone in Ksordia-Akhtaria, nobody more than Tamara, whose plane landed in the Akhtarian capital less than an hour later.

Akhtarian TV devoted the whole evening to the shooting, though to Tamara's intense frustration, they had no actual news about Ruslan's condition. Instead, they kept showing a brief interview with a dishevelled and very distraught Lionidza.

'I can't believe I'm alive. Mingrelsky junior would have shot all of us if Ruslan hadn't saved us.'

Every time Lionidza said Mingrelsky's name, it stung Tamara. How she wished Ruslan had been more afraid of him all those years ago. If only he hadn't kept mocking his 'important papa'. If only he had run when Mingrelsky came for them on the beach that night.

And yet, even now, Ruslan had managed to secure one last victory: he had bamboozled Mingrelsky into leaving ' four eyewitnesses alive. Their testimony would destroy him, Tamara was sure of that.

She just prayed that Ruslan would live to see it.

Soon after ten, Ruslan's sister-in-law Venera telephoned from East Ksordia. She knew even less than Tamara, since Ksordian TV hadn't broadcast the interview with Lionidza. Venera said that Giorgi was on his way to pick Ruslan's mother up and take her to be with him.

The first real news about Ruslan didn't come until gone eleven, when Mikhel Inalipa called from Kvemodishi.

'They've finished operating. He's in a critical condition, but he's stable.'

'What are his injuries?'

'It's pretty grim, Tamara. They shot him four times in the chest.'

'Oh my God. Poor Ruslan.'

'I've got one of the doctors with me. Maybe you should hear it first-hand.'

Mikhel handed the phone over to the surgeon, who gave Tamara full details of Ruslan's injuries, his emergency tracheotomy, the field hospital just one kilometre from where he was shot, the litres of blood that had kept him alive on the way to Kvemodishi and the treatment he was receiving now. Tamara listened in horror, astonished that he had survived at all.

His worst injuries had been caused by a high velocity bullet that had entered his chest just above his second rib, five centimetres to the left of the breastbone. It had destroyed most of his left lung, blasting an exit wound nine centimetres wide through his back, shattering three ribs and the lower part of his shoulder blade, and shredding his back muscles and nerves in the process.

The bullet's impact had also caused some haemorrhaging of other organs, and the surgeons weren't sure how bad this was. Ruslan was still reliant on blood transfusions.

The other three rounds had all been low velocity bullets from Mingrelsky's pistol. The first had all but missed, skimming his left flank, fracturing a rib and causing muscle damage. Then, when Ruslan was lying on the ground, Mingrelsky had fired two more pistol shots into his chest. One had entered through the fourth rib, ricocheting to the right and passing through areas already destroyed by the high velocity bullet. The other had been aimed straight at Ruslan's heart but had been halted by his breastbone.

The surgeons had removed most of Ruslan's left lung. His rib cage would need major reconstruction, and the damage to his muscles and nerves was irreparable. Tamara had never dealt with major trauma like this, but she knew that even if he survived, he was likely to be an invalid for the rest of his life.

But it was far from certain that he would survive. Even if internal haemorrhaging didn't kill him, infection might, despite the heavy doses of antibiotics he was receiving. An equal danger came from necrosis, a chemical reaction that can kill tissues adjacent to major trauma. The doctors doubted that they would be able to save the remainder of his left lung, and if necrosis spread to his heart or his major blood vessels, there would be nothing they could do.

Ruslan had slipped into a coma, with his body shutting down non-essential organs in an effort to stay alive. Tamara knew that the deeper the coma, the greater would be the chances of severe brain damage.

As she listened, tears welled up in her eyes. Eventually, her resistance collapsed and she stopped listening and cried inconsolably.

The North Ksord leadership contacted the Akhtarian government, and next morning an official car came to pick Tamara up and take her to Kvemodishi. She decided to leave her baby son Shota with grandparents he scarcely knew, thinking it would be irresponsible to take him into what could easily become a war zone. She was worried enough about going there herself.

The Akhtarians drove her south along rain-sodden roads choked with military vehicles going one way and refugees coming the other. They kept the radio on in case there was news of Ruslan. There was nothing about his condition, but they did repeat Lionidza's interview several times.

At about ten, Tamara was dozing in the back of the car when her escorts woke her up. A woman's voice was speaking on the radio.

'It's Leila Meipariani,' they told her.

Tamara jolted wide awake.

'...Nina Begishveli. She warned Ruslan that Mingrelsky was planning to kill him, and she begged him to stop crossing from one side to the other. We were all really scared, but Ruslan said a lot of good people were depending on him and he couldn't let them down.'

Tamara's eyes filled with tears at this. 'Why didn't you listen to her?' she asked aloud. 'Why didn't you listen?'

By now, the news was dominated by tales of ceasefire violations by the Ksords, who were said to have started a major movement of men and equipment up from East Ksordia and Central Kubania. Ruslan seemed to feature only for his propaganda value. The Akhtarian authorities clearly wanted to make sure the blame for killing the peace process stuck firmly to the Ksords.

Just before the handover, there was a telephone interview with Nina. She spoke of how Tatar leader Yakub Bovin had warned her of Mingrelsky's intention to kill Ruslan. The interviewer asked her if she thought he had been given the nod by the Ksordian government.

'It wouldn't surprise me. Why hasn't Mingrelsky been arrested? Why aren't the Ksordian press allowed to say what's happened?'

Some 20 kilometres north of Kvemodishi, Tamara was transferred to a Ksordian police car. Ksordian radio was almost a mirror image of the Akhtarian station. It spoke of ceasefire violations by the 'Rebels' and massive movements of 'Rebel' troops and equipment south.

It seemed obvious to Tamara that war was about to begin in earnest. And she had just gone and placed herself in enemy territory.

Ksordian radio had a very different version of the attempt on Ruslan's life. The Ksordian military had allegedly picked up radio traffic which proved that 'Rebel' Minister of Defence Nartshu Sulkavidza had been behind the attack.

The voice of Valentin Dolidza, the Ksordian village leader who had been with Ruslan, came on air to back this story up: 'The assassins would have killed all the Ksords in the car if it weren't for Ruslan,' he said. 'But they weren't planning to shoot the local Rebel leader. That proves they were Rebels.'

Tamara wondered whether he believed what he was saying. Didn't he realise he had been set up? Mingrelsky was going to kill him to make it look as if the Akhtarians had done it. Ruslan had saved his life and that was how he repaid him, by sheltering Mingrelsky. Had the man no shame?

She wanted to scream.

But she thought it better not to get into an argument with the two Ksordian policemen in the front of the car, so she said nothing.

She reached the hospital in the early evening. A nurse led her through the dingy corridors and past three heavily armed police officers to intensive care. There were five beds inside, one of them surrounded by screens. The nurse pulled a screen back to reveal Ruslan, face down on his bed, a large brown patch on his back showing the site of his exit wound, and pipes and tubes protruding from almost every orifice.

Ruslan's mother and Giorgi were already there, along with Leila and another nurse. They all stood up but Tamara scarcely acknowledged them. She made straight for her husband and crouched down beside him.

She checked his temperature and his breathing. A bit clammy, but otherwise okay. No stink of infection, but it was too early for that in any case. There was a little urine in the bottle by his bed. That was a good sign. If his kidneys were working, his coma shouldn't be too deep.

'What do the doctors say?'

'He's stable.'

Tamara kissed his forehead and stroked his hair.

'Please Ruslan,' she whispered, 'stay alive for me, I beg of you. Stay alive for me.'

Later that night, Tamara found herself alone with Leila and the unconscious Ruslan.

'Why didn't he listen to Nina Begishveli?'

'He tried, but he just got sucked back into it.'

They sat in silence for some time, then Tamara asked about Sergo Lionidza. 'Ruslan's mother says he ran away as soon as she turned up. Is that true?'

'Yes. He blames himself, and he's frightened you and Ruslan's mother will blame him.'

'Do you think we should?'

'I honestly don't know. Ruslan didn't trust him.'

'What do you mean?'

'He thought he was working for Comrade Zikladza.'

'And was he?'

'Maybe he was but I don't know. Ruslan wanted you to know about it. He wrote this for you.'

Leila reached into her bag and handed a notebook to Tamara, who opened it. She could see at once that it was a diary Ruslan had written for her.

'Where did you get this?'

'I found it in his room this morning.'

'Have you read it?'

'Some of it, yes. I'm sorry. I had no right to.'

Tamara began to skim through the pages of the diary.

After a few moments, Leila said, 'I might as well tell you. You'll find something in there about me.'

Tamara shot her a hostile glare. 'What?'

'Mikhel and me, we had an affair.'

Tamara looked at her in astonishment. She was also relieved. She had half expected Leila to tell her that she had been sleeping with Ruslan.

Leila sighed. 'I know you must think I'm a stupid slut, but you can't imagine what it was like. All the death threats, they just wore me down. I was so scared. I needed someone to hold me. I needed to feel alive.'

'You don't have to explain yourself to me. It wasn't my husband you were knocking off.'

Leila bowed her head and started to cry.

'I'm sorry,' said Tamara. 'I had no right to say that.'

'Whatever you think of me, believe me, I think ten times worse.'

'What did Ruslan say about it?'

'He didn't say anything to me. He teased Mikhel a bit: "Do you want me to drive? You can't have got much sleep last night." That sort of thing.'

Tamara almost smiled at this. 'You're not in love with Mikhel?'

Leila shook her head.

'Is he in love with you?'

'I hope not.'

'So do I. A girl like you, you could turn a man's head. You should send him home to his wife, and tell him to keep his mouth shut.'

Three days later, Tamara reluctantly accompanied Leila and Giorgi to ask Mataa Bogiani, leader of the North Ksords, why Mingrelsky hadn't been arrested. Tamara fully expected to find Bogiani a loathsome figure, his hands dripping with blood. She was surprised when Leila told her that Ruslan had genuinely liked him.

Bogiani welcomed them warmly and spoke of his admiration for Ruslan, but he refused point blank to move against Mingrelsky.

'I wish I could, but I can't. Mingrelsky has some very powerful friends.'

'So he can just shoot anyone he likes and nobody will touch him?' said Leila.

'I'm sorry. I really do wish I could help.'

'Can't you just go public and say that it was him?'

'I can't. I'm not strong enough to move against him.'

Leila spat out her reply. 'I thought you were supposed to be a leader.'

'Leader?' said Bogiani. 'That's a joke. The North Ksords have gone berserk. I'm just doing what I can to restrain them.'

Tamara interrupted them: 'So what's to stop Mingrelsky coming to the hospital and finishing Ruslan off?'

'He wouldn't dare do that. His impunity only stretches so far.'

'You don't know him. He didn't shoot Ruslan for political reasons, I'm sure of it. It was personal. Me and Ruslan humiliated him once when we were students. He's never forgiven us for it.'

'What do you mean?'

Tamara told the story of the fight on the beach.

'Do you think he might come after you?'

'I wouldn't put it beyond him.'

'How many bodyguards does Ruslan have?'

'Three.'

'Okay, I'll double his bodyguard, and two of them will accompany you when you leave the hospital.'

'Thank you.'

Bogiani turned to Leila. 'My advice to you would be to get out of North Ksordia.'

'Are you threatening me?'

'Far from it, Miss Meipariani. But do you seriously imagine Mingrelsky doesn't know you're trying to get him arrested? I can protect Mrs Shanidza, but I can't be seen to protect you. I'm sorry, I just can't.'

Ruslan's coma lasted for two weeks. When he came round, he wasn't surprised to find himself in hospital: his dreams had told him he would be in a bad state, though he had no idea why. There was no pain for the first few minutes, but then it kicked in and caused him to moan out loud.

His mother, who had been dozing by his bedside, jumped up.

'Ruslan? You're awake?'

'Mama?'

'You've finally woken up. Thank God.'

'Mama, is Nina here?' Ruslan slurred his words, like a drunk.

'No, of course not. You're married to Tamara, not Nina.'

'Tamara?'

'Yes, Tamara.'

'The Akhtarian girl?'

'Yes.'

'But I haven't seen her for years,' he slurred.

'Yes, you have. You're married to her. You have a son, Shota.'

'I have a son?'

'Don't you remember?'

'No.'

By the time the nurses fetched Tamara, Ruslan had retrieved a few memories of her. He could remember her selling flowers in a market, waving to him at a station and sitting with Korgay at a big reception, flashing a smile. Even so, when she came into his line of sight, her appearance surprised him. He had been expecting the teenager he had known in Bogmaperdi rather than the mature woman who crouched beside him.

'Are you a doctor now?'

'Yes.'

'And my mama says we have a baby.'

'Yes. Can't you remember?'

'No. I'm sorry, I can't.'

Ruslan drifted in and out of consciousness for the next few days. Every time he came round, he asked for Nina and expressed surprise when told that he was married to Tamara, who began to worry that she might have to spend the rest of her life reminding him.

On the fifth day, he remembered and was mortified that he had ever forgotten.

134

Over the next few weeks, he would be reminded just how precious Tamara was to him. His only solace was the time she spent with him, when she would regale him with anecdotes about their time together, or read to him from his diary. Only she could take his mind off the excruciating pain, the shortness of breath, the fear of permanent disability and the knowledge that all of this suffering was for nothing, because he could hear the distant sound of fighting from his bed.

Tamara had been working in the hospital since before Ruslan came out of his coma. Keeping busy was the only way she could cope with her worries about her husband and the pain and guilt of separation from her baby son. Besides that, she needed an income.

The hospital gave her responsibility for the post-operative care of troops whose injuries were so severe that they would never be able to fight again. This role protected her from any accusation that she might sabotage their recovery in order to prevent them from rejoining their units. Equally, Akhtarians wouldn't be able to accuse her of patching up enemy troops so that they could return to the battlefield.

She expected some hostility from her patients and colleagues, but in fact there was none. They all knew that she was Ruslan's wife, and it was clear that she was a very competent doctor who had the best interests of her patients at heart.

She was horrified by the wastefulness of war, by the wreckage of the young bodies she encountered. She came across amputation after amputation: fingers, hands, forearms, arms, toes, feet, half legs, whole legs and genitals.

If the men with abdominal injuries turned a ghostly pale and stank of infection, she knew they were heading for a painful and lingering death. The surgeons wouldn't take them back, and Tamara hardly dared to use up her precious supply of painkillers on them.

Just as heart-breaking were the spinal injuries: men paralysed from the waist down, the chest down, the neck down. And the facial injuries: eyes lost, ears blown off, cheekbones and noses smashed in, lower jaws shot off. Tamara was glad that at least she didn't have to deal with burns patients.

She became a focus for the small, frightened remnants of Kvemodishi's Akhtarian population. For the most part, they were women married to Ksords, though there were also a number of elderly people who had not had the means or the strength to flee. They faced harassment and death threats from their neighbours and from troops and militiamen. In some cases, the fact that their husbands or sons were fighting for North Ksordia was no defence.

Tamara called on Bogiani again. He was sympathetic, but once more he was unable to help. 'This whole country has descended into madness. If I gave the police the addresses of Akhtarians to protect, they'd just turn round and harass them themselves.'

'Can't you do anything?'

'If they've got a husband or a son at the front, they should always carry a picture of him in uniform. As for the others, I'm sorry, but the best thing for them would be to leave. Your husband's name will protect you, but I'm afraid there's nothing I can do for anyone else.'

Tamara's inability to do anything for her fellow Akhtarians added to her sense of helplessness. She tried to remind herself that this bleakest of periods in her life wouldn't last forever. Ruslan had survived, and influential friends were working to find a way to take him out of North Ksordia for medical treatment in either Russia or England, where the two of them would be reunited with Shota. Tamara was desperate to escape from the tragedy that their homeland had become so that they could rebuild their lives as a family once more.

But she worried that Ruslan might not wish to do so. He said little about his feelings, but his questions told her what dominated his thoughts. Again and again he asked the same thing: 'Why hasn't Mingrelsky been arrested?' She could see that he thirsted for revenge on the man who had so nearly killed him. She knew that there were days when he thought of little else.

Chapter Seventeen

BY THE beginning of July, Ruslan was well enough to travel. He was taken south to Central Kubania, where crowds lined the streets to applaud his ambulance as it passed through towns and cities. He was still lying on his front and never got to see his supporters, but their presence and Tamara's slightly exaggerated descriptions of their numbers gave a massive boost to his morale. In Khosume, they were reunited with little Shota, who Ruslan by now remembered much better than Shota remembered him.

After a day's rest, Ruslan was deemed fit enough to receive visitors. Tamara acted as gatekeeper, making sure they didn't stay too long and exhaust Ruslan. The first to come was Mikhel.

Ruslan greeted him with, 'I've got a scar on my bloody throat, thanks to you.'

Mikhel laughed. 'God, some people. They're just so ungrateful.'

He knelt down by Ruslan's bed and the two men embraced as best they could.

Mikhel told Ruslan and Tamara that he was scraping a living growing vegetables, driving a taxi and doing odd jobs. The Ksordian government couldn't afford to train athletes any more. The army had offered him work as a trainer but had then withdrawn the offer, presumably under orders from on high.

Ruslan asked if he was in touch with Leila and Lionidza.

'Not really. They live in a different world from me. And in any case, I'm keeping out of Leila's way.'

'Yes, you naughty boy.'

The two of them laughed.

Tamara was sorry to have to split them up after just a few minutes, but the journey had tired Ruslan out, and Tamara was conscious of his need for rest before the flight to Moscow. But she was delighted to see him so happy and relaxed with Mikhel, even though she knew that much of it was bravado.

As she and Mikhel walked towards the hospital exit, Tamara suggested he ask Lionidza to help him find a job.

Mikhel stopped walking. 'Is it true that Lionidza betrayed Ruslan?'

'I don't know. Yakub Bovin told Ruslan he was still working for Comrade Zikladza.'

'I really liked him, you know that? He seemed really genuine. And then you hear these rumours and you think...well, you just don't know what to think.'

That afternoon, it was Leila's turn. She embraced Tamara like an old friend. 'I'm really nervous.'

'Why?'

'I'm scared I'll burst into tears when I see him.'

'He's in a better state than he was when you left Kvemodishi.'

She led Leila into the ward, where she knelt down by Ruslan's bed, kissed his forehead and held his hand. Tamara wasn't sure she liked such physical intimacy between her husband and another woman.

Ruslan and Leila caught up with news, and then Leila asked about Mikhel. 'Did he say anything about me?'

'No, except that he isn't in touch with you.'

'Is he okay? I mean, his wife hasn't found out or anything?'

'I don't think so.'

'Thank God for that. There's one person I am in touch with.'

'Who's that?'

'Sergo.'

Ruslan made as if to speak but said nothing.

'He wants to come and see you.'

'What for? To explain?'

'No, he wants to beg you for forgiveness.'

After a moment, Ruslan said, 'And do you think I should forgive him?'

'One hundred percent yes.'

'You think so?'

'Yes. He told me he was working for Zikladza, but he was working for peace too. He wasn't just using you, using us. He was with us too, helping us. Does that make sense?'

'And you believe him?'

'Yes. The man's an absolute wreck. His wife told me she has to hide his anti-depressants to make sure he doesn't top himself.'

'He's that bad?'

'Yes.'

'When does he want to come?'

'Today or tomorrow, any time.'

'Tell him to come this evening. Let's get it over with.'

Leila returned at eight with Lionidza and his wife, who Ruslan and Tamara had briefly met at his post-medal receptions. Lionidza was clearly very nervous, and Leila almost had to push him into the ward.

He stood by the bed.

'Hello Ruslan.'

'Hi.'

'How are you?'

Ruslan gave a little laugh. 'Not great.'

'No.'

There followed an awkward silence. Then Ruslan said, 'So how are you?'

Lionidza sighed. 'I'm still alive. Thanks to you, I'm still alive.'

He started to cry.

'I hear you held a pen in my throat while Mikhel went to get help. So I suppose I'm still alive thanks to you.'

Lionidza's wife put a chair behind him and he sat down. After a moment, he took out his handkerchief to blow his nose and wipe his eyes. 'I'm so sorry, Ruslan. I'm so so sorry. I should have been honest with you and I'm so sorry I wasn't.'

He covered his face and cried for some time. Eventually he recovered enough composure to say, 'Can you ever forgive me?'

'Was any of it genuine?'

'Yes, absolutely. I was working for peace, you must see that. I didn't see any contradiction between that and working for Comrade Zikladza.'

'But you did lie to me.'

'Yes. I'm sorry.'

139

After a moment, Ruslan said, 'I could say that I forgive you, but then tomorrow I might be angry again.'

'I understand.'

'Shall we just say that our reconciliation is a work in progress?'

Lionidza nodded. 'Thank you, Ruslan.'

'You know my diaries are coming out in a few weeks?' (Murad had collected the diaries Ruslan had kept during his peace missions plus his letters to Tamara and arranged for them to be published. There was just one act of censorship: the removal of all references to Leila's affair with Mikhel.)

'Yes, I heard.'

'You'd better brace yourself. It's all in there.'

'When it comes out, I won't deny anything.'

'Good. That can be part of our little peace process.'

Lionidza clasped Ruslan's hand and thanked him.

He cried and apologised again as he said goodbye to Tamara. Leila turned down his offer of a lift, saying she would wait for her boyfriend to pick her up.

'Is Ruslan going to be okay?' she asked Tamara when Lionidza and his wife had gone.

'It depends what you mean by okay. His back's in a terrible state. If they can reconstruct his ribs, he should be able to walk again, eventually. But he won't be able to roll over for weeks, maybe months. Truth is, he's very lucky to be alive at all. If he hadn't been so fit, I don't think there's any way he could have survived.'

Leila nodded. 'He's even more lucky that he's got you. Just promise me one thing.'

'What's that?'

'Promise me you'll never ever let anyone drag him down here and get him involved in this bloody shit hole again.'

Tamara smiled. 'I'll do my best.'

Leila stepped forward and embraced her. They exchanged kisses and then Leila squeezed Tamara's hands and left. Tamara watched her as she hailed a taxi. There was no sign of any boyfriend.

Two days later, Ruslan flew to Moscow, where the considerable *blat* of Russian TV reporter Sergei Ivanov had secured a bed in the Burdenko Military Hospital for him and a small flat for Tamara, Shota and Ruslan's mother. Sergei's *blat* also found work for Tamara in the ENT department of a nearby municipal hospital.

When Ruslan's diaries and letters were published, they were an instant bestseller in both Ksordia and Akhtaria, giving Tamara a much-needed financial cushion that enabled her to spend her evenings and weekends with Shota and Ruslan rather than with private patients.

Ruslan needed five operations on his back to reconstruct his ribs and his scapula before he could roll over. Only then could he begin a long and often painful course of physiotherapy to build up his wasted muscles and try to reintroduce strength and suppleness to his wrecked back. This gave him something to aim for and brought a long period of helplessness and depression to an end. Even so, he couldn't sit up until October and didn't take his first faltering steps until mid-November.

Just as important to him was his achievement on the first day of December. For the first time since May, he was able to shit and wipe his backside by himself. At long last he felt that he was beginning to regain his independence. (He also now had an alibi for occasional visits to the toilet to relieve his growing sexual frustration.)

By now, his memory had almost completely returned. There were still some blank periods: his recall of the weeks preceding the attempt on his life was very hazy, and he had no memory whatsoever of the day on which he was shot.

One memory that made him shudder was the night he had almost ended up in Leila's bed. He came to think he had had a very lucky escape and wondered if Tamara would ever have forgiven him.

He had only ever had one really serious row with her. A few weeks after they arrived in London, they had gone to a party at a Hungarian colleague's flat, and Ruslan had been furious when he saw Tamara taking a puff on a joint. It had taken her more than a week to forgive him for yelling at her in public.

The war had begun well for the Ksords, who poured forces north the day after the attack on Ruslan. They won a dazzling victory when troops commanded by his friend Colonel Bebur Chikradza surrounded Natsopeli. The town's Akhtarian defenders ran out of ammunition within days.

Colonel Chikradza allowed the Akhtarians to pull all their troops out, minus their heavy weapons. Natsopeli's civilian population fled with them, despite Chikradza's guarantees for their safety. They were wise to leave, however: once Chikradza's regiment had left, the extremist militias plundered the town and murdered many of the elderly Akhtarians who had remained.

Korgay, meanwhile, was finally able to create a legally-constituted Federal government. Comrade Zikladza, the old Communist leader, suffered a stroke at the end of July, and his party promptly disintegrated. More than 20 Communist deputies defected to Korgay in a single day, and Sergo Lionidza, whose stock among the Party faithful had been boosted rather than diminished by the revelations in Ruslan's diaries, was forced to create a new Social Democratic Party to stop others following them.

(In fact, Comrade Zikladza soon recovered from his stroke, but by the time he got out of hospital, his party had disappeared.)

Boosted by the ex-Communists and the support of moderate nationalists who had rallied to the flag, Korgay now had a secure majority in the Federal Assembly, though he still didn't have enough votes to amend the constitution, so Tatar-led Central Kubania retained its autonomy for the time being.

The Ksordian army now swung west to the Sea of Azov in an effort to split Akhtaria in two. They soon reached the coast, but the Russian navy and air force bombarded them, forcing them to retreat. The Russians also started to deliver large quantities of ammunition to an Akhtarian Army whose supplies had become desperately low.

The Ksords responded with a massive artillery attack on Pirvelituri, one of the most picturesque towns on the Azov coast. This would be a public relations disaster for their cause, as film of Pirvelituri's destruction was broadcast throughout the former

Soviet Union. In fact, the Akhtarians could easily have moved their own guns forward to protect the town, but their government realised the propaganda value of its martyrdom.

Less than a week after Ruslan and Tamara arrived in Russia, Akhtarian TV obtained footage of North Ksord leader Mataa Bogiani denouncing the brutality and incompetence of his own forces. He called the war a calamity and said he had begged Korgay to open peace talks with the Akhtarians.

Korgay and his North Ksord allies responded furiously, and the next day Bogiani fled to Russia in fear of his life.

In August, the Ksords mounted another major offensive, this time in the southeast, aimed at Onchi'Aketi. Once more, they used artillery bombardment as their main weapon. As Ruslan had predicted, troops from outside North Ksordia proved very reluctant to take risks, so their commanders had to rely on superior firepower against the highly motivated Akhtarians. They took this policy to its logical conclusion in Onchi'Aketi, where their artillery obliterated the town street by street in an effort to flush out its defenders, who finally capitulated at the end of September.

What happened next was a calamity in every sense of the word. Mingrelsky's White Eagles, acting in concert with regular troops, rounded up 250 POWs and civilians, among them more than 60 dragged from hospital beds. They subjected them to a horrendous beating before shooting them in cold blood, a crime that reverberated around the region, turning many, including the Central Kuban Tatars, decisively against the Ksords.

Ruslan was horrified by this atrocity. Until this point, at some visceral level that he couldn't control, he had celebrated every Ksordian victory and been stung by every reverse, even though on a conscious level he considered the war itself to be a catastrophe. But after Onchi'Aketi, he knew the Ksords would be seen around the world as murderous savages.

It wasn't as if Mingrelsky was the only psychopath for whom this war represented an opportunity to live out his sadistic fantasies. There were hundreds, probably thousands of them out there, Akhtarians and Russian mercenaries as well as Ksords, relishing a once-in-a-lifetime chance to plunder, rape and kill with impunity. And alongside them, there would be otherwise decent people on both sides, driven to a frenzy of hate by propaganda and fear or by a thirst for revenge. They now acted as if the other side had lost their humanity and it was entirely legitimate to drive civilians from their homes, abuse them or even kill them.

Any Ksord could list dozens of atrocities committed by the 'Rebels': old men and women murdered on their doorsteps, whole families locked in their basements and their houses set on fire, POWs found dead with their hands tied behind their back or women and girls as young as ten raped, raped and raped again. And any Akhtarian could list just as many war crimes committed by Ksords.

But nothing on this scale.

Previously the crazies on either side had slaughtered half a dozen here or a score or so there. This was the first time anyone had massacred hundreds at a time or had dragged 60 helpless people from their hospital beds and murdered them *en masse*. It was by far the worst atrocity of the war to date.

The Onchi'Aketi massacre plunged Ruslan into another bout of despondency. He felt a total failure. His great peace mission had done no good to anyone. More than that, he felt an idiot. Nina had warned him about Lionidza, but he had let him use him and manipulate him. And she had warned him about Mingrelsky. But had he listened to her? No, imbecile that he was, he had walked straight into a trap from which he was lucky to escape with his life.

Or rather, half of his life. He might be able to walk unaided one day but he would never run again. He would be a marathon runner who couldn't run for a bus. And even if he managed to stand up straight, his left arm would be all but useless. Within a year or two, his son would be too big for him to pick up. He would never play football or climb a mountain with him, and he would never teach him to ride a bike.

By now, the Ukrainians had reached an accord with the Russians, and they no longer had any incentive to arm their embarrassing Ksordian allies. This, and the profligate use of artillery, meant that it was the Ksords' turn to find their stocks of ammunition running dangerously low.

144

The Akhtarians were at last able to launch their first major offensive. They recaptured Natsopeli, and soon afterwards another attack pressed down towards Kvemodishi itself.

Korgay responded by appointing a leading entrepreneur as his Minister of Munitions. Zviad Qipiani was best known for the introduction of mobile phones into Ronkoni, and as Minister of Munitions he proved to be an inspired choice. In a matter of weeks, he revamped the Ksordian armaments industry, doubling production in November and more than doubling it again in December.

He also toured the countries of the Black Sea and the Caucasus, stressing the importance of Ksordia as a bulwark against renewed Russian expansionism. This helped him secure invaluable supplies from Turkey, Romania, Azerbaijan, Georgia and Iran, as well as clandestine supplies from the Czechs and the Poles.

The result was stalemate on the battlefield, with neither side strong enough to deliver a knockout blow. By mid-December, the war had almost ground to a halt, though mediators from the Organisation for Security and Co-operation in Europe wouldn't secure a formal ceasefire until 23rd.

Nobody was certain exactly how many lives had been lost in the preceding eight months: probably about 10,000. The Ksordian military had lost nearly 2,000 and the Akhtarians more than double that number. About 1,400 Ksordian civilians had been killed, along with over 2,500 Akhtarians. Tens of thousands more had been wounded.

More than 250,000 people had been driven from their homes, two thirds of them Akhtarians. The refugees were housed in squalid refugee camps or billeted on their countrymen, or else they occupied empty houses and flats whose inhabitants had been driven out, in many cases by the refugees themselves. More than a quarter of the total housing stock of southern Akhtaria / North Ksordia had been destroyed. There were also serious food shortages. The harvest hadn't been gathered in many areas and a third of livestock had perished. When agriculture eventually resumed, there would be thousands of unexploded landmines to contend with.

Nobody believed that the current stalemate meant an end to the war. Both sides were simply licking their wounds and husbanding their resources for the spring. Their eyes turned hungrily towards Ruslan's homeland, the multi-ethnic region of Central Kubania, which everybody expected to be the scene of the next big round of fighting.

When the Soviet Union collapsed, Tatar leader Yakub Bovin had been optimistic about the prospects for inter-ethnic co-operation. He thought all would be well provided the Ksords didn't try to dominate the other ethnic groups and the Akhtarians didn't opt for total separation.

After Korgay's Ksords promptly threw their weight around and the Akhtarians hurriedly declared independence, Yakub had done everything he could to support Ruslan's peace missions and had participated in Nina's failed attempt to lock Korgay into the peace process.

When these efforts failed, Yakub travelled to Russia and Ukraine to try to persuade the two regional powers to restrain their allies in Ksordia-Akhtaria. Unfortunately, both of them seemed quite happy to engage in a little proxy war as a way of spicing up their negotiations.

In December, Russian policy took what for the Tatars was a truly catastrophic turn. As the fighting died down, President Boris Yeltsin announced that Russia would give full diplomatic recognition to Akhtarian independence as of 15th January. This would kill off forever any hope that some form of Pan-Kuban confederation might contain the conflict between Ksords and Akhtarians. It would make a war to carve up Central Kubania all but inevitable, forcing the Tatars to choose sides.

Yakub went back to Moscow, where he met Yeltsin and begged him to reverse his decision. The Russian President paid little attention during the meeting, preferring to let his Foreign Minister do all the talking. Then at the end, he leaned forward and said, 'As far as I'm concerned, the Central Kuban Tatars have legitimate national aspirations of their own. If you can get a majority to vote for independence in a referendum, we'll recognise an independent Central Kubania too.'

Yakub now felt that he had no choice but to go for independence and pray that the Russians would protect his people. On 11th December, he convened the full Central Kuban cabinet for the first time in more than a month and put forward his proposal for independence. The Ksords exploded and walked out, threatening insurrection and civil war.

Yakub managed to draft some liberal Ksords into his government, most prominent among them his old friend Nina. This gave him a fig leaf of inter-communal respectability, but everyone knew that independence would ride roughshod over the aspirations of the Ksords, who made up a third of Central Kubania's population. As soon as the independence referendum was called, the Ksordian leadership denounced it as a stitch-up. They said they would boycott it and refuse to recognise the result.

The Central Kuban government was desperate to find a way to bring the Ksords round to the idea of independence but they had very little success. At a cabinet meeting in mid-December, an Akhtarian minister suggested that they should ask Ruslan to help.

Yakub turned to Nina. 'Do you know if he's in a fit state to do anything?'

'Apparently his operations have been successful, but it'll be some time before he gets out of hospital.'

'Do you know how long?'

'I don't, sorry.'

'Do you think he'd be sympathetic?'

'I would have thought so.'

'Could you ask him to help us?'

'It might be better for you to do it. You were in prison together, weren't you?'

'I think you'd be more effective,' the Akhtarian minister interjected. 'You know who he asked for when he woke up?'

Nina shot him a filthy look. 'That was because he'd lost his memory.'

'Maybe we could go together,' said Yakub. 'It'd be worth a go.'

Tamara was waiting for Nina and Yakub just inside the main entrance of the hospital. It would be the second time they had met but the first time their conversation had extended beyond pleasantries.

'Hello Tamara, it's nice to meet you again.'

'Nice to see you too.'

The two women shook hands.

'You've met Yakub Bovin, haven't you?'

'Yes,' Tamara said, shaking his hand. 'I remember Ruslan called you his jailbird friend.'

Yakub smiled at the memory.

'It's this way,' said Tamara. Then she nodded at the receptionist and said, 'Can you let them know we're coming?'

As they walked down the dingy corridors, Tamara told them about Ruslan. 'The physio's going well, but it's hard work, especially with him only having one lung. His posture's coming along, though. His target is to walk six steps with a Zimmer frame by the end of this week. He can manage about three so far.'

'How is he in himself?' Nina asked. 'It must be very hard for him to accept not being an athlete any more.'

'He hasn't accepted it at all. He's a dreadful patient: he always wants to do so much more than the professionals recommend. I keep telling him to slow down, but whatever targets the physiotherapists give him, he has to accelerate them. If they say to do such-and-such in ten days, he says, "No, I'll do it in six." He's driving everybody up the wall.'

Nina smiled. 'It's good that he hasn't given up.'

'Yes, but the trouble is, he sets himself such ambitious targets that he never meets them. And then he sometimes gets very low.'

'I can imagine. How long do you think he'll be in hospital?'

'At least until April.'

Nina and Yakub exchanged a disappointed look.

'What are his long-term plans?' Yakub asked.

Tamara stopped walking and looked Nina in the eye. 'I know why you're here, and I want you to promise me you won't ask him to discharge himself. He isn't ready. He won't be ready for ages. When you see him, he'll be standing with crutches, but they're just

148

for show. He hasn't got the strength to use them. The reason why I sent a message was to get the nurses to prop him up.'

Nina made as if to speak, but Tamara interrupted her.

'It's not fair, Nina. It's just not fair. You've got no idea what he's been through.'

Nina nodded. 'I hear what you say, Tamara. We won't ask him to discharge himself, just to do what he can from here. Maybe a TV interview, something like that.'

'Okay.'

'Do you think he'd be willing to help us?' Yakub asked.

'It's not for me to say,' said Tamara. 'Believe it or not, we try not to discuss politics. He's a Ksord and I'm Akhtarian.'

Yakub laughed. 'I'm married to a Ksord too, you know.'

'You have my deepest sympathies.'

Tamara led them to a small room near his ward, where Ruslan was waiting for them, supported by crutches as Tamara had said.

Chapter Eighteen

RUSLAN WAS unable to move towards Nina or embrace her, but she stepped forward and they exchanged four kisses. Nina's eyes filled with tears. She held on to his arms for a few seconds. Then she let go and stepped back.

'It's good to see you, Ruslan.'

'You too, Nina.'

'I was so worried. I thought we'd lost you.'

'Well, here I am. I wish I looked as good as you do, but at least I'm still alive.'

'Thank God.'

Ruslan greeted Yakub and they kissed.

They all sat down, Tamara taking Ruslan's crutches and guiding him into a stiff armchair that gave lots of support. They spent several minutes catching up on news, including the latest pregnancy of Yakub's wife Marta. Then it was time to get down to business.

Nina looked intently at Ruslan. 'You know why we're here?'

'I can guess.'

Ruslan felt a terrible sadness as Yakub outlined the Tatars' dilemma and the reasons why they had opted for independence. He desperately wanted to agree with his old friend, but Yakub said nothing that could possibly persuade him.

'Our policy isn't anti-Ksord,' Yakub insisted. 'Central Kubania will be a multi-ethnic state with human rights guarantees and representation for all ethnic groups at all levels. It was one of your Principles for Peace, wasn't it? Nobody is to live in a state which isn't theirs.'

'Can you have a multi-ethnic democracy?' Ruslan asked. 'I always thought a democracy was a self-governing community. No community, no democracy.'

'Oh, come on,' said Nina. 'Have you never heard of Switzerland?'

'The Tatars are committed to inclusivity,' Yakub said. 'So are the Akhtarians.'

'Do you think they're sincere?'

'Lazarev is.' (Lazarev was leader of the Akhtarians in Central Kubania.)

'And President Eristov?'

'Yes.'

Ruslan looked sceptical. 'What about their neo-Rebel Defence Minister, Mr Sulkavidza? Is he sincere in his support for multi-ethnic inclusivity?'

Nina answered for Yakub. 'Some of the Akhtarians are sincere. Others just want to carve Central Kubania up. President Eristov's backing the moderates.'

'Publicly.'

'And privately. We've got our ears to the ground.'

'What we're doing follows on from what you did in Akhtaria,' said Yakub. 'We're trying to create a peace without winners and losers. We mustn't fail, Ruslan. If there's war in Central Kubania, it'll make what happened in Akhtaria look like a caviar reception for Party big shots.'

Nina stepped in: 'Ruslan, you could make a difference. People will listen to you.'

'Do you really think so?'

'Yes.'

'I'm not sure, Nina. I've had lots of time to think about it. You know what I think? My peace mission? It was all crap.'

'No, Ruslan.'

'Yes, Nina. You know why we managed to end the War of the Border Posts? Because everybody wanted us to. The Akhtarians were desperate for a way out and so was the Federal government. And you were right about Lionidza: he was working for Comrade bloody Zikladza all the time.'

'I know.'

'And all our negotiations between the North Ksords and the Akhtarians? It was just a facade. Both sides were playing for time.'

'So how come Mingrelsky junior tried to kill you?' said Yakub.

'Because he hates my guts.'

'No, because him and Alavidza were scared that you'd prevent them from having their war.'

Ruslan shook his head. 'You don't know Mingrelsky.' He turned to Nina, 'You told Sergei Ivanov, didn't you? You said when Mingrelsky beat you up it was like he was attacking me by proxy.'

Nina nodded. 'But he wouldn't have dared shoot you without clearance from Alavidza, I'm sure of it.'

'Alavidza hates me.'

'It wasn't personal. He wanted you out of the way.'

They were all silent for a moment, then Ruslan said: 'I tell you this, I don't remember much about the last couple of weeks of my peace mission, but I've read my diary, and it's pretty obvious the whole thing was falling to pieces long before Mingrelsky shot me.'

'I've read your diary too,' said Nina, 'and you knew you still had the Russians and the Ukrainians onside.'

Yakub agreed: 'You shouldn't underestimate the impact you had.'

Ruslan shook his head.

Nina looked at Tamara for support, but Tamara said nothing.

'You shouldn't underestimate yourself,' said Nina. 'It's not like you.'

Ruslan looked at her and they both smiled.

'A lot of people will listen to you.'

'So what do you want me to do? Sell your independent Central Kubania to the Ksords?'

'Yes.'

Ruslan reached out and squeezed Tamara's hand before he gave his answer.

'Yakub, I know where you're coming from. I understand, believe me I do. And Nina, I understand you too. And I understand how the Akhtarians feel. I'd feel the same in their shoes. But you have to understand me. You have to know where I'm coming from. Yakub, do you know what happened to my family in the Great Patriotic War?'

'Yes, of course.'

'And you know what my mother says now? She says, "The Rebels are back." That's what she thinks. All over North Ksordia and Central Kubania, that's what the Ksords think. They think the Rebels are back and they're very very frightened.'

Yakub made as if to speak, but Ruslan interrupted him. 'Yakub, it doesn't matter whether they're right or wrong. That's what they think. That's what my mother thinks. Can't you understand why?'

Yakub and Nina said nothing.

'You want me to sell your independent Central Kubania to the Ksords? I couldn't even sell it to my mother.'

Yakub and Nina's visit came as another massive setback to Ruslan. He felt consumed by guilt, lying in hospital while his homeland continued to tear itself apart. But what else could he do? He wasn't in any fit state to help, and in any case Yakub's strategy was totally wrong. There was no way an independent Central Kubania could survive. The Ksords and the Akhtarians would strangle it at birth. And as for the Akhtarians' commitment to multi-ethnic inclusivity, Ruslan didn't believe a word of it.

A month later, he woke up from a slumber to see Leila Meipariani sitting next to his bed. She looked as gorgeous as ever with her mischievous lipstick grin, but he wasn't entirely pleased to see her. He guessed that the reason for her visit was political.

'Hello Ruslan.'

'Hello. This is a pleasant surprise.'

Leila stood up and they exchanged kisses.

'Can you pull me up?' He raised his right arm and she tugged at it. 'Can you put my pillows up behind me? Thanks.'

'So how are you?'

'Coming along. I walked ten steps with just a walking stick today.'

'That's good.'

'And how are you?'

She told him about her new boyfriend and the new album she had been hoping to record until she had put her music career on one side to get involved in politics again.

'Is that why you're here?'

'Yes.'

'You know I've already said no to Yakub and Nina?'

'Yes, of course. It was all over the papers. You told them you couldn't sell Central Kuban independence to your mother.'

'And I couldn't.'

'I know. I'm half Ksord, remember? I might be able to sell it to my papa, but there's no way I could sell it to any of his relatives.'

'Then why should I be able to sell it to them?'

'Ruslan, don't you know?'

'Know what?'

'Me and Sergo have started a new campaign.'

'What new campaign?'

'For a No vote.'

'A No vote?'

'Yes, if independence is going to provoke civil war, the best thing would be if people voted against in the referendum. Makes sense, doesn't it?'

'I suppose it does. Whose idea was this? Yours or Sergo's?'

'Bit of both really. We were just talking about how awful everything was and then the idea sort of emerged.'

'So how long has this campaign been going?'

'Four days.'

'Ah, that's why I haven't heard about it. The post usually takes a week. Did Sergo send you?'

'No. He absolutely forbade me to come. He said we have no right to ask you to help us. Of course, he's so manipulative, he might have said that just to make me come.'

Ruslan laughed. 'So how is Sergo?'

'Back to his old self. He says he still gets nightmares, but otherwise he's okay now.'

'That's good.'

'It's amazing what you did, Ruslan.'

'I don't remember a thing about it.'

'Well, Sergo does. He cries every time he talks about it. Have you heard about Mikhel, by the way?'

'No?'

154

'He's had a nervous breakdown.'

'Really?'

'Yes. Sergo went to see him. He said he was pretty bad.'

'Poor Mikhel.'

For a moment, neither of them spoke, then Leila said, 'I don't know if some of it might be my fault. Sergo says it was the shooting, but I don't know. I can't have helped. I really screwed up there, didn't I?'

Ruslan almost told her how close she had been to having him but thought better of it. 'We all make mistakes.'

'You know what I'd do to you if you were ever unfaithful to Tamara?'

'What?'

'I'd fucking castrate you.'

'And what would you do to the other woman?'

'I'd shoot her.'

'Well you won't have to because it's not going to happen.'

'It had better not.'

They looked at each other and burst out laughing.

'Thanks for censoring me and Mikhel out of your diary.'

'Thank Fatima. She asked me to.'

'Well thanks anyway.'

'You know Sergo went on TV and admitted everything you said about him was true.'

'I saw it in the papers. He didn't have much choice though, did he?'

'Are you still angry with him?'

'I have good days and bad days. On bad days, I'm angry with everyone.'

'I hope you're not angry with me.'

'No.'

'Or Tamara.'

'No.'

'You shouldn't be too hard on Sergo. He's one of the good guys.'

'So you say.'

'I've spent a lot of time with him since you were shot. He wasn't just using you. He was working for peace. He's your friend. He's my friend too, a very good one, and Mikhel's.'

Ruslan frowned. After a moment, he said, 'Anyway, who's in this campaign of yours?'

'Just Sergo's crusty old Communists and me.'

'Nobody else?'

'I'm in contact with one or two old dissident friends. Trouble is, they don't want to work with Sergo.'

This made Ruslan smile. 'Do you really think you can get people to vote No?'

'Do I think we can get people to vote No? Me and Sergo and his crusty old Communists? Maybe ten percent at best, if we're lucky. But if you joined us, we might stand a chance.'

'I can't see it happening.'

'We have to try.'

'Our shoes are full of shit, Leila. There's going to be another war, and we can't do anything to stop it.'

'For God's sake, we have to do something, otherwise how are we going to face ourselves? You're married to an Akhtarian, aren't you? Your best friend's a Tatar.'

'I'm not even sure I could persuade Tamara to support a No vote. She was angry with me when I turned Yakub and Nina down. She wouldn't admit it, but she was.'

'So she's happy for you to get involved again?'

'I doubt it very much. She was angry because I was sympathetic to the Ksords. She's a bit pro-Akhtarian, believe it or not.'

'I thought you were the perfect couple.'

'We are, most of the time.'

'But a No vote is the only way to bring about a compromise between the Ksords and the Akhtarians.'

Ruslan burst out laughing. 'Politics as marriage guidance counselling. Have you spoken to Murad and Fatima about this?'

'Not yet.'

'I bet there's no way you could persuade them. They're quite nationalistic.'

'Well they're coming to see you on Tuesday, aren't they? Why don't you try and persuade them then?'

'Are you serious?'

'Yes. I'll come and help. If we can persuade them, we can persuade other people too.'

'What about my mother? Do you think we could persuade her?'

'Why not?'

'Have you met my mother?'

'Of course I have.'

'And you think we could persuade her?'

'We could try.'

Ruslan burst out laughing.

'I'm serious.'

'Really?' said Ruslan. 'Well, I'll tell you what. When Murad and Fatima come on Tuesday, I'll get my mother to come, and Tamara too. That'll make two Tatars, a Ksord and an Akhtarian. If we can persuade them, then I'll come to Central Kubania and help you. But if not, there's no point. If we can't persuade them, we can't persuade anybody, can we?'

'All right, it's a deal. I'll bring Sergo too.'

Ruslan spent the rest of that afternoon asking himself the same questions. Could they really do it? Could they really get members of all ethnic groups to vote No? That would mean persuading Akhtarians and Tatars to vote to stay in Ksordia. How on earth were they going to do that?

But then again, what was the alternative? Another war, except this time it would be a three-way conflict in a region frequently described as an ethnic fruit salad. He couldn't think of anything more horrendous.

But if they could win, well that would piss on the plans of his enemies. That might knock them off balance, and then maybe he could find a way to get justice for what they had done to him. A way to get revenge.

But wouldn't that be the worst of motives? Wasn't politics supposed to be a higher calling? Shouldn't he genuinely work for peace rather than use politics to pursue his own personal vendetta?

His thoughts raced round and round. In the end, he wasn't sure what his real motives would be if he did get involved again.

Chapter Nineteen

TAMARA CAME straight from work that evening, arriving before Ruslan's mother and Shota. She found Leila waiting for her outside the ward. Leila embraced and kissed her, but Tamara gave her a very cautious reception.

'What brings you here?'

'Politics, I'm afraid.'

'He won't help you. He doesn't think independence will work.'

'I know. Neither do I.'

Tamara frowned, confused.

'Sergo and I have started a campaign against independence, for a No vote in the referendum.'

'And you want Ruslan to help you?'

'Yes.'

'What? A statement of support, something like that?'

'No, I'm hoping for more than that, I'm afraid.'

'Don't tell me you're expecting him to discharge himself and go back to Ksordia-Akhtaria?'

'That's what I'm hoping, yes.'

'What was it you made me promise, Leila?'

'I know.'

'Remind me. What was it?'

'Never to let anyone get him involved in Ksord-Akhtarian politics again.'

'So what am I supposed to say to you now?'

'I'm sorry, I really am. It's just that everything's falling apart and he's the only one everyone will listen to. Ksords, Akhtarians, Tatars, they'll all listen to him.'

'That's exactly what Lionidza said last time, almost word for word.' Tamara could barely contain her anger.

'I'm sorry. I wouldn't ask if we could do it without him.'

'I thought you were his friend.'

'I am.'

'And that's why you want to drag him out of hospital into all that...' Tamara hesitated; she wasn't in the habit of either raising her voice or using obscenities: '...all that shit, with...fucking Mingrelsky waiting to have another go at killing him.'

'I'm sorry,' said Leila. 'I hate myself for this. I really wouldn't be here if there was any other way.'

'At least last time Lionidza had the balls to ask him himself instead of sending you to flutter your eyelashes at him.'

'It was my idea to come here. Sergo tried to stop me.'

'For God's sake, don't you think he's done enough?' Tamara's eyes were filling with tears.

'I'm sorry.'

'I wish you'd stop saying you're sorry. Why can't you just leave him alone, all of you? Just leave him alone.'

Leila looked down at her feet and then she sighed and said, 'I'll go now. Say goodbye to him for me.' She gave Tamara a thin smile and then left.

Tamara had to retreat to the toilets to compose herself before going in to see Ruslan.

'I suppose you know who I just saw out there.'

'I could hear you from here.'

'So what did you tell her?'

'I said I'd think about it.'

'Think about what? Going back?'

'Yes.'

'God's nails, Ruslan. Haven't you noticed? You're a physical wreck. You know they're not planning to let you out of here until April.'

'I know, but I think maybe I really can make a difference.'

'What you mean is you can just about bring yourself to say no to Nina, but not to Leila if she flutters her eyelashes at you.'

'Please Tamara, don't speak like that. Yakub and Nina were asking me to support Central Kuban independence. Leila's asking me to help her oppose it.'

Tamara, who cared little for the finer points of Central Kuban politics, shook her head. 'Say that again.'

Ruslan explained that Leila and Lionidza had started a campaign to persuade members of all ethnic groups to vote against independence in the forthcoming referendum.

'What? You mean persuade Akhtarians and Tatars to vote to stay in Ksordia?'

'Yes.'

'You're joking, aren't you?'

'No.'

'I'm sorry, but why on earth would anyone who isn't a Ksord do that?'

'Because if they vote for independence, our psychopath of a president will set his army on them.'

'So you're going to get people to vote for what you want by threatening them?'

'No. We're going to try and screw up the warmongers' plans. Korgay and the Akhtarian leadership want a war to carve Central Kubania up, and if people vote for independence, that will give them the excuse they need to start fighting.'

'So it's another peace mission?'

'Indirectly yes, but first and foremost it's a referendum campaign.'

'But why does it have to be you?'

Ruslan hesitated. 'Look, I don't want to sound big-headed, but I do have a certain prestige among the different ethnic groups. You remember the crowds that applauded my ambulance?'

'They weren't massive crowds, you know. It wasn't like after your medals.'

'I know, but shouldn't I try to make a difference if I can?'

'Do you seriously think you can persuade Akhtarians to vote to stay in Ksordia?'

'I don't know.'

'I'm not sure you could even persuade me.'

'Funny you should say that. I told Leila that I'd try and persuade you, my mother and Murad and Fatima next Tuesday. If I can't persuade you, there's no point going back. If I can persuade all of you, then maybe there's hope.'

'You're serious?'

'Yes. Leila's coming with Lionidza to help me out.'

Tamara looked at him in astonishment. 'What, when Murad and Fatima come?'

'Yes.'

'So you're going to get me, your mother, Murad and Fatima in the same room for a political discussion?'

'Yes.'

'I get on very well with your mother, but there are some things we're very careful never to discuss. You know that, don't you?'

'Yes.'

'God help us.'

And so, on Tuesday evening, the 'meeting' Tamara had been dreading assembled. Once the ritual greetings had been gone through, Ruslan invited everyone to sit down, selecting for himself the same stiff-backed armchair he had used when he met Nina and Yakub.

'Mama, Fatima, Murad, I should apologise to you. It's not a coincidence that Sergo and Leila are here too. Leila was here last Friday, and I asked her to bring Sergo today. She put a proposal to me last week and I want to hear your opinions before I make any decision.'

Tamara saw Ruslan's mother stiffen. Murad and Fatima both folded their arms tight and glared at Lionidza.

'I think you all know that Nina came to see me last month,' Ruslan continued. 'She wanted me to go back to Central Kubania to try and add a Ksordian voice to the campaign for Central Kuban independence. I think you all know that I refused.'

'Yes,' said Ruslan's mother, 'and you were right, you know: you couldn't have sold it to me.'

Ruslan smiled at her, and then he nodded at Lionidza, who sat forward in his chair.

'Shall I say my piece?'

'Please,' said Ruslan.

Lionidza fumbled in his jacket pocket and pulled out a cigarette. He didn't light it; he just fiddled with it as he spoke.

'Well, as you know, in two days, the Central Kuban Regional Assembly's going to debate a resolution declaring independence from Ksordia and calling a referendum to ratify it. I have to fly back first thing tomorrow. I'm due to speak in the debate.'

'Against independence,' said Murad.

'Yes, against independence. The debate's going to be horrendous: people yelling abuse and trying to shout one another down. I'm dreading it, because both sides will have a go at me. Some people might even try to beat me up on the floor of the Assembly.

'Anyway, the resolution will be passed; there's no doubt about that. Then the Ksords will stage a walkout and announce a boycott of the referendum. After that, the referendum campaign will be bad-tempered and bloody. Literally bloody, I'm sure some people will get killed. The Ksords won't vote. They'll boycott the referendum. The Tatars and the Akhtarians will all vote Yes. It'll be...' Lionidza looked at Ruslan, '...it'll be a bit like election results under the old regime, a ninety or ninety-five percent Yes vote.

'That's when the Ksords will attack. They'll send three armies from the north and east to sweep the Tatars before them. The plan is for the three armies to meet in a massive assault on Khosume. The Tatars and Akhtarians will try to hold one of the armies up at Timashevsk – you're from near there, aren't you Ruslan? But the first key battle of the war will be for Khosume.

'If they can capture Khosume quickly, the Ksords will go west and attack Siriach'Sichi. They have to go for a speedy victory, or else the Russians will arm the Akhtarians and the Tatars and get them to seize the Taman Peninsula, which the Russians are desperate to control. The Tatars are hoping the Russians will help them further east, but they won't. The Russians don't give a damn what happens there. Nor do the Akhtarians. They'll just use the Tatars to help them in Siriach'Sichi and the west, and then they'll probably turn on them and annex the area into Akhtaria proper.

'It's going to be a bloodbath. Civilians will be a target because it'll be an ethnic war for territory, and the only way you can hold onto the territory you win is to drive the enemy population off. And you do that by generating terror through murder and rape. It's going to be horrendous, unimaginably awful, much worse than southern Akhtaria last year and as bad as anything that happened in the 1940s.'

Murad spoke next. His tone was scathing. 'And we all know what you're proposing. You want us to stay in Ksordia, with that son of a slut Korgay as President. The same Korgay whose friends talk about "transferring" the entire Tatar population out of Central Kubania.'

'I'm no friend of Korgay,' said Lionidza.

'But you're a Ksord.'

'Is that such a crime?' asked Ruslan.

'Don't put words in my mouth. You're all the same, even you, Ruslan. You can only see the Ksordian point of view.'

'So tell me the Tatar point of view.'

'Do you know how the Ksords have behaved? Do you know about two hundred thousand Akhtarians driven out of their homes? Do you know about the massacre in Onchi'Aketi? Do you know about scum like Mingrelsky rampaging round the countryside raping and murdering?'

'I know all that,' said Ruslan. 'I don't excuse it and I don't deny it. Don't forget, I happen to have my own reasons to hate Mingrelsky.'

'And you want us to submit to them?' said Murad. 'Do you honestly think we'll be safe?'

'Will you be safe if you vote for independence?'

'We'll take our chances.'

'You'll get your throats slit.'

'So the Tatars have to submit and just hope the Ksords are merciful.'

Ruslan raised his hands to his head, then groaned at a stab of pain in his left shoulder. Tamara jumped up and told him to lean back in his chair. 'Be careful. Try not to move your left arm.'

Tamara sat down. It was several seconds before Ruslan was able to speak again. 'What's so bad about submitting? I submitted to the Communists. Not completely: I managed to phrase my denunciation of Nina in such a way that she'd know it wasn't genuine if she ever heard it.' He glanced at Lionidza, who gave a knowing grin. 'But I submitted enough to have a life. In fact some of the years when I submitted were very happy years. And it's the same for the Central Kuban Tatars. If you submit and live as a minority in Ksordia, you can have a life. It won't be perfect, but you can have a life.'

Murad shook his head.

'What's the alternative? Do you have any idea how defenceless you are? You've got no heavy weapons at all. The Ksords will drive hundreds of thousands from their homes, and Korgay will give all the psychos a free hand to do whatever they want. You can't imagine the horror that they're going to unleash.'

Murad said nothing. His set his angry face to one side and stared into space.

'I don't know whether you're right or not, Ruslan,' Fatima said, speaking Russian. 'I'm very scared about what's going to happen. But you're never going to persuade us by telling us to submit. We've spent seventy years submitting to the Communists. In fact, we've been submitting to the Russians since 1783.

'You can't imagine how our culture has blossomed since the Soviet Union fell. You know, when Murad organises poetry readings, he can't find rooms big enough to hold them. I can fill any theatre in the country when I sing, and not just me. Do you remember that exhibition of paintings you helped organise two weeks ago, Murad?'

'It was so crowded that nobody could stand far enough back to see the pictures properly.'

'We can't submit again,' said Fatima. 'Not now. It's like asking a baby to crawl back into the womb. You shouldn't be trying to get us to submit; you should be trying to persuade your own people to accept a multi-ethnic Central Kubania.'

'Okay,' said Ruslan. 'Here's my mother, a fairly representative Ksord. Let's hear you persuade her to vote for a multi-ethnic Central Kubania.'

Fatima said nothing. She looked down at the floor.

Ruslan's mother spoke, her voice quivering with anger. 'They murdered my babies, Fatima. You're a mother, so you should understand that. The Rebels murdered my babies and they raped my sister and shot her and her children. And now they're back. I've got nothing against Tatars, or against Akhtarians as individuals, but the Rebels tried to annihilate us. Can't you understand what that does to you, if someone tries to exterminate you? The Communists kept it all under control because they kept everybody down. But now they're gone and the Rebels are back.'

'But Auntie' Fatima protested, 'a multi-ethnic state would include the Ksords. It isn't just for the Tatars and the Akhtarians. It's for everybody, with full guarantees of human rights.'

'You're talking about fine words written on paper. Do you really think we can trust that to protect us?'

'Auntie, the Tatars are as opposed to Akhtarian extremism as we are to Ksordian extremism. We're for a democratic state.'

'I can believe that you mean well, and Murad too. I've known you for a long time and you've always been good friends to Ruslan. But I'm not so sure about your leader, that Yakub Bovin. I don't trust him. Every time I think of him, I just see those Rebel cockroaches Eristov and Sulkavidza standing behind him.'

'So what's the alternative, Mama?' Ruslan asked.

'The Ksords have to stick together.'

'And?'

'If our leaders tell us to boycott the referendum, then that's what we have to do.'

'And when the fighting starts?'

'We have to defend ourselves.'

'Okay, let's imagine I'm living back home and Murad and Fatima are Tatars living in the next village. What should I do about them?'

'What do you mean?'

'Well, should I shoot Murad and drive Fatima and her children away and burn their house down so they can never come back?'

'Don't be ridiculous. We just have to defend ourselves.'

'That's what defending ourselves means. If there's a war, that's what the Ksords will do. That's how it's always been done. Kill a few men and rape a few women. The others will flee, and they'll carry the terror with them. The next village will be empty before we even get there.'

'Ksords would never behave like that.'

166

'Oh for God's sake. You were in Kvemodishi. Even Bogiani was shocked by the way the North Ksords behaved. You told me so yourself.'

Ruslan's mother shook her head. 'Have you forgotten who you are? Have you forgotten what the Rebels did to your family? And now you want us to submit?'

'Mama, haven't you heard anything we've said? We're saying we vote No to keep Central Kubania in Ksordia.'

'You'll never persuade the Ksords to vote in this referendum. It's a stitch-up because the Tatars and the Akhtarians outnumber us.'

Leila spoke: 'Grandma, what about me? I'm half-half, just like your little grandson.'

Ruslan's mother turned on her. 'Shota's not half-half. He's a Ksord.'

Leila put her hands up to her neck and dug a golden necklace out from under her blouse. A little crucifix dangled from it.

'Look at me, Grandma. I'm a Ksord too. I've been baptised and chrismated and occasionally I even remember to go to church. But my mother's a Tatar and I've got lots of Tatar relatives. What am I supposed to do when the Ksords turn on them? Applaud?'

Ruslan's mother said nothing.

'That's why I'm still half-half. So is your grandson and he always will be.'

Ruslan's mother looked away.

Nobody spoke.

After a moment, Ruslan looked at Lionidza. 'I don't think we've persuaded anyone.'

Tamara hesitated for a moment. 'Yes, you have,' she said. 'You've persuaded me. I didn't agree with you before, but now I think you're right. The Tatars have fallen into a trap, and if they vote for independence, then God help them.'

She and Ruslan looked at each other and smiled, though inside, Tamara felt like screaming. She knew she had just given him a green light to put himself in the firing line once more.

She looked nervously at Fatima and Murad. Fatima gave her the most fleeting of smiles. Murad wouldn't even return her glance.

167

'I don't know how many other Akhtarians you'll persuade, but you've persuaded me.' She looked at Ruslan's mother. The time had come to say the things she had always stopped herself from saying.

'Mama, please don't take this the wrong way, because I love you, and I know how much you've suffered. But the Akhtarians suffered too in the Great Repression. And we didn't deserve what they did to us. When Ruslan did his thesis in England, he studied the Rebels and how much support they had. Ruslan, tell your mother.'

Ruslan said, 'The Nazis gave the Rebels permission to recruit ten thousand men, but they didn't get many volunteers. I've done the research, Mama, and I know. They had to use conscription, but even then there was a lot of draft dodging, and desertion rates were very high.'

'Why are you telling me this?' Ruslan's mother asked.

Tamara answered her: 'Because I want you to understand the Akhtarian people never supported the Rebels. But Stalin punished all of us. Hundreds of thousands of Akhtarians died. Ruslan, tell her how many.'

'It's really difficult to give a definitive answer. You have to work on population projections and local records and things like the 1959 census. And you have to factor in collectivisation and the Repression in the 1930s...'

'Ruslan, stop being such an academic and give me a number.'

'About twenty thousand Akhtarians massacred in 1943, and up to four hundred and twenty thousand deaths during the deportation and exile.'

'My family suffered too,' said Tamara. 'My great-grandmother died of thirst before they even got to Kazakhstan. My mother's little brother died a few months later. I've never said this to you before because I know how much you've suffered, and I have so much respect for you. But we're wounded too. We were expelled from our homeland and left to starve. Can you imagine the scars that leaves? And we can see how Korgay and his gang have behaved in southern Akhtaria. It doesn't take much brains to figure out what they're planning to do to us in Central Kubania.'

She looked at Ruslan. 'I'd vote No because it might be a way of avoiding a war. But I don't think you'd get many other Akhtarians to join me.'

Again they all sat in silence.

'I don't know what to think,' said Fatima, her hand on Murad's arm. 'I feel a bit like Tamara. It might be better if you got a No vote, but I just can't see it happening. The Tatars will stick together; we have to. You won't persuade us to abandon our leaders now.'

Murad nodded.

Ruslan looked at his mother.

'I hope someone can do something to stop this war,' she said. 'I really do. But the Ksords will stick together. Otherwise the Rebels will slaughter us.'

Ruslan looked at Lionidza, who sighed.

'So what are you going to do?' said Leila.

Ruslan was silent.

'God's nails, Ruslan,' she said. 'You can't just stay in Moscow feeling sorry for yourself.'

'How dare you say that to my son?' Ruslan's mother shouted. 'How dare you say that? Have you got any idea what he's been through these last eight months?'

Leila bowed her head. A moment later, she stood up and hurried out of the room.

Tamara hesitated and then followed her. When she found her, she was wiping her eyes and nose with a tissue. Tamara put a hand on her shoulder.

'I'm sorry. I didn't mean to say that.'

'It doesn't matter. I think Ruslan's mama was just taking her frustrations out on you.'

Leila turned round. 'You must hate me.'

'No I don't. As a matter of fact, I feel bad about being so rude to you the other day.'

'I don't hold it against you.'

They were silent for a moment, and then Leila said, 'The truth is, I'm desperate. Me and my cousins, we've been such good friends all our lives. But not any more. My Ksordian and Tatar cousins can barely bring themselves to look at each other. I'm so scared of what's

169

going to happen if there's a war. I think they'll end up killing each other.'

Tamara said, 'It was the same with our families when we brought Shota back for his baptism. There was a big punch up between some of the young men, and all my relatives' cars had their lights kicked in. I was so shocked. Maybe Ruslan told you about it.'

Leila nodded.

'Do you really think you can win this referendum?'

'Me and Sergo? No way. There's only one person who might stand a chance.'

'That's a very heavy burden to place on his shoulders.'

Ruslan and Tamara didn't get a chance to discuss the matter alone until the next evening.

'Have you decided?'

'No. It has to be a joint decision.'

'Does it?'

'Yes.'

'Well I've got a few questions. First thing, what about Mingrelsky? He's not going to like having you back on the scene, is he?'

'I don't think Korgay would let him have a crack at me, not while the referendum campaign's on. It would bring us too many votes.'

'Do you really think that would keep Mingrelsky in check?'

'Remember what Bogiani said: his impunity only stretches so far.'

Tamara looked away from him, and then she looked hard into his eyes. 'Are you doing this in spite of Mingrelsky or because of him?'

'What do you mean?'

'I know you, Ruslan. You're so angry it's burning you up. And that ex-KGB man who put him up to it, Alavidza. Don't tell me you don't want revenge on them?'

'Am I angry? You bet I am. You can see what they've done to me. And yes, I want justice, although I doubt that I'm ever going to get it. Those two are guilty of a lot more than just shooting me. This isn't about Mingrelsky or Alavidza. It's about trying to stop a war.'

'But what's the first question everyone's going to ask you when you get home? "Was it Mingrelsky?" And, "Who do you think gave him the green light?"'

'Well I can give a politician's answer to that question. I can say ten thousand people have died since I was shot, and right now the most important thing is to make sure we don't have a war where another fifty thousand get killed.'

It was some time before Tamara spoke again. 'What would you do if I said no?'

'I'd stay in Moscow.'

'And would you hate me for it?'

'How could I ever hate you?'

'Well would you be angry?'

Ruslan hesitated.

'You don't need to answer that. You just have. I can't stop you, can I? Even if I tried, it would eat at you and eat at you, and then I'd end up having to let you go anyway. It's the same as when you asked me to marry you, the same as when Lionidza first dragged you into all this. You always tell me I have a choice but I don't.'

Ruslan said nothing. He thought she might burst into tears at any minute.

'Are you planning a career as a politician?'

'I don't know. Maybe.'

'So do you want me to be your politician's wife?'

Ruslan smiled. 'I kind of assume you'd rather be a doctor.'

'Too right I would.'

'Well that's settled then.'

'Not quite.' For a moment she was silent. Then she looked at him and said. 'If I go to Central Kubania with you, in exchange you have to make me two promises.'

'What?'

'Number one, you say you're not interested in who shot you. You don't want an investigation either now or later. You're only interested in the future and in preventing another war.'

It was several seconds before Ruslan answered. 'So you think I should let him get away with it?'

'No, I just think you should try to stay alive.'

'What's the second condition?'

'If you lose, if Central Kubania does vote for independence, then you don't try another peace mission, because they'll just kill you if you do.'

'Don't worry. I could never do anything like that again.'

'Good. So what this means is that on the day of the referendum itself, you stay at home with me and you help me pack all our things. And the minute the result comes in, if you've lost, if Central Kubania votes for independence, then you take me and Shota and you get us out of there straight away, before the fighting starts. You take us to Russia or England, I don't care which, and you stay there with us. You give up politics and you find work in a university, and you give us a normal family life as a normal husband and father. You have to promise me that.'

Ruslan was astonished. He hadn't expected this.

'Those are two tough conditions.'

'I want you to promise me.'

'No room for negotiation?'

'No.'

'I'm quite good at negotiating, you know. Lionidza taught me.'

Tamara smiled, but Ruslan could see that she had no intention of changing her mind. 'There'll be no negotiation. Those are my terms.'

'Can I think about it?'

'Take your time.'

Ruslan's mother arrived with Shota soon afterwards, terminating their conversation, though Ruslan could think of little else throughout the visit. He was extremely reluctant to let Mingrelsky off the hook, but he could also see that Tamara was right. It wasn't just that avoiding direct conflict with Mingrelsky might be the best way to make sure he wasn't shot again. It would also prevent him from behaving like the kind of politician he hated most, the kind who used politics as a cover for their own personal agenda.

But knowing that it was the right thing to do wouldn't make it any easier.

As for fleeing back to Russia if he lost the referendum, that would feel like the worst kind of betrayal. But then again, he would have failed and war would be inevitable, and he could see that his first responsibility in that situation would be to protect his family.

As his visitors prepared to depart, he touched Tamara's fingers and said, 'I agree to your terms.'

'You have to promise.'

'I promise.'

'You have to mean it.'

'I mean it.'

'Both conditions.'

'I promise. Both conditions.'

She looked into his eyes intently. Then she said, 'In that case, I'll go with you and I'll support you.'

'Thank you.'

'I'll hold you to your two promises, so don't think I won't.'

Ruslan nodded.

'I'll speak to the doctors about getting you ready to be discharged, and I'll hand in my notice at my hospital.'

'Thank you.'

Ruslan got hardly any sleep that night. He was buzzing with excitement. He would soon be out. He would be free. He could start to live again, to do something again. It was a hard task he had set himself, maybe an impossible task. And there would be some very dangerous people who would have a lot to lose if he looked like succeeding. The stakes would be very high. Very high indeed. But at least he had finally found a way of doing something.

And he had managed to persuade Tamara to accept his decision to return home and join the No campaign. That was very important to him. He needed her to believe that he was doing the right thing.

But just two days later, he would learn from his mother that Tamara had also got next to no sleep that night too. She had spent almost the whole of it crying.

February 1993
Khosume, Central Kubania

Chapter Twenty

AS HIS driver turned his Chaikas left into the familiar suburban street, a feeling of dread swept over Sergo Lionidza. But it was too late to get out of it now. 'Best to get it over with,' he said to himself. 'Oh God, the things you do for lost causes.'

He looked at the houses to his left. Nothing much had changed, apart from the bars on the windows and the 'Beware of the Dog' signs by almost every gate. They hadn't expected this, had they, when they voted for their 'freedom'? They hadn't realised that within a year or two they would hardly dare to leave their houses for fear of being burgled. Those who still had jobs to go to, that is. Well Lionidza had news for them: it probably wouldn't be long before they were cowering under their dining tables as the Ksords and the Tatars battled for the city.

The driver parked just outside the largest house on the street and Lionidza put on his hat. It wasn't particularly cold. Indeed, the snow was quite slushy, but Lionidza always wore a hat in winter. Bald heads are cold heads, no matter how much you comb what's left of your hair over them.

He rang the bell by the gate. After a few minutes, the front door opened and an elderly lady peered out. She was Ganna Zikladza, wife of Ksordia-Akhtaria's fallen Communist ruler.

'Is that you, Sergo?' she asked in her native Russian.

'Yes.'

'Just a moment.'

She disappeared into the house, and a buzzing noise issued forth from the lock on the gate. 'Give it a push,' her voice crackled.

Lionidza pushed the gate open, went through and gently closed it. The buzzing stopped and the lock clanged shut. Lionidza's were the first footprints in the snow, which meant the Zikladzas couldn't have had any visitors for two days.

Ganna Zikladza opened the door to let him in. The house was warm and musty inside, and Lionidza stamped the slush and snow off his feet as she took his coat and hat.

'How are you, Ganna?' he asked in Russian.

'A few aches and pains, but not too bad. And you?'

'Nervous.'

'So you should be.'

She put her hand on his shoulder and they exchanged four kisses. He had always liked Ganna. She had been a fine looking woman when he had first met her almost thirty years before.

'How's the boss?'

'He's not your boss any more.'

'How is he anyway?'

'I'll tell you how he feels: old and useless. Thanks in no small part to you.'

Lionidza gave a wan smile. Seven months earlier, he had effectively ended Comrade Zikladza's political career. With Zikladza in hospital following a stroke, the Communist Party he had led for two decades began to disintegrate. After twenty-three Communist members of the Federal Assembly defected to Korgay in a single day, Lionidza hurriedly announced the creation of a new Social Democratic Party in a desperate effort to keep others from joining them. The Communist Politburo met and voted wind up the Party, transferring all its assets to Lionidza's new party and calling on all remaining members to join.

Comrade Zikladza was out of hospital within two weeks, but by then his Party had disappeared. He couldn't even get hold of a membership list. All he could do was call up everyone in his personal phone book and beg them to come back to him. These efforts came to nothing. About half of the Ksords had gone over to Korgay and nearly everyone else had signed up with Lionidza. None showed the slightest inclination to abandon their new leaders.

As Ganna led Lionidza through the cluttered, dusty house, it occurred to him that the Zikladzas were having to survive on a state pension. That wouldn't go far with prices rising as they were. Presumably their children would make sure they didn't starve, but it was obvious that they could no longer afford to have cleaners.

Comrade Zikladza was in the living room at the back of the house. Its decorations and furniture were simple. Apart from the photographs on the wall, there was nothing you wouldn't find in any other house. Zikladza wasn't a kleptocrat like the new rulers of Ksordia and Akhtaria. He was a good, honest man who had given his people twenty years of peace, stability and prosperity. Well, perhaps only fifteen years of prosperity, but never anything as bad as the current shambles.

'Hello Sergo,' said Zikladza, struggling to his feet.

'It's good to see you, comrade.'

They kissed and Zikladza invited Lionidza to sit down while Ganna went to make some tea. Lionidza sat at the side of the sofa nearest to his old boss's armchair and looked at the photographs above the fireplace. As well as pictures of his host with Soviet leaders Brezhnev, Andropov and Chernenko, there were pictures of him with other Party leaders whose steadfastness Lionidza had always admired: Honecker, the architect of the Berlin Wall, Kadar, the gravedigger of the Hungarian uprising, Husak, the terminator of the Prague Spring, and Jaruzelski, the hammer of Solidarity.

As he looked at them now, Lionidza wondered how history would judge these men. After all, everything they had worked so hard to preserve had been washed away, and the next generation would learn that these indefatigable Communists were nothing but puppets of the Russians and traitors to their countries.

Perhaps the same fate would befall Comrade Zikladza too. Lionidza hoped not. That would be so unfair.

'So how are you?' Zikladza asked.

'Busy. And you?'

'Bored, ignored.'

'You don't seem to have a bodyguard?'

'No.'

'That's a disgrace.'

Zikladza shrugged. 'I'm just a normal citizen now, you see.'

'Haven't you even got a dog?'

'No, Ganna's scared of them. She was bitten when she was a child.'

'Leave it with me. If the police won't help, I'll get you a bodyguard from my party.'

Zikladza nodded.

Ganna brought in some tea and handed a glass to Lionidza.

'Would you like a cigar?'

'Oh, thank you.'

She produced a box from which Zikladza and Lionidza each extracted an enormous cigar.

'A gift from Castro.'

Once the cigars were lit, Ganna made her excuses and left.

'I see you've brought your athlete friend back from the dead.'

'Yes.'

'He doesn't look very well.'

'He isn't. He should be in hospital.'

'Did you see what the papers called him? "The Ghost of Ruslan Shanidza."'

'It wasn't my idea to bring him here.'

'Whose was it?'

'Leila Meipariani.'

'Who?'

'That singer.'

'Ah. She's a politician now, is she?'

'Yes.'

Zikladza shook his head and the two of them laughed.

'And I see he's foresworn vengeance against Mingrelsky junior. Does he really think that's going to save him?'

'His wife made him say that.'

'Fat lot of good it'll do. If Korgay and Alavidza decide they need him dead, that'll be the end of him.'

'I suppose he's gambling that they won't have the nerve.'

'He's a brave man,' said Zikladza. 'But you want to be wary of him.'

'You're telling me. He's completely taken over my campaign.'

'What campaign?'

'Against Central Kuban independence.'

'Oh yes of course, that campaign. Well, it serves you right. Now you know how I feel. And tell me this: what do you think his motives are?'

'I think they're good.'

'Oh, so now he's working for the restoration of Socialism, is he?'

'No, that's not what I mean.'

'No, I don't suppose it is.

Lionidza smiled meekly. 'He's got some trade unionists involved.'

'Which ones?'

'Dissidents, not our sort at all. Demna Ksnis and Halil Ametov.'

'God's teeth. How can you bring yourself to work with people like them?'

'Let's just say it's a marriage of convenience.'

Zikladza didn't look convinced. 'So what's your strategy?'

'Meetings, interviews, press conferences. We're sending Shanidza on a speaking tour.'

'Is he up to it?'

'That's a good question. He can only manage one meeting a day, if that. They did their first one last night.'

'They?'

'Yes. Leila, that's the singer, she starts off with a very witty speech about being the child of a Tatar and a Ksord. She really is very funny. She had the audience in stitches. And then she stilled the whole hall with a description of her Ksordian grandfather's funeral and the speech her Tatar grandfather made in his honour. Honestly, I was close to tears at that point.'

'You always were a sentimental fool. Petit bourgeois sentimentalism will not be tolerated, you know.'

They both laughed at this.

Lionidza puffed on his cigar and said, 'Then Leila spoke about the prospect of all her Ksordian and Tatar cousins slaughtering one another if Central Kubania becomes independent. It was very effective. After that Ametov spoke.'

'Who?'

'Ametov, the trade unionist.'

'Oh, him. Does he speak Ksord-Akhtarian?'

'Yes, quite well, actually. But we're conducting the campaign in Russian so as to include the Tatars.'

'I suppose you have to. Was Ametov a good speaker?'

'Not as good as Leila, but he wasn't bad. He told the story of the three wise monkeys.' (Yakub Bovin, Ramaz Kurdanadza and Akakide Lazarev, respectively the leaders of Central Kubania's Tatar, Ksordian and Akhtarian communities.)

'I remember when Lazarev was in the Party,' said Zikladza.

'Yes.'

'We never heard a peep out of him until bloody Gorbachev came along and said, "I say, anyone got any grievances they'd like to air?" Then it was Great Repression this, Great Repression that.'

Lionidza nodded. 'Ametov laid into all of them, especially our Ksordian friend. Do you remember he was leader of the Green Party until he jumped on Korgay's bandwagon?'

'Yes, I'd forgotten that. It was him that said: "Bolshevism's bad, but nationalism is worse."'

'Yes, Ametov quoted that.'

'What about your friend Ruslan Shanidza? How was his speech?'

'Bloody good. He talked about how it's all gone pear-shaped since we lost power. Then he talked about how the Rebels massacred his family and how his wife's family suffered during the Great Repression. After that, what's going to happen if Central Kubania becomes independent, with the Ksords and Akhtarians going for each others' throats and the Tatars in the middle getting massacred. Then he said, "Come on everybody, let's bang all these politicians' heads together and make them come up with a deal." He got a massive ovation at the end, but when we invited questions, all they wanted to ask about was whether it was Mingrelsky who shot him and if he really saved my life.'

Lionidza stopped speaking. His eyes began to fill with tears. 'I'm sorry. I still get very emotional when I think about that.' He took out his handkerchief and wiped his eyes. 'Have you read his diaries?'

'No.'

'You should. They're very good. He knew I was working for you, but still he saved me right when he thought he was about to die. Isn't that amazing?'

Lionidza wiped his eyes again and blew his nose.

Zikladza waited until he had finished. 'No heckling at your meeting?'

'A bit, but it was all very polite.'

'Hecklers won't be so polite outside Khosume.'

'I know.'

Zikladza's cigar had gone out. He spent some time lighting it again and then leaned over towards Lionidza. 'Do you mind if I point out a weakness?'

'Well, our biggest weakness is that we can't get on TV. All the stations are controlled by our opponents.'

'No, I don't mean that. You haven't got any Akhtarians on the platform.'

'Ah, we thought of that. Do you remember Schebet Jeltkov? He's chairing the meetings.'

'Jeltkov? I know the name.'

'He used to be my secretary. Remember last time we met? It was in his flat.'

'Oh, him.'

'You don't approve?'

Zikladza shook his head. 'A lot of people think it was him that spilled the beans about us still being in touch.'

'I hadn't heard that.'

'So how come you aren't going on tour with them?'

'I'm organising, co-ordinating and speaking in the Regional Assembly,' said Lionidza, not mentioning the nightmares that were his real reason for missing the speaking tour. 'And I'm trying to get the authorities to give us some free airtime on TV.'

'Why on earth should they do that?'

'Shanidza's wife says that's what happens when there's an election in the West.'

'Ah, Shanidza's wife? Still the same one?'

'Yes.'

'Rather a pretty little thing if I remember right.'

'Very pretty. Very likeable too.'

'Does Shanidza know about what you did?'

'What? You mean fixing them up?'

'Yes.'

'No, he doesn't know anything.'

'Does your man Jeltkov know?'

'I think so, yes.'

'Well you'd better make sure he keeps his mouth shut.'

'Yes, I'll tell him to stay off the booze. He'll be all right as long as he doesn't get pissed.'

Zikladza stood up slowly and walked over to look out of the window. As Lionidza watched him, he noticed that it was snowing. He was surprised. He hadn't thought it was cold enough.

'Anyway,' Zikladza said, keeping his back to Lionidza, 'I'm getting curious. I'm wondering why my old friend and comrade, who hasn't said so much as a word to me since the day he stole my Party from me, I'm wondering why he's come to see me today.'

Lionidza bowed his head. He felt his whole body burn, with prickles around his cheeks and neck. He put out his cigar, and when he spoke, his voice was almost a whisper. 'I only did it to stop all the Ksords going over to Korgay. There was no other way.'

'Then why didn't you have the decency to come and tell me?'

'I'm sorry. Believe me, I never wanted it and I never planned it. It's just...you're in a situation and you have to make a decision. And then there's no going back. But the last thing I ever wanted to do was to betray you.'

Zikladza walked back over and picked up his tea. He took a sip and twisted his face in disgust. It had gone cold.

'So why have you come to see me?'

'To recruit you.'

'What? To your fucking Social Democratic Party?'

'We'd be honoured if you'd join us, but I'm here to recruit you to the No Campaign.'

'You want me to go round making speeches?'

'Not necessarily. Maybe just make a statement on TV.'

'So you don't want me to go round making speeches? Too much of a liability, am I?'

Lionidza didn't answer.

'Tell me this, Sergo, will a No vote advance the cause of restoring Socialism in Ksordia-Akhtaria?'

'I honestly haven't thought about that. I'm just trying to prevent a war.'

'I don't know what it is with you. I tell you to pretend to be a pacifist and you go and become one. Just like I tell you to pretend to be an ex-Communist and you become one of those too.'

Lionidza closed his eyes.

'And tell me this, Sergo. Do you really think your No Campaign will succeed?'

'I don't know. But I have to do something. I can't just sit back and let all those nationalist sons of sluts destroy everything. Didn't Gramsci say something about pessimism of the intellect and optimism of the will?'

Zikladza snorted. 'You know what happened to him? He died in a fascist gaol.'·

'I can't do nothing.'

'But you don't stand a chance.'

'We might get somewhere if you added your voice to ours.'

'You can piss into the wind if you want to, but don't expect me to join you.'

Ruslan wasn't looking forward to his speaking tour. He was anxious about his back and about the kind of reception he would get from the more militant communities. He had assured Tamara that he would be safe. This was just a referendum campaign with a vote at the end of it. He would be speaking to voters, not to gunmen. He would be travelling from meeting hall to meeting hall, not from armed roadblock to armed roadblock.

He had believed these words when he said them, but now he found himself feeling vulnerable, acutely aware that he now had only one lung, and that if a knife or a bullet ever punctured it, he would be in deep trouble. And he was worried that if he looked like he was going to win, Mingrelsky and all the other crazies might come after him, and things could start to get very scary indeed.

He sometimes wondered if he should have stayed in Russia. But then again, if he could make a difference, surely it was better to do something rather than lie in a Moscow hospital hating himself for doing nothing.

He was also worried about the tension between his companions. Everyone liked Leila, but the other two didn't think much of each other. Schebet Jeltkov, the token Akhtarian, was an old Communist, while Halil Ametov, a short, stocky Tatar in his forties, had spent many years in and out of prison for organising independent trade unions.

They left the restaurant where they had eaten a rather strained lunch together and Jeltkov led them to his car. Ruslan had no choice but to use the walking stick he despised. He could still go no more than a few metres without it.

'That's my car,' Jeltkov said, pointing to a sleek black Volga.

'You know what?' said Ruslan. 'First time I sat in a black Volga, I was under arrest.' He wanted to remind Ametov that he had been to prison too, but that didn't stop him being friends with Communists.

'Me too,' said Ametov. 'It put me off Volga 21s for life.'

'This isn't a Volga 21,' said Jeltkov. 'It's a 23-23.'

'You're joking. Is it yours?'

'Yes. It's a beauty, isn't it?'

They made Jeltkov open the bonnet and crowded round cooing at the engine. Leila stood back, shaking her head.

'It's a Catch Me-Catch Me Car,' Ruslan told her.

'A what?'

'A Catch Me-Catch Me Car,' explained Jeltkov. 'In the Soviet era, only senior ministers were allowed to have a Chaikas. The Volga's a much more beautiful car, but the Chaikas has an amazing V8 engine. So all you had to do was get hold of a Chaikas engine and put it in your Volga.'

'Where did you get the engine?' asked Ametov.

'Well, I sort of accumulated it bit by bit. Took about two years.'

'It must handle beautifully.'

'Like an ocean liner.'

'Yes,' said Jeltkov's driver, 'and it's about as manoeuvrable.'

Jeltkov's Catch Me-Catch Me Car was the main topic of conversation as they left Khosume, boring Leila rigid but dissolving at a stroke the tension between Jeltkov and Ametov.

The road swung northeast, passing through Tatar country where green, white and red flags were intermingled with the new flag of Central Kubania: a blue background to represent the River Kuban, with a shield in the centre representing the protection the new state would offer all its peoples. On the shield were four symbols: a dove of peace, the Ksordian triband, the red and yellow diamonds of Akhtaria and the Tatar flag. Many houses also had blue posters and flags with the word *Yoye*, Tatar for Yes.

After thirty kilometres, the road turned northwest and through mixed countryside, past colourful Tatar villages and sullen Ksordian villages where the graffiti was stark: KTKT (Ksordia United With Korgay) and *Valar Fyetnarbis Tvis* (Death to the Rebels).

As far as many Ksords were concerned, all Akhtarians were Rebels.

They drove through a drab Ksordian town and then headed north towards Timashevsk. They would spend the afternoon in Ruslan's home village so the film crew, who were following in a clapped-out old Moskovich, could record interviews with Ruslan and some of the villagers.

'Turn left here,' said Ruslan, as they approached a narrow, icy road that went off across the plain at a right angle.

The road went by several Ksordian villages, then through one inhabited by Tatars. Finally, they came to Vakesia. They went past the old school building and drove on into what passed for the centre of the village: a shop, a few houses and the church. Ruslan's old house was some 200 metres further along the road. His mother was outside, shovelling snow.

Within minutes Ruslan found himself surrounded by a crowd of villagers, most of them *babushkas* and children. The *babushkas* hugged him and kissed him, some of them with tears in their eyes. The children crowded round excitedly: 'Ruslan's back! Ruslan's back!'

Everyone was full of questions: 'How are you?' 'Why have you got a walking stick?' 'Did you really save your comrades' lives?' 'Where's Tamara?' 'How old's little Shota?'

All of this was recorded by Leila's camera crew. She made Ruslan visit an old Partizan comrade of his father's, who agreed to show them round the sites of the massacre and the battles against the Rebels.

He remembered the Akhtarian Partizan who had helped defend the village. 'Shota was a good comrade,' he said. 'I've often wondered what happened to him.'

A middle-aged woman took them to the school and explained how Ruslan's mother had saved all the children. She stood by the ditch where they had hidden while the Rebels slaughtered their families, and she wept as she remembered their terror as Ruslan's mother crept up and down the ditch hugging and kissing them, telling them to be quiet.

She cried again by the memorial, as she described what she and her brother had found there: their mother, naked from the waist down, their poor little brother, their grandparents and their aunt, all of them dead. Ruslan embraced her and cried too.

'I'm sorry, Auntie. I shouldn't have made you go through it again.'

The woman shook her head. 'Put it on TV for us, Ruslan. You've got to let them know why the Ksords will never accept this new Rebel-Tatar state.'

After they said goodbye and left, Leila made them stop just outside the village to film Ruslan saying something about his visit. He was very reluctant to get out of the car, having only just eased himself into it. Still, at least this time he could manage without his bloody walking stick.

'What do you want me to say?'

'Anything.'

He thought for a moment, and then he said in Russian: 'So this is my home. It's where I belong. Its trauma is my trauma, and I can never escape it.'

That evening in Timashevsk, nearly 300 people turned up in a hall big enough for little more than half that number. (Murad had insisted that all venues should be smaller than the anticipated audience in order to generate a sense of excitement.) Most of the audience were Tatars, with many of them there to heckle, so Ametov and Ruslan had great difficulty making themselves heard. There were militant Ksords in the audience too, and at one stage a fight broke out between them and some of the Tatars.

At the end of the meeting, activists from Lionidza's party and Ametov's trade union federation recruited 38 new people to the No Campaign, all of them Tatars. A very tired Ruslan went round, shaking hands and signing autographs. He was disappointed by the number of new recruits, but greatly encouraged by three students who told him that they had come to the meeting to heckle but would leave convinced of the case for a No vote.

'Well, what do you think?' he asked Ametov as they had a beer afterwards.

Ametov shrugged. 'We have to begin at the beginning, don't we? We've recruited a nucleus, but it's very small. Yakub Bovin spoke to a pro-independence crowd of ten thousand here just two weeks ago.'

Ruslan found it difficult to sleep that night. He wasn't sure if it was adrenalin from the meeting or the hopelessness of the task they had set themselves.

Chapter Twenty-One

THE FOLLOWING day, they drove twenty-five kilometres north towards the city of Bryukhovetskaya. They stopped at a bar a few kilometres outside the town, where Ruslan, Leila and Ametov left Jeltkov and the others. 'Don't get pissed,' were Ruslan's last words to Jeltkov. 'You need to be sober for the meeting tonight.'

They got into a car driven by a swarthy Tatar named Selim Mustafayev, who would take them to the heavily guarded farmhouse inhabited by Timur Sultanov, a leading Tatar whose support Ruslan regarded as crucial to the No Campaign's chances.

Sultanov had risen to prominence in the mid-1980s, when the Soviet economy began to grind to a halt. He had quietly taken over failing state enterprises and created a sizeable business empire, which soon became the biggest employer in Bryukhovetskaya. But capitalist enterprise was illegal during the Communist era, and Sultanov found himself arrested for speculation and sentenced to two years in prison.

He was said to have lived a very luxurious life inside, running his businesses and enjoying regular conjugal visits from both his wife and his mistress. Freed after just eight months, he was then able to continue his activities unmolested.

To the Tatars of Bryukhovetskaya, Sultanov was a hero. He was a paternalistic employer who organised cheap private clinics for his workers and educational scholarships for their children, and who installed running water in the villages that supplied his export businesses. Critics alleged that his philanthropy was 75% publicity and just 25% action on the ground, but the local Tatars remained fiercely loyal.

When the Communists lost power, Sultanov became a minister in the Central Kuban regional government. But in December he had resigned in protest at the moves towards independence. 'It's all well and good for Yakub Bovin to ally himself with the Akhtarians down in Khosume,' he said, 'but up in Bryukhovetskaya, we're surrounded by Ksords. We might as well slit our own throats.'

This made Sultanov an obvious ally for the No Campaign, and Ruslan was optimistic about recruiting him. Ametov, however, was less certain: 'Sultanov was KGB in the Soviet era, and he's in the pockets of the Ksordian Security Police now.'

When they arrived at the farmhouse, it turned out that Sultanov was asleep. Apparently he liked to work late into the night and often needed an afternoon nap. Ruslan and his companions were ushered into a large, ornate room where a number of Tatar big shots were waiting, among them the local police commissioner and the commander of a Tatar militia that was said to have more than a thousand men under arms.

After twenty minutes, a tall, striking young woman appeared. Everyone took this as a sign that Sultanov was awake. Two maids came in and cleared away the teacups and emptied the ashtrays. They placed a bunch of snowdrops on the large table in the middle of the room. The others all sat down around the table, inviting Ruslan, Ametov and Leila to do so too.

Everyone stood up when Sultanov came in, not an easy task for Ruslan. Sultanov was a tall, immaculately dressed man in his late fifties with a full head of grey hair and a thick black moustache. He walked around the table, shaking hands and exchanging a few words with everyone. When he came round to Ruslan, he patted his shoulder warmly. 'It's good to see you alive, young man,' he growled in heavily accented Russian.

'It's a pleasure to be here.'

'Everyone says it was Mingrelsky. What do you think?'

'I couldn't possibly comment.'

Sultanov laughed. 'Very diplomatic.'

With that, he moved on to Ametov, who merited only the briefest of handshakes. Evidently, he didn't think too much of trade unionists.

He kissed Leila's hand. 'Even more beautiful in person than on TV.'

'And you're more handsome in person too.'

Sultanov smiled. Then he sat down, inviting the others to do so.

'So,' he said in Tatar. 'I understand you can speak our language.'

'A little,' said Ruslan. In fact, he found the Bryukhovetskaya accent difficult and would have felt far more comfortable speaking Russian.

'Pity,' said Sultanov. 'We'll have to watch what we say.'

Everybody laughed.

Sultanov sat at the head of the table and invited Ruslan to put forward the case for a No vote in the independence referendum. He did so in Tatar, reverting to Russian or asking Leila and Ametov for help whenever he got in a tangle.

When he had finished, Sultanov asked his companions what they thought. They all spoke at some length, mostly, it seemed to Ruslan, about how wise and wonderful Sultanov was, without committing themselves one way or the other regarding the No Campaign.

As he listened to them, it occurred to Ruslan that Sultanov was well on the way to becoming the modern equivalent of a medieval baron. If the forces unleashed by the collapse of Communism were allowed to bring about the disintegration of the state, Soviet rule in Ksordia would be replaced not by a capitalist democracy but by a brutal new feudalism dominated by Sultanov and other warlords far less benevolent than him.

Finally, it was Sultanov's turn to speak. His voice was deep and gravelly, and he spoke just a little above a whisper so that Ruslan had to strain to hear him at all. If he hadn't also spoken extremely slowly and repeated almost every sentence four or five times, Ruslan would have found what he had to say incomprehensible.

His theme was realism. He started by saying that he wasn't a theoretician and had no great love of ideology. 'When I was a young man with no money and no talent, I joined the Party. Not because I was a Communist, not out of any love for Lenin or the Russians, but because I was a realist. If you wanted to get anywhere in those days, you had to be in the Party.

'Then, years later, when the official economy was dying on its feet, I turned to the black economy. Not foreign cigarettes or pornography, nothing like that. I dealt in textiles, machine tools, agricultural products, the things the people need. Then when they arrested me, I did what I had to do to keep things going. Some people criticised me for it, but I didn't care. I've always been a pragmatist.

'Now we have to be pragmatic again. I agree with you, young man: there's no way an independent Central Kubania can survive. The Ksords and the Akhtarians will tear it apart, and woe betide any Tatar who gets in their way. You and Lionidza are right about that.'

Ruslan nodded and waited for the 'but'.

It came soon enough. 'You may be right, but are you pragmatic? That's the question. Do you really think you can get the Ksords to abandon their leaders? No chance. They'll stick together because they're scared of a return of the Rebels. And the Akhtarians? They think Korgay's planning a second Great Repression. You'll never get them to vote to stay in Ksordia – because that's what a No vote would mean.

'As for the Tatars, Yakub Bovin's got them hooked on this absurd dream of a multi-ethnic state where we'll all suddenly love one another again. You can't reason with them. They'll probably still believe it until the Ksords burn down their houses and rape their wives and daughters.'

'They might listen to you,' said Ruslan.

'Round here yes. But not in Khosume. Everyone there thinks I'm just an ignorant country bumpkin.'

'But we have to try,' pleaded Leila. 'What alternative is there?'

'Pragmatism. Pragmatism. If you live round here, keep quiet and keep your head down. The Ksords will leave you alone if I can convince them you're not a threat. If you live in the west, ally yourself to the Akhtarians. They'll need you, so they'll look after you. Yakub Bovin might just be able to hold on to Khosume, but I doubt it. Best thing for the Tatars in the south and the centre would be to pack their bags and get out until it's all over. Go to West Ksordia or Russia. They'll be safe there.'

'You can't seriously mean that?' said Leila.

'So what else do you suggest? Tell our people to gamble their lives on a romantic gesture by an ex-Communist, an ex-dissident, a half-dead athlete and a singer? Are you telling me that's a pragmatic alternative?'

The failure to recruit Sultanov was a heavy blow. Ruslan and the others didn't speak as they were driven back to the bar where they had left their companions. Then, to make matters worse, Jeltkov and the others were all drunk.

They left Jeltkov's driver and the camera crew in the bar, having extracted a promise from them not to get any more pissed than they already were, and dragged Jeltkov to the Catch Me-Catch Me Car, hoping that some fresh air would sober him up in time for the evening meeting.

Ametov, who was delighted to get his hands on the steering wheel, drove them to the southeast of the town, where they parked and walked along a slushy footpath that followed a silent brook.

'It's not starting well,' said Ametov. 'No Zikladza and now no Sultanov.'

'I know. I was sort of hoping Sergo was still working for Zikladza, but it looks like he isn't.'

'That's what I don't get,' said Ametov. 'How come you and Lionidza are so close? I mean, you were always anti-Communist, weren't you?'

'You should hear them argue about politics,' said Leila. 'Do you remember in Kvemodishi, Ruslan? You and Sergo argued about Communism every night.'

Ruslan told Ametov how Lionidza had spotted him as an athlete and had protected him from the KGB.

'So why did he protect you?'

'I don't know. I've often wondered.'

'He likes you,' said Jeltkov. 'And he was desperate for someone from Ksordia-Akhtaria to get a gold medal.'

'Wasn't he taking a risk, supporting me?'

Jeltkov shook his head. 'Maybe a bit, but he knew everything would be okay as long as you had no contact with Nina Begishveli.'

'I bet he was pleased when I got together with Tamara again.'

'Well, it wasn't exactly a coincidence.'

'What do you mean?'

'Well come on, Ruslan. You weren't even in the same republic. I mean, what were the chances of you meeting by accident?'

'You mean Sergo fixed it?'

'Him and the GRU.'

'Who?' said Leila.

'Soviet Military Intelligence.'

Ruslan said nothing. He had stopped walking, a shocked look on his face. Leila and Ametov froze too, obviously aware that Jeltkov's revelations had gone too far.

Jeltkov remained oblivious. 'The military had a lot to lose. I mean, they'd rehabilitated you, and they kicked up a stink when the KGB sent Mingrelsky's son to break your leg. So they had to make sure they could keep you away from Nina Begishveli.

'The GRU investigated all your old girlfriends, and they decided Tamara was their best bet. So the next question was how to get the two of you together. At one point there was talk of sending you off for a race in Tatarstan and getting her to do the doping test, but Sergo vetoed that. He said testing your urine would hardly be conducive to romance.

'Then the GRU remembered that you were friends with Fatima Dzemileva, and it turned out that not only did she know Tamara, but her husband was angling to take their troupe to Tatarstan. The KGB had blocked them because of their habit of doing Crimean songs and dances.

'So the GRU applied a bit of *blat* and off she went. They made sure Tamara heard she was coming, and they made sure she had a seat near the front so Fatima Dzemileva could see her from the stage. And that's it. That's how Sergo and the GRU fixed you up.'

The public meeting that evening was a lacklustre affair. Jeltkov was a sloppy chairman, Ametov's performance was poor, and Ruslan's heart clearly wasn't in it. The only person up to speed was Leila.

All the new volunteers at the end were marshalled by Tatar baron Sultanov's retainer Selim Mustafayev. Evidently Sultanov wanted to be able to turn the No Campaign in Bryukhovetskaya on or off at will. This area was his fiefdom and he wanted control.

After the meeting, Ruslan went to his hotel room to write up the diary he was keeping for Tamara, including full details of Jeltkov's revelations. Then he got ready for bed and watched the sports roundup on Russian TV.

At eleven thirty, there was a knock at the door. Ruslan struggled to his feet, put a dressing gown on over his pyjamas and went to answer it.

It was Leila. 'Hi. Can I come in?'

'It's very late.'

'Don't worry, I haven't come to seduce you.'

He let her in and turned off the TV. She parked herself on the bed, sitting cross-legged. He eased himself back into the room's one and only chair, grimacing until he found a comfortable position.

'Are you very upset?'

Ruslan shrugged. 'Would you be?'

'I don't know. Nobody's ever handed Prince Charming to me on a platter.'

'I just wonder if there's any part of my life over the last ten years that he hasn't scripted. I mean, anything? I only got to run abroad thanks to his *blat*. And you know about the War of the Border Posts? Him and Comrade Zikladza were just using me. Did I tell you about that?'

'Yes.'

'And they used me in North Ksordia too and now he's sucked me into this.'

'I thought that was me.'

Ruslan smiled. 'Yes, maybe. Did you know he forced us to get married?'

'No?'

'I mean, Tamara wasn't even pregnant but we still had a shotgun wedding.'

'How come?'

'He said the KGB would break my legs if we didn't get married before the running season started.'

'You're joking.'

'No I'm not. And now it turns out he fixed us up in the first place too.'

'Who cares? Just remember how much you love Tamara and how much she loves you. You're perfect for each other. So who cares what Sergo and the bloody GRU were up to? Your motives were good, her motives were good and you came out of it with something special. That's what matters.'

'Do you think I don't know that? All these years I've been so grateful to Fatima and Murad for putting us back in touch. And now am I supposed to feel the same gratitude to Lionidza and the GRU?'

'It doesn't matter. You should be grateful to Fatima and Murad because they did it as an act of friendship. Sergo and the GRU did it for their own reasons. You don't have to thank them. Just enjoy your good luck.'

They sat in silence for a minute, then Leila stood up. 'I'd better go. I don't want anyone to catch me here. We don't want a scandal, do we?'

Chapter Twenty-Two

NEXT DAY they drove back to Khosume to report back on the result of their encounter with Sultanov, the northern Tatar baron. Ruslan, Leila, Ametov and Lionidza met outdoors in a park not far from Lionidza's Social Democratic Party headquarters – they took it for granted that some secret service or other would have bugged his office. After wandering around for a while, they found some broken-down benches near a bandstand that was covered with angry political graffiti.

Lionidza didn't seem surprised to learn that Sultanov had refused to back them but had then made sure he could control the No Campaign in Bryukhovetskaya. 'Sultanov's a very slippery fish. He likes to keep his options open.'

'He was KGB in the old days, wasn't he?' said Ametov.

'So I hear. Believe it or not, I never had much to do with the KGB. Aleksander Mingrelsky was their contact person in the Party leadership, and after he fell, it was Korgay. I liaised with the military. From what I understand, Sultanov went over to the KGB after he got arrested, but by then you had senior KGB officers like Tengiz Alavidza who had virtually gone freelance. It was all very chaotic in the final years.'

'So do you think Sultanov's working for Alavidza now?' Ametov asked.

Lionidza shook his head. 'Not working for him as such, but he's probably working with him. Sultanov will be trying to use Alavidza just as much as Alavidza's trying to use him.'

'If he's working with Alavidza, that means he's working with Korgay,' said Ametov.

'Sultanov will work with anyone if he thinks it's to his advantage.'

'So he may yet work with us,' said Ruslan.

'If we can show him it's to his advantage.'

'Yes,' said Ametov, 'but we can't do that unless we start doing much better than we're doing now.'

Once their meeting was over, Leila and Ametov stood up to go. Lionidza stood up too, but then Ruslan said, 'Sergo, can I have a word in private?'

Lionidza sat down and Ruslan waited until the others were out of earshot before telling him what Jeltkov had said about Tamara.

Lionidza shrugged. 'It's true. She wasn't the first woman we tried to fix you up with.'

'Who else?'

'Oh, I don't know their names. The GRU arranged for you to coach some young female runners, and there was a Ukrainian athlete they kept sending you off to competitions with.'

'Who? Marina Shishova?'

'I can't remember her name, but I know the GRU had high hopes of her.'

'Was it really that important to keep me away from Nina Begishveli?'

'Yes.'

'Tamara will be upset when I tell her.'

'So why tell her?'

'I can never keep secrets from her.'

Lionidza raised an eyebrow. 'I bet she doesn't know that you arranged for Leila to fly Nina Begishveli back from Siberia.'

Ruslan laughed. 'I didn't know that you knew.'

'It took us about ten seconds to find out, and Comrade Zikladza wasn't exactly pleased with me. Anyway, talking about secrets, I didn't want to tell the others, but remember your old lawyer Zourab Orbeliani?' (Orbeliani was leader of the more moderate wing of Ksordian nationalism.)

'He wasn't my lawyer. He was Nina's.'

'Was he? Well, anyway, he's been in touch.'

'Really? Have you spoken to him?'

'Not directly. It's all very cloak and dagger.'

'And?'

'He's very sympathetic. He doesn't think he can stay in Korgay's government much longer, and he might come over to us if we start to make an impact.'

'That's fantastic news. I still think Sultanov might join us one day.'

'You know what? We should get them to join us at the same time, one a Ksord and the other a Tatar. It should be our slogan: "I'll vote No if you vote No."'

'That could make a good slogan.'

'Never forget you're working with a political genius here.'

'A master manipulator, more like.'

'Don't tell me you're complaining.'

Ruslan smiled. 'Not in the least, but Leila tells me I shouldn't thank you because you had an ulterior motive.'

'I did. I was trying to save a promising young athlete from ruining his career.'

They sat in silence. After a moment Ruslan said, 'There's something else you should know. I made Tamara two promises, not one.'

'I know.'

'You know?'

'Yes. You promised her that if we lose, you won't stay and help us clear up the mess. You'll take her and Shota away from Ksordia-Akhtaria and stay out of politics.'

'God's nails. Who told you that?'

'Tamara. She wanted me and Leila to promise we'd help her hold you to it.'

Ruslan laughed. 'And what did you say to that?'

'We said we would.'

'Well in that case we'd better win this bloody referendum.'

That night, it took a long time to get little Shota to sleep, so excited was he to see his father again. Once he was out of the way, Tamara showered and emerged in a cream bathrobe Ruslan had bought for her in England. He signalled that he wanted to speak to her before he joined her in bed.

She sat down on the sofa. He closed the living room door and, with some difficulty, knelt down in front of her, taking her hands in his. 'There's something you should know.'

'What's that?'

'That old guy Jeltkov, on Monday, he got drunk, and he told me something I didn't know. Something about us.'

'What?'

'When you met Fatima and Murad in Menzelinsk, it wasn't a coincidence. Lionidza and the GRU had set it up.'

'Lionidza and who?'

'Military Intelligence. Apparently the GRU arranged Fatima's tour, then they made sure you heard about it and they even arranged for you to sit near the front so that Fatima would notice you from the stage.'

'You're joking.'

'No, I'm not.'

'Were they that desperate to make sure you didn't go back to Nina?'

'Yes.'

That answer hit her like a slap in the face. She looked at him and then looked away. When she looked back at him, there were tears in her eyes. She pulled her hands out of his to wipe them away. For a minute, she tried not to cry, but then she let her tears flood out unhindered.

Ruslan put his right hand up to her neck and pulled her towards him. He held her against his shoulder and kissed her hair. 'I'm sorry my love. I didn't mean to hurt you.'

She took a tissue from the pocket of her bathrobe and wiped her face. 'You were right to tell me. I'm sorry for being so stupid.'

'You're not being stupid.'

She gave him a salty kiss. 'Thank you. It's just that...'

'What?'

'It's just that she never seems to go away. It's like the default is her, and I'm just the one you ended up with when that didn't work out.'

'No, Tamara. No, no, no. You're the love of my life.'

Tamara hesitated and then mentioned something they had never been able to discuss: 'It wasn't my name you said first when you came out of your coma.'

'I know. You have no idea how much I curse myself for that, honestly you have no idea.'

'People always remember their wives when they lose their memories, but you forgot me.' She started to cry again.

Ruslan held her while she sobbed. He stroked her hair and kissed it. He took out his handkerchief and gave it to her so that she could wipe her face again.

'I didn't forget you. I forgot twelve years of my life. I forgot everything from those twelve years: you, Shota, all my medals – the three things that mean most to me in all the world. I didn't just forget you.'

Tamara laughed. 'I'm sorry, Ruslan. If you forgot your medals too, then I should know I wasn't being singled out.' She wiped her tears.

'You don't know how much I love you. How many men have fallen in love with their wives three times? You're the love of my life, you and only you.'

She looked at him and smiled. 'No, I'm not.'

'Yes, you are.'

'I know you love me, but I've always had to share you with something. If it's not your running, it's your thesis and now it's bloody politics.'

'But I only love you. I don't love those things.'

She kissed him on the lips. 'Debatable point.'

'Do you really think I'm so bad?'

'I always knew what I was letting myself in for, so I'm not complaining. Just don't ever ask me to share you with another woman, because I'm not willing to do that.'

'I promise. Absolutely never.'

'And promise me you won't get too close to that Leila.'

'You don't need to worry about her.'

'Promise me.'

'I promise.'

'She likes you and I can see she's just your type.'

'What do you mean she's just my type? My type is you.'

She smiled and kissed him. Then they kissed again, Ruslan stroking his fingers through her hair. She put her arms around his shoulders, while his strong right hand stroked her hair, her ears and her neck.

He brought his hands down and opened up her bathrobe. He kissed her lips, her cheeks and her neck, pushing the bathrobe back as he did so. She brought her arms back, and he slipped the bathrobe off her, revealing her slender body. He brought his fingers up her arms and down the sides of her trunk, then inside to gently caress the soft flesh of her breasts.

She caught his eye and they both smiled. They kissed, and then he broke off, bending his wrecked back as far as it would go and kissing her neck and her shoulder. At that moment he was reminded how precious it was to love one woman and only one woman. There could never be another.

The next morning, it was back to campaigning. Tamara carried Ruslan's bag to the Catch Me-Catch Me Car, while he followed behind with his walking stick. Then he settled down for a long ride to Chitaskiri, a mixed town of Ksords and Akhtarians just south of the border with Akhtaria / North Ksordia. This was one of the most dangerous flashpoints in the whole region. All of its Akhtarian inhabitants had been expelled from the town centre and the eastern suburbs, which were controlled by Ksordian troops and extremist paramilitaries, among them Mingrelsky's White Eagles.

The Akhtarians clung on in the western suburbs, protected by their own lightly armed militia and a contingent of Tatar policemen. It was clear, however, that these forces would be no match for the Ksords when fighting started, so rather than drive Ksordian civilians out, the Akhtarians did everything they could to stop them from leaving, effectively holding them hostage in the hope that this would prevent the Ksords from using all their firepower.

Lionidza's party had no presence in Chitaskiri, so the meeting there was organised by a small group of trade unionists who clung onto the ideal of inter-ethnic solidarity. They persuaded Ruslan and his friends to tour the town, handing out flyers and drumming up support for the meeting.

Jeltkov tried to stop Ruslan going into the eastern suburbs, saying it was too dangerous, but he insisted on doing so. 'Korgay won't let Mingrelsky lay a finger on us. In any case, if I'm scared to campaign there, how can I ask anyone else to?'

He did, however, agree to go nowhere without a bodyguard from either the Ksordian military or the Tatar police.

The crowds who stopped to see him were curious and totally lacking in hostility. Where he had intended merely to give out leaflets, he invariably ended up giving a five-minute version of his speech. People applauded politely and then either went on their way or queued up to shake his hand and get his autograph. He would ask them if they planned to support the No Campaign, and many would smile politely or shrug and make an evasive comment. One old *babushka* gave it to him straight, however: 'No, I'm not going to vote in that filthy referendum, but it's good to see you're still campaigning for peace.'

The meeting that night was a great success. The press and TV were there in force for the first time ever, and Leila, Ametov and Ruslan were on sparkling form. Though there were lots of hecklers, Jeltkov and the three speakers deployed their repertoire of stinging rebukes without mercy. A lot of people signed up that evening.

Afterwards, a journalist told Ruslan that Lionidza had just succeeded in persuading the Tatar and Ksord-Akhtarian TV channels to transmit two No Campaign broadcasts, one the next Sunday and a second one three weeks later, just seven days before the referendum. This was excellent news.

'Something happened today,' said Ametov. 'This was the best day yet. We have to go on the streets everywhere, same as we did here. Just one big meeting in the evening isn't enough.'

'Are you up to it, Ruslan?' Leila asked. 'Don't forget you guys, he should still be in hospital.'

'I'm a marathon runner. If there's one thing I've got, it's stamina.'

'Okay, but I know what I'm talking about here, because I've been on tour. We have to do it properly. Ruslan does speeches and quick interviews and that's all he does. He doesn't get involved in organisation. You have to trust us with that, okay Ruslan?'

Ruslan nodded.

'As far as you're concerned, we just take you to a shopping centre and say "Do your little speech and sign some autographs," or we plonk you in front of a bunch of reporters and tell you to give them five minutes and not a second more, or we take you to a hall and say, "Siriach'Sichi, big speech." It's got to be like that, Ruslan, it's the only way you can do it.'

'Sounds good to me.'

'Second thing, we recruit someone whose job it is to look after Ruslan's every need. He needs a coffee, a bar of soap, something for a sore throat, he just turns to this person and he gets it. Has to be a man, because a woman would probably end up giving him blow jobs too, and that might affect his performance.'

Everybody laughed.

'Now I'm tied up with filming, so all organisation falls on you two, plus Demna.' (The Ksordian trade unionist Demna Ksnis travelled one day ahead of them to co-ordinate their meetings.) 'But really, you can't be expected to perform and organise. We should call Sergo and tell him to come and join us.'

'No. We need him in Khosume.'

'Ruslan, this has got nothing to do with you. You just worry about your performance.'

'He's right, though,' said Ametov. 'Why don't we speak to my people here? We've got loads of good organisers.'

'Don't just get Ksords,' said Ruslan. 'And no I won't shut up if you insist on discussing these things in front of me.'

Leila laughed. 'Fair enough. That's another thing we have to remember. We don't discuss organisational matters in front of Ruslan. We just tell him what he needs to know.'

Leila and Ametov recruited three new people to the team, among them a sports fanatic who would act as personal assistant to Ruslan. He felt they had made an excellent choice. He desperately missed being able to run, and it would be good to be able to get away from politics from time to time and talk about sport.

By eleven thirty next morning, they were ready to go. Ametov went in a Volga 21 with the new road manager and press officer. Ruslan and his personal assistant joined Jeltkov and his driver in the Catch Me-Catch Me Car, while Leila stayed with her film crew in the Moskovich. The press convoy would follow them.

Just before they set off, Leila wandered over to Ruslan's car.

'Well?' he asked her. 'What do I need to know today?'

'Five gigs. First: two o'clock in the eastern suburbs, quick speech, autographs. Second: two forty-five, Kikari town centre, ditto. Then three thirty, western suburbs, ditto. Next, five o'clock, just outside the town, you're going to meet that wounded soldier who Tamara treated. Last one: eight o'clock, town centre, big speech. Think you're up to it?'

'Do I have a choice?'

'Not really.'

Ruslan laughed. He hoped Leila wouldn't stay out of the Catch Me-Catch Me Car for long.

The road south to Kikari took them through Ksordian countryside, a land of fields, farms and wooden villages with tribands and everywhere the same slogans: 'Death to the Rebels' and 'KTKT'.

Here and there, they passed signs of military activity: side roads blocked off with bored soldiers warming themselves by a brazier, M-46 field guns scattered among farm buildings, BTR-60PA armoured personnel carriers parked in a village just off the road. Ruslan wondered how often Tatars or Akhtarians saw these sights, and how well they slept at night when they did.

As their little convoy entered Tatar country, Ruslan was surprised to see a flock of red-breasted geese flying northwards. It must be a very early spring if they were already heading for the Arctic. But then again, perhaps they were wise to depart before their feeding grounds became battlefields once more.

Chapter Twenty-Three

THEIR TOUR ended in Khosume on the Saturday. Fatima had invited everyone for Sunday lunch, and all their wives and children came along, as did Leila's boyfriend, a rather quiet Ksordian bass guitarist. They started to eat once the interminable rituals of kisses and handshakes were over, and before long the house was full of laughter and gossip.

It was a really enjoyable afternoon, and all the stress of the campaign seemed forgotten. Ruslan found it the perfect distraction from his increasing nervousness about the No Campaign broadcast due that evening.

Lionidza revealed that the broadcast had only come about because he had got the Organisation for Security and Co-operation in Europe to lean on Yakub Bovin.

'Can't you ask them to make him give us more time on TV? Maybe some interviews and debates, a bit more than just the odd brief mention on the news.'

'I'm working on it, don't worry.'

Murad had to leave early to go to the TV studio, but all the others stayed and settled down in front of Fatima's TV as seven thirty approached. Ruslan had pride of place on the sofa, with Tamara next to him and Shota sprawled across his knee.

The opening shots of the No Campaign broadcast showed police cars, policemen and a grey Volga 21 riddled with bullet holes. Then Leila's voice in Russian: 'Do you remember when they shot you?' (The whole of the broadcast was in Russian. Any Ksord-Akhtarian or Tatar had Russian subtitles.)

'No, not at all. I just remember waking up half dead in hospital.'

Cut to footage of Ruslan in the Catch Me-Catch Me Car. 'Why do you think they tried to kill you?'

'Because they wanted a war. The extremists on both sides wanted a war, just as now they want to spread it to Central Kubania.'

Next came extracts from his Ruslan's speeches, set against film of Ksordian and Akhtarian troops and heavy weapons, all pushing home the message that independence will lead to war.

Cut to his speech in Siriach'Sichi. 'What lies at the heart of all of this is the relationship between the Ksords and the Akhtarians, poisoned by the terrible events of fifty years ago, poisoned by the inability of people on each side to recognise the wounds of the other.'

This was followed by Ruslan standing by a country road, speaking lines that Leila had given to him. 'I'm going to take you deep into that pain. First the pain of the Ksords, then the pain of the Akhtarians. I ask you to bear with me, and to remember that nothing you see here is contrived. Akhtarians and Tatars must understand that the sufferings of the Ksords are real. Ksords must understand that there's nothing fake in the suffering of the Akhtarians.'

The film then told the story of the Rebel massacre in Vakesia, how his mother had saved the children and how his father's Partizans (among them an Akhtarian) had beaten off two more Rebel attacks. It showed Ruslan in tears, apologising to his former neighbour for making her live through it again. Next it showed him outside the village, again full of emotion: 'So this is my home. It's where I belong. Its trauma is my trauma. I can never escape it.'

Then he was in the Catch Me-Catch Me Car. Leila's voice asked him, 'And this is why you could never sell the idea of independence to your mother.'

'Yes.'

Cut to an Akhtarian village where Ruslan was speaking to Jeltkov's niece, a woman in her mid-sixties. She talked about her fifteen-year-old brother and showed Ruslan the farm buildings where he had hidden throughout the German occupation.

'The Rebel press gangs were after him, but he was determined not to join them. His father and his brother were in the Red Army. How could he fight against them?'

She remembered the short-lived sense of relief when the Germans had fled, and how her brother and the other villagers had cheered the first Red Army units to appear in their wake. But four days later, her brother had been arrested. His name had appeared on a Rebel list in Siriach'Sichi, and it didn't matter how desperately his mother begged the authorities to spare him, that was enough to condemn him.

Jeltkov's niece had taken the camera crew to the ditch where they had made him strip to the waist and kneel down before shooting him in the back of the head. She cried as she remembered him. 'He was never a Rebel. What had he done that he had to die?'

Film of Ruslan, standing by the ditch. 'An innocent young boy died here. Like thousands of others, he was caught up in a collective punishment he had done nothing to deserve.'

After that, Jeltkov's niece spoke about the Great Repression. All three of her surviving grandparents had died during the journey to Central Asia, and her youngest brother had died within a month of their arrival. She said the experience had broken her mother's spirit, and she had died ten months later after a succession of illnesses, leaving behind a daughter of fourteen and a son of twelve trapped in utter destitution. Their father had managed to track them down soon afterwards, and only this had prevented them from starving to death.

The film showed Ruslan speaking in Moidan'Abasha. 'And so here we are, two wounded peoples, each trying to cope with our own trauma, each completely insensitive to the pain of the other. There are so many Ksords, when you speak to them, they say about the Great Repression: "The Akhtarians had it coming to them." No they didn't. No they most definitely didn't. So many of the people who were shot were innocents, and ninety-nine percent of those who were deported were innocent of any crime.

'And so many Akhtarians belittle the horror of Rebel violence. President Eristov himself said it to me. He said that what the Rebels did was nothing compared to what the Akhtarian people suffered. I remember I was shaking with fury and I said: "So it was nothing when the Rebels shot my mother's babies? So it was nothing when they shot my father's wife and children?"'

The soundtrack continued with extracts from his speeches and images of Ksordian and Akhtarian troops and militiamen. 'Each of us has to recognise the other's pain,' said Ruslan's voice. 'Each of us has to respect that pain, and respect the fear that our history can generate. Because if we don't, we'll fight each other and slaughter each other, and God only knows how many of us are going to die.

'Be in no doubt about it, war is very actively being prepared, and there are both Ksordian and Akhtarian extremists who are very much looking forward to having the opportunity to carry on where they left off last year.'

This was followed by footage of Mingrelsky addressing his White Eagles: 'The war in North Ksordia was just a dress rehearsal. The Central Kuban war will be the big one. We have to smash the Rebels once and for all. And we have to make the Tatars pay for daring to oppose us. We'll shoot all the men and "BEEP" all the women and burn all their houses down. There won't be any Tatars left in Central Kubania when we've finished with them.'

Everybody in Fatima's living room gasped.

'Got you, you evil son of a slut,' said Ruslan. He glanced at Tamara, who smiled and squeezed his knee with her hand.

Cut to film of Teimuraz Garashveli, the hard-line Akhtarian Mayor of Siriach'Sichi and a minister in the multi-ethnic Central Kuban government. 'Siriach'Sichi is the capital of South Akhtaria,' he told his audience. 'The Tatars can stay if they accept that this is an Akhtarian city. But as soon as the fighting starts, we have to drive out all the Ksords within a fifty-kilometre radius.'

'God's nails,' Ruslan said to Lionidza. 'Where did you get that?'

Lionidza tapped his nose and said nothing.

Next came an excerpt from one of Ruslan's more recent speeches. 'I'm so afraid of this war because I've seen what it can do to the young men who are sent to fight.'

The following scene was the interview he had filmed with three mutilated Ksordian veterans of the Akhtarian war. One, who Tamara had treated, was paralysed from the waist down. A second soldier had had his lower jaw blown off and wore a mask to make himself presentable. The youngest of the three had lost a leg and his genitals when he stepped on a landmine.

The three soldiers said something about how their injuries had affected them. The eunuch was quite blunt about himself. 'I was seventeen years old when I went off to fight and I was a virgin. And now I always will be. It doesn't matter if I live to be a hundred.'

Ruslan asked them why they wanted to appear in his broadcast. 'The politicians threw our lives away,' said the paralysed soldier. 'And now they want to do the same again in Central Kubania. We know you tried to stop them in Akhtaria and you nearly succeeded. This time you mustn't fail, Ruslan. You have to stop this war.'

He had almost cried when the soldier said that.

The next scene was twenty wounded soldiers waving to Ruslan as he departed, with his voice saying, 'Those fine young men made me feel so humble. I have to confess that I've sometimes felt a bit sorry for myself since I was shot. But their injuries are so much worse than mine and they face their future with such integrity of spirit. I just hope we don't let them down.'

After this came extracts from his speeches in which he spoke about the pogrom he had witnessed in Sumgait and the terrifying speed with which Azeris had turned on their Armenian neighbours. This included interviews with his former Azeri neighbours and the Armenian Mrs Jibotian. They told how Ruslan and Tamara had sheltered one Armenian family and had offered shelter to the Jibotians, who had turned them down. (All this had been part of the documentary about Ruslan shown just before his Olympic triumph.)

Mrs Jibotian described the attack on her family and how Tamara had risked her life to stop her husband bleeding to death. Her words could almost have been scripted for the No Campaign broadcast: 'It's my greatest regret that we didn't listen to Ruslan and Doctor Tamara when they tried to save us.'

The broadcast moved towards its end with Ruslan asking, 'Can you imagine the horror that's going to be unleashed when the peoples of Central Kubania go for one another?'

Cut to film of him in the centre of Khosume, with its mixture of Ksordian and Tatar flags. 'Can you imagine it here?' Then to Timashevsk, again with a mixture of Tatar and Ksordian flags behind him. 'Can you imagine it here?'

Ruslan said to Tamara, 'Everywhere we went, Leila made me say that.'

'Yes,' said Leila. 'And you complained every time.'

They all laughed.

Next was Chitaskiri, with Ksordian flags nearby and Akhtarian flags in the distance. 'Can you imagine it here?' Then Kikari, Tatar and Ksord, and finally Siriach'Sichi, with its mass of Tatar and Akhtarian flags: 'And can you imagine the horror here, when the militant Akhtarian leadership decide they're fed up with their Tatar allies.'

The broadcast returned to film of the scene of the attempt on Ruslan's life. Leila's voice asked him, 'Do you really think it's possible to prevent a war?'

'Yes, it's possible. It's not going to be easy, but if people from all three major communities vote with their head and not with their blood, then maybe we can succeed.'

Finally, a blank screen with a Khosume telephone number and Leila's voice in Russian reading it out.

The phone rang incessantly after Ruslan and Tamara got home. One of the first to get through was Ruslan's mother, who said she had been campaigning in the village and would deliver a No vote if he promised to come home straight after the referendum and take some daffodils to sell in Tatarstan.

Ruslan laughed. 'Do you think they'll be ready?'

'Oh yes, it's a very early spring this year. They'll be at their peak.'

The broadcast completely transformed the situation, and the telephones at campaign headquarters didn't stop ringing for two days. The No Campaign's bandwagon had started to roll, and over the next few days, three heavyweight politicians clambered aboard. Former Communist leader Comrade Zikladza released a statement expressing support. Northern Tatar baron Timur Sultanov said nothing in public, but his retainer Selim Mustafayev moved into action and demanded two seats on the Campaign Committee. And the next day, Nina and Yakub's former lawyer Zourab Orbeliani resigned from Korgay's government and threw his party's full weight behind the campaign.

Of all his new allies, Ruslan was most delighted about Orbeliani, who bought credibility among the Ksords and a strong regional powerbase in the port city of Moidan'Abasha. Orbeliani also had extensive connections throughout the political class: he had after all been defence counsel in almost every major political trial in Ksordia-Akhtaria during the final decade of the Soviet era.

The expanded Campaign Committee met and delegated Murad and Lionidza to prepare the next broadcast, which would be aired just seven days before the referendum. Lionidza's other task would be to press the authorities to give them time on TV. Apart from brief mentions on the news, the two Central Kuban TV channels paid little attention to the No Campaign. They never interviewed anyone or invited them to debate with pro-independence campaigners. As for the TV stations controlled by the Ksordian and Akhtarian governments, they ignored the existence of the No campaign altogether.

The rest of the campaign leadership would devote themselves to a punishing schedule of meetings, rallies, press conferences and interviews, culminating in a rally in the streets of Khosume on the last day of the campaign.

Three groups of speakers would set off on tour. Ruslan and Ametov would take the densely populated south and centre, which meant that Ruslan would be able to go home almost every night. Leila would tour the Ksordian and Tatar communities of the east and northeast, along with Ksordian trade unionist Demna Ksnis and one of Sultanov's allies. Orbeliani, Sultanov's retainer Selim Mustafayev and Jeltkov the token Akhtarian would work in the west, taking in Moidan'Abasha and Siriach'Sichi.

Over the next few days, it became clear to Ruslan that the success of the broadcast had changed the way that their opponents treated them. Hecklers were now both more numerous and more hostile, and Ruslan and Ametov soon learnt to take two changes of clothes to cope with the eggs and flour bombs that came their way.

Where once they had accused him of naivety, Ksordian hecklers now accused Ruslan of treason, and Tatars made the same accusation against Ametov. Hostile crowds also assembled outside some of their meetings in Ksordian areas and pelted the audience with stones as they left.

The two communities were closing ranks. Anyone who stepped out of line was viewed as a traitor, especially among the Ksords.

Ruslan tried to hide from Tamara just how badly all this was affecting him, but in the bedroom his disguise fell away. He couldn't sleep at night. Nor could he give her the satisfaction she was used to, and for the first time in her life she found herself faking orgasms in an effort to salvage her husband's morale.

Ten days after the broadcast, Ruslan and Ametov had to abandon a street meeting when it was attacked by a Ksordian mob.

'That was grim,' said Ruslan as they were driven to the next town.

'Not as bad as Demna and Leila.'

'Why? What happened to them?'

'Haven't you heard? Demna phoned me last night. They've received death threats from Mingrelsky's White Eagles.'

'God's nails. I hope they're taking them seriously.'

'Very. Demna's crapping himself. Leila's thinks they'll be okay as long as they have plenty of TV cameras with them.'

'That's what I thought last time, but it didn't stop him shooting me. Does Sergo know?'

'I don't think so.'

'Let's find somewhere to stop and phone him.'

Lionidza wasn't surprised by the death threats. Orbeliani had received warnings to keep away from Siriach'Sichi. 'I've told Orbeliani not to go anywhere without a police escort and a camera crew.'

'Sergo, this is Mingrelsky we're talking about.'

'I know.'

'And Leila, for God's sake. Can you get hold of her?'

'I should be able to find out where she's staying tonight. I'll tell her to be very cautious.'

'Stress the word "very". Remind her about when Nina phoned me and I didn't listen.'

Ruslan and Ametov spoke at three further meetings that day, all of them marred by hecklers, flour bombs and eggs. The final meeting degenerated into a brawl, and the police had to escort them back to Khosume at the end.

'This isn't working,' Ametov said as they headed home. 'We have to come up with another strategy.'

'Like what?'

'I don't know, but we can't carry on like this.'

Ruslan got home at one o'clock, and this time there was no disguising his fears from Tamara.

'It was pretty scary.'

'Is it safe?'

'I think so. They only wanted to disrupt.'

'You don't look like you feel safe.'

'I'll be all right.'

'Don't you think you should stop having meetings?'

'What else can we do? We have to campaign.'

Ruslan showered and washed the egg out of his hair, and then Tamara massaged him all over. 'Lie still,' she told him. 'You're in my hands now. Doctor's orders.'

If her hands brought him some relief and helped him to sleep for several hours before the nightmares woke him, Tamara gained little solace for herself. She lay awake next to him worrying that it might after all be her destiny to spend half her life a widow.

Chapter Twenty-Four

THE NEXT morning, Ruslan telephoned Lionidza first thing. Lionidza had been unable to contact Leila and Ksnis. Apparently they had switched to another hotel at the last minute as a precaution. 'I've spoken to some party comrades who'll be meeting them this afternoon. They'll get them to phone me.'

'Can you convene a meeting of the campaign committee? These speaking tours aren't working. We have to come up with something else.'

'Like what?'

'I don't know, but we have to come up with something different.'

'Okay, I'll call a meeting for Saturday afternoon.'

'And tell Leila and Ksnis to cancel all their meetings.'

'Okay.'

'Thanks.'

Ruslan and Ametov spent the day touring Tatar towns and villages. The hecklers there were unruly, but not nearly as hostile as Ksords.

Ruslan was almost two thirds of the way through his final speech of the evening when he noticed his personal assistant walk up to Ametov and whisper in his ear. Ruslan tried to ignore them and carry on with his speech, but Ametov stood up and took hold of his arm: 'We have to stop.'

Ruslan stood back and Ametov said, 'Friends, comrades, opponents, we have to end our meeting here. I've just heard that our friends Demna Ksnis and Leila Meipariani have been shot.'

A shock wave swept around the hall.

'I'm afraid I don't have any more information at present,' said Ametov. 'But I think the best thing for everyone here would just be to go home. We can't continue under these circumstances.'

214

A dazed Ruslan was led off the platform and through a side door to a room where one of their aides was holding a telephone. 'It's Comrade Lionidza.'

Ruslan grabbed the telephone. 'Sergo? What's the news?'

'They were shot on the way into their meeting. That's all I know.'

'Meeting? Didn't you tell them to cancel?'

'Yes. They said they'd think about it.'

'Are they going to be all right?'

'I don't know. I only know what it says on TV.'

'Is it on TV? Which channel?'

'Ksord-Akhtarian.'

There was a TV in one of the anterooms at the back of the hall, and Ruslan and his comrades crowded round it. A reporter was outside the hospital in Siterzola, a Ksordian town in the northeast. He said that Leila and Ksnis had been shot and were both seriously injured. There was footage of Leila and her companions walking past a jeering crowd and into the theatre for their meeting. Then shots rang out and there was pandemonium, with the camera crew and the crowd fleeing in all directions. When the cameraman had eventually recovered his nerve, he managed to film policemen carrying Leila and Ksnis into their cars and speeding off with sirens blazing.

Ruslan had hardly spared a thought for Leila at all that day. He cursed himself for not making her halt her speaking tour immediately, and he cursed Lionidza for not insisting that she cancel.

And he knew Mingrelsky was behind it, and probably Alavidza too.

Who else could it be?

Was this another consequence of their feud? Had he brought this upon Leila and Ksnis, the same as he may have brought the KGB down on Nina and the others?

He prayed that Leila and Ksnis would survive.

At eleven thirty, Ksord-Akhtarian TV closed down for the night. Ruslan and the others decided to return to Khosume and keep up with any developments on their car radio.

Some twenty kilometres from home, the radio station broadcast a statement by a hospital spokesman in Siterzola: 'I regret to inform you that at twelve eighteen this evening, Miss Leila Meipariani was pronounced dead. She had suffered a cardiac arrest as a result of two gunshot injuries. The condition of Mr Demna Ksnis remains serious, but the doctors don't think his life is in danger.'

Ruslan closed his eyes. He covered his face with his hands and wept.

Leila's funeral took place three days later in her home town, a small community of Ksords and Tatars twenty kilometres north of Khosume. Ruslan and Tamara went with Murad and Fatima, plus Ruslan's new bodyguard. Ruslan's mother and Giorgi were waiting for them.

They embraced and kissed, straightened their clothes and took the lift up to Leila's parents' flat. One of Leila's cousins met them and accepted their gifts of flowers and fruit. Leila's parents greeted Murad and Fatima as old friends, and they kissed, embraced and cried together. Leila's mother turned to Ruslan and shook his hand. 'Thank you for coming.'

'I'm so sorry, I really am.'

'Thank you,' said Leila's mother. She turned to Tamara: 'You must be Ruslan's wife. Thank you for coming.'

Tamara embraced them and kissed them.

Ruslan introduced his mother and Giorgi. 'She was a lovely girl,' said Giorgi. 'We're so sorry.'

'Thank you.'

'We're having two ceremonies,' Leila's father told them. 'We're going to the mosque first, for Janazah prayers. After that we'll go to the church for a Christian funeral. She'll be buried there, because she was a Christian.' His voice cracked at this point and he stopped speaking.

'Fatima, can you say a few words at the church?' asked Leila's mother.

'Of course.'

'And Ruslan, can you say something too?'

216

'Yes, of course. It'd be an honour.' Ruslan hoped he could do so without breaking down.

Other guests came in and Ruslan's group was swept outside the flat. They met Leila's two brothers and some of the innumerable supply of cousins she had spoken about. Murad and Fatima introduced Ruslan to a string of musicians and TV and record producers, some of them from as far afield as Moscow and Tatarstan. Leila's bass guitarist boyfriend was there. He cried on Ruslan's shoulder when he embraced him.

Lionidza and Jeltkov arrived, then Orbeliani and Ametov, each of them now accompanied by a bodyguard.

Soon afterwards, Nina turned up with Yakub Bovin's wife Marta. Ruslan hesitated for a moment, but then he greeted them both with four kisses and an embrace. Tamara, Giorgi and, somewhat reluctantly, Ruslan's mother embraced and kissed Nina, who introduced them to Marta.

'Do you know her parents?' Ruslan asked.

'I haven't met them.'

'I'll get Fatima to introduce you.'

The last big fish to arrive was northern Tatar leader Sultanov, who came with a large posse of tough looking young men, all of them with bulges under their jackets.

When it was time, Leila's parents and brothers led a lengthy procession of mourners towards the mosque, where Leila's body had been cleansed and wrapped in a shroud. Ruslan noticed her Tatar grandfather in a wheelchair ahead of him. He thought what an awful fate it must be to outlive a beloved grandchild.

The route was lined with Ksords and Tatars of all ages. At first, Ruslan assumed that these were a mixture of fans and friends and neighbours, but then he realised that the whole town was in mourning for Leila. She had been its favourite daughter, just as he was Vakesia's favourite son.

After ten minutes, they arrived at the mosque, a squat building in the Tatar style. Many Tatar guests went inside, along with a few Ksordian relatives and a TV camera crew. Ruslan, Tamara and a large crowd waited outside, listening to the prayers, which were relayed on loudspeakers. All the Tatars raised their hands in prayer, while the Ksords just stood in respectful silence.

Ruslan and Tamara held hands and leaned into each other. Ruslan listened to the prayers without understanding anything but their mournful tone. This made the ceremony more powerful for him than the Christian ceremony could ever be.

He had lost his faith at his father's funeral, which had taken place nearly twenty kilometres from his home in the nearest functioning church his mother could find. The whole village had turned out for Ruslan's father, as did several hundred Ksords and Tatars from neighbouring villages.

Ruslan remembered standing in the church with the priest banging on about resurrection and eternal life and how they would all meet again in Heaven. He just wanted to scream. For him, the whole point was that his father was dead and he would never see him again. The priest then spoke about God's love for us all and Ruslan just thought it was nonsense. His father had had a terrible life. How could God love him and let him have a life like that?

Now he thought the same about Leila. How could God love us all and let Mingrelsky's scum murder Leila? It made no sense to Ruslan.

But he also thought it was wonderful that the local mullah and priest were enlightened men who were prepared to bend the rules a little for this double funeral. If only more people could be like them, then there might never have been a need for this damned referendum in the first place.

After the Muslim ceremony, Leila's shrouded body was transferred to a coffin, which was draped with the Ksordian and Tatar flags and carried to a waiting hearse. Ruslan caught himself hoping that the two flags on her coffin would appear on the TV news that night. They would say something very important.

The funeral procession followed the hearse to the Ksordian church. The people lining the streets applauded as the hearse went by.

Ruslan, Tamara, Fatima and Murad went into the church, where they stood three rows from the front. After prayers, the priest invited one of Leila's cousins, a handsome young Ksord, to speak.

He spoke lovingly of Leila and the scrapes they had got into as children. Ruslan knew his stories from her speeches. She seemed to have been the leader of their gang, which had included both Ksords and Tatars. Ruslan guessed that she had never been a *good* girl. She had always been too full of energy and mischief for that.

Her cousin said how proud they all were when she became a star, but her success had never gone to her head. They had also been very proud when she got involved in politics, first in Akhtaria and then in the referendum campaign. 'We never thought it would come to this,' he said, and then quite suddenly he broke down. He turned away from the congregation and cried uncontrollably. A middle-aged Ksordian woman, perhaps his mother, ushered him back to his position in the front row.

The priest now invited Fatima to speak. She squeezed forward and walked to the front. She spoke in Russian about how they had met when Leila was still an impatient seventeen-year-old student. Leila had no time for the conventions that should have kept her off stage until she was qualified. She wanted to be on stage now. She wanted to sing now.

For a year, Leila had worked as one of her backing singers. 'Some backing singers, you just know they aren't going to be backing you for long. Leila was like that, and half way through our second tour together, my husband promoted her to be my warm-up act. But she was far too good for that, and by the end of the tour, it was obvious that she was ready to strike out on her own.'

Fatima reminded everyone how Leila had struck gold by translating Tatar folk songs into Ksord-Akhtarian and then rearranging them as rock songs. 'Her songs were just like her, half-Ksord, half-Tatar, and full of life and energy and humour. I was so proud of her. I used to boast to people: "Leila Meipariani started out as my backing singer, you know."'

She talked about how Leila had approached her and Murad a year ago, asking them to help her join Ruslan in Kvemodishi. 'She knew that war in Akhtaria would spell danger for Central Kubania, and she wanted to help Ruslan keep a lid on things. She told me how terrified she was of a war that would set her Ksordian and Tatar relatives against one another. And then, when things started to get tense here, it was Leila's idea to bring Ruslan back from hospital to get him involved again. She knew that he was the only one who could save us from ourselves.

'She asked me if I was prepared to help with the No Campaign. I said I'd think about it, but the fact of the matter is that I've never been interested in politics. I'm so ashamed to stand here now, with Leila in her coffin, and admit that I just couldn't be bothered to help.' Fatima paused for a moment. A solitary tear made its way down her cheek.

'Leila, you were the best of all of us, because if you thought it was right, you just went ahead and did it. You were so talented, not just at singing but at giving speeches and organising campaigns too. We'll take up your baton, Leila. I've spoken to lots of singers and musicians here today. We'll hold concerts in your memory all over Central Kubania, and the first one will be in Siterzola. And we'll sing your songs, and we'll honour your memory, and we'll mourn your death and celebrate your life. Goodbye my dear friend. We'll never forget you.'

She stopped talking and stood still for a moment. Then she walked back to stand between Tamara and Murad, who consoled her with a hand on her shoulder.

The priest invited Ruslan to speak and he squeezed through to the front. The TV lights were hot and dazzling. It would be some time before he could see the faces of the congregation.

Ruslan spoke in Ksord-Akhtarian. 'This is just too terrible for words, to see this wonderful young woman cut down. It's just appalling, and my heartfelt sympathies go out to her family and all those who loved her. I share the pain of your loss, and I wish I could find words to bring you some comfort.

'I first heard of Leila when she burst onto the scene with *Daffodils in the Springtime*. It was such a beautiful song and she sang it so well. We were very honoured when she came to sing it at our wedding.

'And then five years later, when she came to Kvemodishi to help me and Sergo Lionidza with our peace mission there, it was a bit of a surprise to have this vivacious young singer with us. But we soon learnt just how talented she was.. Do you remember when

Akhtarian TV tried to discredit us? Me and Sergo Lionidza didn't know what to do. It was only Leila who had the gumption to organise a proper response.

'There wouldn't be any campaign for a No vote if it weren't for Leila. Central Kubania would be sliding towards civil war and nobody would be doing anything to stop it. It was Leila who started everything, and she was a fantastic campaigner. She gave such a brilliant speech. She could silence hecklers by forcing them to laugh at her stories, some of them the same as the stories her young cousin told us here today.

'She talked about her family, Ksords and Tatars, her cousins and her uncles and her grandfathers. And she was so terrified of a war that would set these people she loved against one another.

'She knew that campaigning was dangerous. She knew Mingrelsky's men had threatened to kill her. Don't imagine she wasn't afraid, because I'm sure she was. But she was prepared to take risks for what she believed was right. She was prepared to risk everything.'

He paused and took a few deep breaths.

'We have to remember that Leila risked her life for a reason, and we have to remember that those who want a war took her life for a reason. Well, I've got a message for them. Yes, we're afraid of you, but like Leila, that's not going to stop us. We'll carry on what she started, and we'll draw inspiration from her courage. We're all here: me, Lionidza, Ametov, Orbeliani and Sultanov. And if you want to stop us, well you're going to have to shoot all of us, because we're so determined to prevent you from having your filthy war.'

Ruslan stopped, afraid that he had got carried away. He thought it was the worst speech he had ever given. Not like Fatima, who had struck exactly the right note.

After a moment, he looked at the priest. He walked back to stand by Tamara, who gave his arm a little squeeze. Leila's mother turned round and nodded in his direction. Her face was stained with tears, and when Ruslan saw her, he bowed his head and cried.

After the burial, Leila's parents and her brothers stood outside the churchyard, shaking the hands of the guests as they left. They embraced Murad and Fatima, and Leila's father thanked Fatima for her words.

'There was so much more I wanted to say.'

Then Ruslan's mother, Giorgi and Tamara shook their hands, and finally Ruslan, the last of their group. They all thanked him for coming and thanked him for his words. Ruslan felt so awful to be the object of their gratitude. He thought they should hate him for exposing Leila to danger and getting her killed.

Leila's father embraced Ruslan. 'We'll all be voting No.'

Her mother embraced him too. Then she held his hands and looked him firmly in the eye. Speaking in Tatar, she said, 'Be very careful, Ruslan Shanidza. They'll kill you next.'

Chapter Twenty-Five

RUSLAN RETREATED to a café with Tamara, his mother and Giorgi. His bodyguard sat near the door.

'Do you blame yourself?' Ruslan's mother asked.

'I don't know.'

'Remember you didn't recruit Leila,' said Tamara. 'She recruited you.'

'I know.'

Ruslan's mother spoke next: 'I remember when your father came to Vakesia with the other Partizans, after the massacre. We held a meeting to decide what to do, whether to stay in the village or to flee to East Ksordia. I wanted to go. I was desperate to get out of there.

'Your father was a lot like you, Ruslan. He was a born leader, very charismatic. He said it was our land and we should stay and fight for it. I think if it wasn't for him, we would probably have gone, but he won over most of the doubters. Apart from me. I still wanted to leave.

'About two weeks later, the Rebels attacked again. This time we were ready for them. We lost three men, but we killed seven Rebels and captured two. A few days later, the Rebels had another go, about sixty of them. They came at us from all sides. The Tatars down the road saved us. They tipped us off. Even so, it was touch and go. It really was. The fighting lasted all day, and in the evening, they launched a surprise attack and got into the centre of the village before we managed to beat them off.

'Next morning, we counterattacked. The only reason we could was all the ammunition we'd captured when they fled the night before. But we really caught them napping. We must have killed twenty altogether and we captured six. Your father interrogated them, and then we hanged them, just like we'd hanged the other two.'

Ruslan and Giorgi didn't react to this. Giorgi had witnessed everything, and Ruslan had grown up with the knowledge. Tamara, however, was shocked. Nobody had ever told her about the execution of captured Rebels.

'But we lost nine Partizans in those two days,' Ruslan's mother continued. 'And two more died of their injuries soon afterwards. Five civilians got caught in the crossfire: three children, a young mother and an old man. That's nineteen of our people who died in those battles.

'A few days after the final battle, I went into the church. We hadn't had a priest for years, but your father had reopened the church for funerals. He even insisted on giving the dead Rebels a Christian burial. We also kept the church open so people could have a place to pray. So I went in there, and I saw your father kneeling in front of the altar. He was crying.'

Ruslan and Giorgi both started. They had never heard about this before.

'I thought he was crying over your mother, Giorgi, and your little brother and sister. I nearly went out and left him alone with his tears, but I felt so sorry for him, so I went up and put my hand on his shoulder. Just a little gesture of sympathy. He looked up at me, and he stopped crying and stood up. I think he was embarrassed. I said I was sorry, I hadn't meant to disturb him.

'He shook his head and said, "I'm so sorry. I should have listened to you. It's my fault we stayed here, and now nineteen people are dead. If I'd listened to you, they would all still be alive." It's ironic, isn't it? Everyone in Vakesia thinks your father was a hero, because he led us when we beat off the Rebels. But he never thought that, never. He was always tortured by the thought of five dead civilians and fourteen dead Partizans. He never forgave himself for those nineteen deaths.'

That evening, Murad dropped Ruslan, Tamara and their bodyguard off at their house. They paid off their babysitter and Tamara went to check on Shota. Then the two of them went into the living room to wind down, leaving their bodyguard in the kitchen.

Tamara reached out and took Ruslan's hand. 'You okay?'

224

'No.'

They looked at each other and smiled.

'Do you remember your first promise, about Mingrelsky?'

'Of course.'

'Well I won't hold you to it.'

'Are you serious?'

'Yes. It doesn't make any difference now, does it? If they think they can get away with killing you, they will.' She stopped speaking for a moment so as not to lose control. 'You just have to make it politically impossible for them. That's your only defence.'

'Thank you.'

'I haven't released you from your second promise.'

'I'm not asking you to.' Ruslan was in fact dreading the moment he would have to choose between his marriage and his debt to those who supported him. Most of the time he managed to shelve the issue by telling himself that if he won the referendum he would never have to make that choice. But in his dark, pessimistic moments, fear of his second promise would eat away at him.

He squeezed Tamara's hand. 'You know who Lionidza's going to see tomorrow?'

'Yes.'

'Do you mind if I join him?'

'I think it'd be a good idea.'

'Can you help me stand up? I'll give him a call.'

She got up and pulled him to his feet. He walked out into the hallway and telephoned Lionidza.

'Can you pick me up tomorrow? I'm coming too.'

Lionidza laughed. 'I can't wait to see Tengiz Alavidza's face when you walk into the room.'

'He'll get plenty of warning. If my phone isn't bugged, you can bet yours is.'

The next morning, Ruslan travelled to Ronkoni with Lionidza and one of Leila's uncles, a grey-moustached Ksord in his late fifties. Lionidza had requested an appointment with his old acquaintance Tengiz Alavidza, Korgay's Minister of the Interior. Ruslan had expected Alavidza to refuse to meet him: eight months earlier,

Lionidza had almost caused a riot in the Federal Assembly when he accused Alavidza of being behind the attempt on Ruslan's life.

As they approached the Ministry, Lionidza said, 'I hope you're not going to cause a scene by refusing to shake his hand.'

Ruslan laughed. 'Not this time. I'd dearly love to go for his throat, though.'

The receptionist led them into an ornate room dominated by photographs of Korgay, Lenin and Yuri Andropov, the KGB chief who briefly ruled the Soviet Union from his deathbed in the mid-1980s.

Alavidza and an official came in and tersely shook hands with Ruslan, Lionidza and Leila's uncle, to whom he offered brief condolences. He invited his guests to sit on red and gold armchairs which, to Ruslan's relief, offered his back plenty of support.

Ruslan thanked Alavidza for agreeing to see them at such short notice and explained the reason for their visit. 'As you must know, our friend Leila Meipariani was murdered three days ago, and our colleague Demna Ksnis was seriously injured. There were a lot of witnesses to the shootings, several of whom have given good descriptions of the killers.'

Alavidza was taking this in, nodding his head.

'The descriptions are remarkably consistent, and six witnesses have identified one of the assassins. We have their sworn affidavits here with us.'

Alavidza raised his head a little, a sneer on his face. 'And who's this man these witnesses have identified?'

'Teqire Davidov, commander of the Second Battalion of the White Eagles.'

'Do you have these affidavits?'

Ruslan looked at Lionidza, who fumbled with the latch on his briefcase. He opened it and handed a wad of documents to Alavidza. 'These are copies.'

'Where are the originals?'

'In Siterzola.'

Alavidza spent a minute leafing through the documents. He passed each one to his official after he had skimmed it. 'Very interesting. Do you mind if I ask why you've brought these documents to me?'

'Because Davidov's in Ronkoni. Sergo, have you got the address he's staying at?'

Lionidza fumbled in his bag once more and produced a sheet of paper. He gave it to Alavidza, who glanced at it as if it were a snotty tissue and passed it to his official.

'How do you know he's there?'

'Journalist friends.'

'And what do you expect me to do about it?'

'Have him arrested for murder. I think you should also investigate his boss, while you're at it.'

'You mean Vakhtan Mingrelsky?'

'Yes.'

'He's got immunity from arrest. He's a member of the Federal Assembly.'

'I know, but that doesn't stop you investigating.'

'We'll look into it.'

'We'd appreciate that, but if I may be so bold, I think it would be a mistake for the police not to arrest Davidov immediately. Somebody might tip him off, and then he'd disappear to one of Mingrelsky's strongholds where the police can't touch him.'

Alavidza raised his head and sneered once again. 'You're a remarkable man, Mr Shanidza. As far as I'm aware, the only training you've ever had is in running long distances, but not only do you presume to lecture us about politics, but you also have the gall to tell me, a man who's been fighting political and economic crime for over thirty years, how to do my job.'

'Mr Alavidza, I'm here to secure justice for a woman who's been murdered. The evidence against Davidov is compelling, and there's no doubt about his ability to place himself beyond the reach of the police.'

'And there's no doubt in my mind about the ability of the police to make their own judgements about this case.'

'If Davidov were to flee Ronkoni before he was arrested, people might assume there was collusion.'

'Mr Shanidza, I don't doubt your sincerity, but your lack of political experience is sometimes rather too obvious.' He turned to Lionidza: 'I would have thought you would have learnt to restrain your young protégé by now, Sergo.'

Lionidza smiled. 'I've almost come to enjoy his indiscretions. I'm sure you'll agree that it would be a serious embarrassment for the government if Davidov were to get away.'

'And I'll tell you what else would be a serious embarrassment,' said Alavidza. 'It would be a serious embarrassment if we arrested a leading member of a patriotic militia which served our nation well in North Ksordia, and which may soon be called upon to do so again in Central Kubania, and if it then turned out that he was innocent of any crime and his name had been blackened by a discredited pacifist who was known to have a grudge against his commander, Vakhtan Mingrelsky.'

'But Davidov isn't innocent,' said Leila's uncle. 'He murdered my niece.'

'I can understand your feelings, Mr Meipariani. But you must understand that police work depends on carefully scrutinising the evidence.'

Leila's uncle could barely contain his fury: 'What you mean is that Davidov's your friend, and you plan to let him get away with it.'

'No. I'll tell the police to look into it properly.'

'Okay,' said Ruslan. 'I'll tell you what I'll do. I'll cancel my Ronkoni press conference this afternoon, and I'll call another one in Khosume at two o'clock tomorrow. That'll give the police twenty-four hours, which should be plenty of time. At my press conference, I'll name Davidov as Leila's killer and say that you know all about it. And either I'll praise you for your prompt action to deliver justice for this murder, or I'll say that your failure to take action points to official collusion.'

'Is that a threat, Mr Shanidza?'

'No, Mr Alavidza. It's a description of what's going to happen.'

'Really? Well, as I said, we'll look into the matter. I believe our meeting is now at an end. Good day.'

He left the room without shaking their hands.

'Do you think I cocked it up?' Ruslan asked Lionidza when they were back in their car.

'No, there's no way he was ever going to arrest Davidov.'

'Do you think he ordered the murder?' asked Leila's uncle.

'I don't know,' said Lionidza. 'I doubt it. He's probably pretty angry with Mingrelsky, but he won't move against Davidov.'

'I'm sorry,' Ruslan said to Leila's uncle. 'We've brought you here for nothing.'

'No you haven't. I've seen with my own eyes who's protecting the killers.'

Later that afternoon, they left their hotel and spent some time driving round Ronkoni. They soon worked out that two black Volgas were following them, working in tandem.

'Sergo, what is it with secret policemen and black Volgas,' Ruslan asked. 'They don't exactly make it hard for us do they?'

Lionidza laughed.

They needed to lose the Security Police before their next appointment, but they didn't really know how to do it, so they decided to telephone the Military Intelligence officer who had arranged the meeting to ask him for advice. Ruslan tried to use the enormous mobile that Murad had lent him, but he couldn't get a decent signal, so they stopped and used a phone box instead.

They were instructed to drive to the other side of town, park outside a restaurant and go in. The owner immediately led them out of the back door to an old Moskovich that was waiting. It took them to a small house just over a kilometre away to meet Zviad Qipiani, Korgay's Minister of Munitions.

A tall man in his mid-seventies with a gentle smile and dyed hair, Qipiani greeted Ruslan warmly: 'I've been looking forward to meeting you for so long. I've been a great admirer of yours for many years.'

'That's very kind of you.'

Ruslan introduced Lionidza, who had never actually met Qipiani.

'So you're Ruslan Shanidza's famous fixer.'

'Every Pele needs a Gérson.'

Qipiani shook hands with Leila's uncle and offered his condolences. He asked him about Leila, whether they had been close and how her murder had affected her family. 'I don't think you'll ever get over the grief, but you and her family should also be very proud of her. You should draw strength from that.'

'Thank you. We are proud of her. Very.'

Ruslan and his comrades told Qipiani about their meeting with Alavidza.

Qipiani shook his head. 'That man's such a gangster. He's got a lot of blood on his hands, quite possibly several litres of yours, Ruslan. Orbeliani and I have often felt very uncomfortable in the same government as him.'

'But Orbeliani's left the government now,' said Ruslan.

'Yes, and I suppose you've come here to ask me to do the same.'

'Not necessarily. I hope you do, but today we came to get justice for Leila.'

Qipiani nodded. 'Yes, of course, but I'm afraid Alavidza could never bring Davidov to trial. He knows too much, and so do his friends in the White Eagles.' He looked at Leila's uncle. 'I'm sorry.'

'Then how can you stay in the government with him?' asked Leila's uncle.

'Because we're at war. It's not as if the Rebel government is any better than us. We have to defend the North Ksords against the likes of Sulkavidza.'

'I respect what you're doing,' said Ruslan. 'But there is another strategy.'

'What? To join you?'

'Yes.'

'Orbeliani tried to persuade me, but it's different for him. He's from Central Kubania, but I'm Ronkoni born and bred.'

'But you make a difference. When we argue that Muslim countries won't sell us arms if we attack the Tatars, people just say, "Oh, don't worry. Qipiani will come up with something."'

'Yes, that's what people here say too. And they're wrong. The only way we can win the war is if we deliver a knockout blow right at the start. If not, the enemy will eventually regroup, and they'll have no problems getting supplies.'

'And can we deliver a knockout blow?'

'I doubt it. I can't really see us taking Siriach'Sichi. Can you?'

'So we may lose?'

'I don't think we'll lose as such, but we're unlikely to win. We're bound to capture the northeast and the east. The big losers are going to be the Tatars who live there. But there's a very real danger of Akhtaria winning in the west, and possibly even driving out the North Ksords.'

'But what if there's no war?'

'You mean if you get a No vote?'

'Yes.'

'Do you really think you can?'

'If there was a vote today, we'd get twenty or twenty-five percent. But we've got a bandwagon rolling, and we need to keep finding new recruits to keep it going.'

'And you've only got thirteen more days to do it.'

'Which is why we need people like you.'

'But I'm not a proper politician. I'm a businessman, a technocrat. Orbeliani brought a base of support to your campaign, but I haven't got anything like that. All I have is mobile phones and business acumen. That's what the Minister of Munitions' job is: business, production.'

'You shouldn't underestimate your prestige,' said Lionidza, 'A lot of Ksords will listen to you, especially the military. They trust you.'

'I'll think about it, gentlemen. I promise you I'll think very seriously about what you say. And I'll do what I can for Leila Meipariani at the next cabinet meeting.'

Alavidza, meanwhile, wasted no time in protecting Mingrelsky's man Davidov, who left Ronkoni that afternoon. A journalist tried to follow him, but his car was hijacked at a road junction by a group of armed men, who beat him up and slashed his tyres.

At the same time, in the Central Kuban town of Chitaskiri, the police picked up an Akhtarian who vaguely resembled Davidov. They whisked him to Siterzola, where the eleven witnesses who had named or described Davidov were rounded up for an identity parade. They all picked out the hapless Akhtarian, whose confession to the murder was broadcast on Ksordian TV's lunchtime news the next day.

At his press conference shortly afterwards, Ruslan denounced the arrest of the Akhtarian suspect and named Davidov as Leila's killer and Mingrelsky and Alavidza as his protectors. To Ruslan's left sat the reporter who had attempted to follow Davidov as he fled Ronkoni. His broken nose, black eyes and missing front teeth provided compelling collaboration of his story, but Ruslan deeply regretted having given Alavidza so much warning.

He left Khosume again almost immediately. He, Lionidza and Nina's old lawyer Zourab Orbeliani headed for a small Ksordian village where they had arranged to meet Bebur Chikradza, the Ksordian colonel who had befriended Ruslan during his peace mission the previous year.

Ruslan wondered how Lionidza, a high flyer in the old Communist regime, would enjoy sharing a car with Orbeliani, who had defended just about every dissident the Ksord-Akhtarian Communists put on trial in the 1980s. In fact, the two men got on well, and they discovered that they had something in common. Both of them had served in government with Korgay.

During Comrade Zikladza's years as ruler of Ksordia-Akhtaria, Lionidza, Korgay and, until his downfall, Aleksander Mingrelsky had been his most trusted colleagues. Ruslan asked Lionidza which of the three had been closest to Zikladza.

'I suppose we all wondered that, and we all wondered who would be his eventual successor. Well, I certainly did. Comrade Zikladza liked to keep us guessing. Whenever he bollocked one of us, he nearly always did it in front of the other two.'

Ruslan and Orbeliani laughed.

'So what did he use to bollock you for?' Ruslan asked.

'Me? Petit-bourgeois sentimentality.'

'I can imagine that.'

'You know what it was with Alexander Mingrelsky?'

'I know this,' said Ruslan. 'Women.'

Lionidza grinned. 'He couldn't keep his hands off them. He once told me he would never deflower a virgin but all married women were fair game. He made a lot of enemies in the middle ranks of the Party. Men don't like it when you bed their wives, funnily enough.'

'Was Korgay a womaniser too?' Ruslan asked.

'No, not at all.'

'Do you remember that reception after I won Olympic gold? Tamara couldn't get away from him.'

'Really? It's not what you think. If Korgay chatted up someone's wife, he wouldn't be trying to bed her. He'd just be trying to use her to recruit her husband to his coterie of supporters. Maybe he was hoping to recruit you, Ruslan.'

'What, alongside Mingrelsky and Alavidza? I don't think so.'

'So what did Korgay do that got him into trouble?' Orbeliani asked.

'Comrade Zikladza always called him a chameleon. Korgay never ever disagreed with the boss about anything, but when he was with someone else who criticised him, Korgay might nod his head and hint that he agreed, without actually saying so. If Comrade Zikladza found out, he'd fly into a rage.'

'I can imagine that,' said Orbeliani. 'We could never work him out. Was he the arch villain? Or was he just an ambitious politician who was prepared to ally himself with some very unsavoury characters?'

Lionidza nodded. 'The thing you have to remember about Korgay is that he's not exactly overburdened by scruples.'

Colonel Chikradza greeted Ruslan with an enormous bear hug. 'I thought that cockroach Mingrelsky had killed you,' he said in his gentle West Ksordian accent. 'It's good to see you alive, even if you do look like death warmed up.'

Chikradza introduced his companions, half a dozen senior military commanders, all of them West Ksords. Ruslan recognised two of them from his time in North Ksordia. The officers offered condolences for Leila's death. 'A lot of people in the army are very angry about that, especially the West Ksords among us. There's nothing more shameful than the murder of a woman.'

They questioned Ruslan and his comrades at length about the progress their campaign was making. They weren't hostile but were deeply sceptical.

'Aren't you legitimising the referendum by agreeing to take part?'

'No we're not,' said Ruslan. 'Democracy isn't the dictatorship of the majority. It's a system in which every voice is heard. If the Tatars and the Akhtarians cobble together a majority, that doesn't give them the right to dictate to the Ksords.'

'So you'll be with us if you lose the vote?'

'Yes. At the end of the day I'm a Ksord too.'

'Hear hear,' said Orbeliani.

'That's good to hear.'

Ruslan noticed that Lionidza had remained silent at this point.

'But the thought of the Tatars being driven from their homes just appals us,' said Ruslan. 'We don't know if we could support that.'

'It may not happen,' said Chikradza, 'at least not in the north. Did you know that Sultanov contacted us before he went over to you?'

'No?' Ruslan wondered what the slippery Tatar baron was up to now.

'Yes, he offered us a deal. He'll get the northern Tatars to vote No so as to split them from Yakub Bovin. Then, when the war starts, he'll give us free passage through the areas he controls. In return we have to guarantee the safety of the Tatars in those areas.'

'And did you agree to that?'

'Yes. We signed a treaty.'

'Does the Ksordian leadership know?'

'Oh yes. They signed it too.'

Ruslan, Lionidza and Orbeliani looked at each other in astonishment. They knew nothing of this.

'Sultanov says there's no way you'll win this referendum,' said Chikradza. 'He's just trying to save the Tatars in the north and northeast.'

'But why should the Ksords do a deal with Sultanov?' Orbeliani asked.

'We have to deliver a knockout blow in the first few weeks. We need to avoid getting bogged down in the north. Then, if we can capture Timashevsk and Khosume quickly, we can send all our forces west to take Siriach'Sichi and the Taman Peninsula. If we succeed, the Russians will abandon the Rebels and do a deal with us.'

Ruslan was astonished by the boldness of the Ksords' strategy. He realised that once more he was being used, just as he had been used in Akhtaria. Sultanov was using him to protect his fiefdom, and Korgay was using him to split the Tatars.

'Let them use me,' he thought to himself. 'I'll use them too. And then at the end, we'll see which of us gets what he wants.'

Lionidza steered the conversation onto the topics they had come to discuss. 'We want to ask you two things. First, can the military offer some security for our campaign in Ksordian areas?'

Chikradza frowned. 'The officer corps are divided about you. You've got lots of friends in the army, Mr Lionidza, especially at the top. Military Intelligence are quite sympathetic to your campaign. Maybe thirty percent of army officers like you and another thirty percent are neutral, but there are plenty who hate your guts. And all the various paramilitary groups, they really can't stand you. You should hear what Mingrelsky says about you, Ruslan.'

'What?'

'He says he's going to offer your wife up to his boys for a gangbang.'

Ruslan felt a deep surge of adrenalin course around his body. Tamara was extremely vulnerable alone in the house with Shota. As soon as the meeting was over, he would tell Lionidza to find her some bodyguards.

'If Alavidza gives him the nod again, Mingrelsky will be very happy to kill you,' said Chikradza.

'And he won't cock it up next time,' said another officer.

They got out a map of Central Kubania and, amid much debate, marked out the places that could be made safe for the No Campaign and those that could not. They decided the military could protect them in just over half the Ksordian areas, including most of the large towns and cities.

'That's great,' said Ruslan. 'Thank you very much.'

'You had a second question,' said Chikradza. 'What is it?'

'What happens if we win?'

The officers all looked at each other. 'You mean if you get a No vote?'

'Exactly.'

'Everybody assumes you're going to lose.'

'We're in this to win,' said Ruslan. 'That's why we need to know what you'll do if we're successful.'

'Well, if the Tatars don't take Central Kubania out of Ksordia, we don't really have any reason to go to war with them. But the Rebels in Siriach'Sichi are another matter.'

'Our broadcast has created a lot of tension in Siriach'Sichi,' said Lionidza, 'between the Akhtarians and the Tatars.'

Chikradza and the other officers laughed. Ruslan guessed that they knew the footage of the Mayor of Siriach'Sichi had come from Military Intelligence.

'If we do win the referendum,' said Orbeliani, 'and if relations between the Ksords and the Tatars improve, they might help us to break the Akhtarian grip on Siriach'Sichi.'

'If you win the referendum.'

'If we win. And we'd need some sane people in the Ksordian Army arguing for moderation.'

'You'll get that,' said Chikradza. 'But you have to win the referendum first.'

Ruslan put on his most innocent of smiles. 'If some of the troops were encouraged to vote No, that might help.'

'Encouraged or ordered?'

'Let's say strongly encouraged.'

The officers all laughed. Ruslan knew that Orbeliani didn't approve, but he was only interested in votes. He didn't care how he got them.

After the meeting, Ruslan, Lionidza and Orbeliani headed for Kikari, where they would stay the night. As they sped through the countryside, Ruslan looked out of the car window. Almost all the snow had melted from the fields and the first wave of daffodils was

236

already out, a patchy green and yellow carpet on the embankment leading down from the road. Daffodils held a special place in Ruslan's heart. They reminded him of that beautiful day with Tamara in the market in Menzelinsk. That was why Leila's song had always been special to him, and why it had been so perfect when she had sung it at their wedding.

But now he felt the pain of Leila's death wash over him. He wondered if he would ever be able to look at a daffodil again without this terrible sense of loss and grief.

Chapter Twenty-Six

THE NEXT morning, Ruslan, Lionidza and Orbeliani went to Siterzola for Leila's first memorial concert. After visiting the injured trade unionist Demna Ksnis in hospital, they joined an emotional pilgrimage to the spot where Leila had fallen. Flashlights flashed and cameras whirred as Ruslan made his contribution to the carpet of daffodils that lay there.

Leila's relatives were all there, Ksords and Tatars together. They embraced him and kissed him.

'Thank you for trying to get justice for her,' said Leila's mother.

'We won't stop trying.'

'Thank you.'

He wished they would stop thanking him.

Lionidza came up to Ruslan in a state of great excitement. 'You must come and hear what Fatima's saying.' He looked at Leila's parents. 'Maybe you should come too. We'd need your approval for this.'

He led them to where Fatima and Murad were standing with Ametov and some musicians, but he wouldn't let Fatima say anything until he had assembled the rest of the No Campaign leadership.

'Okay Fatima, tell them.'

'Well, Sergo was saying you should make the campaign slogan "I will if you will." You know, Ksords find a Tatar or an Akhtarian friend, and the Ksord promises to vote No if the other one promises to vote No.'

This was nothing new. Lionidza had been pushing this idea for some time.

'Well, Ruslan, you know your mother said the daffodils would be at their best on polling day.'

'She's always right about that.'

'Well, the daffodil's Leila's flower, isn't it? So as a tribute to her, you should make the daffodil a symbol of the campaign. You know, people give each other a daffodil to say, "I will if you will." You can use Leila's song: *Daffodils in the Springtime*.'

Ruslan smiled his biggest smile for months. 'Fatima, I always said you were a genius.'

The others were all enthusiastic too, apart from Orbeliani, who favoured a greater emphasis on argument and debate.

'Zourab, it's not as if this is all we'll do,' said Ruslan. 'We'll still argue our case. But this is such a good symbol, we'd be mad if we didn't use it.'

'All right, I'll go along with it.'

Lionidza looked at Leila's parents. 'Do we have your permission?'

'Of course,' said her mother. 'She'd be so proud if you used her song.'

'Right,' said Murad, 'this is what we'll do: we do the concert as planned, but with *Daffodils* as the finale, with everyone on stage. Ruslan, you give a little speech, very short, about Leila and daffodils, "I will if you will" and what have you. Fatima, you do the verses and everyone does the chorus. Apart from you, Ruslan. I don't want you singing.'

Ruslan smiled. 'Nor do I, believe me.'

'Hey,' said Lionidza, 'we should send some people round the local markets to buy all the daffodils we can find and then hand them out after the song.'

'Good thinking,' said Murad. 'And we should send some people to harvest wild flowers by the roadside too. I saw thousands on my way here.'

Ametov took hold of Lionidza's arm. 'Have you got many activists here?'

'Loads.'

'Okay, let's get your people and my people onto it.'

Lionidza nodded eagerly.

'I've got lots of people too,' said Sultanov's man Selim Mustafayev.

'Great,' said Lionidza. 'I'll get some cash out of the bank. We're going to need it.'

The three of them strode off together, the ex-Communist, the ex-dissident trade unionist and the Tatar capitalist baron's retainer. It amused and delighted Ruslan to see their unity of purpose.

The concert, which was held in Siterzola's Park of Rest and Culture, began at three in the afternoon, an odd time to hold such an event in the middle of the week, but the organisers were concerned that the audience should be able to get back home before dark. Even though the local Ksordian military had guaranteed their safety, everyone was nervous about such a large number of Tatars venturing into militant Ksordian territory at a time of great tension. They were particularly afraid of Mingrelsky's White Eagles.

(In fact the military had devised a foolproof plan to prevent trouble from that direction. They arrested a dozen of Mingrelsky's senior officers and informed him that they would be shot at once if anyone attending the concert were molested.)

The concert was a triumph, with a massive crowd that filled the park to bursting. Most were Ksords and Tatars, with just a sprinkling of Akhtarians. This reflected the ethnic composition of the performers, whose number didn't include any major Akhtarian artists. However, Murad had assembled enough big names to get the concert broadcast live on several radio stations. Tatar TV would show a half-hour programme of highlights the following evening.

At the end of the concert, when all the artists had assembled onstage for their finale, Ruslan went out to give his speech, a bunch of daffodils in his hand. The audience gave him an enormous ovation, as big as anything they had given any of the performers.

'Friends,' he said in Russian once the tumult had died down. 'Ksords, Tatars, Akhtarians.'

This brought forth another lengthy round of applause and cheering.

'Six days ago, something terrible happened in this town.'

The audience was suddenly silent.

'Six days ago one of my dearest friends and one of the most exceptional people I've ever met was brutally cut down. And we know who killed her."

Pandemonium. Shouts of 'Da!' 'Ha'a' and 'Yoye' ('Yes' in Russian, Ksord-Akhtarian and Tatar), 'Down with Mingrelsky!'

'And we know why they killed her. Because she proved, by her very existence, that people of different ethnic backgrounds don't need to hate one another.'

Applause.

'We don't need to fear one another.'

Applause.

'Just sometimes, we need to listen to one another.'

Applause.

'And if our leaders won't listen to one another, then we have to bang their heads together. Hard.'

Applause and cheering that seemed to go on forever.

'We're here today to celebrate the life of Leila Meipariani, and we'll finish with the song that made her famous.'

The audience applauded and cheered.

'But first, I'd like to say that in honour of Leila, we're going to make the daffodil the symbol of our campaign. We ask every Ksord to find a Tatar or an Akhtarian friend or neighbour or workmate, and give them a daffodil and say: "I will if you will. I'll vote No if you promise to vote No." And we ask every Tatar and every Akhtarian to find a Ksordian friend or neighbour or workmate. Give them a daffodil and say: "I will if you will."'

Ruslan was silent. For a moment, the crowd didn't respond. It was as if it took a little time for the idea to sink in. And then someone applauded and soon the whole audience was clapping, cheering and whistling.

'And if you take your friend's daffodil,' Ruslan realised that they couldn't hear him, so he repeated himself, this time much louder. 'And if you take your friend's daffodil, your neighbour's daffodil, your workmate's daffodil, then remember, that's your solemn vow. Because Leila died so that we could make this promise.'

Silence descended on the park.

Ruslan broke it by saying, 'Thank you' and throwing his daffodils into the crowd. They cheered and clapped and shouted, 'Shanidza, Shanidza, Shanidza.' He stood and accepted their applause for a minute. Then he waved and turned round, embraced Fatima and some of the other artists and finally left the stage.

Fatima walked up to the microphone. 'Ladies and gentlemen: Ruslan Shanidza.'

More thunderous applause.

She waited until it died down, and then she nodded to the musicians, and as they played, she began to sing in her wondrous voice.

'Give me daffodils in the springtime
As a token of your love.
Hold my hand in the gentle sunshine
While the birds sing their songs for us.
We'll walk together in the fairs and markets,
So that everyone can see we are one.'

Fatima sang the verses and the other artists and the audience joined in for the chorus. When the song was over and the applause had died down, Lionidza's, Ametov's and Selim Mustafayev's activists ran and pushed their way around and through the audience, handing out bunches and bunches of daffodils, throwing them from the stage, asking people to pass them round to make sure that everyone in the audience had one.

Fatima took the microphone again. 'Ksords, find a Tatar or an Akhtarian. Give them your daffodil. Say, "I will if you will." Tatars, Akhtarians, find a Ksord. Give them your daffodil. "I will if you will."'

And then in the park, there unfolded the extraordinary scene of thousands of people walking up to strangers and offering them their daffodil. They swapped flowers and shook hands, embraced and exchanged four kisses. And almost at once, many of them would go off in search of another person with whom they could exchange their newly acquired flower. Lots of them had tears in their eyes as they embraced people they had never met before and would most likely never meet again.

The leaders of the No campaign met the next morning. They started with a two-minute silence for Leila that reduced both Ruslan and Lionidza to tears. They and Orbeliani reported back on their meetings with Alavidza, Qipiani and the army officers. This was followed by a debate on whether or not they should resume their public meetings.

'Even if we do,' said Ametov, 'it's not enough. We won't win if we confine ourselves to public meetings. We need to get on TV.'

'And how are we going to do that?' said Lionidza. 'It turns out that the post-Communist governments are no better than we were when it comes to giving the opposition airtime on TV.'

Ruslan couldn't resist teasing him: 'Do I detect a hint of self-justification there?'

'Far be it from me.'

Everyone laughed.

'With Korgay and the Akhtarians it's hardly a surprise,' said Ruslan. 'But Yakub Bovin really should know better.'

'So why don't you say that to him,' said Orbeliani. 'Put it in an open letter.'

The leadership delegated Ruslan to do precisely that, and he drafted the letter that afternoon. Lionidza persuaded him that he would be more likely to generate headlines if he addressed Nina too.

'Dear Nina and Yakub,
'I write to you in the spirit of a friendship that goes back many years, a friendship which I hope will survive our finding ourselves on opposite sides in this referendum campaign.
'Eleven years ago, when I was your co-defendant at the trial of the Ronkoni Committee for Truth, we were critical of many aspects of Communist rule, among them the Party's stranglehold over the media. We all dreamed of a day when every voice would be

heard, including, or perhaps even especially, those that were critical of the government.

'Today I find myself part of a campaign against the policies of a regional government of which you are leading members. And yet our campaign is all but excluded from the Central Kuban TV channels. The news features the sometimes tragic events surrounding our campaign but never deals with our arguments. Under pressure from the Organisation for Security and Co-operation in Europe, you have granted us two broadcasts. But in almost two months of campaigning, we have not been interviewed on TV or radio once and have never been invited to a studio debate with any representative of the regional government.

'The TV stations controlled by Korgay and the Akhtarian government pretend that we do not exist. I expected as much from them, but I have to say that I expected better from you.

'With affection and respect.

'Yours,

'Ruslan'

The letter made the front pages of several pro-independence newspapers, and within days it began to bear fruit. Lionidza was subjected to a ferocious grilling by one of the Ksord-Akhtarian TV station's senior correspondents, though he was enough of an old pro to more than hold his own.

Tatar TV sent Ruslan and Ametov an invitation to a studio debate with leading members of Yakub's party. Ruslan was reluctant to take part, fearful that his Tatar wasn't up to the task, but the TV station agreed to let him bring an interpreter to help out if he got into difficulty.

The Ksord-Akhtarian channel invited him to debate against Nina. Ruslan insisted that all shades of Ksordian opinion should be represented, including someone from the pro-boycott camp. Nina concurred, and the deputy leader of the Central Kuban Ksords, a professor of English literature who had once been one of the Soviet Union's leading Shakespeare scholars, agreed to take part.

Meanwhile, Ruslan's gruelling schedule of meetings and rallies had resumed. He felt much safer now. Not only were the army on hand to offer protection, but audiences had more than quadrupled in size and supporters now vastly outnumbered troublemakers.

Between meetings came hour after hour of coaching for the debates, plus an intensive course in the Tatar words and expressions he was going to need.

The Tatar debate itself turned out to be something of an anti-climax. Both sides managed to stay courteous and polite, even when things got heated. Ruslan found it hard to keep up and had to call upon his translator or revert to Russian several times. He felt that both sides had scored points, the No campaigners with the defencelessness of the Tatars against the onslaught the Ksords were preparing, the Yes campaigners with the question of how it was proposed to make Korgay engage in serious peace talks. Ruslan knew he would need a better answer to this point.

The Ksordian debate was billed by the press as something of a soap opera, and Ruslan was sure it would attract a large audience. He, Nina and the professor greeted each other cordially before the start. Their opening statements were predictable and moderate. Then the three of them laid into one another. Nina said the professor had fallen into the company of gangsters and murderers and Ruslan was guilty of crushing naivety. The professor accused both Ruslan and Nina of being traitors to the Ksordian nation.

Ruslan did his best to calm things down and get his points across, but he half expected Nina and the professor to come to blows at any minute.

He tried to use the vociferousness of their argument to his advantage. 'Can't you see it, Nina? Can't you see how angry the Ksords are? There's no way you can get them to accept an independent Central Kubania.'

'You think we can sit down with the likes of Korgay, Alavidza and Mingrelsky and come to a deal? Come on, Ruslan, get real. Who do you think ordered the attempt on your life? Who do you think was behind Leila Meipariani's murder?'

Ruslan had his answer ready. 'The Ksordian government is the same as the Akhtarian government. Both of them contain extremists with blood on their hands and both contain decent people. What we have to do with a No vote is to compel Korgay and Eristov to back the moderates.'

Nina answered back, but Ruslan felt he had beaten off her heaviest weapon.

After closing statements and the moderator's rather anxious winding up, the studio lights darkened and the three participants sat still for the closing credits. The professor then departed without so much as a glance at the other two. Ruslan and Nina stood up and faced each other uneasily.

'Thanks for the debate, Nina.'

'I could happily throttle you right now.'

'You'd better not. Your friends and my friends are going to need to be on speaking terms after the vote.'

She smiled. 'Okay. I'll make a very big sacrifice for my principles and not throttle you.'

They then exchanged four kisses and parted.

Someone at the TV station leaked their conversation to the press. Several newspapers gave it almost as much prominence as they gave to the substance of the debate.

After that it was back to the campaign: an almost non-stop procession of meetings, press conferences and interviews that would take Ruslan to Kikari, Timashevsk, Siriach'Sichi, Moidan'Abasha, Abinsk, and finally, on the day before the referendum, to a rally in the streets of Khosume.

By now, the regional government and the Ksordian leadership were taking the No Campaign very seriously indeed. There were no reliable opinion polls, but all the evidence pointed to the beginnings of a seismic shift in Tatar and Ksordian opinion, particularly among those communities most likely to be vulnerable in the event of civil war. Akhtarians, however, remained stubbornly pro-independence.

The daffodil had become a very popular fashion accessory, and the weekend before the referendum, many Ksords could be seen with one pinned to their breast on the spring promenades. Attendance at the No Campaign's public meetings had grown exponentially. Ruslan could fill the main square in any town or city he went to, and the local peasants would flood in to sell daffodils. Ruslan would sometimes joke that the peasantry would vote No because they were making so much money that it would seem churlish to do otherwise.

He found the campaign exhausting but exhilarating. The huge meetings gave him an enormous buzz. There were very few hecklers now. Any who dared to raise their voices would be jeered, and the crowd would applaud Ruslan's putdowns enthusiastically.

He didn't worry about death threats, largely because he never knew anything about them. Working on the assumption that an attempt on his life before the referendum was highly unlikely, he had instructed his bodyguard to keep any death threats from him. 'Don't say anything to me unless you decide I have to cancel an appearance.'

Tamara was receiving death threats too. She told Lionidza but asked him to keep it secret from Ruslan.

He was very reluctant: 'He'll skin me alive if anything happens to you.'

'They're only threatening me to get at him. He's got enough on his plate.' She soon discovered, however, that knowing you are unlikely to be attacked doesn't make you feel safe, and she began to have problems with her nerves once more.

Ruslan saw nothing of Tamara and Shota for five days between his press conference and first Sunday in March, when he finally had a chance to go home. An excited Shota jumped and clambered all over him, delighted to see him in the flesh rather than on TV. He was irrepressible, and Ruslan had to watch much of the No Campaign's second broadcast lying on the floor playing rough and tumble with him.

The broadcast contained two strands. The first was a potted visual history of the campaign. This was interwoven with the second strand: shots of people raising daffodils to the camera and saying, 'I will if you will.'

The potted history started with the smaller early meetings. Then came excerpts from Zikladza and Orbeliani's statements of support, followed by shots of better attended meetings with fighting in the audience and Ruslan and the others splattered by eggs and flour bombs. After this came film of the attack on Leila and Ksnis, with the scenes of panic and policemen carrying the dying Leila. Her funeral was next, with the Ksordian and Tatar flags on her coffin and Ruslan's challenge to her killers.

This was followed by Fatima at the concert, instructing people to find a partner for the exchange of daffodils. Next came Ruslan debating in Tatar and then Nina and the Ksordian professor furious with each other. After this, there were scenes from the huge open-air meetings of the last few days.

Murad had re-edited drastically on the morning of the broadcast, after Korgay's Minister of Munitions Zviad Qipiani dramatically resigned from the Ksordian government the previous evening. Not entirely sober, Qipiani had called a dozen reporters to his house and informed them of his decision to resign, a decision that he had not yet communicated to the President. Lionidza had insisted that Murad should include as much of Qipiani's statement as possible: 'It's pure dynamite.'

'For the last nine months,' Qipiani had said. 'I've remained a member of President Korgay's government despite serious misgivings about the conduct of the war in Akhtaria and the gangsterism with which President Korgay has been so willing to associate himself, most recently in the shameful protection offered to Leila Meipariani's killer. I remained in the government because Ksordia was at war, and I believed that I had to do what I could to help protect the North Ksords.

'For some time now, President Korgay has pursued a foolish and aggressive policy towards the Central Kuban Tatars, a policy that couldn't have been more disastrous if it had been deliberately designed to drive them into the arms of our Akhtarian enemies.'

Ruslan was surprised to see the word 'enemies' included. It meant the No Campaign had given up all hope of winning over

Akhtarian opinion. A No vote could only come from Ksords and Tatars, and this broadcast was aimed at them.

'I've tried to make President Korgay and his ministers understand that this policy is suicidal. Let there be no doubt about this: we would have lost the Akhtarian war were it not for the military supplies we received from Islamic countries such as Turkey and Iran. And if we attack the Tatars, these countries won't sell us a single bullet. We'll find ourselves isolated and fighting a war we cannot win.

'President Korgay is planning a genocidal war against the Tatars that will blacken the name of Ksordia for generations. I've done everything in my power to persuade him to change course, but I'm sorry to say I've failed. Now I've examined my conscience, and I've concluded that I can no longer be a part of this government. I am consequently resigning. There's now only one thing that can prevent President Korgay's futile and disastrous war, and that's a No vote by the people of Central Kubania.'

Ruslan thought Lionidza had miscalculated. The broadcast had wasted too much valuable time on Qipiani.

He was much happier with the second strand of the broadcast: film of a seemingly random mix of ordinary citizens and celebrities raising their daffodils to the camera. This was woven into the potted history so that the broadcast flitted between the two. Near the beginning two old men, one a Tatar, the other a Ksord, raised their daffodils and said 'I will if you will.' Then came two pop singers and two shop assistants, followed by former Communist strongman Comrade Zikladza and a senior Tatar ex-Communist and then Tatar trade unionist Ametov and his injured Ksordian colleague Ksnis.

Next came three factory workers, a heavy metal rock group, four traffic policemen, a group of five actors, six students, seven bus drivers, seven of the Spartak Khosume football team, a group of eight teachers, nine stars of a Tatar soap opera. Gradually the groups were getting bigger, reinforcing the impression of an unstoppable bandwagon. Next came all of the Bryukhovetskaya football team, a dozen firemen, peasants in a market, a large group of doctors and nurses, a studio full of pop stars, the crowd at one of Orbeliani's rallies, the crowd at one of Ruslan's.

Towards the end, Ruslan detected the faintest trace of the music from Leila's daffodil song. This gradually got louder and louder, until right at the end, there was film of Leila singing at an open-air concert. Tears came to Ruslan's eyes as he watched her.

She finished her song and bowed to rapturous applause. The camera focused on her face as it was lit up by that lipstick grin. The image faded to black, but the applause continued. Then silence, and in Russian the words: 'This broadcast is dedicated to the memory of Leila Meipariani, 1968-1993.'

Qipiani's defection may have made little impact on public opinion, but it induced near panic among the senior ranks of the Ksordian military. All their plans had been based on the assumption that he would be there to make sure they could use enough ammunition to win decisive victories in the early stages of the war. Without Qipiani, there was a strong possibility that they would never be able to mount a massive offensive against the Akhtarians in the west. If as a result, the Akhtarians held onto Siriach'Sichi and the Taman Peninsula, the Ksords might run out of ammunition, leaving the Akhtarians in a position to drive them out of North Ksordia and all of western Central Kubania.

Publicly at least, the Ksordian high command continued to support the boycott. But Military Intelligence began to give the No Campaign active assistance, and several senior commanders decided to order their troops to vote No.

However, the Ksordian political leadership wasn't finished yet. The day after the broadcast, they announced that they would prevent the referendum from being held at all in the areas they controlled.

This threatened to hand victory to the Yes campaign. Ksords, after all, could almost be guaranteed to vote No if they voted at all, and those Tatars who lived as a threatened minority in Ksord-controlled areas were precisely the members of their community most likely to vote No.

The Campaign Committee gave Ruslan, Lionidza and Orbeliani the task of frustrating this boycott-from-above. And so, instead of the endless round of rallies and interviews that he had been expecting, Ruslan found himself dispatched to militant Ksordian strongholds in the north and east, where he spent much of his time talking to groups of army officers, police chiefs and local politicians, trying to persuade them to allow the referendum to go ahead.

Ksordian Military Intelligence set up many of the meetings. They also advised the No Campaign to cancel all public meetings and rallies planned in Ksordian areas. 'Alavidza's got Mingrelsky on your case. First chance they get, the White Eagles are going to throw a hand grenade into the crowd and blame it on the Rebels.'

There was more to come. On the Friday before polling, the bodyguards cancelled all Ruslan, Lionidza's and Orbeliani's appointments. 'Military Intelligence say you'll be dead before you get to the first one.'

'Can't we surround ourselves with troops?'

'It wouldn't help, Mingrelsky's planning to zap your cars with anti-tank missiles.'

And so, on the penultimate morning of the campaign, Ruslan found himself kicking his heels in campaign headquarters with little to do. There would be one more press conference, a final round of interviews and a massive No rally in Khosume on Saturday afternoon whose size would be matched by the Yes crowd in another part of the city centre that evening.

At the end of the No rally, Lionidza gestured Ruslan to have a private word. They retreated to one of the vans that had brought the loudspeakers.

'Are you going to keep your promise to Tamara?'

'I honestly don't know. I have to choose between betraying all the people who've put their trust in me or betraying the woman I love.'

'You've sacrificed enough, Ruslan. We can't ask any more of you.'

'Leila died for peace. She fucking died, Sergo. How can I just run away?'

'Do you have any idea who much it tore her apart to drag you back into this? Do you have any idea? She hated herself for doing it. If there's one thing I am very very sure of, it's that Leila would have wanted you to keep your promise.'

Ruslan shook his head. 'I don't know if I can.'

'If we lose this referendum,' said Lionidza, 'I never want to see your face again until whatever happens next has happened and it's all settled down. If I do see you before that, I'll fucking hit you and that's a promise.'

Ruslan and Tamara went to vote early the next morning in front of a blaze of flashlights and TV camera crews. And that was it. The marathon was over. It only remained to see who had won.

They returned home, where, to Tamara's astonishment, Ruslan helped her pack everything that would fit into their car, leaving their bags and boxes just inside the front door. They didn't speak as they packed. Tamara was afraid that if she opened her mouth, she would end up giving him the excuse he needed to stay. She hardly dared to imagine the inner turmoil he must have been feeling.

They settled down to wait for the result. They would know before morning, and then either the No Campaign would have won, or else it would have lost, and Ruslan would keep his promise and flee to Russia with Tamara and Shota before the peoples of Central Kubania fell upon each other in a grim festival of death.

April 1993
Ronkoni, East Ksordia

Chapter Twenty-Seven

PRESIDENT KORGAY rolled his eyes. 'Oh, God. What does he want now?'

'I don't know, sir,' said the official. 'He just said it was urgent.'

'It's always bloody urgent with Alavidza.'

The official nodded obediently.

'I mean, you were there, weren't you? Remember when he said the people had turned against us because every motorist who saw him gave him a dirty look? Do you remember that?'

'Yes, sir.'

'And why did they all give him a dirty look? Because he'd stopped all the traffic so he could whiz across town during the rush hour. People were angry because he'd made them late for work.'

'Indeed, sir.'

'And remember when he said the economic crisis was turning everyone against us, just because the opposition had a new slogan: *Ksordia Maka Korgaytan Tad* (Ksordia Hungry With Korgay)?'

'Yes, sir.'

Korgay sighed. Alavidza had been a real asset until recently but now he had lost his bottle. Something had frightened him very badly.

And Korgay knew what it was.

It was Ruslan Shanidza.

The irony was that if it wasn't for Alavidza's cock-ups, Shanidza would never have won that bloody referendum.

Mistake number one: 'Let's get Sultanov to support the No Campaign. That'll split the Tatars.' Except, of course, that Sultanov ended up getting rather too many Tatars to vote No.

Mistake number two: 'Why don't we use the paramilitaries to make sure the Ksords in the northeast stay loyal?' Except, of course, that Mingrelsky's White Eagles were a bunch of useless baboons, and they went and killed that bloody singer. Shanidza would never have won if he hadn't been able to milk her death with all that daffodil crap.

And then, to cap it all, easily avoidable mistake number three: turn your back on Qipiani for five minutes and let him defect to the opposition so half the top brass in Central Kubania panic and order their troops to vote No.

One phone call. Just one phone call. That was all that was needed.

'Hello Mr Qipiani. You know that whore who ties you up and spanks you? Well, we've got it on video, so stay in the government and stop causing trouble, will you? There's a good chap.'

Korgay shook his head in despair. Alavidza was becoming a serious liability.

'You'd better let him in and see what he wants this time.'

The official opened the door and Alavidza hurried in.

'Tengiz, good to see you.'

'Hello, Mr President.'

Korgay got up from his desk and stepped forward. The two men exchanged kisses and Korgay patted Alavidza's slender shoulders and invited him to sit down.

'How can I help you?'

'Mr President, the situation is very serious. Shanidza intends to destroy us. He's said so in as many words.'

'Yes, I know,' said Korgay, leaning back in his chair. 'But look at me. I'm not exactly crapping myself, am I?'

'He's already managed to get twenty-two opposition parties lined up against us, plus the Tatars.'

'Ha. Just look at who he's got together. The Tatars? Don't make me laugh. Yakub Bovin and Timur Sultanov won't even speak to each other. And the rest of them? Sergo Lionidza and Nina Begishveli? What a joke. Those two can barely stand to be in the same room. As for Kakhi, they all detest that fascist lunatic, and Orbeliani's such a two-faced piece of shit that nobody will ever trust him again.

'And who are they planning to put up against me in the November elections? Qipiani? Come on, Tengiz, we'll eat that fucking pervert for breakfast. In any case, they've peaked too soon.

Do you seriously imagine Shanidza's going to be able to hold that rabble together until November? No chance.'

'Mr President, Shanidza knows he can't keep the opposition together until November, so he plans to bring us down before then.'

'Oh yes? How's he going to do that?'

'He's going to demand something so reasonable that no sane person can possibly oppose it, but something that he knows you can't deliver.'

'Oh yes, and what's that?'

'My head on a platter.'

'And how's he going to dress this up to make it look reasonable?'

'They're going to demand the removal of organised crime from the government.'

Korgay snorted.

'And, they're going to try to get me prosecuted as an accessory to the murder of Leila Meipariani.'

'And how are they going to do that?'

'How do you think?'

'How?'

'Well who do you think got Mingrelsky's man out of Ronkoni?'

'They can't prove a thing.'

'Shanidza's got Military Intelligence working on it, and the Tatar police.'

Korgay frowned. He would have to smash those treacherous sons of sluts in Military Intelligence first chance he got. But not yet. Timing was everything.

He looked at Alavidza and said nothing.

'Mr President, there's something I think I should tell you.' Alavidza's voice was weak and shaky.

'What's that?'

'I've been a great admirer of yours for many years. I've always admired the way you know how to divide the opposition with the right combination of repression and timely concessions.'

'And?'

'With all due respect, sir, it would be a grave mistake for you to try to split the enemy by sacrificing me. I absolutely refuse to be made a scapegoat. I will not allow it, sir. It would stretch my loyalty to breaking point and beyond, and that would put the whole government in a very weak position.'

Korgay's eyes widened and his nostrils flared. Was Alavidza threatening him? For a moment, he thought of challenging him, but he decided to bide his time. He would protect him for now, until he had seen off Shanidza and his rabble, but then Alavidza would have to go. There was no way that Korgay could tolerate insubordination like that.

He stood up and went to look out of the window, his hands clasped behind his back. 'Tengiz, my old friend, we've been together for too long to speak to each other like that. We'll see this half dick off and we'll see him off together. We're a good team, me and you, and it'll take a great deal more than him and his bunch of cretins to beat us.'

'Thank you, sir.'

'I'll tell you what. Why don't you send Shanidza a little signal? Just let him know that you're not a man to be trifled with.'

'Yes, sir. Good idea. I think I know exactly how to do just that.'

The result of the Central Kuban referendum had stunned the whole region. Everyone from Moscow to Ankara had been working on the assumption that Central Kubania would vote for independence. Nobody had any contingency plans for what to do if the No Campaign won, but in the end, it did by a margin of 44,514 votes.

Ruslan joked that the historians of the future would devote whole careers to arguing over the result and trying to work out which way the different ethnic communities had voted in different parts of the region.

The Akhtarians had been very solid in their support for independence from Ksordia, that much was evident. And everyone agreed that most Ksords had either boycotted the referendum or been prevented from voting, but those who did turn out had voted No. And so the result had hinged on the Tatars, who had been split right down the middle, with a very slight bias towards the No camp.

The biggest shock of all had come from Siriach'Sichi, the epicentre of militant Akhtarian nationalism. Here, relations between Akhtarians and Tatars had deteriorated sharply during the campaign, and the Tatars had combined with the small Ksordian and Armenian communities to outvote their Akhtarian neighbours. This city, which Akhtarians regarded as the linchpin of their strategy, voted by the slenderest of margins to reject independence.

Ruslan's health collapsed almost as soon as the results came in, and he spent a week in bed with flu-like symptoms. None of this came as any surprise to Tamara, who thought it was a miracle that he had been able to undertake such a gruelling campaign at all. What did surprise her was the apathy and lethargy that accompanied his sickness.

She was determined that he should have the space to recover. She kept all his colleagues away and refused to let the press speak to him. The only thing she passed on were messages from Lionidza and others telling him to stay in bed.

On the political level, it was Lionidza and Nina's old lawyer Orbeliani who held everything together. They realised that the main threat came from the stunned Akhtarians, particularly in Siriach'Sichi, where the mayor asked his police and military chiefs to draw up plans to expel all the Tatars from the city.

Orbeliani gave interview after interview to Akhtarian reporters, constantly repeating the same mantra: 'Nobody's going to force a settlement down anybody's throats. We've got a long and difficult period negotiations ahead of us, but the final settlement has to be acceptable to all communities.'

Meanwhile Lionidza travelled to Moscow, where he managed to persuade the Akhtarians' Russian patrons to restrain them, at least for the time being.

Ten days after the referendum, Orbeliani and Tatar leader Yakub Bovin arranged a meeting with Akakide Lazarev, the relatively moderate leader of the Central Kuban Akhtarians. The delegation included Nina and two senior Tatars from the regional government and Lionidza and Ametov from the No Campaign. At the last minute, Ruslan decided to join them. He was still feeling shaky but his lethargy had left him.

Everyone greeted him warmly, even Yakub and Lazarev, who were generous in defeat, offering him their congratulations on a brilliant campaign. Nina held onto his hands after she gave him four kisses. 'I hated having you as an opponent but I admired your campaign.'

'I thought you wanted to throttle me.'

Nina laughed. 'There were times, yes.'

Unfortunately, if everyone was warm towards Ruslan, they were very frosty towards one another. The only other person they all seemed happy to tolerate was Orbeliani, who had after all represented most of them at their trials during the Soviet era.

'We have a mandate from our people,' said Akhtarian leader Lazarev as they sat round his dining table, Akhtarians on one side, Ksords and Tatars on the other. 'There's no way we'll ever submit to Korgay. We will not be part of a Greater Ksordia.'

'I understand your concerns,' said Orbeliani. 'I really do. But what we're saying is that all of this has to be settled through dialogue. We have to avoid war.'

'How can we have dialogue with Korgay? We can't trust him a millimetre. And don't talk to me about confidence-building measures. They won't work. We know we can never trust him. Never.'

The room was silent.

Eventually Ruslan spoke: 'What if you didn't have to deal with Korgay?'

Everyone looked at him.

'What are you saying?' asked Yakub.

'Well I happen to think Lazarev's right. Korgay isn't interested in peace, so there's no reason why the Akhtarians should ever trust him, or why the Tatars should for that matter. I remember Nina said it to me once, Korgay could never bear to share power with the leaders of other ethnic groups. That's why there'll never be a just peace while he's in power.'

'You're talking about getting rid of him?' said Orbeliani.

'Well why not?' Ruslan looked round the table. 'It's what we all want, isn't it? Why don't we cobble together a temporary deal here, just for the time being, to give us a breathing space in Central

Kubania. Then the Ksords among us turn our guns on Korgay. And when we've got rid of him, the Ksords, the Tatars and the Akhtarians, including Zeda'Anta, we all sit down and thrash out a deal.'

There was silence. Everyone looked at Ruslan in astonishment.

Nina was the first to speak. 'Ruslan, I hate Korgay and everything he stands for. I think everyone in this room does. But he's no fool. If we threaten his position, he'll just start a war to rally the Ksords behind him.'

'He might want to, but he can't, at least not in the short term. The Ksordian military won't agree to go to war without Qipiani.'

Everyone was staring at him.

'I don't think it would take long to build a very broad anti-Korgay coalition. Ex-Communists, democrats, moderate nationalists, trade unionists, students, people in the new bourgeoisie. Lots of Korgay's former allies might join us – Bogiani still has friends in North Ksordia. And don't forget the army. There was a lot of support for the No Campaign in the Ksordian army. All we need is patience from the Akhtarians, maybe half a million Tatar votes in the presidential elections, a lot of determination and our fair share of luck. Korgay's more vulnerable now than he's ever been.'

'You know what?' said Nina. 'I think we might just be able to do it.'

Lionidza nodded. 'It might be worth a go.'

Orbeliani leaned forward. 'Now's as good a time as any. But we'd need Central Kubania to be quiet.'

Yakub glanced at his Tatar companions and then said, 'We'll do what we can, but we'll expect real autonomy in return.'

'We'll agree to that, won't we?' said Ruslan.

The Ksords all nodded.

Ruslan turned to the Akhtarians: 'So what about it?'

'Can we discuss it in private?'

The Ksords and Tatars agreed and the Akhtarians left the room.

There was little conversation among those left behind. They divided into the former Yes and No camps at opposite ends of the room, each group speaking quietly so that the other couldn't hear.

The Akhtarians came back after twenty minutes. Presumably they had telephoned Zeda'Anta for orders.

Everybody sat down again.

'There'll be no Akhtarian uprising while you're working to get rid of Korgay,' said Lazarev. 'Provided, that is, that there are no provocative troop movements by the Ksords. If you succeed, then we'll negotiate with you, as long as you negotiate in good faith. But you won't find us a pushover, so don't imagine you will. And if you fail to get rid of Korgay, then we reserve the right to defend ourselves, and we'll take South Akhtaria out of Ksordia by force of arms.'

Ruslan smiled. 'You won't find us a pushover in negotiations either, but we'll be there in good faith.'

He leaned across the table as far as his wounded back would let him, his hand outstretched. Lazarev took his hand and shook it, and then there were smiles and handshakes all round.

The elation didn't last long, however, and Ruslan found it impossible to sleep that night. He knew Korgay wouldn't give in without a fight, and there were plenty of others who had a lot to lose if he fell, Alavidza and Mingrelsky among them.

It was going to get very scary.

Ruslan decided that he needed to prepare for the worst. Whenever he spent the night away from Tamara, he would sleep on the floor without a pillow or blanket so as to toughen himself up for prison. And he would start every day with visualisation exercises in which he imagined every form of torture he could think of, from beatings to having his head ducked under water, from mock executions to having a pencil thrust up his penis, and he would visualise himself resisting it.

The visualisations would be a real challenge in themselves, but Ruslan knew he would never be able to resist torture if he didn't train himself for it.

He had a fantasy in which he destroyed Korgay, Alavidza and Mingrelsky and then gave it all up for the quiet and simple life of an academic, just like Lucius Quinctius Cincinnatus, who led ancient Rome to victory in war and promptly surrendered all his powers and returned to obscurity on his farm.

But in his heart Ruslan knew it could never be like that. He could have victory and the responsibilities that came with it, or he could have defeat and its consequences: prison, exile or death.

There was no going back now. His old life was lost to him forever.

Chapter Twenty-Eight

TAMARA DIDN'T like shopping in the markets of Ronkoni. Her North Akhtarian accent made her feel extremely vulnerable, despite the fact that people who heard her were never hostile. In fact, many recognised her and said, 'Tell your husband the people are with him,' or 'We're all against Korgay here too.'

Nevertheless, Tamara preferred to go to a small private supermarket a few kilometres from her house. She could simply walk round the shop, fill her basket up and pay at the till without having to say anything much, particularly if she got her bodyguard to take Shota to the little playground by the car park. She wished she could go shopping just once a week, as she had in England, but freezers were impossible to get hold of in Ronkoni, and in any case the regular power cuts made storing food difficult.

On this particular occasion, she had only been in the shop for a few minutes when she heard a woman scream near the entrance. She looked and saw three hooded men striding towards her.

She recognised one of them at once.

It was Mingrelsky.

Tamara dropped her basket and fled in terror.

She turned into the next aisle and ran towards the exit, calling out to her bodyguard. Just as she reached the end, Mingrelsky stepped out in front of her and punched her hard in the stomach.

She doubled up and fell to her hands and knees. He kicked her flank and the others rushed up and joined in, kicking her legs and her sides.

Other shoppers screamed as she fell to the floor. She curled into a foetal position as the kicks rained down upon her. Then Mingrelsky took hold of her hair and almost lifted her off the ground, pulling her head up until her face was right next to his.

'Tell your husband this is just the fucking start,' he said and threw her to the floor.

'Get away from her!' It was Tamara's bodyguard, standing by the entrance, pointing his Makarov pistol at her attackers.

Shoppers screamed and ran for cover as the three men pulled out their APS machine pistols. Two of them aimed at the bodyguard. Mingrelsky aimed at Tamara's head.

'Drop your gun or I'll blow her fucking brains out.'

The bodyguard hesitated for a moment and then slowly put his pistol on the floor. He stood back and put his hands up. One of the men stepped forward and picked up his gun, then the three of them laid into him, kicking, punching and stamping.

'Come on, let's go,' shouted Mingrelsky and they all ran outside.

After a few seconds, shoppers and shop assistants gingerly approached Tamara and her bodyguard.

'Are you all right?'

'Do you need an ambulance?'

They helped a shaky Tamara to sit up. Others helped her bodyguard. Tamara thought he looked a lot worse off than she did. They had hit him in the face and his nose was obviously broken.

She crawled over to him and knelt by him, her hand on his shoulder. 'Where's Shota?'

'I gave him to a *babushka* outside.'

'Are you okay?'

The bodyguard nodded. 'I'll live.'

Tamara looked up and saw the nervous old lady holding Shota by the door. He was crying. 'I want my mama. I want my mama.'

Tamara wiped the tears from her eyes. Two shoppers helped her up and she hobbled towards the exit. 'Shota, come and see Mama.'

The *babushka* let him go, and he ran to Tamara, who bent down and tried to pick him up but couldn't. She knelt down instead, hugging her little son tight. After a minute, she looked up and saw the supermarket's manager standing in front of her.

'Shall I call the police?'

Tamara hesitated. She would rather have hushed the whole thing up and kept it from Ruslan, but that was obviously impossible. He was due back from a trip to West Ksordia that evening, and even if none of her ribs were broken, her bruises would probably keep her in bed for a few days.

'Yes, please. And I think my bodyguard needs an ambulance. Maybe I do too. And have you got some ice?'

The manager nodded and went off.

'You're Ruslan Shanidza's wife, aren't you?' said one of the shoppers.

'Yes.'

'And was that Vakhtan Mingrelsky?'

'Yes.'

'I used to really admire him.'

'I can't say I ever did.'

Tamara's bodyguard was by now trying without success to get a signal on his mobile phone.

She limped towards him, Shota trailing by her side. 'You'd better let me have a look at you. I'm a doctor you know.'

He shook his head. 'Don't worry about me. Are you okay?'

'I'm black and blue.'

'God, Tamara, I'm so sorry.'

'Don't worry about it. At least Shota's okay, aren't you, poppet?'

Shota gave a disapproving look at the bodyguard. 'He got a nosebleed. He been picking his nose.'

Tamara and several of the shoppers laughed. She turned to one of the shop assistants. 'Have you got a phone we can use? His mobile's useless.'

'Yes, you can never get a signal round here.'

It proved impossible for Ruslan's staff to contact him because he was already on his way back to Ronkoni. His mobile wouldn't work until he got to the capital, and even then there wouldn't be many places where he could get a decent signal.

As his car approached the capital, his chief bodyguard tuned in to Provisional Radio, a pro-democrat station that was banned from broadcasting news or commenting on current events. Even so, the broadcast soon told them what had happened

Ruslan was busy preparing a speech, so he paid no attention to the songs on the radio until the driver asked: 'What are they playing this crap for?'

It was Ray Charles' *Hit the Road Jack*.

'What was the last song?'

'*Bek Ga'a-Dyett Iida Guora Tyi*.' (Hit Me on the Dance Floor.)

'They've both got the word "hit" in the title,' said Ruslan, using the Ksord-Akhtarian *dyett*. 'Someone's been beaten up.'

After the Ray Charles song had finished, the DJ came on air. 'We've been talking about mixed marriages, like Ruslan Shanidza and his wife, and whether a mixed marriage can really work. While that song was playing we got an interesting phone call from a lady who didn't want to give her name, but she's married to a Tatar.' He then proceeded to play a recording of their conversation (Provisional Radio didn't dare to run live phone-ins, in case the caller said something that got them closed down).

'Do you think it was Tamara?' asked Ruslan's chief bodyguard.

'Oh my God. Give me the mobile.'

Ruslan turned it on and waited for a signal. At last he got one and phoned home.

'Hello? Ruslan here. Hello? Hello? God's fucking nails. I've lost the signal.'

'Do you want me to stop?' asked the driver.

'No, let's get there as quick as we can.'

The radio played Ian Dury's *Hit Me with your Rhythm Stick* as Ruslan tried again and again to get through on the mobile. Every time he started to dial, he would lose the signal. 'Blood and damnation,' he said, 'Qipiani's got a lot to answer for with these useless mobile phones.'

'Try again when you're nearer home,' said his bodyguard. 'You can sometimes get a good signal there.'

He got through just a couple of minutes from home. 'Has something happened?'

'Tamara's been beaten up.'

'Is she okay?'

'She'll have to stay in bed for a few days but she's okay.'

As they turned into his cul-de-sac, Ruslan hardly noticed the gaggle of reporters standing by his gate. He jumped out of the car and hurried straight past them and into the house.

'Is she upstairs?'

'Yes.'

Lionidza and Orbeliani were in his living room but Ruslan barely said hello to them. He rushed upstairs and into the bedroom, where Tamara was lying in bed. His sister-in-law Venera was sitting near her, keeping Shota from clambering over his mother.

'Papa!' Shota leapt at the breathless Ruslan, who caught him and held him with his strong right arm. He kissed his child and sat next to Tamara as Venera got up to make room.

'Are you okay?'

'I'll survive.'

'Where are you hurt?'

'I've got bruises all down my sides and my back and the top half of my legs. My bodyguard's much worse off than me. He's got a broken nose and a cracked rib.'

'Oh God Tamara, I'm so sorry.'

'It's not your fault.'

'It probably is. Alavidza must be behind it, and it was my idea to go for him.'

'So it's his fault, not yours.'

'Tamara I'm so sorry. I had no right to expose you to this.'

Tamara was so sore she could hardly move, but she managed to stroke his face with her hand and wipe away the tears that were forming in his eyes. 'It's okay. It's not your fault.'

'We've got to get you and Shota out of here. You could go to Zeda'Anta or Moscow. You'd be safe there.'

'No way. We belong here with you and this is where we're staying.'

'Tamara, Alavidza's as dangerous as they come. He'll stop at nothing. You have to get out of here.'

'No, I'm not leaving and that's my final word. You'll just have to get me more bodyguards.'

As he listened to their conversation, Security Police Captain Lemash Kafeveli's contempt for Ruslan Shanidza grew. Not only was he a treacherous pacifist who didn't have the balls to tell his wife what to do, but he couldn't recognise a decent patriot when he saw one. Tengiz Alavidza would never stoop so low as to order an attack on a woman, the most shameful act imaginable in the eyes of a West Ksord like Kafeveli. Impossible. He would never do anything of the sort.

When Ruslan had moved his family to Ronkoni at the end of March, Kafeveli had been detailed to supervise the surveillance of his house. He was greatly assisted in this by the presence among Shanidza's bodyguards of an informant who had planted listening devices all over the place.

Kafeveli set up a listening post in the back bedroom of a house almost directly behind Shanidza's, their high-walled gardens separated by a small alleyway. The occupants of the house were long-standing KGB informants who had no objection to the comings and goings of the Security Police.

Surveillance was in fact a very tedious business, and this case was even more so than usual since Shanidza was hardly ever home. He spent all his time at meetings and rallies and sometimes stayed outside Ronkoni for days on end. Consequently, Kafeveli and his colleagues squandered most of their time listening to his wife and their two-year-old son as they chatted, played, sang songs, listened to the radio and watched TV. Shanidza's wife cooked and cleaned and washed the clothes. She fed her little child, coaxed him onto the potty, told him it was time for a bath or bed and periodically told him off when he was naughty. The little boy talked and talked and talked and followed his mother everywhere.

It wasn't exactly demanding work for the Security Police.

Shanidza's wife liked to wander into the staff common room to chat with the bodyguards and the office staff. They all seemed to like her, and some of them would seek her out and talk to her about their very boring problems in their very boring lives. Kafeveli had to write it all down in case there was anything that could be used to blackmail them, but there never was.

He noticed that Shanidza's wife never seemed to offer any advice. She would just listen and give support, and perhaps help them to clarify their feelings and weigh up their options. Kafeveli found himself liking her ability to listen, just as he liked the fact that she would never divulge anything that had been told to her in confidence.

There was never any useful information even when Shanidza was at home. If he discussed politics with his wife, it was more in the sense of describing events that other informants would have witnessed, or blowing off steam about other politicians. Even here, there was never anything of any use. When he played his boss a tape of Shanidza moaning about Kakhi's rudeness towards Nina Begishveli, he shook his head: 'He's already said the same thing to Kakhi face-to-face.'

Kafeveli also soon learned that most of the myths about Shanidza were untrue. Fearless and heroic? He was nothing of the sort. He had trouble sleeping at night and frequently woke up with nightmares. Kafeveli's team passed this on to their commanders but they already knew.

Another myth that turned out to be false was that Shanidza was a patriot who had been led astray by his Rebel wife. In fact, Kafeveli and his team never once heard her offer her husband political advice of any kind. As with their staff, she would simply listen, offer support and help him to work through his feelings.

Sergo Lionidza was a frequent visitor, and it was obvious that Shanidza relied on his judgement. But this was hardly a revelation. Other visitors included the leaders of various political parties, business and professional associations, trade unions and student groups, plus newspaper editors and the owners of pro-democrat radio stations, including Provisional Radio, which Shanidza's wife liked to listen to, both for its irreverence and for the Western songs that reminded her of the time she had spent in England.

At all these meetings, Kafeveli never once heard anything of any use like Shanidza slagging off one of his allies. He always stressed the common ground that united his fractious coalition.

When Nina Begishveli visited Shanidza and his wife, Kafeveli and his team hoped for an encounter dripping with tension, but they got nothing of the sort. Nina Begishveli brought her latest lover, a Tatar film director, and the two couples appeared to get on very well.

The listening device in the bedroom inevitably brought some entertainment. If any of his colleagues were there, they would bet quite large sums of money on the length of time between the first sounds of humping and Shanidza's climax. Kafeveli quite enjoyed listening to their bedroom antics at first, but eventually he began to find it depressing, and if he were alone, he would turn the sound down, confident that he wouldn't get into trouble for missing a crucial political discussion.

Kafeveli wasn't an introspective man, and he didn't think too deeply about why he took no pleasure in what for most of his career he had regarded as one of the few perks of surveillance work. The fact was that he was becoming very fond of Shanidza's wife and sometimes gazed longingly at the photographs of her pinned on his wall. He had come to admire her approachability and her honesty, and he was also beginning to admire her courage. The more he liked her, the more it hurt to listen to her giving herself to a man he despised.

The garrotte was beginning to tighten around Alavidza's neck. The Central Kuban police, Ksordian Military Intelligence and pro-opposition journalists pooled their resources and soon found evidence linking him to organised crime and a string of gangland murders. Korgay's media ignored all of it, and his censors kept all but the most oblique references out of the opposition press. But they couldn't bury the news. Most Ksords could pick up Central Kuban, Akhtarian or Russian TV and radio, all of which covered the story extensively.

The opposition organised huge rallies all over Ksordia calling for Alavidza's downfall. The official media ignored these too, or else they would show images of small groups of stragglers and depict them as the whole demonstration.

This didn't worry Ruslan. Nor did he worry about the way the pro-Korgay media picked at the deep divisions within the opposition, portraying Lionidza as a Communist dinosaur, Ruslan his performing monkey, Nina a treacherous pacifist, Orbeliani a two-faced hypocrite, Kakhi a fascist lunatic and Qipiani a money-grubbing plutocrat. Bogiani and other former allies of Korgay were portrayed as embittered opportunists and the Tatars as the eternal enemies of the Ksordian people.

Ruslan was aware that all too many opposition supporters would agree with these descriptions of those who had become their allies, but this didn't worry him much. The prospect of power and a focus on Alavidza would keep such divisions submerged for the time being.

What worried Ruslan was the lack of a reaction from Alavidza. There were no more attacks on Tamara (thank God), no baton charges or teargas attacks on opposition demonstrators, no agents provocateurs attacking the police to give them an excuse to crack down, no violence from the paramilitaries, no hand grenades or shots aimed at the crowds and no credible death threats.

Alavidza had to be up to something, and the fact that Ruslan had no idea what it was unnerved him.

Chapter Twenty-Nine

'JUST SIT it out,' said Korgay. 'Sit it out until they fall apart like they always do.'

But it was no good. His government was already beginning to crumble.

Five Socialist Federal Assembly Members had defected to Lionidza. A sixth would have joined them had the Security Police not had photographs of him canoodling with a pretty young research assistant.

Other Socialists were becoming increasingly restive: 'Drop Alavidza,' they told Korgay.

'Sack him.'

'Get rid of him.'

'Dump him.'

'Send him to bloody Georgia. Just get him out of the way.'

Three nationalist cabinet ministers had hinted that they might defect to Orbeliani if Korgay didn't find a way to resolve the Alavidza situation, and the Army Commander-in-Chief had publicly promised that his men wouldn't take part in any crackdown. General Napashidza told Korgay his officers were so deeply divided that any involvement in politics would lead to civil war.

Behind his calm facade, Korgay was starting to panic. He didn't dare to sack Alavidza while the opposition were calling for his head. Not only would that be a sign of weakness, but Alavidza had powerful friends who Korgay couldn't afford to offend.

Alavidza requested a meeting with Korgay. He said he had found a way to outmanoeuvre Shanidza. 'My Security Police have been investigating him,' Alavidza said, eying an official who had stayed in a corner of the room.

'Have they come up with anything?'

'Not much. Sex? Nothing. His wife has a past, but most people won't give a damn, and they've been faithful to each other since they got married.'

'Any corruption?'

'Nothing much. He used to speculate in daffodils and gladioli. He got them from his mother's neighbours and sold them at inflated prices. Nothing to get very excited about, I'm afraid.'

'No, and speculation isn't a crime any more. It's the driving force of the economy.'

Alavidza snorted his disgust. 'So they say.'

'Anything political?'

'Well, ideological.'

'What?'

'He supports the Gothic Hypothesis.'

'The what?'

'Well,' said Alavidza, looking distinctly uncomfortable, 'the Rebels claimed that Akhtaria was founded by the Black Sea Goths. Shanidza once wrote an article in an historical journal that supported that claim.'

'Tengiz, what the fuck are you on about?'

'Nothing, sir.'

'And this is the best you can come up with?'

'There is his sordid little deal with the Rebels in Central Kubania.'

'Tengiz, he boasts about that openly.'

'Yes, sir. For a while I thought we had nothing on him, but then it turns out that his wife's been a very naughty girl.'

'Really? What?'

'Drugs.'

'You're joking.'

'No, I'm not. She took amphetamines when she was a student, and a Hungarian informant said she took marijuana when she was in England.'

'What? Are you trying to tell me she's a drug addict?'

'Well, that's an interesting question. I mean, what if Shanidza got involved in the drug trade to keep his Rebel wife supplied, and then he realised he could make a lot of money out of it. After all, he does have a history of speculating. And so he set up a drug smuggling network with the help of a certain corrupt member of Comrade Zikladza's inner circle.

'But then came reform in Ksordia and the Rebel takeover in Zeda'Anta, and this buggered up their smuggling routes, so they launched all their so-called peace initiatives to protect their business interests, helped by a well-known junkie singer he was shagging. And of course, some of the other drugs gangs were very upset by their activities, so they shot Shanidza and killed the singer.'

Korgay got up from behind his desk and walked over to the window. He stood there for some time, saying nothing.

Alavidza stood up and approached him. 'What do you think, Mr President?'

'Tengiz, not only is it donkey shit, it's pathetic donkey shit.'

'We have a lot of evidence.'

'Like what?'

'His driver from when he was in North Ksordia will admit everything, plus one of his current bodyguards will do so too.'

'Oh, for Christ's sake. I can imagine how you got that crap. Nobody's ever going to believe it.'

'Why shouldn't they? Anyway, why should we give a shit what people think? Who rules this country? You or the baying mob?'

'I don't mean the bloody public, Tengiz. I mean people who matter: Socialist Assembly Members, military top brass, Ukrainian diplomats, the OSCE. None of them are going to believe a word of it.'

'I don't give a shit what they think.'

'Well you should, because if many more of my Assembly Members defect, I'll lose my power to govern legally.'

'Well govern illegally then.'

'It's a bit difficult if half the military support the fucking opposition. And you always forget the bigger picture. The good old days of one-party rule have gone forever. The international community won't stand for it.'

'Who cares what they think?'

274

'I do. We happen to need the Ukrainians and the Poles and the Czechs. We'll need their arms supplies when fighting breaks out again. And we'll need to have the OSCE onside, otherwise the Russians will be able to shell us and bomb us like they did last time. And in the long term, we're going to need the World Bank and the IMF to help us sort out the economy.'

'Mr President, what if we get Shanidza to confess on TV? People will have to believe us then.'

'And how are you going to do that?'

'When the KGB arrested him back in 1980, he crumbled within two days. He told them everything he knew and signed anything they put in front of him.'

'I thought he refused to testify.'

'That was Aleksander Mingrelsky's fault, sir. He wanted Shanidza locked up, so he told his friends in the KGB not to make him testify. But he did crumble under interrogation.'

'Oh, for Christ's sake, he was just a kid. Don't you think he'll be a tougher nut to crack now?'

'No I don't, sir. You've seen the reports on him. He's a bag of nerves. If I get my best interrogators on him, we can crack him within days, I'm sure of it.'

'We can't afford another mess like last time, when your goons nearly killed Kakhi.'

'We don't need to torture him. Good interrogators can break anyone without laying a finger on him.'

'Forget it, Tengiz. It won't work.'

'So what do you suggest? What alternative is there?'

'You tell me.'

Alavidza was silent for a moment. 'Well, the obvious alternative is to stir it up with the Rebels. If there's fighting, everyone will rally round the flag.'

'God's nails, Tengiz. Do you never listen to a word that General Napashidza says?'

'He's just a wet lettuce.'

'Maybe he is, but the fact is the army's is no state to fight. The conscripts all think that bloody referendum's got them off the hook, and the officer corps is in a panic because you let Qipiani resign from the government.'

'That wasn't my fault, sir.'

'Rubbish. It was your job to keep an eye on him and warn me if he was planning to quit. That was a major cock-up. We could have kept him in and you know it.'

'He just did it on the spur of the moment when he was pissed. We didn't have time to stop him.'

'One bloody phone call. That's all it needed. One bloody phone call and you'd have stopped him.'

Alavidza made as if to say something, but then stopped.

'So?' said Korgay. 'What do you suggest?'

'Shoot him.'

'Don't be ridiculous.'

'Mingrelsky's itching to have a crack at him.'

'If we did that, half my assembly members would defect. We'd have to crack down on everyone. We'd have to smash all the opposition parties and close down all their papers.'

'So let's do it. It would do this country good.'

'For God's sake, don't you get it? Those days are over.'

'More's the pity.'

'So what do you suggest, Tengiz?'

'I don't know, sir.'

'There is one other alternative.'

'What's that?'

Korgay stepped forward, bringing himself right up to his Interior Minister. 'Go to Georgia. You'll be safe there.'

'No.'

'It won't be forever. You can come back when it's blown over.'

'No.'

'I can't protect you, Tengiz.'

'I won't let you sacrifice me, sir.'

'Won't you?'

'No, sir.'

'And I'll tell you what I won't do,' said Korgay, his face right next to Alavidza's. 'I won't sacrifice this government for the sake of one man. I refuse to let those cockroaches destroy everything that's been achieved over the last four years. Not even for you, Tengiz. Is that clear?'

Alavidza didn't back down. His face white, his whole body trembling, he stood his ground. 'I'd like to show you something, Mr President.'

'What's that?'

'Alone, sir.' Alavidza glanced at the official in the corner of the room.

Korgay nodded towards him. 'Leave us.'

When the official had gone, Alavidza went over to his briefcase and pulled out a small Japanese cassette recorder. He took a cassette out of his pocket and put it in. He pressed play, and two muffled but instantly recognisable voices came out of the machine.

'Tengiz, good to see you,' said the first voice.

'Hello, Mr President,' said the second.

Sounds of footsteps and chairs being moved.

'How can I help you?'

'Mr President, the situation is very serious. Shanidza intends to destroy us. He's said so in as many words.'

'Yes, I know. But look at me. I'm not exactly crapping myself, am I?'

Alavidza pressed stop. 'Have I played enough, sir?'

'You recorded me? You recorded the President?'

'I took out an insurance policy, sir. And that isn't the only conversation I recorded.'

'You recorded the fucking President? I don't believe it.'

'It was my insurance.'

'How many conversations did you record, you scumbag?'

'A lot.'

'You recorded the fucking President?' Korgay's voice was becoming hysterical.

'It was my insurance and now I'm cashing it in.'

'You fucking traitor.' Korgay punched his right fist into his hand as he spoke.

'I had to do it, sir.'

'You treacherous piece of shit.'

Korgay stepped up to Alavidza and punched him in the stomach. Then he grabbed his head in an arm lock and punched him hard in the face.

Alavidza fought back, and the two men staggered around the room, sending a chair and table flying. The official put his head round the door and then ran back out again. 'Help! Guards! The President's being attacked.'

Two uniformed members of the Presidential Guard ran into the room. Korgay had his back to them. He had Alavidza in a full nelson, pressed against the far wall of the room. 'You fucking traitor,' he was saying. 'You fucking traitor.'

'Mr President? Mr President?' shouted the guards.

Korgay released Alavidza and punched him in the kidney. Alavidza screamed and sank to the floor.

Korgay turned round and adjusted his jacket and tie. 'Arrest that man.'

The two guards looked at each other in alarm. 'Permission to call our Commander, sir?'

Korgay nodded, and the guard took out his walkie-talkie and called for reinforcements and the Commander of the Presidential Guard to come quickly. After a few minutes, the Commander came rushing in with half a dozen guards, their APS pistols all drawn.

Korgay pointed to Alavidza, who had by now dragged himself onto a chair and was trying to stem the blood from his nose with his handkerchief. 'Arrest that man.'

The guards all looked at their Commander, who hesitated. 'Mr President, sir, I'm afraid we can't do that.'

'What?'

'I'm sorry, sir, but we take orders from the Minister of the Interior.'

Alavidza shot what was obviously a triumphant grin at Korgay, who yelled at the Commander, 'What the fuck did you say?'

'I'm very sorry, sir, but that's how it is. We're under the Minister's command.'

'But I'm the fucking President. I'm fucking ordering you.'

'I'm sorry, sir.'

Korgay looked around the room, waving his arms in frustration. Then he turned round to Alavidza. 'Tengiz Alavidza, I hereby dismiss you from my government without notice. You're no longer the Minister of the Interior. I'm taking over your functions until I can find a suitable replacement.'

'You won't get away with this.'

Korgay went to punch him in the face. Alavidza raised his arms to protect himself, and Korgay hit him again and again, until finally he knocked him off his chair. He turned to the Commander.

'Now fucking well arrest that man.'

'Yes, sir.'

The Commander nodded to his men, who picked Alavidza up and took him out of the room.

Chapter Thirty

THE SECURITY POLICE came for Ruslan just four days later. A score of them, led by a man with bushy, frowning eyebrows that met in the middle, raided the house and arrested him shortly after dinner. All the shouting and the chaos terrified poor Shota, and Ruslan could see that Tamara was very frightened too.

'Don't worry,' he told her. 'I'm not afraid.'

In fact, he was very afraid, despite all his nights on floors and his hours of visualisations.

When Alavidza had had been sacked and arrested for unspecified 'abuses of power', it had thrown the opposition into confusion. Their strategy had, after all, been based on the assumption that Korgay would be unable to dismiss him, and they were divided about what to do next. Kakhi favoured a mammoth rally that brought opposition supporters from all over the country to Ronkoni for an insurrectionary *putsch*. Nina and Lionidza, on the other hand, favoured extreme caution. They feared that with Alavidza gone, the Security Police and the extremist militias might well go berserk.

And now, as if to confirm these fears, Ruslan found himself handcuffed to a Security Police officer in the back of a black Volga 21.

They took him down into the bowels of Security Police Headquarters. Ruslan knew the building well enough, just as he knew the routine they would follow. He wouldn't see daylight again until his interrogation was over. They would keep him awake and fight him with tiredness, hunger and thirst.

They would interrogate him in shifts, and he remembered all too well how good they were at their job. He knew how easily they had outwitted him last time and was determined not to make the same mistakes again. He would refuse to answer their questions with anything but abuse. He would refuse to engage them in conversation, even the so-called good cops. Especially the good cops. They were the most dangerous of all.

This was a risky strategy. After all, if they couldn't defeat him by exhausting him and tripping him up during his interrogation, then they might resort to physical force. That would be the real test. Ruslan hoped he was ready for it.

They made him strip in front of half a dozen men. Ruslan was in fact more self-conscious about the mass of scar tissue on his back than he was about being naked below the waist. The gloved finger up his backside was unpleasant but not unexpected, and this time at least they didn't make him roll back his foreskin.

They gave him a uniform: old dirty-white underpants, ill-fitting black trousers and a blue shirt. No socks, no shoes, no pullover. Next he had his fingerprints and photographs taken. After that, they let him piss and then frogmarched him into a room where the man with the bushy eyebrows was waiting for him, a thick file on his desk, a younger officer by his side.

'Surname?'

'You know my bloody name.'

'Surname?'

'I'm not playing your stupid games.'

'What's your surname?'

'Go fuck your mother.'

'It's for the record. It's procedure.'

'Look in my fucking file then. I'm sure it's got it there.'

The interrogator looked at Ruslan, who had obviously given him a surprise.

'What about you?' said Ruslan. 'What's your name?'

'That's for me to know and you to find out.'

'Have it your way. What's the charge?'

The interrogator grinned. 'Drug smuggling and racketeering.'

'What?'

'Drug smuggling and racketeering. You're facing up to fifteen years in prison, so I suggest you co-operate.'

'Who the hell came up with that?'

'Witnesses.'

'Donkey shit.'

'We've got rather a lot of evidence against you. So, let's start at the beginning. What's your surname?'

Ruslan stared at him. He couldn't believe it. Drug smuggling? Where had that come from?

'Surname?'

Ruslan shook his head to bring himself back to the present. 'You're joking, aren't you?'

'I've never been more serious.'

'Look, either you know as well as I do that this is just pure lies, or else you're the thickest cop in the whole of Ronkoni and you actually believe it. It doesn't bother me which, but you'd better get one thing into your head: I have no intention whatsoever of playing your stupid game.'

'Surname?'

'Go fuck yourself.'

Seven Security Police officers stayed behind and ransacked the house after Ruslan and all his staff had been taken away. They ripped the sofa open, lifted up floorboards and stomped around the attic. They took all of Ruslan and Tamara's papers, including their wedding certificate and old love letters.

After almost an hour, one of the Security Police officers came downstairs with a triumphant look on his face and a small plastic bag in his hand. He waved it in front of Tamara's face: 'Got you!'

'What?'

'Heroin if I'm not mistaken.'

'What are you talking about?'

The officer handed the bag to an elderly officer, who looked into it and smiled. 'We've got the son of a slut,' he said. He put the bag in his pocket and called off the search. Within minutes, the Security Police had gone, leaving the house an absolute shambles.

Tamara sat down on what was left of their sofa, he infant on her knee. She wanted to cry but was keeping as cheerful as she could for his sake.

'Those nasty mans made a big mess.'

'They certainly did. Never mind. We'll tidy it up tomorrow.'

She put Shota on the sofa and went to plug the phone back into the wall, but the Security Police had ripped out the wiring. They had confiscated both of their mobile phones too. Tamara picked up Shota and went over the road to the house of a friendly young couple. She knocked on the door, and the husband opened it, his wife standing behind him, looking very afraid.

'Hi, can I use your phone? They've wrecked mine.'

The young couple looked at each other. 'Don't let her in,' the woman whispered.

'You can't come in.'

'Please. My husband and all our staff have been arrested, our house has been wrecked and I need to phone someone.' Tamara was suddenly finding it very difficult to keep her emotions in check.

'You can borrow my mobile,' said the woman. She disappeared and came back after a few seconds. Her husband handed it to Tamara.

'Thanks.'

She waited until the signal was clear and then telephoned Orbeliani.

'Tamara! We've been trying to call you for ages. Is Ruslan there?'

'He's been arrested. The Security Police have got him.'

'Oh, God, that's terrible. Are you okay?'

'I'm more worried about Ruslan.'

'We'll get him out, don't worry.'

'I hope so.'

'Did you see the TV programme?'

'What TV programme?'

'They're accusing Ruslan of being a drug dealer.'

'But that's ridiculous.'

'I know. Look, I'll be round as soon as I can, okay?'

Orbeliani arrived after twenty minutes, accompanied by eight armed bodyguards, four for him and four for Tamara.

Soon afterwards Lionidza and then Nina arrived. Lionidza was shocked by the state the Security Police had left the house in, but Nina and Orbeliani had experience of KGB searches and evidently knew what to expect.

They briefed Tamara on what the TV programme had said. It was Alavidza's story: she was a heroin addict. Ruslan had got involved in drug smuggling to keep her supplied but then found it was a good way to make money. All his political work had been a front for his drug smuggling activities. Leila had been an addict too and was Ruslan's lover to boot.

'Honestly, Tamara, I swear that Ruslan and Leila were never lovers,' Lionidza reassured her.

'I know. Don't worry about that.'

Orbeliani told Tamara about the 'witnesses', including Ruslan's friend and former driver Mikhel Inalipa and one of his current bodyguards.

She shook her head in disbelief. 'Do you think people will believe it?'

'I doubt it,' said Orbeliani.

'So what happens now?'

Nobody answered.

Orbeliani nodded at Shota. 'We'll talk about that later.'

'Yes,' said Tamara. 'Bedtime for you, little poppet.'

'Don't want to.'

'Well, if you promise to be a good boy, you can sleep in Mama's bed tonight.'

'Okay.'

While Tamara was putting Shota to bed, Nina motioned the others to go out into the garden.

'Lionidza,' she hissed. 'Did she use to take drugs or something?'

'How am I supposed to know?'

'Oh come on. Don't tell me the KGB didn't tell you everything about her. You used to be very friendly with them, didn't you?'

'Don't come holier than thou with me, Nina. I'm not ashamed to have been part of the only government that ever treated all the ethnic groups in Ksordia-Akhtaria fairly.'

'What? When you weren't deporting them, you mean?'

'I'm not talking about Stalin and you know it. And just remember this: unlike some people here, I protected Ruslan.'

'You don't know what you're talking about.'

Orbeliani stepped in. 'Nina, Sergo, can you save it for another day? We're supposed to be on the same side.'

Nina took a deep breath. 'Look, I know the KGB mentality. When they want to discredit someone, they don't just make things up. They take a half-truth and they twist it and exaggerate it. So what about it, Lionidza? Did she use to take drugs?'

'I'm not sure,' said Lionidza. 'Maybe she did, when she was a student. The informant said she was with a group of people who were all pissed, and one of them got some amphetamines out. The informant didn't say she took any, but she was a bit wild in those days, so it's possible that she did.'

'It's true, I did.' They all turned round and saw Tamara standing by the door. 'I was very ashamed afterwards and I never did it again.'

'So you just took drugs just once?' said Nina. 'We have to know the truth.'

'Isn't it in my file, Sergo? The time I tried marijuana in England.'

'I don't know. As a matter of fact, I've never seen your file.'

Tamara stepped forward and put her hand on Lionidza's arm. 'I'm sorry. I had no right to say that to you.'

'It's okay.'

She turned to Nina. 'I took three puffs of a joint at a party. Ruslan was furious, and I knew better than to do it again, I can tell you. But that's all, Nina. That's all I ever did.'

The next morning Tamara held a news conference. Orbeliani had rehearsed everything with her, but even so, she was extremely nervous as she made her brief statement.

'I'm not a politician. I'm a doctor and a mother and a woman who married an athlete. I've never sought the limelight, and I don't seek it now, but I'm here because Ksordian TV has made outrageous allegations about me in order to attack my husband.

'According to them, I'm a heroin addict. Well, I'd like to invite you all to photograph my arms.' She rolled up the sleeves of her top and held her arms forward as the flashlights flashed. 'You can see there isn't a single scar on either of them. If I were a heroin addict, there would be a mass of scars from all the times I injected myself. These bruises are from when Vakhtan Mingrelsky beat me up last month, but there are no scars.'

To her surprise, some of the reporters applauded her. This gave her extra confidence to continue, though her voice remained very shaky. 'Do we have anyone here from Russian TV?'

A second's delay while the Russian reporter's translator whispered into his ear, then he shouted 'Yes.'

'And Ukrainian TV?'

'Yes.'

'Right. A nurse is going to take a sample of my blood. We'll give it to the Russian and Ukrainian reporters, and ask them to take it somewhere reliable to get it tested for heroin or any other drug they like. They'll find it negative, because I'm not a drug addict.'

A nurse then went onto the platform and took a blood sample from her arm. When she finished, the Russian and Ukrainian reporters came up and took it. Many of the journalists applauded again.

'You've got a scar now,' one of them shouted and everybody laughed.

Most of the questions were directed at Lionidza, Orbeliani and Nina, but a few came Tamara's way. She refused to answer all political questions, apart from one, where a journalist asked which side she had wanted to win the Ksord-Akhtarian War.

'The war tore me apart. I'm Akhtarian and my husband and my son are both Ksords.'

'But which side did you want to win?'

'I've answered that question. The war tore me apart.'

Two other questions were more personal. 'What's your reaction to reports that Leila Meipariani was your husband's lover?'

Tamara didn't flinch. 'I know this is absolutely untrue. I spent some time with Leila after Ruslan was shot, and I know.'

Then came the question she had been dreading. 'Have you ever taken drugs?'

Lionidza had wanted her to deny it, but Nina and Orbeliani had advised her to be totally honest. 'If you lie, they'll find out, and that'll just undermine everything else you say.'

Tamara took a deep breath. 'Yes, I have. Twice. A long time ago. When I was a student, a friend produced some amphetamines when we'd been drinking. I took a couple. I felt very guilty afterwards and I never did it again. And soon after we went to live in England, I was at a party and I took a couple of puffs of marijuana. Ruslan saw me, and he was absolutely livid. I've never seen him so angry before or since and I never did it again. I can't pretend I'm a saint. I've done some stupid things in my life. But I'm not a drug addict, and my husband is an honest man.'

Tamara felt very depressed after the press conference, convinced that she was a liability. She had heard what Nina said about the KGB always taking a half-truth and using it against their enemies. She bitterly regretted her foolishness and the danger it had placed Ruslan in.

Meanwhile President Korgay was feeling equally despondent. Everything had gone wrong, and it was all Alavidza's fault. All he had to do was disappear to Georgia for a few months. But no, he was bigger that the President, wasn't he? He was more important than the government, more important than the future of the fucking country.

But even then, with Alavidza locked up, everything should have been okay. Just sit back and wait for the opposition to disintegrate, like every other opposition coalition had disintegrated before it. They were already bickering. They didn't have a clue what to do next. Just sit tight, keep our nerve. That was all we had to do.

But Alavidza's friends weren't prepared to do that. They wanted macho posturing. They wanted action. They wanted blood. The Security Police and the paramilitaries were itching to lash out. There would be assassinations and bombings against the opposition and attacks on the Rebels too. Before Korgay knew it, he would be embroiled in a war on two fronts, one internal, the other external.

He had to do something. He had to take a lead.

But what could he do? Crush the opposition and impose a dictatorship? Declare a state of emergency, ban the opposition parties, shut their newspapers and lock up all their leaders? Then brace himself for a wave of riots and strikes and use the army to crush them?

But the army was too divided to do that. He couldn't even rely on his own party, especially with fucking Lionidza's supporters out there, circling like vultures, wining and dining Socialist Party members, telling them that they too had picked up the banner of Lenin.

Or maybe he could start a war and rally the country round the flag.

Except they would probably lose the war. Morale was rock bottom, thanks to fucking Shanidza convincing the conscripts that they wouldn't need to fight. And the supply situation was disastrous, thanks to Alavidza. All he had to do was make sure Qipiani didn't resign. One phone call, that was all it would have taken. One phone call. Useless moron.

So Korgay couldn't impose a dictatorship, and he couldn't pick a fight with the Rebels.

What could he do?

Oh God's fucking bollocks.

He had always known it would never work.

Nobody was ever going to believe it.

And for God's sake, why didn't he let them arrest his wife? How could he let her pull off a stunt like that?

What a mess.

And now the head of the Security Police had come to tell him that Shanidza was proving very difficult to crack. It might take longer than a week.

'It would help if we could rough him up a little.'

'No way. I'm not having another situation like Kakhi. We're lucky you didn't kill him.'

'I'm not saying we kick the shit out of him, sir. Just rough him up a little, as and when appropriate.'

'And you can get a confession in less than a week?'

'Yes, sir.'

'And no serious injuries.'

'Yes, sir.'

'Do whatever you have to do.'

Chapter Thirty-One

AFTER TWO days of relentless interrogation by shifts of Security Policemen, Ruslan was completely disoriented. He had lost track of time and had no idea how much sleep he had had. But he knew it was desperately important to concentrate, despite the tiredness, the hunger and the thirst. It was desperately important not to answer their questions.

'Tell me about your father,' said his chief interrogator an hour into yet another session.

'Go fuck your mother.'

'Okay then, I'll tell you about your father. He was a Partizan, a not very effective one.' The interrogator paused, but Ruslan said nothing. 'He ended up in a punishment unit and lost a leg clearing mines.'

Ruslan said nothing.

'And then in 1946, he was arrested for counter-revolutionary agitation. I suppose you know the story, don't you? He got drunk and told his neighbour he hated the Party because they sacked your mother. But I bet you didn't know that his neighbour never denounced him. It was his neighbour's wife.'

Ruslan said nothing, but his interrogator was right: he hadn't known it was the wife who had denounced his father. He suddenly felt sorry for all the faces he had pulled at her husband when he was a boy.

'Actually, there's quite a lot you don't know about your father. You're very proud of him, aren't you? I can't think why. If you ask me a Partizan commander who just uses his men to protect his own village is a selfish coward.'

Ruslan made no response.

'Would you like me to tell you something you don't know about your father?'

Ruslan stared malevolently at the interrogator. 'Go bugger a goat.'

'Well, I'll tell you anyway.'

He rummaged around among the files in front of him and eventually produced some old sheets of paper whose age Ruslan could smell from a metre or more away. 'Here it is. "Tuesday 17th September. TS" – that's your father – "checked in at 02:45. Interrogation 03:10 – 04:50: TS denied all knowledge of counter-revolutionary comments or conspiracy. Interrogation 05:10 – 07:30: TS continued denial." Your father was a stubborn man, Shanidza. I've counted it, they interrogated him for thirteen hours that day, and he managed to deny everything. The next day was the same, and the next. He didn't admit a thing for five whole days. Rather better than you, if I may say so. You only lasted two days.'

He smirked in a way that made Ruslan want to hit him.

'Now, here it gets interesting. "Friday 20th September. Permission to use physical influence granted." Can you guess what physical influence means? Well, use your imagination. "Interrogation 10:30 – 14:50: physical influence applied. TS continued denial." He was a brave man. You have to take your hat off to him. He was interrogated for fourteen hours that day, and they physical influenced him in five different sessions.'

Ruslan said nothing.

'They broke him the next day. "Interrogation 03:20 – 05:40: physical influence used. TS admitted anti-Soviet comments but denied conspiracy. Interrogation 05:55 – 07:00: physical influence applied. TS admitted taking part in counter-revolutionary conspiracy. Named Lieutenant Filipp Makharadza and Captain Mikha Tskhakaya of the 563rd Independent Battalion as co-conspirators."

'They interrogated him for quite a long time after that, and they applied physical influence again, but those were the only two names they got out of him. So on Tuesday 24th, exactly one week after his arrest, your father met with the prosecutor and signed his full confession, and his interrogation came to an end. And that would have been the end of that, except that it turned out that the names your father gave were two officers who'd been killed in action in 1942. He was trying to fool us.

'So you can imagine what happened next, can't you? "Wednesday 9th October: TS returned for further interrogation. Permission to use physical influence given. Interrogation 09:50 – :30: Physical influence applied. TS admitted lying but denied conspiracy. Interrogation 13:15 – 15:00: Physical influence applied. TS confessed to conspiracy and implicated Sergeant Mamiya Orakhelashveli and rankers Nestor Lakoba and Lavrenty Kartvelishveli of 563rd Independent Battalion."

'It turned out that these three men were still alive, so they were hauled in. Your father got eight years as the leader of the conspiracy. The other three got five.'

Ruslan could remember seeing his father crying as he tended their private plot. Perhaps he hadn't been crying for the wife and children murdered by the Rebels but for the friends he had betrayed under torture. He recalled what his mother had said, that he had been a broken man when he was finally released. But perhaps it wasn't the torture that had broken him, or the harsh conditions in the Gulag.

It was guilt.

How many years of self loathing had he endured before he had managed to salvage some self respect?

'I don't blame your father,' said the interrogator. 'The point is, if they're tortured, anyone'll crack sooner or later. And then they'll say absolutely anything, whether it's true or not, just to stop the pain. Your father did and so will you. Because we really want to get a confession out of you, and it doesn't bother us how we get it.'

Ruslan said nothing. He was concentrating on collecting some saliva in his parched mouth. When he had enough, he leaned forward and spat in his chief interrogator's face.

'That's for my father.'

The interrogator took out a handkerchief and wiped the spittle away. 'You'll wish you hadn't done that.'

'Do your worst. I'm ready for you.'

Tamara had been reluctant to leave Ronkoni, but Lionidza had insisted: 'You have to do it, Tamara. You owe it to him.'

They travelled in a convoy of four cars, one with Tamara and Lionidza, the others full of armed bodyguards, as was a fifth car that followed far enough behind to keep an eye on the inevitable black Volga that tailed them as they headed for the mountains of West Ksordia.

Mikhel Inalipa and his wife lived in a dreary little village some five kilometres south of Ormi. Mrs Inalipa came out of their small wooden house as soon as Tamara's convoy pulled up outside. She was a handsome woman in her fifties, tall and straight in her bearing, like the former athlete that she was.

'Thank you for coming,' she said to Tamara. 'I'm very grateful.'

'How is he?'

'It's like his spirit's died.'

Mikhel's wife had contacted Lionidza two days earlier, after her husband had swallowed half a bottle of pills. She had found him soon afterwards, and she and a neighbour had dragged him into her car and rushed him to hospital.

'What would you like me to do?' Tamara asked.

'I want you to forgive him for all the lies he's told about your husband.'

'Of course I forgive him. He saved Ruslan's life.'

'Will you speak to him?'

'Alone or with you?'

'It's probably better if you see him alone. He won't speak to me.'

Tamara nodded.

Mikhel was at the back of the house, in what must once have been a bedroom for their children. He was sitting looking out of the window when Tamara went in and didn't turn round to see who it was.

'Hello, Mikhel.'

Mikhel swung round and greeted Tamara with a look of horror.

'I've come as a friend.'

Mikhel's eyes filled with tears. 'Tamara, I'm so sorry.' He covered his face with his hands and began to cry.

Tamara sat down on his bed.

It was two or three minutes before he regained enough control to speak. 'They made me do it, Tamara. I didn't want to, I really didn't want to, but they made me.'

'I know.'

'They blackmailed me.'

'I know.'

He took a handkerchief out of his pocket and wiped his face. 'You know?'

'Leila told me.'

'She told you?'

'Yes, a long time ago.'

'The irony is that it wasn't me she wanted. She wanted Ruslan, but he pulled back at the last minute. I think she only jumped into my bed as a way of getting at him.'

Tamara flinched at his words.

'I'm sorry. I should never have told you that.'

She shook her head. 'It doesn't matter.'

'Why didn't you say anything at your press conference?'

'Sergo made me promise not to.'

Mikhel bowed his head. 'My wife doesn't know. Do you think she'll ever forgive me?'

'You know her better than me.'

'That's why I'm so afraid. God has abandoned me. I can't even pray for help.'

'Why ever not?'

'When I did Ruslan's tracheotomy, I promised God that if he helped me then, I'd never ask him to help me again.'

Tamara put her hand on his knee. 'It wasn't God that saved Ruslan that night. It was you, you and the doctors. You knew what to do and you got it right.'

Mikhel shook his head.

'Then I'll ask God to help you. I'm allowed to, aren't I?'

'Would you really do that?'

'Of course.'

Tamara put her hands together and closed her eyes. 'Heavenly Father, I ask you to give your protection to my friend Mikhel Inalipa. He's a good man. He's made mistakes, but he's a good man, and he deserves your love and protection. And I ask you to release him from the promise he made never to ask you for anything. He made this promise to save my husband, but now he's in trouble and he needs you. I ask this in the name of our Lord Jesus Christ. Amen.'

Tamara opened her eyes. She hadn't prayed aloud like this since she was a child, and, unbeliever that she was, she found it a strangely moving experience.

'Thank you,' said Mikhel. 'God bless you and thank you.'

They sat in silence for a moment.

'Tamara, can you do one more thing for me? Can you speak to my wife? Can you tell her and ask her to forgive me?'

'Don't you think it might be better coming from you?'

'I can't. I can't do it. Please, you do it for me. If she can't forgive me, I'll just leave. I'll go and stay with my brother.'

'Okay, if you really want me to.'

She went out of the bedroom and walked into the living room, where Lionidza was waiting with Mikhel's wife.

'Sergo, can I speak to Mrs Inalipa alone, please?'

Lionidza nodded and went to join the bodyguards in the garden.

Tamara sat down on the sofa next to her. If there was one thing being a doctor had taught her, it was how to give bad news.

'This is going to be very painful for you, so prepare yourself for a shock.' She paused for a second. 'The Security Police blackmailed your husband into telling lies about Ruslan. They said that if he didn't, they'd tell you about the affair he had with Leila Meipariani when he was in Kvemodishi.'

Mrs Inalipa breathed in sharply and closed her eyes.

'I'm sorry,' said Tamara.

Mrs Inalipa's eyes were full of tears when she opened them. 'And that's why he tried to kill himself?'

'Yes. He's afraid that you won't be able to forgive him.'

She looked away and for a moment wrung her hands. Then she turned back to Tamara. 'Would you forgive your husband if it was him?'

'I don't know. Sometimes I think I love him so much that I could forgive him anything. At other times I think I'd cut his you-know-whats off if he was ever unfaithful.'

Mrs Inalipa laughed in the way that people sometimes do when they are trying not to cry. 'And which do you think right now?'

'My husband's in a desperate situation. He needs my love right now.'

'Mine too.'

The two women looked at each other and smiled.

Mrs Inalipa stood up. 'I'll go and speak to him.'

Tamara went out into the garden. 'Sergo, can I have a word?'

They went into the Inalipas' kitchen to get away from the bodyguards.

'Be honest with me Sergo: what happened between Ruslan and Leila in Kvemodishi?'

'Between Ruslan and Leila? Nothing.'

'Don't donkey shit me. Something happened.'

'Nothing happened.' Lionidza reduced his voice to a whisper. 'She had an affair with Mikhel, not with Ruslan.'

'Didn't it strike you as odd? I mean Mikhel's not a bad looking man, but he's fifteen years older than Ruslan and he hasn't got a tenth of his charisma. Do you seriously think he's the kind of man who gets pop stars throwing themselves at him every day of the week?'

Lionidza sat down at the breakfast table. 'Leila and I became very close after Ruslan was shot. We spent a lot of time together, and to a certain extent she got me through it. I was in a bad way. I mean, one thing, I only just escaped with my life. You don't just go home and forget about something like that. And the other thing, I had a lot of guilt to work through. You know what for. You've read his diary.'

'Yes.'

Tears welled up in Lionidza's eyes. He took his handkerchief out, wiped his eyes and blew his nose. He looked at Tamara and gave an embarrassed smile. 'I don't know if I'm crying for me or Ruslan or Leila.'

Tamara sat next to him.

'So what happened? I need to know.'

'They flirted. I should think we all flirted with Leila, but with him, she flirted back. It was pretty obvious she'd taken a shine to him.'

'And him to her?'

'He's a red-blooded man, Tamara. And she was a very attractive woman.'

'And?'

'Well I was surprised when she ended up in Mikhel's bed. I asked her about it weeks later, after the shooting. She told me she'd made a pass at Ruslan and he didn't want to know. She said she wasn't sure why she jumped on Mikhel. Maybe partly as a way of getting at Ruslan and partly just because she was desperate. Not desperate for sex. Desperate for companionship. We were all desperate by that stage. Everything was falling to pieces and we didn't know how to extricate ourselves.'

They were silent for some time. Then Lionidza said, 'Shall I tell you what else she told me?'

'What?'

'She said she really liked you when she met you in Kvemodishi, and you were so perfect for Ruslan. She said she was really glad he'd been impervious to her charms.'

'I've never thought he was a hundred percent impervious.'

'Impervious enough. He's always been loyal to you.'

Tamara smiled. 'Well, I was specially chosen for him, wasn't I?'

'We just got you together. Cupid did the rest.'

'I don't think it was cupid who told him to marry me quick or else the KGB would break his legs.'

'I have to admit that was me. I hope you don't regret it.'

'I won't say I wouldn't have liked a bit more time to decide, but I don't regret it, no.'

'And please don't hate Leila.'

'As a matter of fact I liked her very much. Just not quite as much as my husband did.'

Ruslan was on his knees.

'Come on, Shanidza,' said his chief interrogator. 'Save yourself a lot of trouble.'

'Go fuck your mother.'

The interrogator nodded, and another operative whacked Ruslan's arm with a short piece of hosepipe. Ruslan moaned.

'We've got a free hand with you. We can do anything we want.'

'Oh yes?' said Ruslan, lifting his head. 'Why don't you hit me in the face, then? Come on, break my nose and knock a few teeth out. Or else break my ceramic ribs. One good kick should do it.'

They hit him with their hosepipes again, on the chest, arm and back. Each time, Ruslan cried out in pain. But they didn't hit him in the face or kick him in the ribs.

'He pongs a bit, doesn't he, lads?' said the interrogator. 'Don't you think it's time he had a bath?'

They lifted him to his feet and took him down some stairs and into the bathrooms. Ruslan looked along the rows of grey washbasins, and then at the end, he saw a young officer standing by a bath full of water. Two men grabbed hold of Ruslan, one holding his shoulders, the other his hair. They rushed him towards the bath and plunged his head into the cold water, banging his crown against the side. Ruslan barely had time to take in a breath.

He opened his eyes under water and struggled to raise his head. They kept him under. He waited a few seconds and tried to rise again, but they wouldn't let him. And then they kept him there and they kept him there some more. Ruslan began to panic. He didn't know how much longer he could hold out. He emptied his single lung of most of the air it held, and still they kept him there. He struggled and still they held him under.

And then he was up, gasping for air. And suddenly he was down again. He had hardly any air in his lung and was terrified that they would let him drown. And then, just when he thought he might, they lifted him up for a few seconds, and then down, down into the cold and the panic of that bath.

Ruslan tried to keep count of the seconds, to detach himself from the fear, to pull back from the immediacy of the terror, but as they held him down, down and down again, fear took over. Every time they submerged him, he was terrified that they would miscalculate, that this time he was going to drown.

And then they did miscalculate.

They kept him under as the last of the air in his lung bubbled to the surface, and then they kept him down as he breathed in water and coughed it out and breathed in more.

And then he stopped.

His chest pulsed in an effort to cough, but nothing came out.

It was the drowning reflex. His throat muscles had gone into spasm.

They pulled him up, but this time he couldn't breathe.

His body convulsed in an effort to cough, but nothing came out.

They let go of him.

He put his hands to his throat and fell to his knees.

They all stood round him in a circle.

He thrashed about in desperation and fell to the floor.

And then his throat muscles relaxed and he gasped. The noise of it was frightful.

He lay on the ground, coughing and gasping for air.

Nobody hit him. Nobody kicked him. They just stood there as he coughed and gasped and gasped for what seemed an eternity. The pain in his chest and his throat was almost unbearable.

He coughed and gasped and coughed.

Eventually, he was able to raise himself to his hands and knees, and then to sit on the floor. He looked at his captors and tried to speak, but this just led to another fit of coughing. After a minute, one of the Security Police officers handed him a cup of water (his first drink in over eight hours) and he sipped it cautiously.

'You fucking imbeciles,' he finally managed to say. 'Don't you know I've only got one lung?'

This near-drowning came as a dreadful shock to Ruslan, and for the next few hours, he was extremely vulnerable. If they had resumed at once, they might easily have broken him.

But it had obviously frightened them as much as it frightened him. They were clearly under orders not to kill him, because they left him alone for the rest of that shift. By the time they resumed, he was ready for them.

The near-drowning left its mark, however. Ruslan coughed all the time, and he was more afraid of the threat of drowning than anything else they might do to him.

They kept him awake almost round the clock and kept him hungry and thirsty all the time. They yelled abuse at him, screamed at him and threatened him with death. And again and again they beat him, kicked him and squeezed his testicles. They stripped him naked and hit him with wet towels and short lengths of hosepipe. They loved to pull his hair and his ears, and to twist his arms behind his back.

And then they left him alone with the good cops, who gave him sympathy and offered him deals: a short, token prison sentence, that was all, and then he could go into exile.

Ruslan fought back with sheer brute stubbornness. When he wasn't coughing, he would swear at them and curse them. He would threaten them with long prison sentences when the opposition came to power. And he would taunt them: 'Go on, break my nose, smash my teeth in. Or stick my head under water again, why don't you?'

And when they threatened Tamara, he would remind them of all the West Ksords in the army who would regard any attack on a woman as shameful, and asked them whether they really wanted to provoke a *coup d'état*.

By now he had no idea how long he had been in prison, and he knew nothing about what was happening outside. He was ignorant of the diplomatic pressure on Korgay, the panic that gripped the government, the continuing defections to Lionidza and Orbeliani, or the massive demonstration calling for his release that had turned into a riot less than 100 metres from Security Police headquarters (they put earphones on him and played white noise into his ears throughout).

He just knew that he was in the middle of the defining struggle of his life, and he also knew that they were still holding back. They were still under orders not to harm him. This was kilometre thirty-five of his marathon. The worst was yet to come.

'Well?' said Korgay. 'How much more time do you need?'

'Just a few more days.'

'I haven't got a few more days.'

'We can pile on the pressure a bit more.'

'No. No serious injuries.'

'There is another option, sir.'

Korgay shook his head. 'It's too risky.'

'I'm sorry, sir, but in that case you have to give us a few more days.'

Korgay looked up to the heavens. Had it really come to this?

His thoughts took him back to the first time he had met Shanidza, just after he won his Olympic gold medal. Korgay and Comrade Zikladza had been very wary of this former dissident and the mass adulation he was attracting. Lionidza assured them there was nothing to worry about. He had everything under control. Well, he was right about that. Shanidza still danced to his tune, after all.

What Korgay hadn't been prepared for was his own reaction when he encountered Shanidza's wife. She had quite simply knocked him out. He hadn't been able to take his eyes off her throughout all the interminable speeches of the reception. First chance he got, he made straight for her and spent most of the rest of the evening talking to her.

Korgay couldn't understand it. There were so many beautiful women in the world, so why did he make a fool of himself over this one? He had never behaved like that since he was a young man. Indeed, he had always prided himself on the fact that he wasn't a slave to his cock, unlike that idiot Aleksander Mingrelsky.

Two years later, when Shanidza came back from the European Championships, there was no way Korgay could attend his reception, even if he had wanted to. By then, he and Zikladza had become venomous rivals, and Korgay knew he might be arrested or even assassinated if he placed himself in territory Zikladza controlled.

By the time of Shanidza's third triumph, Zikladza had been defanged. The Ksord-Akhtarian capital was once again safe for Korgay, who felt he had no choice but to pay public homage to his least favourite athlete. Shanidza's wife was there, of course, and

Korgay's heart jumped at the sight of her, much to his chagrin. But this time he had a lot of bridges to rebuild after the debacle of the Moscow coup, so he put her out of his mind and concentrated on ingratiating himself with some of the political heavyweights whose support he had lost.

Since then, Shanidza had become his most dangerous enemy, but what very few people knew was that Korgay had extended protection to his wife on more than one occasion. It was he who had granted her permission to go to North Ksordia after Shanidza was shot. He had also let all the paramilitaries know that she was not to be touched.

When Alavidza had her beaten up the previous month, Korgay made it very clear that there must be no repetition, and no other opposition leaders' wives were to be attacked either. All the West Ksords in the officer corps had been most upset by it. They had queued up to inform Korgay that such an attack on a woman violated their code of chivalry.

It was fear of their reaction that led Korgay to veto the arrest of Shanidza's wife when the Security Police brought him in. That had been a mistake, and one that he had good cause to regret.

Well the situation was now desperate. Korgay could no longer afford to bow to sentiment. Tamara Shanidza was his enemy, however sublime her cheekbones. She was Akhtarian and was married to the most treacherous of Ksords. They both wanted to destroy him. They both wanted to wreck everything he had achieved for his nation.

Well, he wasn't going to let them do that. The time had come to get serious. Either Shanidza would give him the confession he needed or his wife would suffer the consequences.

Tamara woke up as soon as they arrived in the cul-de-sac. She heard the slamming of car doors and the shouting as they smashed in her front and back doors and overpowered her startled bodyguards. Shota woke up and screamed in terror. Tamara picked him up and hugged him. She turned on the bedroom light and opened the door. She didn't want them to have an excuse to smash it in.

Two Security Police officers rushed up into the room. They pointed their guns at Tamara and told her to put up her hands.

'I can't. I've got to look after my son.'

'Well stand over there by the bed, away from the window.'

Tamara did as she was told and spoke softly to Shota as the Security Police ransacked the house yet again. Shota was terrified and shook and sobbed uncontrollably. Somehow Tamara managed to stay calm for him, but she was very afraid too. Had they come to arrest her this time? What would happen to Shota if they did?

And she felt very vulnerable wearing nothing but her nightdress. She could see the lust in their eyes and it scared her.

Two officers opened all her bedroom cupboards and flung their contents all over the floor. And then she saw their commander, the man with the frowning eyebrows. He leered at her and grinned, surveying the mess on the floor. 'We're just looking for one more mobile phone. We've found four. We know you've got one more.'

Tamara wondered how they knew. Did they have another informer among her replacement staff? Or was the house bugged?

A few minutes later, one of them came into the bedroom with a mobile phone in his hand.

'Where was it?' asked the man with the eyebrows.

'The little kid's bedroom, in his toy box.'

'Okay, let's go.' He took a radio out of his jacket pocket and spoke into it. 'We're just leaving. Tell Mingrelsky to give it five minutes, then we'll give him and his men twenty.'

A voice on the radio said, 'Yes, sir.'

The Security Police left as quickly as they had arrived. Tamara turned off her light and watched them leap into their black Volgas and speed off.

Funnily enough, she was sure she didn't see their leader get into any of the cars.

The whole street was silent, apart from Shota's continued whimpering.

What had happened to her bodyguards and all the other staff? Tamara still knew nothing about the fate of those who had been arrested with Ruslan, apart from the three who had subsequently given 'evidence' against him on TV. How foolish she had been to stay in Ronkoni and put them all at risk.

Shota was quiet now, and soon he would go back to sleep. Tamara wondered how all of this appeared in the mind of a two-year-old. Would he suffer any long-term effects?

And what had that Security Police officer meant? 'Tell Mingrelsky we'll give him and his men twenty minutes.'

Give him twenty minutes for what?

To gang rape her?

Hell and damnation.

Suddenly Tamara realised that she really was in danger.

Chapter Thirty-Two

IF CAPTAIN Lemash Kafeveli's superiors had had access to his thoughts, they would long since have taken him off surveillance of Shanidza's house. He had come to enjoy listening to Tamara too much, and often when she was at the back of the house, Kafeveli would surreptitiously stand near the window and watch her.

He spent many of the tedious hours when there was nothing to listen to concocting elaborate fantasies in which he befriended her. These fantasies were entirely chaste. He imagined that Tamara would treat him as a good friend, a favourite uncle. Sometimes in his fantasies she would embrace him and kiss his cheek, and he would feel her delicate sensuality but would restrain himself, just as she, perhaps, would restrain herself.

Kafeveli was horrified by the allegation that Tamara was a drug addict. He knew that she was nothing of the sort, though he believed the accusations against Shanidza until one of his commanders told him they were pure fiction, just a way of getting him.

Tamara campaigned tirelessly for the release of her husband and his staff. Kafeveli admired her press conference blood test stunt and the incessant interviews she gave to Ksordian and foreign reporters. She had telephoned just about every leading athlete and historian in the former Soviet Union to enlist their help and had used her English to make dozens of calls abroad.

When Tamara addressed a mass rally in Central Ronkoni, Kafeveli went along to watch her, even though it was his day off. He was astonished at the size of the crowd, the vehemence of their hatred for President Korgay and the enthusiasm with which they applauded the short, impassioned speech she made in an accent that would have seemed hateful just a few months ago.

The rally eventually turned into a bloody riot and Kafeveli made himself scarce. It would have been very embarrassing if he had got caught up in it and been arrested, or even worse if he had been recognised as a Security Police officer and lynched, a fate that befell two men that afternoon, both of them lucky to escape with their lives.

For hour after hour, Kafeveli sat at his listening post while Tamara told people that her husband was being tortured. He knew she believed what she was saying, but it wasn't true. The old KGB had never tortured anyone and neither would the Security Police. To be sure, they would use hunger and tiredness to wear him down, but there would be no torture.

On the eleventh night after Shanidza's arrest, Kafeveli was sleeping on duty at three in the morning when noises downstairs woke him up. Four Security Policemen had let themselves into the house. They came into the listening post and turned on the light. Kafeveli stood up blinking.

Their leader, he of the bushy eyebrows that met in the middle, greeted him brusquely: 'Hello Kafeveli.'

'Hello, Colonel Ambalek, sir.'

'We need a chair with a straight, hard back.'

'You can use this one, sir.'

'Yes, okay.' The Colonel turned round to his subordinates. 'Bring him in.'

'Yes, sir.'

Two of them disappeared downstairs. Soon afterwards, Kafeveli heard them walking up the stairs with a man who coughed frequently. They brought him into the room. He was a prisoner, blindfolded and handcuffed to one of the officers, walking very stiffly, as if he had been beaten up.

It was Shanidza.

The Colonel motioned Kafeveli to keep quiet.

The officers led Shanidza to the chair. They pushed him onto it and handcuffed his right arm to the back.

The Colonel turned towards Kafeveli. 'Is it on earphones or speakers?'

'Earphones.'

'Put it on the speakers.'

'Yes, sir.' Kafeveli pulled the earphone plug out. A faint hiss came from the speakers. Everyone in Shanidza's house would be asleep, except perhaps for one of the bodyguards.

The Colonel looked at the other officers and pointed to Shanidza. 'Gag him if he makes any noise.'

'Yes, sir.'

The Colonel left with one of his men, telling him to unbolt the gate at the end of the back garden: 'I'll come back that way when we've finished.'

'What's going on?' Kafeveli asked the other two officers.

'You'll see.'

A few minutes later, he heard the sound of cars in the street in front of Shanidza's house. Then the noise of a well organised raid came through the speakers: shouting, doors being smashed in, a baby crying hysterically, and then agents rushing up the stairs.

Shanidza raised his head. 'That's my baby.'

'Keep quiet.'

'What are you doing?'

'Shut your fucking mouth.'

Through all the noise of the raid, Kafeveli heard the crying of the infant, and the soft murmurings of Tamara's voice as she tried to calm him down. He looked at Shanidza, sitting stiff and upright in the chair, his eyes covered, trying to catch her words.

Looking at him, Kafeveli had no sympathy for him, but he felt angry nonetheless. Beating him up was all so unnecessary, and if word ever came out, it would blacken the name of the Security Police.

And then, as always happened, the raid ended suddenly when they found what they were looking for, in this case a mobile phone, of all things. Kafeveli heard a voice he recognised as the Colonel's say, 'We're just leaving. Tell Mingrelsky to give it five minutes, then we'll give him and his men twenty.'

Kafeveli wasn't sure that he understood, but he didn't like the sound of it.

A couple of minutes later, the Colonel came panting into the house and up the stairs. He opened the door and entered with a triumphant grin.

'Enjoy that, Shanidza?'

'What's going on?'

'You'll see.' He looked at one of the other Security Policemen. 'Take his blindfold off.'

He obliged, and Shanidza blinked in the brightness of the room.

'What's all this about Mingrelsky?'

'I'll give you one guess.'

'You're joking.'

'Wait and see.'

'Oh Jesus. Oh Jesus no. Call him off. Call him off.'

'Why should we?'

'You sons of sluts. Oh Jesus, you sons of sluts.'

'You'd better make your mind up quickly, Shanidza.'

Shanidza was silent.

'You'd better be quick.'

Kafeveli wanted to hit him. What the hell was he waiting for?

Finally, Shanidza bowed his head. 'I'll do anything you want. Just call Mingrelsky off.'

The Colonel pointed to Kafeveli. 'Turn the speakers off.'

'No!' Shanidza yelled. 'I have to hear that she's safe.'

'No. You do whatever I say. That's the deal.'

'Please. Let me hear that she's safe.'

At that moment, the doorbell downstairs rang. It rang again and again.

'Who the hell's that?' said the Colonel. 'Kafeveli, go and see who it is.'

Kafeveli stepped out of the room and down the stairs. Behind him Shanidza was still pleading, and the Colonel was insisting on complete submission to his will.

The bell didn't stop ringing until Kafeveli turned on the kitchen light. He unlocked the back door and opened it.

It was Tamara.

She still had her nightdress on under her coat, and she was carrying her sleeping infant in her arms.

For a moment, she and Kafeveli stared at each other.

'Please,' said Tamara. 'Help me.'

Kafeveli put his finger to his lips. 'Keep quiet,' he whispered. He thought for a moment and then said, 'Come with me. Keep your head low and don't look at anyone.'

He led her through a gate and round to the front of the house.

Just as they reached the front, the back door opened. They heard someone run out and sprint towards the gate at the far end of the back garden.

'It's okay,' said Kafeveli. 'Let's go.'

In the street, two Security Police officers were leaning on their car and smoking.

Kafeveli walked towards them as Tamara headed the other way, her face determinedly pointing in the other direction.

'All right, comrades?'

'All right, Lemash? What are you doing here?'

'Been here for weeks. Surveillance. Now the Colonel says he wants the lady of the house out of earshot.'

The two officers nodded.

Kafeveli caught up with Tamara and led her to his Volga, which was parked some way up the street. He opened the door and Tamara got in the back.

He started the engine and drove off.

Ruslan heard his cell lock clunk. The door opened and three Security Police officers walked in.

'Come on then.'

They led him to the lift and up to a large, sunlit office on the third floor that had been turned into a TV studio. There they eased him into a chair in front of the cameras. The make-up girl brushed his hair and touched up his face while the Colonel told him which bits of his confession they wanted him to go through again.

Ruslan nodded.

This would be the third time.

His 'interviewer' sat down across the desk in front of him. He had been a senior TV reporter since the Soviet era and had actually interviewed Ruslan once when he was an athlete. But this was no interview. They were just repeating lines scripted by the Security Police.

'Try and get it right this time,' said the reporter. 'We've got a tight schedule.'

These were the first unscripted words he and Ruslan had exchanged all morning and they infuriated Ruslan.

Once more, they made him put his hands on the desk in front of him, the left hand cupping the right. It seemed very contrived to him, but presumably they thought it looked natural. Well this time, he would shit on their tight schedule. As he spoke his lines, he crossed the middle finger of his left hand onto the nail of the index finger, in imitation of the way English children sometimes cross their fingers when they tell a lie.

Then, after a few seconds, his nerve gave out.

What would they do if they found out?

Fortunately, they didn't notice. After reshooting, they kept him waiting in the other office for fifteen minutes, and then they led him back down to his bed in the bowels of the building, leaving him to wallow in the misery of defeat.

Chapter Thirty-Three

PRESIDENT KORGAY nodded. It would have to do. The whole thing was a complete mess, but at least this would give him a bit of breathing space. And with any luck, the sight of their hero broken would demoralise the opposition.

It had been also an excellent idea to use one of Ksordian TV's most respected news reporters. That would bring real credibility.

Shanidza's answers had been well scripted. He had admitted all the charges but had refused to finger Lionidza ('the perfect front man because he was too stupid to realise what was going on') and Sultanov ('I don't want to name names'). That would help Korgay to appease those in his own party who still had a soft spot for Lionidza, and it would keep the possibility of a rapprochement with Sultanov open. And it gave the whole thing an air of authenticity. That was good.

Shanidza had admitted that, like the attempt on his life, the killing of Leila Meipariani had been drug-related. But the best part of all was where he said that though he had started dealing in drugs to feed his wife's heroin addiction, he had continued in the trade long after she kicked her habit, just to make money. This negated her blood sample stunt very effectively.

At the end of the interview, the reporter had asked Shanidza why he had decided to confess. 'I held out until I saw all the evidence the police have got against me. There comes a point when you have to cut your losses and co-operate in the hope of a reduced sentence.'

'And how have you been treated since your arrest?'

'The food's lousy and the bed's too hard, but apart from that I haven't got any complaints.'

Very good.

Korgay had to smile. 'Yes, it'll do. Let's broadcast it.'

'We can get it on the one o'clock news, sir,' said the head of the Security Police.

'No, wait until the evening news. People will be at home then. It'll be harder for troublemakers to sow doubts.'

'There is one little problem, sir.'

'What's that?'

The Security Policeman gulped quite audibly. 'It's Shanidza's wife, sir. She's disappeared.'

'What do you mean, disappeared?'

The Security Policeman gave a long and convoluted explanation, the gist of which was that the captain in charge of surveillance had disappeared while Colonel Ambalek was arguing with Mingrelsky, who was so furious at being denied his little gangbang that he was threatening to shoot all the Security Police. Everybody assumed that Captain Kafeveli had lost his nerve and fled. It wasn't until mid-morning that they noticed Tamara was missing and put two and two together.

'So let me get this straight,' said Korgay. 'We're talking about your man, who you left to keep an eye on her, yes? Your man has taken her away? Am I right?'

'I'm afraid so, sir.'

'Oh Jesus fucking Christ, I just don't believe this.' Korgay stood up, kicked his chair away and started to pace around the room. 'This is just one blunder after another. "Three or four days," you said. You'd have a confession out of him in three or four days, and you wouldn't need to lay a finger on him. Except you cover him in bruises, and even then you get nothing. You only get a confession out of him by threatening to gangbang his fucking wife. And then you lose her. Not only that, it's your fucking operative who takes her away. This just goes from bad to worse.'

'We'll find her, sir.'

'Use your fucking brain. Where would you go if you were her?'

'We're searching the house of everyone she knows in Ronkoni, and we're stopping every car that passes into Russia.'

'I'm surrounded by morons. Fucking morons. When did she leave?'

'Quite a long time ago, sir.'

'When?'

'Possibly two, two-thirty in the morning.'

'And now it's gone eleven. She'll be in Central Kubania by now, snug in the arms of the fucking Tatars. Get that confession on TV before they call a press conference. I don't care how you do it. Interrupt programmes for a special announcement, do whatever you want. But we have to get to the TV stations first.'

'Yes, sir.'

'And one other thing – that operative of yours who's taken her. Make sure he keeps his mouth shut. You are capable of doing that, aren't you?'

'Yes, Mr President.'

The plan for the press conference was for Kafeveli to read out a statement detailing exactly what he had seen and heard. Then Tamara would tell the story from her angle, after which she and Central Kuban President Yakub Bovin would answer questions from the press. They would run the press conference in Russian in order to reach the largest possible audience.

They had written Tamara's statement and were busy trying to shorten it when an official put his head round the door and said something in Tatar. Tamara picked out the word 'Shanidza'.

'Come quick,' said Yakub. 'Ruslan's going to make a statement on Ksordian TV.'

They hurried into a nearby office that had a television set. Kafeveli was already there. He stood up and greeted Tamara.

'Hello.'

'Hi.'

'How are you?'

'I'm okay, thanks to you.'

Kafeveli nodded.

Murad and Fatima, who had been looking after Shota, came in and handed him back to Tamara just as a newsreader announced that Ruslan Shanidza had confessed to drug smuggling in an interview with Ksordian TV.

'Papa! Papa!' shouted Shota as Ruslan's face appeared on the screen.

'Shush,' said Tamara. 'Let's see what Papa says.'

As she watched, Tamara scrutinised her husband's face for clues as to his condition. He had lost weight, and his posture seemed to be stiffer than usual. Most of the shots of him were head and shoulders only. There were just a few more distant shots, but Tamara thought he was definitely sitting just a little too upright.

But the worst thing of all was his eyes. They were harsh and haunted, like his mother's. It was as if the beautiful light that had always shone from them had been extinguished. It made Tamara want to cry.

As she watched, Murad leaned forward and whispered in her ear. 'This isn't a real interview.'

'What do you mean?'

'They needed at least two takes to get this, maybe more. Look at his hair. One minute it's really tidy, the next minute it isn't, and then it's really tidy again. There! Did you see that?'

Tamara nodded. 'Yes.'

'It's not just that. The lighting isn't consistent. It's a really shoddy piece of work.'

The interview finished, and then the reporter added that Ruslan had given the police the names of some of his accomplices. There were shots of three of them in police custody: a middle aged Ksordian woman and two young men who looked as if they might be her sons. Tamara had no idea who they were, though there was something familiar about the young men.

Ksordian TV then returned to the old Russian movie it had been showing, and Yakub told the officials to turn it off. He led Tamara back to his office. 'I'm sorry, we should have got onto TV first. It's my mistake and I'm sorry. I thought we had more time.'

They continued their preparations nonetheless. Yakub coached Tamara on the delivery of her statement and gave her practice in answering awkward questions, while Murad sought out examples of poor continuity editing in Ruslan's interview. Then, when they were just about to set off for the conference room, the official came back and said something to Yakub.

Yakub swore in Tatar. Then he turned to Tamara and said, 'That secret policeman, Kafeveli, he's refusing to read out his statement.'

313

'Why?'

'He won't say.'

'Oh no.'

'Can you speak to him, Tamara?' said Fatima. 'See if you can change his mind.'

'Are you sure we've got time?'

'We need him,' said Yakub. 'See what you can do.'

Tamara picked up Shota, and the official led her back to the office where Kafeveli was sitting in front of the TV with his head in his hands.

Tamara remembered the moment she had first clapped eyes on him.

It had been such a shock to see a fully dressed man. She knew he was Security Police at once: he just looked the part. She had half expected him to drag her back to her fate at Mingrelsky's hands and was astonished when he had helped her.

She had asked him to take her to Giorgi and Venera's flat, or else to Orbeliani's house, but he vetoed both of these. 'It's not safe.' Her in-laws' flat would be the first place they would look, and Orbeliani's house was bound to be under observation. So they decided to leave the city. They would be safe once they made it to Central Kubania.

For a long time, she and Kafeveli didn't speak to each other. Tamara didn't feel entirely safe in his presence. He was one of *them* after all. She wondered if he was acting on his own initiative, or was this part of whatever it was they were up to? Would he betray her at some stage, or even sell her to one of the paramilitary groups?

She noticed he kept looking at her in his mirror. Tamara was used to men staring at her, but he was positively creepy.

She decided to engage him in conversation, to make him see her as a human being. That way, she might be safer. She got him to say what had happened in the listening post and what kind of condition Ruslan was in. He told her about the infiltration of their bodyguard and how the Security Police had been able to listen to them for weeks, and yes they had bugged the bedroom too.

Tamara found it difficult to continue the conversation after that. The thought of them listening to her making love to Ruslan made her feel sick.

As she looked at Kafeveli now, Tamara felt that she had treated him rather shabbily.

He looked round and saw her standing there with Shota in her arms. He stood up instantly. 'Hello again.'

'Hello. They say you don't want to speak at our press conference?'

'No.'

'Do you mind if I ask why not?'

Kafeveli hesitated. 'I can't. I have my reasons.'

'Is something wrong?'

Kafeveli turned away from her and covered his face with his hands. Was he crying?

Tamara put her free hand on his shoulder.

He turned round and looked at her. There were no tears in his eyes, but his face was full of despair. 'They've arrested my wife and children.'

'Oh my God. Are you sure?'

'Yes. They showed them on TV, just after your husband. They said they were accomplices.'

'I'm so sorry. Let my friends help.'

'No, you mustn't. You must promise me you'll never tell anyone what I've just told you. Please. Let me deal with it.'

'Are you sure we can't help?'

'No. Leave it to me. I know what I have to do.'

'Okay, I owe you that. In fact, I owe you a lot more than that.'

Kafeveli bowed his head.

'If there's anything I can do, just let me know.'

Kafeveli nodded.

Tamara returned to Yakub and simply said that Kafeveli wouldn't change his mind.

Yakub telephoned Orbeliani and told him what had happened. Orbeliani suggested they postpone the press conference until he arrived.

'But that'll take hours,' said Tamara.

'I know. We'll just have to wait.'

'Do you think you should call Nina and Lionidza too? Ruslan always says to include as many people as possible.'

'In that case, do you mind if I get as many people here as I can? There's something else I need to discuss with them.'

'It's up to you.'

Yakub called every major opposition leader he could think of. Lionidza told him he had a stick of dynamite that would blow the case against Ruslan sky high. 'Whatever you do, don't hold your press conference until I get there.'

Tamara and Shota spent most of the afternoon with Fatima. They went to buy some clothes, surrounded by a dozen heavily armed policemen who wouldn't let the inevitable autograph hunters get anywhere near Fatima.

'It'd be nice to have a bodyguard like this all the time,' Fatima said.

'You can say that again.'

They went back to the President's Palace, where Tamara and Shota had a short nap on a sofa in one of the reception rooms. Yakub's wife Marta came and woke her up after twenty minutes.

'Nina and Orbeliani are here.'

Tamara went to freshen herself up before meeting them.

'How are you, Tamara?' Nina asked as they exchanged kisses.

'I'm okay. I feel much safer here.'

'Are you ready for the press conference?' Orbeliani asked.

'Yes. I just want to get it over with.'

'Yes, I understand,' said Orbeliani. 'But I think it would be best to wait for Lionidza. Yakub says he's got some information that'll be very useful to us.'

'More like he's anxious to get his fat face on TV,' said Nina.

Orbeliani smiled. 'I think we should wait to hear what he's got to say.'

Lionidza arrived half an hour later.

'Are you all right, Tamara?'

'I'm fine.'

'I've got something that might cheer you up,' Lionidza said, crossing his fingers and holding them up in front of her. 'Ever seen this before?'

'Well, yes. English children do it behind their backs when they're playing a trick on you.'

Lionidza smiled. 'And a certain athlete of our acquaintance did it when he was forced to make a false confession on TV.'

'You're joking.'

'No I'm not. Have you got it on video, Yakub?'

'Yes, of course.'

'Well, let's have a look.'

They all went into the room with a TV, leaving a rather nervous official to keep an eye on the sleeping Shota. And sure enough, there it was, just under two minutes into the interview, a shot of Ruslan sitting with his hands on a desk, the second finger of his left hand slightly but definitely crossed over the index finger.

'Make sure there's an English reporter at the press conference,' said Lionidza. 'Ask him what the gesture means and then show this extract. It's a signal from Ruslan to you, Tamara, something that only you would understand. He wanted you to be able to reveal it when you were safe.'

'Thank you, Sergo. That's wonderful.'

'How come you know about it?' Nina asked.

Lionidza laughed. 'I don't know. I must have seen it in his file.'

Korgay was livid. Why hadn't anybody spotted it? The fucking morons. How could they be so stupid?

He called the head of the Security Police to see him and spent ten minutes yelling at him and cursing his incompetence.

'What are we supposed to do now?'

'Just hold onto him, sir. Sit it out.'

'That's what I should have done in the first place, without any of this crap about drug smuggling. God's nails, why I ever listened to you idiots I'll never know.'

The twelve of them sat around a long table: Yakub and a senior Tatar policeman, plus Orbeliani, Nina, Lionidza, former Minister of

Munitions Zviad Qipiani, the erstwhile leader of the North Ksords Mataa Bogiani, the militant nationalist Kakhi and one of his aides, two student leaders and a trade unionist.

The Tatar policeman gave each of them a dossier and talked his way through it, explaining how his men had pieced together the story of the massacre at Onchi'Aketi, where the Ksords had butchered 250 Akhtarian POWs and civilians.

'So as you can see,' the policeman said, speaking in Russian, 'it wasn't just Mingrelsky and the Third Motor Rifle Regiment. The evidence points right to the top: Korgay and Alavidza gave the order and General Napashidza knew what was going on and did nothing to stop it.'

'You're a lawyer,' said Yakub, looking at Orbeliani. 'In international law, that makes General Napashidza a war criminal too, doesn't it?'

'Yes, it does,' said Orbeliani. 'But I think Napashidza's case is different. Yes, he received two messages about what was going on, but one was from a complete stranger, and the other was from Colonel Bebur Chikradza. Everyone knows Chikradza and Mingrelsky detest one another. Napashidza could argue...'

'For Christ's sake,' said Kakhi. 'You're not Napashidza's lawyer now, are you?'

Nina stepped in: 'Never mind about that. The point is, we have to make that dossier public right away.'

'No,' said Lionidza. 'We must do nothing of the sort.'

'Why the hell not?' said Nina.

'I'll tell you why not: the majority of Ksords can't even bring themselves to admit that this massacre took place at all, let alone that their Commander-in-Chief is a war criminal. We have to keep quiet about Onchi'Aketi until we're in power. Then we can do something about it.'

The others all argued against this, but Lionidza was adamant: 'This will destroy us if we try to use it.'

In the end, his arguments won them round, and everybody handed back their dossiers and agreed never to breathe a word of what had been said.

As they left, one of the student leaders went to the toilets on the ground floor. In the second cubicle, he removed a small recording device from his jacket and placed it on the floor behind the toilet.

Korgay could hardly believe his luck. He had been wondering whether to flee to Georgia before Saturday's demonstration, but then the opposition had given him just what he needed. He could barely contain his glee as he played the tape to his Commander-in-Chief, General Napashidza.

'So as you can see,' a Tatar voice said in Russian. 'it wasn't just Mingrelsky and the Third Motor Rifle Regiment. The evidence points right to the top: Alavidza gave the order and General Napashidza knew what was going on and did nothing to stop it.'

'You're a lawyer,' said Yakub Bovin's voice. 'In international law, that makes General Napashidza a war criminal too, doesn't it?'

'Yes, it does,' said Orbeliani.

Nina Begishveli spoke next: 'We have to make that dossier public right away.'

'No,' said Lionidza's voice. 'We must do nothing of the sort. We have to keep quiet about Onchi'Aketi until we're in power. Then we can do something about it.'

Ashen-faced, Napashidza agreed to transfer all the unreliable army units out of the capital and bring in the whole Third Motor Rifle Regiment in preparation for a crackdown.

Korgay then took other steps his military commander wouldn't need to know about. This would be his last chance to save Ksordia from Shanidza's rag-tag coalition of appeasers and defeatists. The stakes couldn't be higher, and this time there could be no restraint. This time there would be no holding back. None whatsoever.

He called the various paramilitary leaders to a meeting: 'Bring all your men to Ronkoni before Saturday, but make sure they're quiet about it. No getting pissed and shooting off their guns or anything like that. You'll get plenty of shooting practice on Saturday. When the opposition have their rally, we're going to provoke a riot. The police will let it get out of control, and then we're going to call in the army, just like April the twenty-fifth last year.

Except this time, there'll be no fucking about. With your help, we're going to smash the enemy once and for all.'

He spoke to Mingrelsky privately afterwards. 'I've got a job that I think you might enjoy. I'd like you to supply the provocation.'

Chapter Thirty-Four

NINA AND Lionidza wanted to cancel Saturday's demonstration. They were unnerved by the military movements and the very conspicuous massing of extremist paramilitaries. Orbeliani and the other opposition leaders insisted that it was essential to keep up the pressure on Korgay. Tamara trusted Orbeliani's judgement, so she and Shota returned to Ronkoni on Thursday. She was determined to do her bit and address the rally herself.

A lot of people were worried that she was putting herself in danger again. Orbeliani arranged for a dozen armed activists to stay and guard her. A trade unionist gave her a telephone number to call. 'Ring this number and we can have thirty men here in less than fifteen minutes.' Kakhi promised a detachment of armed men just as quickly. The head of Provisional Radio gave her his direct line. 'Ring this and I'll put you live on air.'

Tamara programmed the numbers into three mobile phones that she hid around the house and kept them on a scrap of paper in her pocket at all times.

On the Friday, just sixteen hours before the start of the demonstration, Orbeliani telephoned Nina and invited her to his home.

'I'm beginning to wish we had cancelled the demonstration,' he said as they sat on a bench in his garden.

'Why the change of heart?'

'I've been speaking to Bebur Chikradza.'

'The colonel?'

'Yes.'

'The one who ordered his troops to vote No?'

Orbeliani smiled. 'That wasn't my idea.'

'I can guess whose idea it was.'

'It wasn't Lionidza's if that's what you think. Anyway, Colonel Chikradza says General Napashidza's come off the fence. There's going to be a provocation tomorrow, and when the riot starts, they'll call in the troops, just like April the twenty-fifth. Except this time they plan to smash the entire opposition, not just one party.'

'Do you think they're strong enough?'

'Napashidza's brought loyal troops in and ordered Colonel Chikradza to remove all his men from the city, but Chikradza's only moved them about twenty kilometres to the south. He says he's bringing another battalion in bit by bit, in civvies. They'll be in place by Saturday. When the fighting starts, General Napashidza will seize the city centre, but Chikradza's planning to take control of the bridges over the River Kuban and all the suburbs to the south.'

Nina instinctively looked around to make sure nobody was listening. She leaned towards Orbeliani. 'He's talking about civil war.'

'Yes.'

'Zourab, we have to call this rally off.'

'It's too late.'

'There must be something we can do.'

'You must have lots of stewards.'

'Of course.'

'Well,' said Orbeliani, 'we have to make sure our stewards know there's going to be a provocation, and they have to do everything they can to prevent a violent response.'

'Agreed. Why don't you get in touch with Lionidza? He's pretty sensible about things like that. I'll try to get the students and the trade unionists onside. The one who scares me is Kakhi. There's nothing that mad cretin would like more than a rematch of April the twenty-fifth.'

Two uniformed officers came into Ruslan's cell and threw his civilian clothes at him. 'Put these on.'

'What's happening?'

'You'll see.'

Once he was dressed, they took him up to the ground floor, where they handcuffed him to one of their number and took him outside for the first time in over two weeks.

Ruslan blinked in the midday sunshine. 'Where are you taking me?'

'You'll see.'

The Security Police took him to yet another black Volga and set off south through the city streets. They must be taking him home. Were they going to free him?

A thunderbolt struck him. What if they had noticed his crossed fingers and were planning to punish Tamara? He broke out into a cold sweat, closed his eyes and prayed frantically. Please God, please, not that. Anything but that. I don't care if they kill me, but don't let them hurt Tamara.

They stopped outside his house.

'Okay, Shanidza. Go and find yourself a donkey to fuck.'

They were setting him free.

He eased himself out, and the Volga and its escort sped off.

Ruslan walked up to his house. It seemed to be empty, but then the door opened and his sister-in-law Venera stepped out, a distressed looking Shota in her arms.

'Papa!' Shota cried. 'Want to go see Papa.'

Ruslan kissed Shota and Venera and Shota clambered onto him.

'Where's Tamara?'

'She's at the demonstration.'

'What demonstration?'

Venera smiled. 'Calling for your release.'

'Are you two here alone?'

'Yes.'

'Haven't you got any bodyguards?'

'No. The Security Police came about ten minutes ago and made them all leave.'

Korgayo, Korgayo, Wadwaz, Wadwaz (Korgay, Korgay, Down, Down).

The crowd was enormous and the din tremendous: slogans, whistles and drums, and empty pots and pans banged by the once prosperous housewives of Ronkoni. Lionidza wondered how many people there were. Kakhi said more than 350,000, but he was probably counting feet rather than heads. Even so, everyone agreed that it was bigger than April 25th last year, bigger even than the great mass rallies that had swept Korgay to power just four years earlier.

The sheer size of the demonstration gave Lionidza a real buzz, a sense of excitement and confidence that smothered his feelings of dread.

Korgayo, Korgayo, Wadwaz, Wadwaz.

Korgayo, Korgayo, Wadwaz, Wadwaz.

How the people hated him now.

Ruslanis Shanidzis Muka'Dagodi (Free Ruslan Shanidza).

Lionidza wasn't used to demonstrations. He didn't understand how the crowd's slogan could suddenly change like that. The whole thing seemed to be completely random.

Ruslanis Shanidzis Muka'Dagodi.

Nobody shouted this with more fervour than the woman marching next to him, right at the head of the demonstration. It was Tamara, her arms linked to Lionidza on one side and Nina Begishveli, of all people, on the other.

Lionidza had given very specific instructions to a group of his burliest supporters just a few rows behind. If violence broke out, they were to take hold of Tamara and escort her to safety at once.

Ksordia Maka Korgaytan Tad.

Ksordia Maka Korgaytan Tad.

The slogan had changed again.

Then, beneath the noise of the demonstration, Lionidza thought he heard a beeping noise. At first he ignored it, until he realised it was a mobile phone. It certainly wasn't his: he abominated the things.

'Tamara, is that your mobile?'

'Pardon?'

'Is that your mobile phone?'

'Oh God, yes.'

Tamara fumbled in her bag and brought out her enormous mobile. She put it to one ear, her finger in the other. Then she stopped walking, doubled up and crouched down.

The front ranks of the demonstrators came to a halt.

'Ruslan!'

Everyone around her went quiet.

'Ruslan, are you okay?...No, I'm fine...It's all right, my love, I'm fine...They didn't lay a finger on me...There's nothing to forgive...Ruslan? Ruslan? Oh, God's nails, I've lost the signal.'

She looked up at Lionidza and Nina, tears in her eyes.

'He's at home. They've freed him.'

The news rippled back through the crowd, followed by a great wave of cheering.

Tamara stood up.

'I'll take you home,' said Lionidza.

'No,' said Tamara. 'You're needed here.'

'Okay, I'll get my bodyguards to take you.'

And so Tamara left the demonstration, hurrying off down a side street with Lionidza's toughs.

Lionidza's men used their mobiles to call up a converted UAZ ambulance, which drove Tamara south, away from the noise of the demonstration. Here and there, she saw Zil and Ural lorries full of grey-uniformed policemen, and down one street, she thought she saw what looked like military lorries.

She tried to phone home time and time again, but either she lost the signal before she finished dialling or else the line was engaged. Once her own phone rang, but all she heard was Ruslan's voice saying her name and then the signal went again. She didn't get through to him properly until they were less than half a kilometre from her house.

'Ruslan?'

'Hi, Tamara. Got you at last.'

'I'm on my way now. I'll be with you in a few minutes.'

'Don't come without bodyguards.'

Then the signal went again.

'God's teeth,' said Tamara. 'These things are useless.'

Korgayo, Korgayo, Wadwaz, Wadwaz.

'I can't understand it,' Lionidza yelled into Nina's ear. 'Why would he release Ruslan now?'

'I know, it's very odd.'

'Korgay never does anything without a reason. He's up to something.'

'Yes, the question is: What?'

The Security Police halted Tamara some 200 metres from her house. They said she could continue on foot and alone, but her bodyguards would have to leave the area. Lionidza's men had strict orders not to let her out of their sight, but she was insistent. She had to be with her husband.

There were dozens of uniformed Security Policemen all along her route, standing smoking by their black Volgas, blocking the pavements and forcing Tamara to walk in the middle of the street. They leered at her silently as she walked past.

She reached the end of the cul-de-sac. The door opened and Ruslan stepped out, Shota in his strong right arm.

Shota wriggled and Ruslan let him down. He ran up to Tamara. 'Papa's home.'

'Yes, poppet.'

Tamara ruffled his hair and embraced Ruslan.

'Are you okay?' she asked.

'I'll survive. What about you?'

'Never felt better.'

They went into the house, away from the prying eyes of the Security Police. Ruslan said nothing, but he wished Tamara had stayed where there were bodyguards.

Lionidza stood at the back of the temporary platform and listened as Nina Begishveli pointed out the riot policemen skulking behind the tail end of the crowd.

'There are too few of them,' she told him. 'I've spoken at God knows how many rallies, all of them smaller than this one. But there have always been more riot police on duty than today.'

The crowd applauded a trade union leader who had just finished speaking, and Orbeliani, who was acting as master of ceremonies, announced that Nina would be next to speak. Everyone applauded.

Lionidza grabbed her arm as she approached the microphone. 'For God's sake calm them down. There's going to be a provocation and they mustn't respond with violence.'

'Don't worry, Sergo, I'm just as scared as you are.'

That was the first time she had ever called him by his first name.

The knock on the door came after just ten minutes. It was the Security Police.

Shota started to cry.

'He's really scared of them,' said Tamara, picking him up.

'We'd better stay together,' Ruslan said in Russian. 'And stay calm.'

Ruslan, Tamara and Venera remained in the living room, trying to distract Shota while the Security Police ransacked the house yet again. Within ten minutes they had found all but one of Tamara's mobile phones.

'They're up to something,' Tamara told Ruslan in English. 'That's why they're taking my mobiles.'

Ruslan's interrogator, the colonel with the bushy eyebrows, appeared. He approached Tamara, grabbed hold of the front of her top and pushed her against the wall. Shota screamed and covered his eyes.

'Leave her alone,' said Ruslan, stepping forward.

Two Security Policemen leapt on him and pushed him to the floor.

'There's another one,' the Colonel said. 'Where is it?'

'I don't know what you mean.'

'Don't fuck me about, or I'll beat it out of you. We've found your mobile phones in the kitchen and bathroom. Where's the other one?'

'I'll show you, but stop frightening my little boy.'

He let go of Tamara and she led him up the stairs to her bedroom, Shota whimpering and covering his eyes in fear.

She pointed to the far side of the bed. 'I taped it under there.'

The colonel nodded, and one of his men went and crouched down by the bed, his hand feeling until he found the mobile phone. 'Got it,' he said. He yanked it out and threw it to his commander.

'Right. Downstairs.'

As they opened the door to the living room, Tamara noticed the pungent smell of chloroform.

Chloroform?

Inside the room, the smell was almost overpowering. Ruslan and Venera were lying unconscious on the floor, three Security Policemen standing over them.

One of them grabbed Tamara from behind, and another took out a small bottle and poured chloroform onto a cloth. With one hand he took hold of Tamara's hair. With the other, he covered her face and nose with the cloth.

Tamara held her breath as soon as she realised what they were about to do. At the same time, she held onto the struggling, screaming Shota.

What to do? What to do? She couldn't hold her breath forever.

She had to pretend to fall unconscious. That was the only way.

She let Shota slip to the floor.

Shota dug his nails hard into Tamara's arms. It was difficult not to scream with the pain of it, but she knew that if she breathed in once she would be lost. She was already feeling giddy.

Oh God, she was going under.

She made her body go limp, and they removed the cloth from her mouth. One of the Security Policemen slapped her across the face, but she was too far gone to react. The pain felt very distant, their voices and Shota's screams far away.

They let go of her, and she slumped to the floor, still holding her breath with grim determination.

'What about the kid?' she heard one of them say.

'Leave him. Come on, let's go.'

Tamara heard their footsteps echo in the distance. From somewhere she heard Shota's hysterical voice: 'Mama! Mama! Wake up, Mama!'

Then came a noise half way between a sigh and a scream. Tamara realised that it came from herself. She had started to breathe again, and this made her fall further towards unconsciousness.

Of course, there was chloroform around her nose and mouth.

She held her breath again and somehow managed to get to her feet. Shota grabbed hold of her leg but Tamara shook him off. She staggered towards the kitchen. It was like walking into a vortex, the air grinding noisily as it went round and round in front of her.

She turned on the tap and splashed water onto her face, feeling nothing but a slight sensation of cold around the temples. She splashed more and more, frantically washing the chloroform away from her nose and mouth.

The air stopped spinning and she began to breathe again, gasping, out of breath.

Shota put his arm round her leg. 'Mama!'

Tamara picked him up. She would have to be quick.

'Come on, let's go.'

The front door was open but not smashed. Tamara ran outside. All the Security Police had disappeared.

She hurried over the road to the house of the frightened couple. She saw them watching through their living room window.

She hammered on the door. 'Please! I'm desperate!'

'Go away,' the man's voice said.

'Just take my baby and give me your mobile phone. Then I'll go away.'

A few seconds later, the door opened. Tamara tried to give Shota to the husband, but he hung onto her and almost fell to the floor.

'Stay with Mama! Stay with Mama!'

Tamara pushed him away from her and grabbed the mobile phone from the wife. Then she ran back into the house, shutting and locking the door behind her.

She ran into the living room. Ruslan and Venera were still unconscious.

She turned on the mobile phone. It seemed to take ages to get a signal.

She took the paper out of her pocket. Which number? The trade unionists and Kakhi's people were no use to her. She only had a couple of minutes at most before the assassins came. It had to be Provisional Radio.

Tamara's hands were shaking so much that it took three attempts to dial the number. She pressed the 'OK' button and heard short tones with a longer pause between.

She sighed with relief. They weren't engaged. Come on. Answer me for God's sake.

'Hello, Provisional Radio.'

'Can I speak to the boss? It's urgent, very urgent.'

'He's at the demonstration.'

'Oh God. Look this is Ruslan Shanidza's wife. He promised he'd put me live on air if I was in danger. Please, get me on air, quick.'

'What's happening?'

'No time to explain. Just get me on air. For God's sake, get me on air.'

'Hold on.'

Come on come on come on. Hurry up.

'Hello?' Tamara recognised the voice at once. It was Tembot Ksansky, one of her favourite DJs.

'Are we on air?'

'Yes, and are you Tamara Shanidza?'

'Yes.'

'What's going on Tamara?'

'They're coming to kill us.'

Ksansky was silent.

'Hello, are you still there?'

'Yes, sorry. Who's coming to kill you?'

'I don't know. Probably Mingrelsky. The Security Police have set it up. They've left us here alone and they've knocked Ruslan out with chloroform.'

'Oh my God.'

'I need you to help us.'

'What do you want me to do?'

'Keep me on air. When Mingrelsky comes, you have to speak to him. Tell him he's on air.'

'Oh blood and damnation.'

'Can you do that?'

It took Ksansky some time to reply.

'Yes.'

330

'Oh Jesus,' said Tamara. 'They're here. I can hear their cars. They're outside. Can you hear their voices?'

'No.'

Just then there was a bang.

'I heard that,' said Ksansky. 'What was it?'

'They're kicking the door in.'

Tamara opened the living room door, holding the mobile phone to her cheek.

'Mingrelsky!' she shouted.

And then she saw him, instantly recognisable despite his hooded face.

It was him.

It could only be him.

'Mingrelsky!'

There were four or five others too, all armed with AKM assault rifles.

'Ah, Tamara. So you've come round already.' He grabbed her by the hair. He didn't seem to notice the mobile phone. 'I'll tell you what, when we've shot your husband, we'll take you with us, and this time I'll make sure every White Eagle in Ronkoni fucks you before we slit your throat.'

'Mingrelsky, you can't.'

'And why the fuck not?'

'Because this is going out live on the radio.'

'What?'

'I've got Provisional Radio on the other end of this phone. We're going out live.'

Mingrelsky hung his gun over his shoulder and snatched the mobile phone from Tamara, his other hand still clutching her hair.

'Who the fuck's that?'

'Hi there. Erm, this is the Tembot Ksansky show on Provisional Radio. We're going out live to a hundred thousand listeners all over the Ronkoni region.'

Mingrelsky's eyes widened. Tamara wasn't sure whether it was horror or fury.

'Think about it,' she said. 'If you kill us in front of a hundred thousand witnesses, even Korgay won't be able to protect you.'

Mingrelsky paused for a moment.

'You fucking Rebel slut!' he shouted and pushed Tamara to the floor. Then he turned the mobile phone off and threw it against the wall.

Lionidza never thought he would approve of a speech by Nina Begishveli.

'We will defeat Korgay,' she said. 'When a regime is so discredited that it has to threaten to rape the wife of an opposition leader, then you know that regime has had it.'

Everybody cheered.

'We just have to be patient. Soon the whole rotten edifice will come crashing to the ground.'

Cheers and applause.

'But don't imagine Korgay's lost his teeth, because he hasn't.'

The crowd were silent again.

'He's transferred all the democratic units of the army out of Ronkoni, and he's brought the Third Motor Rifle Regiment in. Plus the White Eagles and the Ksord Home Army and all the other fascists. He wants to fight, and he wants to fight now, when he thinks he's still strong enough to beat us.'

Nina raised her voice to a shout. 'We mustn't give him what he wants. No matter what the provocation, we mustn't give him an excuse to send the army and the fascists in against us. Whatever happens today, no violence. We mustn't be provoked, not under any circumstances whatsoever.'

Some of the audience cheered, but here and there, Lionidza noticed a commotion among the crowd. They weren't listening to Nina. It was as if they were listening to something else.

Nina tried to continue her speech, but the commotion seemed to be spreading. 'Provocateurs,' thought Lionidza. 'There must be provocateurs in the crowd.'

The trade union leader who had just spoken pushed forward, a transistor radio in his hand. He took the microphone from Nina. 'Excuse me.'

'Friends,' he shouted. 'I've got Provisional Radio here. You have to listen. They're going to kill Ruslan Shanidza.'

He held the radio to the microphone, and Lionidza instantly recognised Tamara's muffled voice: 'Oh Jesus. They're here. I can hear their cars. They're outside. Can you hear their voices?'

'No.'

Then there was silence for a moment as the trade unionist unplugged the microphone and plugged the lead straight into the radio.

'They're kicking the door in.' Now Tamara's voice was clear. It boomed around the square as 150,000 or more people listened in absolute silence.

Lionidza heard four more bangs, then Tamara's voice came over, very loud.

'Mingrelsky!'

Oh Jesus, no. Not him. Please no, not him.

'Mingrelsky!'

Lionidza wanted to scream. He saw Nina standing in front of him, tears in her eyes, her face a picture of despair.

'Ah, Tamara. So you've come round already.' It was Vakhtan Mingrelsky's voice. Unmistakable.

There was a little scream of sorts from Tamara, then Mingrelsky continued: 'I'll tell you what, when we've shot your husband, we'll take you with us, and this time I'll make sure every White Eagle in Ronkoni fucks you before we slit your throat.'

Nina sank to her knees, covering her head with her hands.

'Mingrelsky, you can't,' said Tamara's voice.

'And why the fuck not?'

'Because this is going out live on the radio.'

'What?'

'I've got Provisional Radio on the other end of this mobile phone. We're going out live.'

For a moment there was silence.

Mingrelsky's voice boomed out again. 'Who the fuck's that?'

'Hi there. Erm, this is the Tembot Ksansky show on Provisional Radio. We're going out live to a hundred thousand listeners all over Ronkoni.'

Silence again.

'Think about it,' said Tamara's voice. 'If you kill us in front of a hundred thousand witnesses, even Korgay won't be able to protect you.'

'Oh, please,' whispered Lionidza.

'You fucking Rebel slut!' Mingrelsky shouted. There were some indeterminate noises, and then silence.

Lionidza heard Nina wail, 'Oh no no, please God, no.'

Silence.

Then Tembot Ksansky's voice: 'Tamara? Tamara? Mingrelsky? Tamara? Are you there?'

No answer. Ksansky asked again, this time it was obvious that he was crying. 'Tamara? Tamara? She's been cut off. Tamara, please for God's sake ring us back.'

Nina was crying, her hands covering her face.

For several minutes, Ksansky's tearful voice called out in vain to Tamara. At first the crowd was silent, but then came a strange noise that Lionidza had never heard before, the sound of thousands of people crying.

'Come on, Sergo,' said Orbeliani. 'We have to make sure there isn't a riot.'

They went to speak to Kakhi. There were no tears on his face, just an expression of fury. Meanwhile, on the radio, Ksansky's voice was still begging Tamara to ring him back.

Orbeliani put his arm on Kakhi's shoulder. 'We'll get them for this, but we can't do it today. Korgay's filled the city with his goons.'

'Fuck them,' said Kakhi.

Qipiani joined them, along with the trade unionist and a student leader.

'We have to prevent a riot,' said the trade unionist. 'They'll massacre us.'

Everyone murmured their agreement, with the exception of Kakhi.

'You fucking cowards,' he yelled at them. 'There'll never be a better time than now.'

'I respect your point of view,' Orbeliani said. 'You'll have every right to pin the blame on us.'

'I will, don't worry.'

Lionidza knew Kakhi was just manoeuvring, making sure he could blame the others for this 'lost opportunity'.

'What about Tamara?' said Nina, who had joined them. 'She must still be alive. We have to do something for her.'

'Oh, God,' said Lionidza. 'You're right. We have to let them know we hold them accountable.'

'Yes,' said Orbeliani, 'and we end the demonstration now. Then they can devote all their energies to finding Tamara.'

Orbeliani went back to the radio and turned it off. He unplugged the loudspeaker lead and plugged it back into the microphone, tapping it once or twice to make sure it was working. 'Friends,' his voice boomed across the square, 'if Ruslan Shanidza is dead, then his murder will not go unpunished, but that's not our priority today. Not now, because we know that Tamara Shanidza's still alive, and we know what Mingrelsky's planning to do with her.'

A restless murmur came from the crowd.

'We have to give this warning to Mingrelsky, to the Security Police and to Korgay: we hold you accountable for her life. We hold you accountable for her safety.'

People applauded and cheered.

'We have to make sure they have no excuse. We have to make sure they can't say they were too busy dealing with us to go after Mingrelsky. So this demonstration ends, now. We just go home. We don't riot. We don't throw stones at the police. We just go home and bear witness, and leave the authorities with no excuse for not rescuing Tamara Shanidza from Mingrelsky. Is this agreed, friends?'

Shouts of approval came from the crowd.

'Then please join me in two minutes of silent prayer for our dear friend Ruslan Shanidza and for his wife Tamara.'

Lionidza closed his eyes and bowed his head. It was all too much for him. Perhaps it wasn't until that moment that he realised how much he loved them, both of them.

Then there came a noise from the crowd.

How dare they make a noise?

'They're cheering,' Nina whispered.

Something was happening, like ripples in a pond, a cheer was spreading out from various points in the square.

'Put the radio on! Put the radio on!' shouted voices in the crowd.

Orbeliani clumsily hooked up the radio once more, and Tamara's voice boomed out form the loudspeakers: 'Sorry it took so long to get back to you. I couldn't get a signal.'

An enormous cheer erupted. Nina raised her arms in triumph. She embraced Lionidza and kissed him. Then she embraced Orbeliani and almost everyone on the platform, even Kakhi.

Lionidza could just make out Tamara's voice above all the din: 'We're both fine. Ruslan looks as if he'll be coming round soon. Tembot, I have to thank you. You saved our lives. You were brilliant.'

'No, Tamara,' said Ksansky's voice. 'You were brilliant.'

Epilogue

IN MARCH 1995, just as the daffodils reached their peak, the new Ksordian political élite descended upon the village of Vakesia for the baptism and chrismation of little Mariam Shanidza. Almost all the Federal government squeezed into the small church, along with General Bebur Chikradza, the new Commander-in-Chief of the armed forces, and Central Kuban Regional President Yakub Bovin. The guest of honour was Zourab Orbeliani, the first ever directly elected President of the Federal Republic of Ksordia.

If Ruslan had been the catalyst who united the opposition against Korgay, Orbeliani had been the hero of the endgame. He had somehow managed to prevent a major riot in the aftermath of the attempt on Ruslan's life, as the great majority of demonstrators obeyed his pleas to return to their homes. Those who didn't go home swarmed south to throw up a human shield around Ruslan's house.

Meanwhile Colonel Chikradza brought his two battalions into the capital, seizing the southern suburbs and all the bridges over the river. Korgay's troops and the paramilitaries took control of the city centre and a tense standoff ensued. Other military units declared for one side or the other and prepared to make their way to Ronkoni. A bloody battle for the capital seemed inevitable.

Orbeliani then contacted General Napashidza, Korgay's Commander-in-Chief. They had a long, wide-ranging discussion, emerging with the compromise that would defuse the crisis. Korgay would remain President, but General Napashidza would become Prime Minister with full executive powers. He would restrain the Security Police and the paramilitaries and give the opposition proper access to the media until November's presidential elections.

Korgay accepted this, but, much to the opposition's surprise, he insisted on bringing the elections forward until the beginning of July. He knew that Zviad Qipiani, his former Minister of Munitions, was the only candidate around whom the whole opposition could unite, and he planned to wait until it was too late for them to nominate anyone else and then broadcast his footage of Qipiani being spanked by a prostitute.

Fortunately for the opposition, Military Intelligence knew what Korgay was up to. They passed details on to Colonel Chikradza, who met Qipiani privately and persuaded him to withdraw his candidature.

Qipiani's sudden and unexplained withdrawal threw the opposition into turmoil, and for a while it looked as three or four candidates would split the anti-Korgay vote. But Ruslan, Nina, Lionidza and others came out strongly in support of Orbeliani, who eventually received backing from every opposition grouping except Kakhi's party and some West Ksordian separatists.

Orbeliani won the presidential election with 52% of the vote, scoring highly everywhere except among the militant North Ksords. Korgay got less than 40%.

Ruslan played only a bit part in all these momentous events. He roused himself to campaign vigorously for Orbeliani's nomination after Qipiani's withdrawal, but the rest of the time, he suffered from a lethargy that he was unable to shake off. He found it difficult to sleep and had terrifying nightmares about his torture, especially the near drowning.

He hated it when everyone told him he was a hero, especially when they said his crossed fingers during his 'confession' had been a masterstroke. He had never told anyone, not even Tamara, how utterly defeated he had been and how his crossed fingers had been nothing more than a fleeting gesture of defiance.

Then, one night just after they had gone to bed, he turned his back on Tamara and told her.

'So it wasn't a signal to me?'

'No.'

She put her hand on his shoulder and tugged. He resisted for a moment and then rolled onto his back.

She kissed him. 'So what? It doesn't matter.'

'I just feel such a fraud.'

'Ruslan, I know you. I know how determined you must have been to beat them. You were winning, and then you surrendered for my sake. Can't you see how that makes me feel?'

'How?'

'You chose me. You chose your love for me.'

Ruslan raised his hand and stroked her face. 'What I did was nothing to what you did for me. You could have run.'

'No, I couldn't. There was no way I could have abandoned you.'

Ruslan threw himself into the final weeks of the presidential election, and the campaigning and the rousing reception he received from supporters did him a lot of good.

The new President wasted little time in calling elections to the Federal Assembly, which produced a landslide victory for his allies. Ruslan, who had decided to join Orbeliani's party rather than start one of his own, received an overwhelming endorsement from the voters of Timashevsk. Much to his disappointment, however, Orbeliani refused to give him responsibility for negotiating a settlement with the Akhtarians and the Tatars.

'You're seen as too neutral. It's got to be somebody the North Ksords can trust.'

Orbeliani gave Ruslan a seat on the cabinet committee that supervised the negotiations, but as minister responsible, he selected the North Ksords' former leader Mataa Bogiani. To Ruslan's delight, Bogiani's first act was the resurrection of his Four Principles for Peace as the basis for a settlement, though he told Ruslan he was determined to drive a very hard bargain, in the belief that to do otherwise would only store up trouble for the future.

Orbeliani and Lionidza, his Foreign Minister, worked hard to isolate the Akhtarians from their Russian protectors. They mounted an aggressive diplomatic campaign that contrasted the new democratic and multi-ethnic government of Ksordia with an Akhtarian regime that still included neo-Rebel fascists like Sulkavidza.

These efforts were so successful that the Akhtarian president was recently heard to remark that it was no longer a question of securing Russian support for expansion into Central Kubania. It was more a question of persuading the Russians to accept any form of Akhtarian independence at all (the deepening crisis in Chechnya was making Boris Yeltsin less and less sympathetic to breakaway republics).

Ruslan reluctantly accepted Bogiani's view that lasting peace could only come through partition and a new border that took most of the North Ksords out of Akhtaria and as many Akhtarians out of Ksordia as possible. The Tatars, meanwhile, were demanding that they remain united within a Ksordia that would give them so much autonomy that they would be all but independent.

Bogiani had only recently begun to make real progress. Just two weeks ago, the neo-Rebel Sulkavidza had resigned from the Akhtarian government, accusing President Eristov of selling out. The Russians had twisted Eristov's arm, and with Sulkavidza gone, the Akhtarians were now negotiating seriously.

Ruslan, meanwhile, had swallowed his disappointment at not running the negotiations and flung himself into his own work. Orbeliani had made him Minister of the Interior and had charged him with the task of clearing out the Augean stench left behind by Alavidza and Korgay. The Ksordian state was infested with gangsterism at every level, and the police and security services were riddled with links to organised crime and extreme nationalist paramilitary groups.

Korgay fled Ksordia soon after Orbeliani's election victory. He surfaced briefly in Georgia before finding a haven in Belarus. His former Interior Minister Tengiz Alavidza continued to languish in the prison cell to which Korgay had consigned him. Ruslan's chief interrogator was just three doors down.

As for Mingrelsky, nobody saw or heard anything of him until after the election, when investigators discovered his body in a shallow grave not far from Ronkoni. It turned out that the Security Police had offered to whisk him out of Ksordia after his botched attempt on Ruslan's life, but as soon as he and his companions fell into their hands, they overpowered them and garrotted them. Apparently, in a casual act of sadism, they made Mingrelsky watch the murder of his men before they killed him.

'Are you glad he's dead?' Ruslan asked Tamara after they heard the news.

'You bet.'

'I bet you feel guilty about it though, don't you?'

'Not really. I think we're entitled to be relieved.'

'I think we're entitled to break out the champagne.'

'Yes, but we mustn't sink to his level.'

'I suppose not.'

How to deal with Korgay, Alavidza and other war criminals was a question that Orbeliani spent long hours discussing with Ruslan and other senior ministers. Orbeliani and Ruslan were convinced that they mustn't have impunity, but they weren't certain that prison sentences that made martyrs of them would do anything to challenge the view of both Ksords and Akhtarians that their side was only and always the victim of aggression by the other. They were intrigued by the South African Truth and Reconciliation Commission and hoped that something of the sort could force people on both sides to confront their own side's guilt by discrediting rather than martyring those who were guilty of war crimes.

But that would mean offering the possibility of amnesty to Leila's killer and the men who had tortured Ruslan and tried to have both him and Tamara murdered. This was something Ruslan was loath to do, though he knew that he couldn't ask others who had suffered to travel the path of reconciliation if he wasn't prepared to do so himself.

Even now, almost two years after his release, Ruslan still suffered from frequent nightmares, and when he made mistakes in his work, or when the cronyism that characterised Ksordia's very imperfect democracy disgusted him, he could be plunged into short but debilitating bouts of depression when that terrible harshness would return to his eyes. These episodes were becoming less frequent, however, and he was hopeful that his psychological wounds would eventually heal. As for his physical limitations, he felt he had come to terms with them. He missed being fit and he missed running, but he consoled himself with long walks and mobility exercises.

Tamara tended to stay out of the limelight as much as she could. She didn't seek or enjoy the role of political wife and preferred to devote her energies to her lively and mischievous little son. By the beginning of 1994, she felt ready to have another child, and she gave birth to a daughter in November. Ruslan would have been happy to stop there, but Tamara wanted to have a third child, and she was anxious to do so quickly. 'I want to make sure I get back to work as a doctor before you're president. Otherwise I might not be able to.'

In fact, Tamara knew that she wouldn't be able to work as a doctor for a very long time. Ruslan had the most dangerous job in the whole government, and for some time to come, both of them would have to randomise their movements and surround themselves with bodyguards wherever they went.

She was only half joking about the possibility of him becoming president. Many assumed that the top job would eventually be his, but Ruslan tried not to let this distract him. Indeed, he felt it would be a disaster to be promoted too far too soon. He saw his political career as a long-term vocation, and his major concern was to do his job effectively without sacrificing his integrity.

In fact, Lionidza was likely to be Ksordia's next president. His party had mopped up almost half of Korgay's Socialists and was now the largest party in Ksordia. If the economy continued to contract at the present rate, Ruslan expected Lionidza to go into opposition and challenge Orbeliani at the next elections.

Ruslan would probably stick with Orbeliani when that happened, but he wouldn't worry too much about a Lionidza-led government. He might even join it if Orbeliani did too. Lionidza wasn't a real Communist any more, and if necessary, Ruslan, Orbeliani and Nina would have every chance of beating him at some future election.

In the meantime, Lionidza and Nina somehow managed to coexist in the same cabinet. They never seemed to agree about very much, but a degree of mutual respect had grown between them, even a friendship of sorts. Ruslan liked to tease them about it.

'We have something in common,' Lionidza once told him. 'You abandoned Nina for Tamara and you abandoned me for Orbeliani.'

Nina and Tamara didn't meet very often, but when they did, they were relaxed in each other's company. Tamara once told Ruslan that Nina treated her like a little sister for whose welfare she felt some responsibility.

All of Ruslan's relatives were in the church, among them his mother, who wasn't so strong as before, but was still resisting his and Giorgi's efforts to persuade her to come and live in Ronkoni. Among the many friends invited was Fatima, who had promised to sing her Crimean lament and Leila's *Daffodils* after the service. Several of Leila's relatives were there too. They all embraced Ruslan warmly, saying how proud they were that Leila had been part of his success.

All of Tamara's family and dozens of her friends came down from Akhtaria. They drove right through North Ksordia, whose highways were now safe for Akhtarians, though refugees wouldn't be allowed to return to their shattered homes until a final peace settlement had been concluded.

The Ksords of Vakesia welcomed their Akhtarian guests, and some of the neighbours put them up in their houses overnight. Their cars, with their Zeda'Anta number plates and tax discs that bore the red and yellow diamonds of Akhtaria, spent over twenty-four hours parked in the streets of the village. And this time, there was no punch-up after the ceremony, and when the Akhtarians came to drive their cars home, not a single one of them had been vandalised.

If you have enjoyed this book

- Please tweet about it to your followers

- Recommend it to your friends on Facebook

- Write a review on Amazon or rate it Goodreads

Author's Note

THE KSORDS and Akhtarians do not exist. Their imaginary country more or less corresponds to the Russian region of Krasnodar, which does not have a substantial Tatar population. My apologies to Krasnodar's inhabitants for borrowing their homeland. No insult is intended.

The reader may notice some parallels between events in this novel and events in the former Yugoslavia. These parallels are not accidental, but they are not accurate and nor are they intended to be. The roles played by Boris Yeltsin, Russia and Ukraine in this novel are entirely fictitious and do not in any way correspond to their roles in the Yugoslav tragedy.

This book is a work of fiction. All the events in it are fictional, as are all the characters. No inference should be drawn from this novel about any historical events, any nation or any person living or dead.

Acknowledgements

I need to thank a number of people who have helped and encouraged me in the writing of this novel. First and foremost my late agent, Paul M Muller, whose encouragement, advice and detailed criticisms have been crucial. Also David Fox for advice on matters medical and Michael Nutt, my late mother Sheila Clark and Angela Osmond for constructive criticisms of early drafts, and my daughter Penny Clark for criticising and proofing the text, plus Steve Downs, Sandra Stella and others for their encouragement.

Most of all, I would like to thank my wife and daughters for putting up with a husband and father who neglected them for the sake of his book.